Mary Cowden Clarke, Charles Cowden Clarke

Recollections of Writers

Mary Cowden Clarke, Charles Cowden Clarke

Recollections of Writers

ISBN/EAN: 9783337386450

Printed in Europe, USA, Canada, Australia, Japan

Cover: Foto ©Andreas Hilbeck / pixelio.de

More available books at **www.hansebooks.com**

RECOLLECTIONS OF WRITERS

BY

CHARLES AND MARY COWDEN CLARKE,

AUTHORS OF "THE COMPLETE CONCORDANCE TO SHAKESPEARE,"
"RICHES OF CHAUCER," ETC.

WITH LETTERS OF

CHARLES LAMB, LEIGH HUNT,
DOUGLAS JERROLD, AND CHARLES DICKENS;

AND A

PREFACE BY MARY COWDEN CLARKE.

NEW YORK:

CHARLES SCRIBNER'S SONS,

743 AND 745 BROADWAY.

CONTENTS.

PREFACE.

A PORTION of these "Recollections" appeared in the *Gentleman's Magazine;* but appeared there in imperfect form. They were written by the Author-couple happily together. One of the wedded pair has quitted this earthly life; and the survivor now puts the "Recollections" into complete and collected form, happy at least in this, that she feels she is thereby fulfilling a wish of her lost other self.

The earliest and best of these "Recollections" (the one on John Keats, written entirely by the beloved hand that is gone) gave rise to the rest. Friends were so pleased and interested by the schoolfellow's recollections of the poet, that they asked for other recollections of writers known to both husband and wife. The task was one of mingled pain and pleasure; but it was performed

—like so many others undertaken by them—in happy companionship, and this made the pleasure greater than the pain.

Charles and Mary Cowden Clarke may with truth be held in tender remembrance by their readers as among the happiest of married lovers for more than forty-eight years, writing together, reading together, working together, enjoying together the perfection of loving, literary consociation; and kindly sympathy may well be felt for her who is left to singly subscribe herself,

Her readers' faithful servant,

MARY COWDEN CLARKE.

VILLA NOVELLO,
GENOA, 1878.

Broadstairs.

Nineteenth September 1848.

Dear Mrs Clarke and Miss Novello.

We, the undersigned, truly mindful in our hearts of hearts, of your kind remembrance of us in; beautiful and ever-careful to. present gift, and of the happy hours we have passed together entreat you to accept our hearty thanks, proffered in all love and friendship. They have been (like Royal Charlie in the Jacobite song) "lang o comin'"; but they will be longer still o' going—

out of our minds. at least we hope so, for
such remembrances can only go out with
our five senses, and we hope to keep
ours for these many years.

dear friends

Yours ever

Shallow
Cus Valorum

Abraham Slender

Robert Flexible

Charles Goldstream

Young Fast
Doctor Blank

Bobadil

Charles Dickens

(The musical Manager.)

RECOLLECTIONS OF WRITERS.

CHAPTER I.

John Clarke—Vincent Novello—John Ryland—George Dyer —Rev. Rowland Hill—Dr. Alexander Geddes - Dr. Priestley —Bishop Lowth —Gilbert Wakefield—Mason Good— Richard Warburton Lytton—Abbé Béliard—Holt White— Major and Mrs. Cartwright—John Keats—Edward Holmes —Edward Cowper—Frank Twiss—Mrs Siddons—Miss O'Neil—John Kemble—Edmund Kean—Booth—Godwin.

To the fact of our having had pre-eminently good and enlightened parents is perhaps chiefly attributable the privilege we have enjoyed of that acquaintance with gifted people which has enabled us to record our recollections of many writers. Both John Clarke the schoolmaster and Vincent Novello the musician, with their admirable wives, liberal-minded and intelligent beyond most of their time and calling, delighted in the society and friendship of clever people, and cultivated those relations for their children.

By nature John Clarke was gentle-hearted, clear-headed, and transparently conscientious—supremely suiting him for a schoolmaster. As a youth he was articled to a lawyer at Northampton ; but from the first he felt a

growing repugnance to the profession, and this repugnance
was brought to unbearable excess by his having to spend
one whole night in seeking a substitute for performing the
duty which devolved upon him from the sheriff's unwill-
ingness to fulfil the absent executioner's office of hanging
a culprit condemned to die on the following morning.
With success in finding a deputy hangman at dawn, after
a night of inexpressible agony of mind, came his determination to seek another profession, and he finally found
more congenial occupation by becoming usher at a school
conducted by the Rev. John Ryland, Calvinistic minister
in the same town. My[1] father's fellow-usher was no other
than George Dyer (the erudite and absent-minded Greek
scholar immortalized in Elia's whimsical essay entitled
" Amicus Redivivus "); the one being the writing-master
and arithmetical teacher, the other the instructor in classical languages. Each of these young men formed an
attachment for the head master's step-daughter, Miss Ann
Isabella Stott ; but George Dyer's love was cherished
secretly, while John Clarke's was openly declared and his
suit accepted. The young couple left Northampton with
the lady's family and settled in Enfield, her step-father
having resolved upon establishing a school near London.
For this purpose a house and grounds were taken in that
charming village—among the very loveliest in England,—
which were eminently fitted for a school ; the house being
airy, roomy, and commodious, the grounds sufficiently
large to give space for flower, fruit, and vegetable gardens,
playground, and paddock of two acres affording pasturage

---

[1] These are Charles Cowden Clarke's reminiscences. When
the first person plural is not used the context will indicate
whether it is Charles or Mary Cowden Clarke who speaks.

for two cows that supplied the establishment with abundant milk.

One of the earliest figures that impressed itself upon my childish memory was that of my step-grandfather—stout, rubicund, facetious in manner, and oddly forcible when preaching. The pulpit eloquence of John Ryland strongly partook of the well-recorded familiarities in expression that have accompanied the era of the all but adored Rowland Hill. Upon one occasion, when delivering a sermon upon the triumph of spiritual grace over Evil, in connexion with the career of the Apostle Paul, John Ryland's sermon concluded thus :—" And so the poor Devil went off howling to hell, and all Pandemonium was hung in mourning for a month." His favourite grace before meat was :—" Whereas some have appetite and no food, and others have food and no appetite, we thank thee, O Lord, that we have both!" Old Mr. Ryland was acquainted with the Rev. Rowland Hill ; and once, when my grandmother expressed a wish to go up to London and hear the famous preacher, her spouse took her to the chapel in the morning and afterwards to Rowland Hill's own house, introducing her to him, saying, " Here's my wife, who prefers your sermons to her husband's ; so I'll leave her with you while I go and preach this afternoon." Between the old gentleman and myself there existed an affectionate liking, and when he died, at a ripe age, I declared that if " old sir " (my usual name for him) were taken away I would go with him ; but when the hearse came to the door to convey the remains to Northampton, for burial, according to the wish of the deceased, my boyish imagination took fright, and I ran to my mother, exclaiming, " I don't want to go with old sir *in the black coach !*"

It has been said that " Every one should plant a tree who can ;" and my father was a devoted believer in this axiom.   While still a little fellow, 1 used to be the companion of his daily walks in the green fields around our dwelling ; and many a tree have I seen him plant.   I had the privilege of carrying the bag containing his store of acorns : he would dibble a hole in the earth with his walking-stick, and it was my part to drop an acorn into the opening.   It was a proud day for me when, the walking-stick chancing to snap, I was permitted to use the ivory-headed implement, thus fortunately reduced to a proper size for me ; so that when my father had selected a spot, it was *I* who dibbled the hole as well as dropped in the acorn !

In many respects my father was independent-minded far in advance of his time ; and an improvement systematized by him in the scholastic education of the boys, which testifies the humanity of his character as well as the soundness of his judgment, added considerably to the prosperity of his later career.   Instead of the old custom of punishing with the cane, a plan was drawn up of keeping an account-book, for and by each scholar, of each performance at his lessons; " B " for bene, " O " for optime, and on the opposite page an " X " for negligence or wrong conduct ; and rewards were given at the end of the half-year in accordance with the proportion of good marks recorded.   A plan was also adopted for encouraging " voluntary " work in the recreative hours. For French and Latin translations thus performed first, second, and third prizes were awarded each half-year in the shape of interesting books.   John Keats (if I mistake not) twice received the highest of these prizes.   In his last half-year at school he commenced the translation of the Æneid, which he completed while with his medical master at Edmonton.

My father was intimate with the celebrated Roman Catholic writer, Dr. Alexander Geddes, and subscribed to all the portions of the Bible that Geddes lived to translate. He was upon equally familiar terms with Dr. Priestley; and such was my father's Biblical zeal that he made a MS. copy of Bishop Lowth's translation of Isaiah, subjoining a selection of the most important of the translator's notes to the text. This MS., written in the most exquisitely neat and legible hand (the occasionally occurring Hebrew characters being penned with peculiar care and finish), bound in white vellum, with a small scarlet label at the back, the slight gilding dulled by age but the whole of the dainty volume in excellent preservation, is still in my possession. He took a peculiar interest in the work, much pursued at that time, of Biblical translation, and closely watched the labours of Gilbert Wakefield, the translator of the New Testament; and the eminent surgeon Mason Good—a self-educated classic—who produced a fine version of Job, the result of his Sunday morning's devotion.

I remember accompanying my father on one occasion in a call upon Dr. Geddes. We found him at lunch; and I noticed that beside his basin of broth stood a supply of whole mustard-seed, of which he took alternate spoonfuls with those of the broth: which he said had been recommended to him as a wholesome form of diet. He had a thin, pale face, with a pleasant smile and manner; and told us several droll, odd things during our stay, in an easy, table-talk style. But Dr. Geddes was irritable in controversy, for we heard from George Dyer that at a party given by Geddes, at his lodging, to some literary men, the subject of James II. arose, and the Doctor was so furious at the unfavourable estimate of the King's character expressed by his guests that he kicked over the table upon them in his wrath. In those days men's ire "grew fast and furious" in discussion.

I was but a mere child, wearing the scarlet jacket and nankeen trousers of the time, with a large frilled cambric collar, over which fell a mass of long, light-brown curls reaching below the shoulders, when, encouraged by himself and my father, I used to visit Mr. Richard Warburton Lytton, and was hardly tall enough on tip-toe to reach the bell-handle at the front garden-gate. Mr. Lytton, although the owner of Knebworth, one of those old-fashioned mansions built with as many windows as there are days in the year—for some reason known only to himself—dwelt for many years at Enfield, and afterwards at Ramsgate, where he died. He was maternal grand-father to the late Lord Bulwer Lytton, his daughter having married a Mr. Bulwer; and after Warburton Lytton's death the author of "Pelham" adopted the maternal name.

Richard Warburton Lytton was educated at Harrow, and latterly attained the first class, in which were himself, the eminent Sir William Jones, and Bennett, Bishop of Cloyne. I have heard my father say that Mr. Lytton has read to him long portions of the Greek histories into English with such clear freedom that his dialect had not the least effect of being a translation made at the time of perusal. He was a man of the most amiable and liberal spirit. Several Frenchmen having emigrated to Enfield at the outbreak of the Revolution, Mr. Lytton displayed the most generous sympathy towards them ; and they were periodically invited to entertainments at his house, especially on their fast days (more properly speaking, abstinence days), when there was sure to be on his table plenty of choice fish. Among these gentlemen *émigrés* was a certain delightful Abbé Béliard, who became French teacher at our school, and who was so much esteemed and even loved by his pupils that many of them were grieved almost to the shedding of tears—an unusual tribute from schoolboy feeling—when he took leave of them all to return to his native land. The bishop of his district required his return (peace between France and England having been declared), giving him the promise of his original living. Mr. Lytton, upon visiting Rouen, having found poor Béliard in distress (his Diocesan having forfeited his promise), with characteristic generosity received his Enfield guest in his Normandy lodging till the abbé had obtained the relief that had been guaranteed to him.

Mr. Lytton had a very round, fat face, he was small-featured and fresh-coloured ; in person he was short, fat, and almost unwieldy. I used to see him, taking such exercise as his corpulence would permit, in his old-fashioned so-called " chamber horse "—an easy chair with so rebounding a spring cushion that it swayed him up and down when he leaned his elbows on its arms—while I stood watching him with the interest of a child, and listening with still greater interest to the anecdotes and stories he good-naturedly related to me—stories and anecdotes such as boys most love to hear—adventurous, humorous, and wonderfully varied.

Another house in our vicinity that I enjoyed the privilege of visiting was that of Mr. Holt White, nephew to the Rev. Gilbert White, the fascinating historian of the parish and district of Selborne, of which he was the vicar.

Mr. Holt White had purchased a handsome property on the borders of the Chase—then unenclosed—and came there to reside. He made the acquaintance of my father, and placed his little son under his tuition. Mr. White was in person, manner, accomplishments, and intercourse a graceful specimen of the ideal aristocrat. As an author he was strictly an amateur. He made himself one among the band of Shakespearian commentators, and I have a slight recollection that in the latter period of his life he was engaged in editing one of the Miltonian essays —I believe the Areopagitica. He also made an effort to be elected member of Parliament for Essex, but failed. His political opinion was of a broad Liberal character, and one of his most intimate associates was the heartily respected, the bland and amiable Major Cartwright, whose intercourse and personal demeanour in society and on the public platform secured to him from first to last the full toleration of his political opponents. I used to meet Major and Mrs. Cartwright at Mr. Holt White's house; and it was either he himself or Mr. Holt White who told me that, having lost a formidable sum at the gaming-table, Cartwright made a resolution never more to touch card or dice—a resolution that he faithfully kept. Mrs. Cartwright had a merry, chatty way with her, and on one occasion at dinner, when she and her husband were present, I remember, the conversation having turned upon the great actors and actresses, Mrs. Cartwright enlarged upon the talent of " *the* Pritchard " (a talent commemorated by Churchill, as overcoming even the disadvantages of increasing age and stoutness, in a passage containing the couplet—

> Before such merit all objections fly ;
> Pritchard's genteel and Garrick's six feet high)—

and on my asking if she were equal in talent with Mrs. Siddons—" Siddons ! " echoed Mrs. Cartwright, " Siddons was not fit to brush Pritchard's shoes " !   So much for the passionate partialities of youth.

Mr. Holt White had an ingenious arrangement by which he converted the more important works of his collected library into an extensive and useful common-place book. In the course of his reading either an original work or a new translation of a celebrated classic, if he came upon a casual and new opinion upon the general character of an established author he would make an allusion to it, and, with a very brief quotation, insert it in the blank leaves of the work referred to. Thus some of his works—and particularly the popular ones—possessed a fine and interesting catalogue of approbations. For the memory of Mr. Holt White my gratitude and affection will continue with my days.   Such was my social freedom and his kind licence that I had only to show him the volume when I had borrowed one of his books, and I had welcome to help myself from his splendid library— a rare and incalculable advantage for a youth of my age in those days.

I had several favourite chums among the boys at my father's school ; but my chief friends were John Keats, Edward Holmes, and Edward Cowper. Of the first I have spoken fully in the set of " Recollections " specially dedicated to him.[2] The second I have mentioned at some length in the same place. There was a particularly intimate school-fellowship and liking between Keats and Holmes, probably arising out of their both being of ardent and imaginative temperament, with a decided artistic bent in their several predilections for poetry and music.

[2] See pages 120 and 142.

Holmes, besides his passionate adoration of music and native talent for that art, had an exquisitely discerning taste in literature. His choice in books was excellent; his appreciation of style in writing was particularly acute —his own style being remarkably pure, racy, and elegant. He had a very handsome face, with beaming eyes, regular features, and an elevated expression. His mouth and nose were large, but beautifully formed. Thick masses of sunny brown hair, and his inspired look, lent him the air of a young Apollo. We who remember him in youth—one of us even recollecting him in child's frock when he first came to school—felt strangely when, in after years, he was presiding at the pianoforte, and one of his enthusiastic young lady hearers present said, "Dear old man! how delightfully he plays!" The words disenchanted us of the impression we had somehow retained that he was still young, still "Ned Holmes," although the Phœbus clusters were touched with grey, and their gold was fast turning to silver.

Edward Cowper, even as a boy, gave token of that ingenuity and turn for mechanical invention which, as a man, rendered him eminent. I recollect his fashioning a little windmill for winding the fibre from off the cocoons of the silkworms that he and I kept at school, and for winding my mother's and sisters' skeins of sewing silk. He used to open the window a certain width that the air might act properly upon his miniature mill, and would stand watching with steady interest the effect of setting in action the machinery. He was a lively, brisk boy, with an alert, animated, energetic manner, which he maintained in manhood. His jocular school-name for me was "Three-hundred," in allusion to my initials, C. C. C. He had a fluent tongue, was fond of talking, and could talk well. Once he joined us in a walk through Hyde Park from Bayswater to the Marble Arch, where we took an omnibus to the east end of Oxford Street; he delivering a kind of lecture discourse the whole way without ceasing, on some subject in which we were all interested. He gave lectures to young lady pupils in a scientific class, telling us that he always found them especially intelligent hearers, and we had the good fortune to be present at a lecture he delivered in the first Crystal Palace, erected for the International Exhibition of 1851, before it was opened. His subject was the great strength of hollow tube pillars, on the principle of the arch, which he prettily illustrated by piling up, on four small pieces of quill set upright, heavy weights one after another to an amount that seemed incredible. He was the inventor of an important improvement in a celebrated German printing-press, brought over and used by the *Times* newspaper; and it was Applegarth, the printer, who helped him to take out the patent for this improvement.

Among our scholars was a boy named Frank Twiss, who was the son (if I mistake not) of Richard Twiss, the author of various tours and travels. I remember the lad being visited by his father, whose antique courtesy engaged my boyish notice when, as he walked round our garden, he held his hat in his hand until my father begged he would put it on; upon which Mr. Twiss replied, " No, sir ; not while you are uncovered ;" my father having the habit of often walking bare-headed in our own grounds.

While at Enfield my father received more than one visit from his fellow-usher in the old—or rather young— Northampton days ; and I well remember George Dyer's even then eccentric ways, under-toned voice, dab-dab mode of speaking, and absent manner. He had a trick of filling up his hesitating sentences with a mild little monosyllabic sound, and of finishing his speeches with the incomplete phrase " Well, sir; but however—." This peculiarity we used to amuse ourselves by imitating when we talked of him and recalled his oddities, as thus:— " You have met with a curious and rare book, you say ? Indeed, sir; abd—abd—abd—I should like to see it, sir; abd—abd—abd—perhaps you would allow me to look at it; abd—abd—abd—Well, sir; but however—" Or: " You have been ill, sir, I hear. Dear me! abd—abd—abd—I'm sorry, I'm sure; abd—abd—abd—Well, sir; but however—" Once when he came to see us he told us of his having lately spent some time among a wandering tribe of gipsies, he feeling much desire to know something of the language and habits of this interesting race of people, and believing he could not do so better than by joining them in one of their rambling expeditions. He once wrote a volume of French poems. During a long portion of his life his chief income was derived from the moderate emolument he obtained by correcting works of the classics for the publishers; but on the death of Lord Stanhope, to whose son he had been tutor, he was left residuary legatee by that nobleman, which placed him in comparatively easy circumstances. Dyer was of a thoroughly noble disposition and generous heart; and beneath that strange book-worm exterior of his there dwelt a finely tender soul, full of all warmth and sympathy. On one occasion, during his less prosperous days, going to wait at the coach-office for the Cambridge stage, by which he intended to travel thither, he met an old friend who was in great distress. Dyer gave him the half-guinea meant for his own fare, and walked down to

Cambridge instead of going by coach. His delicacy, constancy, and chivalry of feeling equalled his generosity : for, many years after, when my father died, George Dyer asked for a private conference with me, told me of his youthful attachment for my mother, and inquired whether her circumstances were comfortable, because in case, as a widow, she had not been left well off he meant to offer her his hand. Hearing that in point of money she had no cause for concern, he begged me to keep secret what he had confided to me, and he himself never made farther allusion to the subject. Long subsequently he married a very worthy lady : and it was great gratification to us to see how the old student's rusty suit of black, threadbare and shining with the shabbiness of neglect, the limp wisp of jaconot muslin, yellow with age, round his throat, the dusty shoes, and stubbly beard, had become exchanged for a coat that shone only with the lustre of regular brushing, a snow-white cravat neatly tied on, brightly blacked shoes, and a close-shaven chin—the whole man presenting a cosy and burnished appearance, like one carefully and affectionately tended. He, like Charles Lamb, always wore black smalls, black stockings (which Charles Lamb generally covered with high black gaiters), and black shoes; the knee-smalls and the shoes both being tied with strings instead of fastened with buckles. His hair, white and stiff, glossy at the time now spoken of from due administration of comb and brush, contrasted strongly with a pair of small dark eyes, worn with much poring over Greek and black-letter characters ; while even at an advanced age there was a sweet look of kindliness, simple goodness, serenity, and almost child-like guileless-ness that characteristically marked his face at all periods of his life.

Before leaving Enfield I used often to walk up to town from my father's house of an afternoon in good time to go to the theatre, and walk back after the play was over, in order to be ready for my morning duties when I had become usher in the school. Dark and solitary enough were the "Green Lanes," as they were called, that lay between Holloway and Enfield—through picturesque Hornsey, rural Wood Green, and hedge-rowed Winchmore Hill—when traversed in the small hours past midnight. Yet I knew every foot of the way, and generally pursued that track as the nearest for the pedestrian. I seldom met a soul; but once a fellow who had been lying under a hedge by the way-side started up and began following me more nearly than I cared to have him, so I put on my cricketing speed and ran forward with a swiftness that few at that time could outstrip, and which soon left my would-be co-nightranger far behind. Well worth the fatigue of a twelve-mile walk there and another back was to me then the glorious delight of seeing Mrs. Siddons as Lady Macbeth or Queen Constance (though at a period when she had lost her pristine shapeliness of person, for she had become so bulky as to need assistance to rise from the ground in the scene where she throws herself there as her throne, bidding "kings come bow to it")! of seeing Miss O'Niel as Juliet, Belvidere, Monimia, and such tender heroines, which she played and looked charmingly; of seeing John Kemble as Coriolanus or Brutus, which he impersonated with true stateliness and dignity both of person and manner. But the greatest crowning of my eager "walks up to town to go to the play" was when Edmund Kean came upon the London stage; and I saw him in all his first perfection. The way in which he electrified the town by his fire, his energy, his vehement expression of natural emotion and passion, in such characters as Othello (in my opinion his masterpiece during his early and mature career), Lear, Hamlet, Richard III., Sir Giles Overreach, Sir Edmund Mortimer, and Shylock (certainly his grandest performance in his latter days), after the comparatively cold and staid propriety of John Kemble, was a thing never to be forgotten. Such was the enthusiasm of his audiences that the pit-door at as early an hour as three o'clock in the afternoon used to be clustered round, like the entrance to a hive of bees, by a crowd of playgoers determined to get places; and I had to obtain extra leave for quitting school early to make me one among them. The excitement rose to feve -pitch when—about two years after Kean's first appearance at Drury Lane Theatre—and Booth had been " starring it " as his rival at Covent Garden —it was announced that the two stage-magnates were to act together in the same play, Shakespeare's perhaps grandest tragedy being selected for the purpose—Booth playing Iago to Kean's Othello. Both tragedians, of course, exerted themselves to their utmost, and acted their finest ; and the result was a triumph of performance. The house was crammed ; the most dis tinguished of theatrical patrons, the most eminent among literary men and critics, being present. I remember Godwin, on coming out of the house, exclaiming, rapturously, " This is a night to be remembered !"

CHAPTER II.

Leigh Hunt—Henry Robertson—Frederick, William, Henry, and John Byng Gattie—Charles Ollier—Tom Richards — Thomas Moore—Barnes—Vincent Novello—John Keats— Charles and Mary Lamb—Wageman—Rev. W. V. Fryer— George and Charles Gliddon—Henry Robertson—Dowton —Mrs. Vincent Novello—Horace Twiss—Shelley—Walter Coulson.

THE elder of my two sisters having married and settled in London, I was now able to enjoy something of metropolitan society, and to indulge in the late hours it necessarily required me to keep, by sleeping at my brother-in-law's house, after an evening spent with such men as I now had the privilege of meeting. I was first introduced to Leigh Hunt at a party, when I remember he sang a cheery sea-song with much spirit in that sweet, small, baritone voice which he possessed. His manner— fascinating, animated, full of cordial amenity, and winning to a degree of which I have never seen the parallel— drew me to him at once, and I fell as pronely in love with him as any girl in her teens falls in love with her first-seen Romeo. My father had taken in the *Examiner* newspaper from its commencement, he and I week after week revelling in the liberty-loving, liberty-advocating, liberty-eloquent articles of the young editor ; and now that I made his personal acquaintance I was indeed a proud and happy fellow. The company among which I frequently encountered him were co-visitors of no small merit. Henry Robertson—one of the most delightful of associates for good temper, good spirits, good taste in all things literary and artistic; the brothers Gattie—Frederick, William, Henry, and John Byng Gattie, whose agreeable tenor voice is commemorated in Hunt's sonnet addressed to two of the men now under mention, and a third, of whom more presently; Charles Ollier—author of a graceful book called " Altham and his Wife," and publisher of Keats' first brought-out volume of " Poems ;" and Tom Richards—a right good comrade, a capital reader, a capital listener, a capital appreciator of talent and of genius.

My father so entirely sympathized with my devoted admiration of Leigh Hunt, that when, not very long after I had made his acquaintance, he was thrown into Horsemonger Lane Gaol for his libel on the Prince Regent, I was seconded in my wish to send the captive Liberal a breath of open air, and a reminder of the country pleasures he so well loved and could so well describe, by my father's allowing me to despatch a weekly basket of fresh flowers, fruit, and vegetables from our garden at Enfield. Leigh Hunt received it with his own peculiar grace of acceptance, recognizing the sentiment that prompted the offering, and welcoming it into the spot which he had converted from a prison-room into a bower for a poet by covering the walls with a rose-trellised papering, by book-shelves, plaster casts, and a small pianoforte. Here I was also made welcome, and my visits cordially received; and here it was that I once met Thomas Moore, and on another occasion Barnes, the then sub-editor of the *Times* newspaper, "whose native taste, solid and clear," Leigh Hunt has recorded in a charming sonnet. Barnes had been a schoolfellow of Leigh Hunt's at Christ's Hospital: he was a man of sound ability, yet with a sense of the absurd and humorous; for Leigh Hunt told me that a foolish woman once asking Barnes whether he were fond of children, received the answer, " Yes, ma'am ; boiled."

It was not until after Leigh Hunt left prison that my father saw him, and then but once. My father and I had gone to see Kean in " Timon of Athens," and as we sat together in the pit talking over the extraordinary vitality of the impersonation—the grandeur and poetry in Kean's indignant wrath, withering scorn, wild melancholy, embittered tone, and passionate despondency—Leigh Hunt joined us and desired me to present him to my father, who, after even the first few moments, found himself deeply enthralled by that bewitching spell of manner which characterized Leigh Hunt beyond any man I have ever known.

I cannot decidedly name the year when I was first made acquainted with the man whose memory I prize after that only of my own father. The reader will doubtless surmise that I am alluding to my father-in-law, the golden-hearted musician Vincent Novello. It was, I believe, at the lodging of Henry Robertson—a Treasury Office clerk, and the appointed accountant of Covent Garden Theatre. My introduction was so informal that it is not improbable my acquaintance with Leigh Hunt may have been known, and this produced so agreeable an interchange of courtesy that a day or two after, upon meeting Mr. Novello in Holborn, near Middle Row, I recollected having that day purchased a copy of Purcell's song in the "Tempest," "Full Fathom Five," and observing that the symphony had only the bass notes figured, I asked him to have the kindness to write the harmonies for me in the correct chords more legible to my limited knowledge of music. His immediate answer was that he " would take it home with him ;" and, with an unmistakable smile, he desired me to come for it on the morrow to 240, Oxford Street, where he then resided. This was the opening of the proudest and the happiest period of my existence. The glorious feasts of sacred music at the Portuguese Chapel in South Street, Grosvenor Square, where Vincent Novello was organist, and introduced the masses of Mozart and Haydn for the first time in England, and where the noble old Gregorian hymn tunes and responses were chanted to perfection by a small but select choir drilled and cultivated by him ; the exquisite evenings of Mozartian operatic and chamber music at Vincent Novello's own house, where Leigh Hunt, Shelley, Keats, and the Lambs were invited guests ; the brilliant supper parties at the alternate dwellings of the Novellos, the Hunts, and the Lambs, who had mutually agreed that bread and cheese, with celery, and Elia's immortalized " Lutheran beer," were to be the sole cates provided ; the meetings at the theatre, when Munden, Dowton, Liston, Bannister, Elliston, and Fanny Kelly were on the stage ; and the picnic repasts enjoyed together by appointment in the fields that then lay spread in green breadth and luxuriance between the west-end of Oxford Street and the western slope of Hampstead Hill —are things never to be forgotten. Vincent Novello fully shared my enthusiastic admiration for Leigh Hunt ; and it was at the period of the poet-patriot's leaving prison that his friend the poetical musician asked Leigh Hunt to sit for his portrait to Wageman, the artist who was famed for taking excellent likenesses in pencil-sketch style.   One of these pre-eminently good likenesses is a drawing made by Wageman of the Rev. William Victor Fryer, Head Chaplain to the Portuguese Embassy, to whom Vincent Novello's first published work—"A Collection of Sacred Music"—was dedicated, who stood god-father to Vincent Novello's eldest child, and who was not only a preacher of noted suavity and eloquence, but a man of elegant reading, refined taste, and most polished manners.   The drawing (representing Mr. Fryer in his priest's robes, in the pulpit, with his hand raised, according to his wont when about to commence his sermon) is still in our possession, as is that of Leigh Hunt ; the latter—a perfect resemblance of him as a young man, with his jet-black hair and his lustrous, dark eyes, full of mingled sweetness, penetration, and ardour of thought, with exalted imagination—has for many years held its place by our bedside in company with the portraits of Keats, Chaucer, Shakespeare, Jerrold, Dickens, and some of our own lost and loved honoured ones, nearer and dearer still.

Vincent Novello had a mode of making even simplest every-day objects matter for pleasant entertainment and amusing instruction ; and the mention of the consentedly restricted viands of those ever-to-be-remembered supper meals, reminds me of an instance.   As "bread-and cheese" was the stipulated "only fare" on these occasions, Vincent Novello (who knew Leigh Hunt's love for Italy and all things pertaining thereto) bethought him of introducing an Italian element into the British repasts, in the shape of Parmesan, a comparative rarity in those days.   He accordingly took one of his children with him to an Italian warehouse kept by a certain Bassano, who formed a fitting representative of his race, renowned for well-cut features, rich facial colouring, and courteous manner. Even now the look of Signor Bassano, with his spare but curly, dark hair, thin, chiselled nose, olive complexion, and well-bred demeanour, remains impressed on the memory of her who heard her father address the Italian in his own language and afterwards tell her of Italy and its beautiful scenery, of Italians and their personal beauty. She still can see the flasks labelled "finest Lucca oil" ranged in the shop, relative to which her father took the opportunity of feeding her fancy and mind with accounts of how the oil and even wine of that graceful country were mostly kept in flasks such as she then saw, with slender but strong handles of dried, grassy fibre, and corked by morsels of snowy, cotton wool.

This "Lucca oil" made an element in the delicious fare provided for a certain open-air party and prepared by the hands of Mrs. Novello herself, consisting of a magnificently well-jellied meat pie, cold roast lamb, and a salad, the conveyance of which to the spot where the assembly met was considered to be a marvel of ingenious management; a salad being a thing, till then, unheard of in the annals of picnic provision. The modest wines of orange and ginger—in the days when duty upon foreign importations amounted to prohibitory height—more than sufficed for quaffers who knew in books such vintages as Horace's Falernian, and Redi's Chianti and Montepulciano, whose intellectual palates were familiar with Milton's—

> Wines of Setia, Cales, and Falerne,
> Chios, and Crete ;

or whose imaginations could thirst "for a beaker full of the warm South," and behold—

> The true, the blushful Hippocrene,
> With beaded bubbles winking at the brim
> And purple-stained mouth.

This memorable out-door revel originated in one of the Novello children having the option given to her of celebrating her birthday by a treat of "going to the play," or "a day in the fields." After grave consideration and solemn consultation with her brothers and sisters, the latter was chosen, because the month was June and the weather transcendently beautiful. The large and happy party was to consist of the whole Novello family, Hunt family, and Gliddon family, who were to meet at an appointed hour in some charming meadows leading up to Hampstead. "The young Gliddons" were chiefly known to the young Novellos as surpassingly good dancers at their interchanged juvenile balls. and as super-excellently good rompers at their interchanged birthday parties, but one of the members of the family, George Gliddon, became celebrated in England for his erudition concerning Egyptian hieroglyphics, and in America for his lectures on this subject; while his son Charles has since made himself known by his designs for illustrated books. The children frolicked about the fields and had agile games among themselves, while their elders sat on the turf enjoying talk upon all kinds of gay and jest-provoking subjects. To add to the mirth of the meeting, Henry Robertson and I were asked to join them; both being favourites with the youngsters, both possessing the liveliest of spirits, and known to be famous promoters of fun and hilarity. To crown the pleasure Leigh Hunt, as he lay stretched on the grass, read out to the assembled group, old and young—or rather, growing and grown up —the Dogberry scenes from "Much Ado about Nothing," till the place rang with shouts and shrieks of laughter. Leigh Hunt's reading aloud was pre-eminently good. Varied in tone and inflection of voice, unstudied, natural, characteristic, full of a keen sense of the humour of the scenes and the wit of the dialogue, his dramatic reading was almost unequalled : and we can remember his perusal of the Sir Anthony Absolute scenes in Sheridan's "Rivals," and Foote's farce of "The Liar," as pieces of uproarious merriment. Even Dowton himself—and his acted impersonation of Sir Anthony was a piece of wonderful truth for towering wrath and irrational fury— hardly surpassed Leigh Hunt's reading of the part, so masterly a rendering was it of old-gentlemanly wilfulness and comedy-father whirlwind of raging tyranny. The underlying zest in roguery of gallantry and appreciation of beauty that mark old Absolute's character were delightfully indicated by Leigh Hunt's delicate as well as forcible mode of utterance, and carried his hearers along with him in a trance of excitement while he read.

Having referred to Mrs. Vincent Novello's long-famed meat-pie and salad, I will here "make recordation" of two skilled brewages for which she was renowned : to wit, elder wine—racy, fragrant with spice, steaming with comfortable heat, served in taper glasses with accompanying rusks or slender slices of toasted bread—and foaming wassail-bowl, brought to table in right old English style, with roasted crab apples (though these were held to be less good in reality than as a tribute to antique British usage) : both elder wine and wassail-bowl excellently ministering to festive celebration at the Novellos' Christmas, New Year, and Twelfth Night parties. Mrs. Vincent Novello was a woman of Nature's noblest mould. Housewifely—nay, actively domestic in her daily duties, methodical to a nicety in all her home arrangements, nurse and instructress to her large family of children—she was nevertheless ever ready to sympathize with her husband's highest tastes, artistic and literary; to read to him when he returned home after a long day's teaching and required absolute rest, or to converse with him on subjects that occupied his eager and alert mind. Not only could she read and converse with spirit and brilliancy, but she wrote with much grace and fancy. At rarely-gained leisure moments her pen produced several tasteful Tales, instinct with poetic idea and romantic imagery. She had an elegant talent for verse, some of her lines having been set to music by her husband. She was godmother to Leigh Hunt's *Indicator*, supplying him with the clue to the information which he embodied in the first motto to that periodical,[1] and suggesting the felicitous title which he adopted. Mrs. Novello contributed a paper to the *Indicator*, entitled "Holiday Children," and signed "An Old Boy;" also some papers to Leigh Hunt's *Tatler* and a large portion of a novel (in letters), which was left a fragment in consequence of this serial coming to an abrupt close. Per-

[1] "There is a bird in the interior of Africa whose habits would rather seem to belong to the interior of Fairyland, but they have been well authenticated. It indicates to honey-hunters where the nests of wild bees are to be found. It calls them with a cheerful cry, which they answer; and on finding itself recognized, flies and hovers over a hollow tree containing the honey. While they are occupied in collecting it, the bird goes to a little distance, where he observes all that passes; and the hunters, when they have helped themselves, take care to leave him his portion of the food. This is the Cuculus Indicator of Linnæus, otherwise called the Moroc, Bee Cuckoo, or Honey Bird."

fectly did Mrs. Vincent Novello confirm the assertion that the most intellectual and cultivated women are frequently the most gentle, unassuming, and proficient housewives ; for few of even her intimate friends were aware that she was an authoress, so perpetually was she found occupied with her husband and her children. Horace Twiss, who was acquainted with the Novellos and often visited them at their house in Oxford Street, near Hyde Park, proclaimed himself a devoted admirer of Mary Sabilla Novello, as the next among women to Mary Wolstonecraft, with whom he was notedly and avowedly "deeply smitten." He used to knock at the door, and, when it was opened, inquire whether he could see Mrs. Novello ; while she, from the front-parlour—which was dedicated to the children's use as nursery and play-room—hearing his voice, and being generally too busy of a morning with them to receive visitors, would put her head forth from amid her young flock, and call out to him, with a nod and a smile, " I'm not at home to-day, Mr. Twiss ! " Upon which he would raise his hat and retire, declaring that she was more than ever adorable.

Over the low blind of that front-parlour and nursery play-room window the eldest of the young Novellos peeped on a certain afternoon to see pass into the street a distinguished guest, whom she heard had been in the drawing-room upstairs to visit her parents. She watched for the opening of the street door, and then quickly climbed on to a chair that she might catch sight of the young poet spoken so highly and honouringly of by her father and mother—Percy Bysshe Shelley. She saw him move lightly down the two or three stone steps from the entrance, and as he went past the front of the house he suddenly looked up at it, revealing fully to view his beautiful poet-face, with its clear, blue eyes surmounted by an aureole of gold-brown hair.

It was at Leigh Hunt's cottage in the Vale of Health, on Hampstead Heath, that I first met Shelley; and I remember our all three laughing at the simplicity of his imagining—in his ignorance of journals and journal construction—that Leigh Hunt wrote the whole of the *Examiner* himself—right through—" Money Market," " Price of Coals," and all! On another occasion I recollect a very warm argument in favour of the Monarchy upheld by Leigh Hunt and Coulson, and in favour of Republicanism by Shelley and Hazlitt.

Walter Coulson was editor of the *Globe* newspaper. He was a Cornish man: and these " pestilent knaves " of wits used to tease him about " The Giant Cormoran," some traditionary magnate of his native country whose prowess he was supposed to exaggerate. They nevertheless acknowledged Coulson to be almost boundless in his varied extent of knowledge, calling him " a walking Encyclopædia ; " and once agreed that next time he came he should be asked three questions on widely different subjects, laying a wager that he would be sure to be able to give a satisfactory answer upon each and all—which he did. If my memory rightly serve me, the questions were these :—The relative value of gold coin in India with sterling money ? The mode of measuring the cubic feet contained in the timber of a tree ? And some moot point of correctness in one of the passages from an ancient classic poet.

It was on a bright afternoon in the early days of my visits to Leigh Hunt at the Vale of Health that the authors of these " Recollections " first saw each other.

Had some prescient spirit whispered in the ear of each in turn, "You see your future wife!" and, "That is your future husband!" the prediction would have seemed passing strange. I was in the fresh flush of proud and happy friendship with such men as Leigh Hunt and those whom I met at his house, thoroughly absorbed in the intellectual treats I thus constantly enjoyed; while she was a little girl brought by her parents for a day's run on the Heath with the Hunt children, thinking that " Charles Clarke "—as she heard him called—was "a good-natured gentleman," because, when evening came and there was a proposal for her staying on a few days at Hampstead, he threw in a confirmatory word by saying, " Do let her stay, Mrs. Novello; the air of the Heath has already brought more roses into her cheeks than were there a few hours ago."

It must have been a full decade after our first meeting that we began to think of each other with any feeling of deeper preference; and during those ten years much that profoundly interested me took place; while events occurred that carried me away from London and literary associates. When my father retired from the school at Enfield, he went to live in the Isle of Thanet, taking a house at Ramsgate, where he and my mother had frequently before made pleasant sea-side sojourns during " the holidays." Here my younger sister and myself dwelt with our parents for a somewhat long period; and it was while we were at Ramsgate that I remember hearing of Charles Lamb and his sister being at Margate for a " sea change," and I went over to see them. It seems as if it were but yesterday that I noted his eager way of telling me about an extraordinarily large whale that had been captured there, of its having created lively interest in the place, of its having been conveyed away in a strong cart, on which it lay a huge mass of colossal height; when he added with one of his sudden droll penetrating glances :—The *eye* has just gone past our window.

I was at Ramsgate when Leigh Hunt started the "Literary Pocket-Book," asking his friends for prose and verse contributions to that portion of its contents 'ich was to form one of its distinguishing characteristics from hitherto published pocket-books. I was among those to whom he applied ; and it was with no small elation that I found myself for the first time in print under the wing of Leigh Hunt. The work appeared in red morocco case for four consecutive years, 1819, '20, '21, and '22, in the second of which he put No. I of "Walks round London," where I described my favourite haunts to the south-west of Enfield, and contributed a small verse-piece entitled " On Visiting a Beautiful Little Dell near Margate,"both signed with my initials. Under various signatures of Greek characters and Roman capitals, Shelley, Keats, Procter ("Barry Cornwall"), Charles Ollier, and others, together with Leigh Hunt himself, contributed short poems and brief prose pieces to the "Literary Pocket-Book ;" so that I ventured forth into the world of letters in most "worshipful society."

Leigh Hunt afterwards paid me a visit at Ramsgate, when the ship in which he and his family were sailing for Italy put into the harbour from stress of weather ; and it was on this occasion that my mother—who had long witnessed my own and my father's enthusiasm for Leigh Hunt, but had never much shared it, not having seen him—now at once understood the fascination he exercised over those who came into personal communion with him. "He is a gentleman, a perfect gentleman, Charles! He is irresistible!" was her first exclamation to me, when he had left us.

Another visitor made his appearance at Ramsgate, giving me vivid but short-lived delight. Vincent Novello, whose health had received a severe shock in losing a favourite boy, Sydney, was advised to try what a complete change would do towards restoration, and he came down with the intention of staying a few days; but, finding that some old friends of my father and mother were on a visit to us, his habitual shyness of strangers took possession of him, and he returned to town, having scarcely more than shaken hands with me.

Not long after that, anguish kindred to his assailed me. In the December of 1820 I lost my revered and beloved father; and in the following February my friend and schoolfellow John Keats died.

CHAPTER III.

Samuel Taylor Coleridge—Jefferson Hogg—Henry Crabbe
Robinson—Bryan Waller Procter (" Barry Cornwall ")—
Godwin—Mrs. Shelley—Mrs. Williams—Francis Novello
—Henry Robertson—Edward Holmes—Mary Lamb—
The honourable Mrs. Norton—Countess of Blessington.

IT was in the summer of 1821 that I first beheld Samuel
Taylor Coleridge.   It was on the East Cliff at Ramsgate.
He was contemplating the sea under its most attractive
aspect : in a dazzling sun, with sailing clouds that drew
their purple shadows over its bright green floor, and a
merry breeze of sufficient prevalence to emboss each
wave with a silvery foam.   He might possibly have
composed upon the occasion one of the most philoso-
phical, and at the same time most enchanting, of his
fugitive reflections, which he has entitled " Youth and
Age ;" for in it he speaks of "airy cliffs and glittering
sands," and—

> Of those trim skiffs, unknown of yore,
>   On winding lakes and rivers wide,
> That ask no aid of sail or oar,
>   That fear no spite of wind or tide.

As he had no companion, I desired to pay my respects
to one of the most extraordinary—and, indeed in his
department of genius, *the* most extraordinary man of his
age.   And being possessed of a talisman for securing

his consideration, I introduced myself as a friend and admirer of Charles Lamb. This pass-word was sufficient, and I found him immediately talking to me in the bland and frank tones of a standing acquaintance. A poor girl had that morning thrown herself from the pier-head in a pang of despair, from having been betrayed by a villain. He alluded to the event, and went on to denounce the morality of the age that will hound from the community the reputed weaker subject, and continue to receive him who has wronged her. He agreed with me that that question never will be adjusted but by the women themselves. Justice will continue in abeyance so long as they visit with severity the errors of their own sex and tolerate those of ours. He then diverged to the great mysteries of life and death, and branched away to the sublimer question—the immortality of the soul. Here he spread the sail-broad vans of his wonderful imagination, and soared away with an eagle-flight, and with an eagle-eye too, compassing the effulgence of his great argument, ever and anon stooping within my own sparrow's range, and then glancing away again, and careering through the trackless fields of etherial metaphysics. And thus he continued for an hour and a half, never pausing for an instant except to catch his breath (which, in the heat of his teeming mind, he did like a schoolboy repeating by rote his task), and gave utterance to some of the grandest thoughts I ever heard from the mouth of man. His ideas, embodied in words of purest eloquence, flew about my ears like drifts of snow. He was like a cataract filling and rushing over my penny-phial capacity. I could only gasp and bow my head in acknowledgment. He required from me nothing more than the simple recognition of his discourse ; and so he went on like a steam-engine—I keeping the machine oiled with my looks of pleasure, while he supplied the fuel : and that, upon the same theme too, would have lasted till now. What would I have given for a short-hand report of that speech ! And such was the habit of this wonderful man. Like the old peripatetic philosophers, he walked about, prodigally scattering wisdom, and leaving it to the winds of chance to waft the seeds into a genial soil.

My first suspicion of his being at Ramsgate had arisen from my mother observing that she had heard an elderly gentleman in the public library, who looked like a Dissenting minister, talking as she never heard man talk. Like his own " Ancient Mariner," when he had once fixed your eye he held you spell-bound, and you were constrained to listen to his tale ; you must have been more powerful than he to have broken the charm ; and I know no man worthy to do that. He did indeed answer to my conception of a man of genius, for his mind flowed on " like to the Pontick sea," that " ne'er feels retiring ebb." It was always ready for action ; like the hare, it slept with its eyes open. He would at any given moment range from the subtlest and most abstruse question in metaphysics to the architectural beauty in contrivance of a flower of the field ; and the gorgeousness of his imagery would increase and dilate and flash forth such coruscations of similies and startling theories that one was in a perpetual aurora borealis of fancy. As Hazlitt once said of him, " He would talk on for ever, and you wished him to talk on for ever. His thoughts never seemed to come with labour or effort, but as if borne on the gust of Genius, and as if the wings of his imagination lifted him off his feet." This is as truly as poetically described. He would not only illustrate a theory or an argument with a sustained and superb figure, but in pursuing the current of his thought he would bubble up with a sparkle of fancy so fleet and brilliant that the attention, though startled and arrested, was not broken. He would throw these into the stream of his argument, as waifs and strays. Notwithstanding his wealth of language and prodigious power in amplification, no one, I think (unless it were Shakespeare or Bacon), possessed with himself equal power of condensation. He would frequently comprise the elements of a noble theorem in two or three words; and, like the genuine offspring of a poet's brain, it always came forth in a golden halo. I remember once, in discoursing upon the architecture of the Middle Ages, he reduced the Gothic structure into a magnificent abstraction,—and in two words. " A Gothic cathedral," he said, " is like a petrified religion."

In his prose, as well as in his poetry, Coleridge's comparisons are almost uniformly short and unostentatious; and not on that account the less forcible : they are scriptural in character ; indeed it would be difficult to find one more apt to the purpose than that which he has used ; and yet it always appears to be unpremeditated. Here is a random example of what I mean : it is an unimportant one, but it serves for a casual illustration of his force in comparison. It is the last line in that strange and impressive fragment in prose, " The Wanderings of Cain :"—" And they three passed over the white sands, and between the rocks, silent as their shadows." It will be difficult, I think, to find a stronger image than that, to convey the idea of the utter negation of sound, with motion.

Like all men of genius, and with the gift of eloquence, Coleridge had a power and subtlety in interpretation that would persuade an ordinary listener against the conviction of his senses.   It has been said of him that he could persuade a Christian he was a Platonist, a Deist that he was a Christian, and an Atheist that he believed in a God. The Preface to his Ode of "Fire, Famine, and Slaughter," wherein he labours to show that Pitt the Prime Minister was *not* the object of his invective at the time of his composing that famous war-eclogue, is at once a triumphant specimen of his talent for special pleading and ingenuity in sophistication.

In a lecture upon Shakespeare's "Tempest" Coleridge kept his audience in a roar of laughter by drawing a ludicrous comparison between the monster Caliban and a modern Radical.   It was infinitely droll and clever ; but like a true sophist, there was one point of the argument which he failed to illustrate—and, indeed, never alluded to—viz. that Caliban, the Radical, was inheritor of the soil by birth-right ; and Prospero, the aristocrat, was the aggressor and self-constituted legislator.   The tables thus easily turned upon Mr. Coleridge, would have involved him in an edifying dilemma.   The fact is, that Coleridge had been a Jacobin, and was one of the marked men in the early period of the French Revolution.   It was at this period of his life that he served as a private in a regiment, and used to preach Liberalism to his brethren ; and I believe he quickly had his discharge.   He had also been a professor of Unitarianism, and delivered sermons.   He once asked Charles Lamb if he had ever heard him preach; who replied that he "never heard him do anything else."   All these opinions he afterwards ostensibly abjured ; and doubtless he had good reason for making manifest his conversion from what he conceived to have been error.   Like the chameleon, he would frequently adopt and reflect the hue of his converser's pre-judices, where neither opinions (religious or political) were positively offensive to him; and thus, from a tranquillity —perhaps I might say, an indolence—of disposition, he would fashion his discourse and frame his arguments, for the time being, to suit the known predilections of his companion. It is therefore idle to represent him as a partisan at all, unless it be for kindness and freedom of thought; and I know no other party principle worth a button.

The upper part of Coleridge's face was excessively fine. His eyes were large, light grey, prominent, and of liquid brilliancy, which some eyes of fine character may be ob-served to possess, as though the orb itself retreated to the innermost recesses of the brain. The lower part of his face was somewhat dragged, indicating the presence of habitual pain; but his forehead was prodigious, and like a smooth slab of alabaster. A grander head than his has not been seen in the grove at Highgate since his neighbour Lord Bacon lived there. From his physical conformation Coleridge ought to have attained an ex-treme old age, and he probably would have done so but for the fatal habit he had encouraged of resorting to the stimulus of opium. Not many months before his death, when alluding to his general health, he told me that he never in his life knew the sensation of head-ache; adding, in his own peculiarly vivid manner of illustration, that he had no more internal consciousness of possessing a head than he had of having an eye.

My married sister having gone to reside with her hus-band and their young family in the West of England, my mother and my unmarried sister went to live near them; while I returned to London and to delightful friendships already formed there. In renewing my old pleasant relations with men previously named I had the good fortune to come into contact with others of literary reputation and social attraction. Jefferson Hogg, author of "A Hundred and Nine Days on the Continent," with his dry humour, caustic sarcasm, and peculiar views of men and things, I met at Lamb's house ; who, one night when Jefferson Hogg sat opposite to him, fastened his eyes on his throat and suddenly asked, "Did you put on your own cravat this morning ?" and receiving an answer in the affirmative, rejoined, "Ay, I thought it was a *hog-stye !*" There I also met Henry Crabbe Robinson ; that agreeable diarist and universal keeper-up of acquaintance. I suppose never man had a larger circle of friends whom he constantly visited and constantly received than he had, or one who was more generally welcome as a diner-out, and better liked as a giver of snug dinners, than himself. Now too, I saw Bryan Waller Procter, whom I had known and admired in his poetry, in his "Dramatic Scenes," and "Sicilian Story," published under his pen-name of "Barry Cornwall," and subsequently knew in his poetically beautiful tragedy of "Mirandola" and his collection of lovely "Songs." He had a modest —nay, shy—manner in company ;· heightened by a singular nervous affection, a kind of sudden twitch or contraction, that spasmodically flitted athwart his face as he conversed upon any lofty theme, or argued on some high-thoughted topic. I again also occasionally met Godwin. His bald head, singularly wanting in the organ of veneration. (for the spot where phrenologists state that "bump" to be, was on Godwin's head an indentation instead of a protuberance), betokened of itself a remarkable man and individual thinker ; and his laugh—with its abrupt, short, monosound—more like a sharp gasp or snort than a laugh—seemed alone sufficient to proclaim the cynical, satirical, hard-judging, deep-sighted, yet strongly-feeling and strangely-imaginative author of " Political Justice," " Caleb Williams," " St. Leon," and " Fleetwood." His snarling tone of voice exacerbated the effect of his sneering speeches and cutting retorts. On one occasion, meeting Leigh Hunt, who complained of the shortness of his sight and generally wore attached to a black ribbon a small single eye-glass to aid him in descrying objects, Godwin answered his complaints by saying sharply, " You should wear spectacles." Leigh Hunt playfully admitted that he hardly liked yet to take to so old-gentlemanly-looking and disfiguring an apparatus ; when Godwin retorted, with his snapping laugh, " Ha ! What a coxcomb you must be !"

The Novellos, after leaving Oxford Street, and residing for a few years at 8, Percy Street, had taken a large, old-fashioned house and garden on Shacklewell Green ; and it was here that they made welcome Mrs. Shelley and Mrs. Williams on their return from Italy, two young and beautiful widows, wooing them by gentle degrees into peace-fuller and hopefuller mood of mind after their storm of bereavement abroad. By quiet meetings for home-music ; by calmly cheerful and gradually sprightlier converse ; by affectionate familiarity and reception into their own family circle of children and friends, Vincent and Mary Sabilla Novello sought to draw these two fair women into reconcilement with life and its still surviving blessings. Very, very fair, both ladies were : Mary Wolstonecraft Godwin Shelley, with her well-shaped, golden-haired head, almost always a little bent and drooping ; her marble-white shoulders and arms statuesquely visible in the per-

fectly plain black velvet dress, which the customs of that
time allowed to be cut low, and which her own taste
adopted (for neither she nor her sister-in-sorrow ever
wore the conventional " widow's weeds " and " widow's
cap "); her thoughtful, earnest eyes ; her short upper lip
and intellectually curved mouth, with a certain close-
compressed and decisive expression while she listened, and
a relaxation into fuller redness and mobility when speaking ; her exquisitely-formed, white, dimpled, small hands,
with rosy palms, and plumply commencing fingers, that
tapered into tips as slender and delicate as those in a
Vandyk portrait—all remain palpably present to memory.
Another peculiarity in Mrs. Shelley's hand was its singular flexibility, which permitted her bending the fingers
back so as almost to approach the portion of her arm
above her wrist. She once did this smilingly and repeatedly, to amuse the girl who was noting its whiteness
and pliancy, and who now, as an old woman, records its
remarkable beauty. Very sweet and very encouraging
was Mary Shelley to her young namesake, Mary Victoria,
making her proud and happy by giving her a presentation
copy of her wonderful book " Frankenstein " (still in
treasured preservation, with its autograph gift-words), and
pleasing her girlish fancy by the gift of a string of cut-
coral, graduated beads from Italy. On such pleasant
terms of kindly intimacy was Mrs. Shelley at this period
with the Novellos that she and Mrs. Novello interchanged
with one another their sweet familiar name of " Mary ; "
and she gave the Italianized form of his name to Mr.
Novello, calling him " Vincenzo " in her most caressing
tones, when she wished to win him into indulging her
with some of her especially favourite strains of music.
Even his brother, Mr. Francis Novello, she would address

as " Francesco," as loving to speak the soft Italian syllables.   Her mode of uttering the word " Lerici " dwells upon our memory with peculiarly subdued and lingering intonation, associated as it was with all that was most mournful in connexion with that picturesque spot where she learned she had lost her beloved " Shelley " for ever from this fair earth.   She was never tired of asking "Francesco " to sing, in his rich, mellow bass voice, Mozart's " Qui sdegno," " Possenti Numi," " Mentre ti lascio," " Tuba mirum," " La Vendetta," " Non piu andrai," or " Madamina ;" so fond was she of his singing her favourite composer.   Greatly she grew to enjoy the " concerted pieces " from " Così fan tutte," that used to be got up " round the piano."   Henry Robertson's dramatic spirit and vivacity and his capacity and readiness in taking *anything*, tenor or counter-tenor—nay, soprano if need were—that might chance to be most required, more than made up for the smallness of his voice.   His fame for singing Fernando's part in the opening trio, " La mia Dorabella," with the true chivalrous zest and fire of his phrase, "*fuore la spada !*" accompanied by appropriate action, lasted through a long course of years. Henry Robertson was one of the very best amateur singers conceivable : indefatigable, yet never anxious to sing if better tenors than himself chanced to be present ; an almost faultless " reader at sight," always in tune, invariably in good temper, and never failingly " in the humour for music," qualities that will at once be appreciated by those who know what the majority of amateur singers generally are.   Edward Holmes was among the enthusiastic party of enjoyers so often assembling at Shacklewell in those days.   His rapturous love of music, his promptly kindled admiration of feminine beauty, caused him to be in a perpetual ecstasy with the Mozart evenings and the charming young-lady widows. He used to be unmercifully rallied about his enamoured fantasies with regard to both; and he took to rallying his old school-mate, "Charles Clarke," in sheer self-defence, on the same score. But the latter was comparatively heart-whole, while "Ned Holmes" was riddled through and through by "the blind bow-boy's butt-shaft." Charles Clarke admired, Ned Holmes adored; Charles Clarke fluttered like a moth round the brilliant attractions, while Ned Holmes plunged madly into the scorching flames and recked not possible destruction. We used often and through a long train of years to laugh at Edward Holmes for his susceptible heart, lost a dozen times in a dozen months to some fair "Cynthia of the minute," some prima-donna who sang entrancingly, some sparkler who laughed bewitchingly, or some tragedy beauty who wept with truth and passion. He confided these ephemeral captivations with amusing candour to the first hearer among his favourite associates, often choosing for his confidante the eldest daughter of his friend and master-in-music, Vincent Novello, when he shared his opera ticket or his playhouse order with her (in turn with one of her brothers or sisters) by her parents' leave.

By the time I (C. C. C.) renewed my visits to her father and mother's house, when Mrs. Shelley and Mrs. Williams were first welcomed there, this "eldest daughter" was growing into young girlhood, and I (M. C. C.) had changed from the "little girl" allowed to "sit up to supper as a great treat"—when Leigh Hunt, "the Lambs," and other distinguished friends met at 240, Oxford Street, in the times of the Parmesan there, or of the "ripe Stilton" at the Vale of Health, or of the "old crumbly Cheshire" at the Lambs' lodgings—into a damsel approaching towards the age of "sweet sixteen," privileged to consider herself one of the grown-up people. Whereas formerly I had been "one of the children," I now spoke of my younger brothers and sisters as "the children ;" and whereas at the Vale of Health I used to join the Hunt children in their games of play on the Heath, I now knew of the family being in Italy, and was permitted to. hear the charming letters received from there; and whereas it was not so very long ago when I had been sent with Emma Isola by Mary Lamb into her own room at Great Russell Street, Covent Garden, to have a girlish chat together by ourselves unrestrained by the presence of the graver and cleverer talkers, I was now wont to sit by preference with my elders and enjoy their music and their conversation, their mutual banter, their mutual and several predilections among each other. Always somewhat observant as a child, I had now become a greater observer than ever; and large and varied was the pleasure I derived from my observation of the interesting men and women around me at this time of my life. Certainly Mary Wolstonecraft Godwin Shelley was the central figure of attraction then to my young-girl sight ; and I looked upon her with ceaseless admiration—for her personal graces, as well as for her literary distinction. The daughter of William Godwin and Mary Wolstonecraft Godwin, the wife of Shelley, the authoress of "Frankenstein," had for me a concentration of charm and interest that perpetually excited and engrossed me while she continued a visitor at my parents' house. My father held her in especial regard ; and she evinced equally affectionate esteem for him. A note of hers, dated a few years after the Shacklewell days, sending him the priceless treasure of a lock of her illustrious mother's hair, and written in the melodious tongue so dear to both writer and receiver, shall be here transcribed, for the reader to share the pleasure of its perusal with her who has both note and hair carefully enshrined beneath a crystal covering: —

"Tempo fà, mio caro Vincenzo, vi promisi questa treccia dei capelli della mia Madre—non mi son scordata della mia promessa e voi non vi siete scordato di me—sono sicurissima. Il regalo presente adunque vi farà rammentare piacevolmente lei chi ama per sempre i suoi amici—fra di quali crederà di sempre trovarvi quantunque le circonstanze ci dividono.
"State felice—e conservatemi almeno la vostra stima, vi prega la vostra amica vera,
"11 March, 1828."   " MARY SHELLEY."

To my thinking, two other women only, among those I have seen who were distinguished for personal beauty as well as for literary eminence, ever equalled in these respects Mary Shelley; one of them was the Honourable Mrs. Norton, the other the Countess of Blessington; but these two latter-named stars I never beheld in a familiar sphere, I merely beheld them in their box at the Opera, or at the Theatre. Mrs. Norton was the realization of what one might imagine a Muse of Poesy would look like,—dark-haired, dark-eyed, classic-browed, and delicate-featured in the extreme, with a bearing of mingled feminine grace and regal graciousness. Lady Blessington, fair, florid-complexioned, with sparkling eyes and white, high forehead, above which her bright brown hair was smoothly braided beneath a light and simple blonde cap, in which were a few touches of sky-blue satin ribbon that singularly well became her, setting off her buxom face and its vivid colouring.

CHAPTER IV.

Leigh Hunt—William Hone—The elder Mathews—John
Keats—Charles and Mary Lamb—Sheridan Knowles—
Bryan Waller Procter.

LATE in the year 1825 Leigh Hunt returned from Italy
to England. The enthusiastic attachment felt for him by
his men friends was felt with equal ardour by the young
girl who had always heard him spoken of in the most
admiring terms by her father, her mother, and many of
those she best loved and esteemed. His extraordinary
grace of manner, his exceptionally poetic appearance,
his distinguished fame as a man of letters, all exercised
strong fascination over her imagination. In childhood
she had looked up to him as an impersonation of all that
was heroic in suffering for freedom of opinion's sake, of
all that was comely in person, of all that was attractive
in manner, of all that was tasteful in written inculcation
and acted precept. He was her beau-ideal of literary and
social manhood.

As quite a little creature she can well remember creep-
ing round to the back of the sofa where his shapely
hand rested, and giving it a gentle, childish kiss, and his
peeping over at her, and giving a quiet, smiling nod in
acknowledgment of the baby homage, while he went on
with the conversation in which he was engaged. Afterwards, as a growing girl, when she used to hear his

removal to Italy discussed, and his not too prosperous means deplored, she indulged romantic visions of working hard, earning a fabulously large sum, carrying it in fairy-land princess style a pilgrimage across the Continent barefoot, and laying it at his feet, amply rewarded by one of his winning smiles. Strange as it seems now to be recounting openly these then secretly cherished fancies, they were most sincere and most true at the time they were cherished. If ever were man fitted to inspire such white-souled aspirations in a girl not much more than a dozen years old, it was Leigh Hunt. Delicate-minded as he was, rich in beautiful thoughts, pure in speech and in writing as he was ardently eloquent in style, perpetually suggesting graceful ideas and adorning daily life by elevated associations, he was precisely the man to become a young girl's object of innocent hero-worship. When therefore I met him for the first time after his return from Italy, at the house of one of my parents' friends, all my hoarded feeling on behalf of him and his fortunes came so strongly upon me, and the sound of his voice so powerfully affected me, that I could with difficulty restrain my sobs. He chanced to be singing one of the pretty Irish melodies to which his friend Moore had put words, "Rich and rare were the gems she wore,"—and, as I listened to the voice I remembered so well and had not heard for so long, the silent tears fell from my eyes in large drops of mingled pain and pleasure. He was the man in all the world to best interpret such an ebullition of feeling had he observed it; but I was thankful to perceive that he had no idea of the agitation I had been in, when he finished his song and began his usual delightful strain of conversation. Leigh Hunt's conversation was simply perfection. If he were in argument—however warm it might be—he would wait fairly and patiently to hear "the other side." Unlike most eager conversers, he never interrupted. Even to the youngest among his colloquists he always gave full attention, and listened with an air of genuine respect to whatever they might have to adduce in support of their view of a question. He was peculiarly encouraging to young aspirants, whether fledgling authors or callow casuists; and treated them with nothing of condescension, or affable accommodation of his intellect to theirs, or amiable tolerance for their comparative incapacity, but, as it were, placed them at once on a handsome footing of equality and complete level with himself. When, as was frequently the case, he found himself left master of the field of talk by his delighted hearers, only too glad to have him recount in his own felicitous way one of his "good stories," or utter some of his "good things," he would go on in a strain of sparkle, brilliancy, and freshness like a sun-lit stream in a spring meadow. Melodious in tone, alluring in accent, eloquent in choice of words, Leigh Hunt's talk was as delicious to listen to as rarest music. Spirited and fine as his mode of narrating a droll anecdote in written diction undoubtedly is, his mode of telling it was still more spirited, and still more fine. Impressive and solemn as is his way of writing down a ghost-story or tragic incident, his power in telling it was still better. Tender and affecting as is his manner of penning a sad love-story, or a mournful chapter in history, and the "Romance of Real Life," his style of telling it went beyond in pathos of expression. He used more effusion of utterance, more mutation of voice, and more energy of gesture, than is common to most Englishmen when under the excitement of recounting a comic story ; and this produced corresponding excitement in his hearers, so that the " success " of his good stories was unfailing, and the laughter that followed him throughout was worked to a climax at the close. Those who have laughed heartily when merely reading his paper entitled " On the Graces and Anxieties of Pig-driving," will perhaps hardly credit us when we assert that Leigh Hunt's own mode of relating the event he there describes of the pig-driving in Long Lane far surpassed the effect produced by the written narration,— polishedly witty and richly humorous as that written narration assuredly is. The way in which Leigh Hunt raised his tone of voice to the highest pitch, hurling himself forward the while upon air, as if in wild desire to retrieve the bolting pig, as he exclaimed, " He'll go up all manner of streets ! " brought to the hearers' actual sight the anguish of the "poor fellow," who was "not to be comforted in Barbican," and placed the whole scene palpably before them.

In the summer of 1826 my father and mother went down to a pretty rural sea-side spot near Hastings called Little Bohemia, taking me, the eldest of my brothers, and one of my younger sisters, with them for the change of air that these members of our family especially needed ; and when we returned home to Shacklewell it chanced that Charles and I met very frequently during the autumn ; so frequently, and with such fast-increasing mutual affection that on the 1st of November in that year we became engaged to each other. As I was only seventeen, and my parents thought me too young to be married, our engagement was not generally made known. This caused a rather droll circumstance to happen. Charles, having occasion to call on business connected with the

' Every-day Book," upon William Hone,—who was then under temporary pressure of difficulties and dwelt in a district called "within the rules " of the King's Bench prison,—took me with him to see that clever and deservedly popular writer. Our way lying through a region markedly distinguished for its atmosphere of London smoke, London dirt, London mud, and London squalor, some of the flying soots chanced to leave traces on my countenance ; and while we were talking to Mr. Hone, Charles, noticing a large smut on my face, coolly blew it off, and continued the conversation. Next time they met, Hone said to Charles, " You are engaged to Miss Novello, are you not ? " " What makes you think so?" was the rejoinder. "Oh, when I saw you so familiarly puff off that smut on a young lady's cheek, and she so quietly submitted to your mode of doing it, I knew you must be an engaged pair."

By the time Hone's " Every-day Book " had been succeeded by his " Table Book," I resolved that I would quietly try whether certain manuscript attempts I had made in the art of composition might not be accepted for publication; and I thought I would send them, on this chance, to Mr. Hone, under an assumed signature. The initials I adopted were " M. H."—meaning thereby " Mary Howard ; " because my father had once when a young man enacted Falstaff, in a private performance of the First Part of Henry IV., as " Mr. Howard." Taking into my confidence none but my sister nearest to me in age (whom I always called "my old woman " when she did me the critical service rendered by Molière's old maid-servant to her master), and finding that she did not frown down either the written essay or the contemplated enterprise, I forwarded my first paper, entitled " My

Armchair," and to mine and my sister Cecilia's boundless joy found it accepted by Hone, and printed in one of the numbers of the " Table Book " for June, 1827, where also appeared some playful verses by Elia, headed " Gone, or Going," and No. XXII. of his series of extracts from the old dramatists, which he called " Garrick Plays." I shall not easily forget the novice pride with which I showed the miniature essay to Charles, and asked him what he thought of it as written by a girl of seventeen ; still less can I forget the smile and glance of pleased surprise with which he looked up and recognized *who* was the girl-writer.

These are some of the bygone self-memories that such " Recollections " as we have been requested to record are apt to beguile us into ; and such as we must beg our readers to forbear from looking upon in the light of egoism, but rather to regard as friendly chit-chat about past pleasant times agreeable in the recalling to both chatter and chattee.

My father and mother had left Shacklewell Green and returned to reside in London when Mr. and Mrs. Leigh Hunt and their family lived at Highgate, and invited me (M. C. C.) to spend a few days with them in that pretty suburban spot, then green with tall trees and shrub-grown gardens and near adjoining meadows. Pleasant were the walks taken arm-in-arm with such a host and entertainer as Leigh Hunt. Sometimes towards Holly Lodge, the residence of an actress duchess,—successively Miss Mellon, Mrs. Coutts, and the Duchess of St. Albans ; of whose sprightly beauty, as Volante in the play of " The Honeymoon," Leigh Hunt could give right pleasant description : or past a handsome white detached house in a shrubbery, with a long low gallery built out, where the elder Mathews lived, whose "Entertainments" and "At Homes" I had often seen and could enjoyingly expatiate upon with Leigh Hunt, as we went on through the pretty bowery lane—then popularly known as Millfield Lane, but called in his circle Poets' Lane, frequented as it was by himself, Shelley, Keats, and Coleridge—till we came to a stile that abutted on a pathway leading across by the ponds and the Pine-mount, skirting Caen Wood, to Hampstead, so often and so lovingly celebrated both in prose and verse by him I was walking with. Then there was the row of tall trees in front of Mr. Gilman's house, where Coleridge lived, and beneath which trees he used to pace up and down in quiet meditation or in converse with some friend. Then there was Whittington's Stone on the road to the east of Highgate Hill, in connexion with which Leigh Hunt would discourse delightfully of the tired boy with dusty feet sitting down to rest, and listening to the prophetic peal of bells that bade him tarry and return as the best means of getting forward in life. And sometimes we passed through the Highgate Archway, strolling on to the rural Muswell Hill and still more rural Friern Barnet, its name retaining an old English form of plural, and recalling antique monkish fraternities when rations of food were served forth, or rest and shelter given to way-weary travellers. Leigh Hunt's simultaneous walk and talk were charming; but he also shone brilliantly in his after-breakfast pacings up and down his room. Clad in the flowered wrapping-gown he was so fond of wearing when at home, he would continue the lively subject broached during breakfast, or launch forth into some fresh one, gladly prolonging that bright and pleasant morning hour. He himself has somewhere spoken of the peculiar charm of English women, as "breakfast beauties," and certainly he himself was a perfect specimen of a "breakfast wit." At the first social meal of the day he was always quite as brilliant as most company men are at a dinner party or a gay supper. Tea to him was as exhilarating and inspiring as wine to others; the looks of his home circle as excitingly sympathetic as the applauding faces of an admiring assemblage. At the time of which I am speaking, Leigh Hunt was full of some translations he was making from Clement Marot and other of the French epigrammatists; and as he walked to and fro he would fashion a line or two, and hit off some felicitous turn of phrase, between whiles whistling with a melodious soft little birdy tone in a mode peculiar to himself of drawing the breath inwardly instead of sending it forth outwardly through his lips. I am not sure that his happy rendering of Destouches' couplet epitaph on an Englishman,—

> Ci-gît Jean Rosbif, Ecuyer,
> Qui se pendit pour se désennuyer,

into

> Here lies Sir John Plumpudding of the Grange,
> Who hung himself one morning, for a change,

did not occur to him during one of those after-breakfast lounges of which I am now speaking. Certain am I that at this time he was also cogitating the material for a book which he purposed naming "Fabulous Zoology;" and while this idea was in the ascendant his talk would be rife of dragons, griffins, hippogriffs, minotaurs, basilisks, and "such small deer" and "fearful wild fowl" of the genus monster, illustrated in his wonted delightful style by references to the classic poets and romancists.

Belonging to this period also was his plan for writing a book of Fairy Tales, some of the names and sketched plots of which were capital—" Mother Fowl " (a story of a grimy, ill-favoured old beldam) being, I remember, one of them. Leign Hunt had an enchanting way of taking you into his confidence when his thoughts were running upon the concoction of a new subject for a book, and of showing that he thought you capable of comprehending and even aiding him in carrying out his intention; at any rate, of sympathizing heartily in his communicated views. No man ever more infallibly won sympathy by showing that he felt you were eager to give it to him.

- The one of Leigh Hunt's children who most at that period engaged my interest and fondness was his little gentle boy, Vincent; who, being a namesake of my father's used to call me his daughter, while I called him " papa." Afterwards, when the news of my being married reached the Hunt family, Vincent was found crying; and when asked what for, he whimpered out, " I don't like to have my daughter marry without asking her papa's leave."

Our marriage took place on a fine summer day— July 5th, 1828. The sky was cloudless ; and as we took our way across the fields that lie between Edmonton and Enfield—for we had resolved to spend our quiet honeymoon in that lovely English village, Charles' native place, and had gone down in primitive Darby-and-Joan fashion by the Edmonton stage, after leaving my father and mother's house on foot together, Charles laughingly telling me, as we walked down the street, a story of a man who said to his wife an hour after the wedding, " Hitherto I have been your slave, madam ; now you are mine "—we lingered by the brook where John Keats used to lean over the rail of the foot-bridge, looking at the water and watching

> Where swarms of minnows show their little heads,
> Staying their wavy bodies 'gainst the streams,
>   To taste the luxury of sunny beams
>   Temper'd with coolness :

and stayed to note the exact spot recorded in Keats' Epistle to C. C. C., where the friends used to part

> Midway between our homes : your accents bland
> Still sounded in my ears, when 1 no more
> Could hear your footsteps touch the grav'ly floor.
> Sometimes I lost them, and then found again ;
> You changed the footpath for the grassy plain ;

and loitered under a range of young oak-trees, now grown into more than stout saplings, that were the result of some. of those carefully dropped acorns planted by Charles and his father in the times of yore heretofore recorded. So dear to us always were Enfield and its associations that they were made the subject of a paper without C. C. C.'s signature entitled " A Visit to Enfield," and a letter signed " Felicia Maritata," both of which were published by Leigh Hunt in his Serials : the former in the number of his *Tatler* for October 11, 1830; the latter in the number of *Leigh Hunt's London Journal* for January 21, 1835.

Dear Charles and Mary Lamb, who were then residing at Chase Side, Enfield, paid us the compliment of affecting to take it a little in dudgeon that we should not have let them know when we "lurked at the Greyhound" so near to them ; but his own letter,[1] written soon after that time, shows how playfully and how kindly he really

---

[1] See page 164.

took this "stealing a match before one's face." He made
us promise to repair our transgression by coming to spend
a week or ten days with him and his sister ; and gladly
did we avail ourselves of the offered pleasure under name
of reparation.

During the forenoons and afternoons of this memorable
visit we used to take the most enchanting walks in all
directions of the lo ely neighbourhood. Over by Winchmore Hill, through Southgate Wood to Southgate and
back : on one occasion stopping at a village linendraper's
shop that stood in the hamlet of Winchmore Hill, that
Mary Lamb might make purchase of some little household requisite she needed ; and Charles Lamb, hovering
near with us, while his sister was being served by the
mistress of the shop, addressed her, in a tone of mock
sympathy, with the words, " I hear that trade's falling
off, Mrs. Udall, how's this ? " The stout, good-natured
matron only smiled, as accustomed to Lamb's whimsical
way, for he was evidently familiarly known at the houses
where his sister dealt. Another time a longer excursion
was proposed, when Miss Lamb declined accompanying
us, but said she would meet us on our return, as the
walk was farther than she thought she could manage. It
was to Northaw ; through charming lanes, and country
by-roads, and we went hoping to see a famous old giant
oak-tree there. This we could not find; it had perhaps
fallen, after centuries of sturdy growth ; but our walk
was delightful, Lamb being our conductor and con-
fabulator. It was on this occasion that—sitting on a felled
tree by the way-side under a hedge in deference to the
temporary fatigue felt by the least capable walker of the
three—he told us the story of the dog * that he had *tired*

* See the chapter " Some Letters of Charles Lamb," page 170.

out and got rid of by that means. The rising ground of the lane, the way-side seat, Charles Lamb's voice, our own responsive laughter—all seem present to us as we write. Mary Lamb was as good as her word—when was she otherwise? and came to join us on our way back and be with us on our reaching home, there to make us comfortable in old-fashion easy-chairs for "a good rest" before dinner. The evenings were spent in cosy talk; Lamb often taking his pipe, as he sat by the fire-side, and puffing quietly between the intervals of discussing some choice book, or telling some racy story, or uttering some fine, thoughtful remark. On the first evening of our visit he had asked us if we could play whist, as he liked a rubber; but on our confessing to very small skill at the game, he said, "Oh, then, you're right not to play; I hate playing with bad players." However, on one of the last nights of our stay he said, "Let's see what you're like, as whist-players;" and after a hand or two, finding us not to be so unproficient as he had been led to believe, said, "If I had only known you were as good as this, we would have had whist every evening."

His style of playful bluntness when speaking to his intimates was strangely pleasant—nay, welcome : it gave you the impression of his liking you well enough to be rough and unceremonious with you : it showed you that he felt at home with you. It accorded with what you knew to be at the root of an ironical assertion he made—that he always gave away gifts, parted with presents, and *sold* keepsakes. It underlay in sentiment the drollery and reversed truth of his saying to us, " I always call my sister Maria when we are alone together, Mary when we are with our friends, and Moll before the servants."

He was at this time expecting a visit from the Hoods, and talked over with us the grand preparations he and his sister meant to make in the way of due entertainment: one of the dishes he proposed being no other than "bubble and squeak." He had a liking for queer, out-of-the-way names and odd, startling, quaint nomenclatures; bringing them in at unexpected moments, and dwelling upon them again and again when his interlocutors thought he had done with them. So on this occasion " bubble and squeak " made its perpetual reappearance at the most irrelevant points of the day's conversation and evening fire-side talk, till its sheer repetition became a piece of humour in itself.

He had a hearty friendship for Thomas Hood, esteeming him as well as liking him very highly. Lamb was most warm in his preferences, and his cordial sympathy with those among them who were, like himself, men of letters, forms a signal refutation of the lukewarmness—nay, envy—that has often been said to subsist between writers towards one another. Witness, for example, his lines to Sheridan Knowles "on his Tragedy of Virginius." Witness, too, his three elegant and witty verse compliments to Leigh Hunt, to Procter, and to Hone. The first he addresses "To my friend the Indicator," and ends it with these ingeniously turned lines :—

> I would not lightly bruise old Priscian's head,
> Or wrong the rules of grammar-understood ;
> But, with the leave of Priscian, be it said,
> The *Indicative* is your *Potential Mood.* .
> Wit, poet, prose-man, party-man, translator—
> Hunt, your best title yet is *Indicator.*

The second, addressed "To the Author of the Poems published under the name of Barry Cornwall," after

praising his " Marcian Colonna," " The Sicilian Tale,"
and " The Dream," bids him

> No longer, then, as " lowly substitute,
> Factor, or PROCTER, for another's gains, "
> Suffer the admiring world to be deceived ;
> Lest thou thyself, by self of fame bereaved,
> Lament too late the lost prize of thy pains,
> And heavenly tunes piped through an alien flute.

And the third, addressed " To the Editor of the ' Every-
day Book,' " has this concluding stanza :—

> Dan Phœbus loves your book—trust me, friend Hone—
>   The title only errs, he bids me say ;
> For while such art, wit, reading there are shown,
>   He swears 'tis not a work of *every day.*

There is another point on which we would fain say a
word in vindication of noble, high-natured, true-hearted
Charles Lamb; a word that ought once and for ever to
be taken on trust as coming from those who had the
honour of staying under his own roof and seeing him day
by day from morning to night in familiar home intercourse—a word that ought once and for ever to set at
rest accusations and innuendoes brought by those who
know him only by handed-down tradition and second-
hand report. As so much has of late years been hinted
and loosely spoken about Lamb's " habit of drinking "
and of " taking more than was good for him," we avail
ourselves of this opportunity to state emphatically—from
our own personal knowledge—that Lamb, far from taking
much, took very little, but had so weak a stomach that
what would have been a mere nothing to an inveterate
drinker, acted on him like potations " pottle deep."
We have seen him make a single tumbler of moderately
strong spirits-and-water last through a long evening of

pipe-smoking and fireside talk ; and we have also seen
the strange suddenness with which but a glass or two of
wine would cause him to speak with more than his usual
stammer—nay, with a thickness of utterance and impeded
articulation akin to Octavius Cæsar's when he says,
" Mine own tongue splits what it speaks." As to Lamb's
own confessions of intemperance, they are to be taken
as all his personal pieces of writing—those about himself
as well as about people he knew—ought to be, with more
than a " grain of salt." His fine sense of the humorous,
his bitter sense of human frailty amid his high sense of
human excellence, his love of mystifying his readers even
while most taking them into his confidence and admitting
them to a glimpse of his inner self—combined to make
his avowal of conscious defect a thing to be received
with large allowance and lenientest construction. Charles
Lamb had three striking personal peculiarities : his eyes
were of different colours, one being greyish blue, the other
brownish hazel ; his hair was thick, retaining its abundance and its dark-brown hue with scarcely a single grey
hair among it until even the latest period of his life ; and
he had a smile of singular sweetness and beauty.

CHAPTER V.

Godwin—Horace Smith—William Hazlitt—Mrs. Nesbitt—
Mrs. Jordan — Miss M. A. Tree — Coleridge — Edmund
Reade—Vincent Novello—Extracts from a diary; 1830—
John Cramer—Hummel — Thalberg — Charles Stokes—
Thomas Adams—Thomas Attwood—Liszt—Felix Men-
delssohn.

WE had the inexpressible joy and comfort of remaining
in the home where one of us had lived all her days—in
the house of her father and mother. Writing the "Fine
Arts" for the *Atlas* newspaper, and the "Theatricals"
for the *Examiner* newspaper, gave us the opportunity of
largely enjoying two pleasures peculiarly to our taste.
Our love of pictorial art found frequent delight from
attending every exhibition of paintings, every private view
of new panorama, new large picture, new process of
colouring, new mode of copying the old masters in
woollen cloth, enamel, or mosaic, that the London season
successively produced, while our fondness for "going to
the play" was satisfied by having to attend every first
performance and every fresh revival that occurred at the
theatres.

This latter gratification was heightened by seeing frequently in the boxes the bald head of Godwin, with his
arms folded across his chest, his eyes fixed on the stage,
his short, thick-set person immovable, save when some
absurdity in the piece or some maladroitness of an actor

caused it to jerk abruptly forward, shaken by his single-
snapped laugh ; and also by seeing there Horace Smith's
remarkable profile, the very counterpart of that of Socrates
as known to us from traditionally authentic sources.
With these two men we now and then had the pleasure
of interchanging a word, as we met in the crowd when
leaving the playhouse ; but there was a third whom we
frequently encountered on these occasions, who often sat
with us during the performance, and compared notes with
us on its merits during its course and at its close.   This
was William Hazlitt, then writing the " Theatricals " for
the *Times* newspaper.   His companionship was most
genial, his critical faculty we all know ; it may therefore
be readily imagined the gladness with which we two saw
him approach the seats where we were and take one beside us of his own accord.   His dramatic as well as his
literary judgment was most sound, and that he became
a man of letters is matter of congratulation to the reading
world ; nevertheless, had William Hazlitt been constant
to his first intellectual passion—that of painting, and to
his first ambition—that of becoming a pictorial artist, there
is every reason to believe that he would have become
quite as eminent as any Academician of the eighteenth
century.   The compositions that still exist are sufficient
evidence of his promise.   The very first portrait that he
took was a mere head of his old nurse ; and so remarkable are the indications in it of early excellence in style
and manner that a member of the profession inquired of
the person to whom Hazlitt lent it for his gratification,
" Why, where did you get that Rembrandt ? "   The upper
part of the face was in strong shadow, from an over-
pending black silk bonnet edged with black lace, that
threw the forehead and eyes into darkened effect ; while

this, as well as the wrinkled cheeks, the lines about the mouth, and the touches of actual and reflected light, were all given with a truth and vigour that might well recall the hand of the renowned Flemish master. It was our good fortune also to see a magnificent copy that Hazlitt made of Titian's portrait of Ippolito dei Medici, when we called upon him at his lodgings one evening. The painting—mere stretched canvas without frame— was standing on an old-fashioned couch in one corner of the room leaning against the wall, and we remained opposite to it for some time, while Hazlitt stood by holding the candle high up so as to throw the light well on to the picture, descanting enthusiastically on the merits of the original. The beam from the candle falling on his own finely intellectual head, with its iron-grey hair, its square potential forehead, its massive mouth and chin, and eyes full of earnest fire, formed a glorious picture in itself, and remains a luminous vision for ever upon our memory. Hazlitt was naturally impetuous, and feeling that he could not attain the supreme height in art to which his imagination soared as the point at which he aimed, and which could alone suffice to realize his ideal of excellence therein, he took up the pen and became an author, with what perfect success every one knows. His facility in composition was extreme. We have seen him continue writing (when we went to see him while he was pressed for time to finish an article) with wonderful ease and rapidity of pen, going on as if writing a mere ordinary letter. His usual manuscript was clear and unblotted, indicating great readiness and sureness in writing, as though requiring no erasures or interlining. He was fond of using large pages of rough paper with ruled lines, such as those of a bought-up blank account-book—as they were.   We are so fortunate as to have in our possession Hazlitt's autograph title-page to his "Life of Napoleon Buonaparte," and the proof-sheets of the preface he originally wrote to that work, with his own correcting marks on the margin.   The title-page is written in fine, bold, legible hand-writing, while the proof corrections evince the care and final polish he bestowed on what he wrote.   The preface was suppressed, in deference to advice, when the work was first published : but it is strange to see what was then thought "too strong and outspoken," and what would now be thought simply staid and forcible sincerity of opinion, most fit to be expressed.

Hazlitt was a good walker; and once, while he was living at Winterslow Hut on Salisbury Plain, he accepted an invitation from a brother-in-law and sister of ours, Mr. and Mrs. Towers, to pay them a visit of some days at Standerwick, and went thither on foot.

When Hazlitt was in the vein, he talked super-excellently; and we can remember one forenoon finding him sitting over his late breakfast—it was at the time he had forsworn anything stronger than tea, of which he used to take inordinate quantities—and, as he kept pouring out and drinking cup after cup, he discoursed at large upon Richardson's "Clarissa" and "Grandison," a theme that had been suggested to him by one of us having expressed her predilection for novels written in letter-form, and for Richardson's in particular.   It happened that we had once heard Charles Lamb expatiate upon this very subject; and it was with reduplicated interest that we listened to Hazlitt's opinion, comparing and collating it with that of Lamb. Both men, we remember, dwelt with interest upon the character of John Belford, Lovelace's trusted friend, and upon his loyalty to him with his loyal behaviour to Clarissa.

At one period of the time when we met Hazlitt so frequently at the theatres Miss Mordaunt (afterwards Mrs. Nesbitt) was making her appearance at the Haymarket in the first bloom and freshness of her youth and beauty. Hazlitt was "fathoms deep" in love with her, making us the recipients of his transports about her; while we, almost equal fanatics with himself, " poured in the open ulcer of his heart her eyes, her hair, her cheek, her gait, her voice," and " lay in every gash that love had given him the knife that made it." He was apt to have these over-head-and-ears enamourments for some celebrated beauty of the then stage : most young men of any imagination and enthusiasm of nature have them. We remember Vincent Novello ecstasizing over the enrapturing laugh of Mrs. Jordan in a style that brought against him the banter of his hearers ; and on another occasion he, Leigh Hunt, and C. C. C. comparing notes and finding that they had all been respectively enslaved by Miss M. A. Tree when she played Viola in " Twelfth Night ;" and, on still another, Leigh Hunt and C. C. C. confessing to their having been cruelly and woefully in love with a certain Miss (her very name is now forgotten !)—a columbine, said to be as good in private life as she was pretty and graceful in her public capacity,— and who, in their " salad days," had turned their heads to desperation.

William Hazlitt was a man of firmly consistent opinion ; he maintained his integrity of Liberal faith throughout, never swerving for an instant to even so much as a compromise with the dominant party which might have made him a richer man.

In an old diary of ours for the year 1830, under the

date Saturday, 18th September, there is this sad and simple manuscript record :—"William Hazlitt (one of the first critics of the day) died. A few days ago when Charles went to see him during his illness, after Charles had been talking to him for some time in a soothing undertone, he said, ' My sweet friend, go into the next room and sit there for a time, as quiet as is your nature, for I cannot bear talking at present.'" Under that straightforward, hard-hitting, direct-telling manner of his, both in writing and speaking, Hazlitt had a depth of gentleness—even tenderness—of feeling on certain sub-jects ; manly friendship, womanly sympathy, touched him to the core ; and any token of either would bring a sudden expression into his eyes very beautiful as well as very heart-stirring to look upon. We have seen this expression more than once, and can recall its appealing charm, its wonderful irradiation of the strong features and squarely-cut, rugged under portion of the face.

In the same diary above alluded to there is another entry, under the date Friday, 5th March :—"Spent a wonderful hour in the company of the poet Coleridge." It arose from a gentleman—a Mr. Edmund Reade, whose acquaintance we had made, and who begged we would take a message from him to Coleridge concerning a poem lately written by Mr. Reade, entitled " Cain,"— asking us to undertake this commission for him, as he had some hesitation in presenting himself to the author of " The Wanderings of Cain." More than glad were we of this occasion for a visit to Highgate, where at Mr. Gilman's house we found Coleridge, bland, amiable, affably inclined to renew the intercourse of some years previous on the cliff at Ramsgate. As he came into the room, large-presenced, ample-countenanced, grand-fore-headed, he seemed to the younger visitor a living and moving impersonation of some antique godlike being shedding a light around him of poetic effulgence and omnipercipience. He bent kindly eyes upon her, when she was introduced to him as Vincent Novello's eldest daughter and the wife of her introducer, and spoke a few words of courteous welcome : then, the musician's name catching his ear and engaging his attention, he immediately launched forth into a noble eulogy of music, speaking of his special admiration for Beethoven as the most poetical of all musical composers ; and from that, went on into a superb dissertation upon an idea he had conceived that the Creation of the Universe must have been achieved during a grand prevailing harmony of spheral music. His elevated tone, as he rolled forth his gorgeous sentences, his lofty look, his sustained flow of language, his sublime utterance, gave the effect of some magnificent organ-peal to our entranced ears. It was only when he came to a pause in his subject—or rather, to the close of what he had to say upon it—that he reverted to ordinary matters, learned the motive of our visit and the message with which we were charged, and answered some inquiries about his health by the pertinent bit already quoted in these Recollections respecting his immunity from headache.

A few other entries in the said old diary,—which probably came to be exceptionally preserved for the sake of the one on Coleridge, and the one on Hazlitt,—are also of some interest :—" 15th February. In the evening we saw Potier, the celebrated French comedian, in the 'Chiffonnier,' and 'Le Cuisinier de Buffon ;' a few hours afterwards the English Opera House was burnt to the ground. God be praised for our escape !" " 4th March.

One of the most delightful evenings I ever enjoyed,—John Cramer was with us." "25th March. Saw Miss Fanny Kemble play Portia, in the 'Merchant of Venice,' for her first benefit." "21st April. Went to the Diorama, and saw the beautiful view of Mount St. Gothard. In the evening saw the admirable Potier in 'Le Juif' and 'Antoine.'" "21st June. Heard the composer Hummel play his own Septet in D Minor, a Rondo, Mozart's duet for two pianofortes, and he extemporized for about twenty minutes. The performance was for his farewell concert. His hand reminds me of Papa more than of John Cramer." "21st September. Witnessed Miss Paton's first reappearance in London after her elopement. She played Rosina in ' The Barber of Seville.' Mr. Leigh Hunt was with us." " 1st October. Saw a little bit of Dowton's Cantwell on the opening of Drury Lane; the house was so full we could not get a seat." " 18th October. Saw Mac-eady in ' Virginius ' at Drury Lane." "21st October. Saw Macready's ' Hamlet.'"

The references to two great musical names in the above entries recall some noteworthy meetings at the Novellos' house. John Cramer was an esteemed friend of Vincent Novello, who highly admired his fine talent and liked his social qualities. Cramer was a peculiarly courteous man : polished in manner as a frequenter of Courts, as much an adept in subtly elegant flattery as a veteran courtier; handsome in face and person as a Court favourite, distinguished in bearing as a Court ruler, he was a very mirror of courtliness. Yet he could be more than downright and frank-spoken upon particular occasion : for once, when Rossini and Rossini's music were in the ascendant among fashionable coteries, and

Cramer thought him overweening in consequence, when he met him for the first time in society, after something of Rossini's had been played, and he looked at Cramer as if in expectation of eulogy—the latter went to the pianoforte and gave a few bars from Mozart's "Nozze di Figaro" (the passage in the finale to the 2nd Act, accompanying the words, " Deh, Signor, nol contrastate"); then turned round and said in French to Rossini, " That's what *I* call music, caro maestro."

As a specimen of his more usually courtly manner, witty, as well as elegant, may be cited the exquisitely-turned compliment he paid to Thalberg, who, saying with some degree of pique, yet with evident wish to win Cramer's approval, " I understand, Mr. Cramer, you deny that I have the good left hand on the pianoforte which is attributed to me ; let me play you something that I hope will convince you ;" played a piece that showed wonderful mastery in manipulation on the bass part of the instrument. Cramer listened implicitly throughout, then said, " I am still of the same opinion, Monsieur Thalberg; I think you have no left hand—I think you have *two right hands.*"

John Cramer's own pianoforte-playing was supremely good, quite worthy the author of the charming volume of Exercises—most of them delightful pieces of composition —known as " J. B. Cramer's Studio." His " *legato* " playing was singularly fine : for, having a very strong third finger (generally the weak point of pianists), no perceptible difference could be traced when that finger touched the note in a smoothly equable run or cadence. We have heard him mention the large size of his hand as a stumbling-block rather than as an aid in giving him command over the keys ; and probably it was to his consciousness of this, as a defect to be overcome, that may be attributed his excessive delicacy and finish of touch.

Hummel's hand was of more moderate size, and he held it in the close, compact, firmly-curved, yet easily-stretched mode which forms a contrast to the ungainly angular style in which many pianists splay their hands over the instrument. His mere way of putting his hands on the key-board when he gave a preparatory prelude ere beginning to play at once proclaimed the master—the *musician*, as compared with the mere pianoforte-player. It was the *composer*, not the performer, that you immediately recognized in the few preluding chords he struck— or rather rolled forth. His improvising was a marvel of facile musical thought; so symmetrical, so correct, so mature in construction was it that, as a musical friend— himself a musician of no common excellence, Charles Stokes—observed to us, "You might count the time to every bar he played while improvising."

Hummel came to see us while he was in London, bringing his two young sons with him ; and we remember one of them making us laugh by the childish abruptness with which he set down the scalding cup of tea he had raised to his lips, exclaiming in dismay, "Ach ! es ist heiss ! "

The able organ-player Thomas Adams, and Thomas Attwood, who had been a favourite pupil of Mozart, by whom he was pettingly called " Tommasino," were also friends of Vincent Novello ; and Liszt brought letters of introduction to him when he visited England. The first time Liszt came to dinner he chanced to arrive late : the fish had been taken away, and roast lamb was on table, with its usual English accompaniment of mint sauce. This latter, a strange condiment to the foreigner, so pleased Liszt's taste that he insisted on eating it with the brought-back mackerel, as well as with every succeeding dish that came to table—gooseberry tart and all !—he good-naturedly joining in the hilarity elicited by his universal adaptation and adoption of mint sauce.

Later on we had the frequent delight of seeing and hearing Felix Mendelssohn among us. Youthful in years, face, and figure, he looked almost a boy when he first became known to Vincent Novello, and was almost boyish in his unaffected ease, good spirits, and readiness to be delighted with everything done for him and said to him. He was made much of by his welcomer, who so appreciated his genius in composition and so warmly extolled his execution, both on the organ and on the pianoforte, that once when Mr. Novello was praising him to an English musical professor of some note, the professor said, "If you don't take care, Novello, you'll spoil that young man." "He's too good, too genuine to be spoiled," was the reply.

We had the privilege of being with our father when he took young Mendelssohn to play on the St. Paul's organ; where his *feats* (as Vincent Novello punningly called them) were positively astounding on the pedals of that instrument. Mendelssohn's organ pedal-playing was a real wonder,—so masterful, so potent, so extraordinarily agile. The last piece we ever heard him play in England was Bach's *fugue* on his own name, on the Hanover Square organ, at one of the concerts given there. We had the good fortune to hear him play some of his own pianoforte compositions at one of the Dusseldorf Festivals; where he conducted his fine psalm " As the hart pants." On that occasion, calling upon him one morning when there was a private rehearsal going on, we had the singular

privilege of hearing him *sing* a few notes,—just to give
the vocalist who was to sing the part at performance an
idea of how he himself wished the passage sung,—which
he did with his small voice but musician-like expression.
On that same occasion, too, we enjoyed the pleasure of
half an hour's quiet talk with him, as he leaned on the
back of a chair near us and asked about the London
Philharmonic Society, &c., having, like ourselves, arrived
at an exceptionally early time before the Grand Festival
ball began that evening. And on the same occasion
likewise, we spent a pleasant forenoon with him in the
Public Gardens at Dusseldorf, where he invited us, in
true German social and hospitable style, to partake of
some " *Mai-Trank*," sitting in the open air, listening to
the nightingales that abound in that Rhine-side spot;
he laughing at us for saying this Rhenish beverage was
" delicious innocent stuff," and telling us we must beware
lest we found it not so " innocent " as it seemed. Once in
England, he came to us the morning after Beethoven's
opera of " Fidelio" had been produced for the first time
on the English stage, when Mdme. Schrœder-Devrient
was the Leonora, and Haitzinger the Florestan. Mendelssohn was full of radiant excitement about the beauty
of the music : and as he enlarged on the charm of this
duet, this aria, this round-quartet, this prisoner's chorus,
this trio, or this march,—he kept playing by memory bits
from the opera, one after another, in illustration of his
words as he talked on, sitting by the pianoforte the
while. On his wonderful power of improvisation, and
that memorable instance of it one night that we witnessed
we have elsewhere enlarged ;[1] and certainly that was a
triumphant specimen of his skill in extempore-playing.

[1] " Life and Labours of Vincent Novello," page 37.

Felix Mendelsohn was a gifted man, a true genius; and he might have shone in several other fields, as well as in that of music, had he not solely dedicated himself to that art. He was a good pictorial artist, and made spirited sketches. He was an excellent classical scholar; and once at the house of an English musical professor, whose son had been brought up for the Church, and had been a University student, there chancing to arise a difference of opinion between him and Mendelssohn as to some passage in the Greek Testament, when the book was taken down to decide the question Mendelssohn proved to be in the right. He was well read in English literature, and largely acquainted with the best English poets. Once, happening to express a wish to read Burns's poems, and regretting that he could not get them before he left, as he was starting next morning for Germany, Alfred Novello and C. C. C. procured a copy of the fine masculine Scottish poet at Bickers's, in Leicester Square, on their way down to the boat by which Mendelssohn was to leave, and reached there in time to put into his hand the wished-for book, and to see his gratified look on receiving the gift. It is perhaps to this incident we owe the charming two-part song, " O wert thou in the cauld blast."

CHAPTER VI.

Fanny Kemble—Mr. and Mrs. Charles Kemble—Dowton—
Perlet—Macready—Potier—Lablache — Paganini — Don-
zelli— Madame Albert—Mdlle. Mars—Mdlle. Jenny Vertpré
—Cartigny— Lemaitre — Rachel — " Junius Redivivus"—
Sarah Flower Adams—Eliza Flower—Mrs. Leman Grim-
stone — Leigh Hunt — Isabella Jane Towers — Thomas
James Serle—Douglas Jerrold—Richard Peake—The elder
Mathews—Egerton Webb—Talfourd—Charles Lamb—
Edward Holmes—John Oxenford.

THE occurrence of Fanny Kemble's name reminds us to
narrate the interest created by her first appearance on
the stage, to retrieve the fortunes of the theatre of which
her father was then lessee. It was one of those nights
not to be forgotten in theatrical annals. The young girl
herself—under twenty—coming out as the girl-heroine ot
tragedy, Shakespeare's Juliet ; her mother, Mrs. Charles
Kemble, after a retirement from the stage ot some years
playing (for this especial night of her daughter's *début*
and her husband's effort to re-establish the attraction ot
Covent Garden Theatre) the part of Lady Capulet ; her
father, Charles Kemble, a man much past fifty years ot
age, enacting with wonderful spirit and vigour the mer-
curial character of Mercutio ; combined to excite into
enthusiasm the assembled audience. The plaudits that
overwhelmed Mrs. Charles Kemble, causing her to stand
trembling with emotion and melted into real tears that

drenched the rouge from her cheeks, plaudits that assured her of genuine welcome given by a public accustomed to a long esteem for the name of Kemble, and now actuated by a private as well as professional sympathy for her—these plaudits had scarcely died away into the silence of expectancy, when Juliet had to make her entrance on the scene. We were in the stage-box, and could see her standing at the wing, by the motion of her lips evidently endeavouring to bring moisture into her parched mouth, and trying to summon courage for advancing ; when Mrs. Davenport, who played in her own inimitable style the part of the Nurse, after calling repeatedly " Juliet ! what, Juliet ! " went towards her, took her by the hand, and pulled her forward on to the stage—a proceeding that had good natural as well as dramatic effect, and brought forth the immediately recognizant acclamations of the house. Fanny Kemble's acting was marked by much originality of thought and grace of execution.   Some of the positions she assumed were strikingly new and appropriate, suggestive as they were of the state of feeling and peculiar situation in which the character she was playing happened to be. . For instance, in the scene of the second act, where Juliet is impatiently awaiting the return of her nurse with tidings from Romeo, Fanny Kemble was discovered in a picturesque attitude standing leaning on the back of a chair, earnestly looking out of a tall window opening on to a garden, as if eager to catch the first approach of the expected messenger ; and again, in " The Provoked Husband," where the scene of Lady Townley's dressing-room opens in the fifth act, Fanny Kemble was found lying upon her face, stretched upon a sofa, her head buried in the pillow-cushions, as if she had flung herself there in a fit of sleepless misery and shame, thinking of her desperate losses at the gaming-table overnight. She proved herself hardly less calculated to shine as a dramatic writer than as a dramatic performer; for in about a year or two after she came out upon the stage, her tragedy of " Francis the First " was produced at the theatre and appeared in print — a really marvellous production for a girl of her age. She showed herself to be a worthy member of a family as richly endowed by nature as the one whose name she bore. One of us could remember John Kemble and Sarah Kemble Siddons; the other could just remember seeing Stephen Kemble play Falstaff (without *stuffing*, as it was announced), and frequent'y witnessed Charles Kemble's delightful impersonation of Falconbridge, Benedick, Archer, Ranger, Captain Absolute, Young Marlowe, Young Mirabel, and a host of other brilliant youngsters, long after he had reached middle age, with unabated spirit and grace and good looks; and who both lived to see yet another Kemble bring added laurels to the name in the person of Adelaide Kemble.

Dowton's Cantwell was one of those fine embodiments of class character that would alone suffice to make the lasting fame of an actor. Had Dowton never played any other part than this, he would have survived to posterity as a perfect performer; his sleek condition, his spotless black clothes, his placidly-folded hands, his smooth, serene voice, his apparently cloudless countenance, with nevertheless a furtive, watchful look in the eye, a calmly-compressed mouth, with nevertheless a betraying devil of sensuality lurking beneath the carefully-maintained compression—these sub-expressions of the eye and lip uncontrollably breaking forth in momentary flash and sudden, involuntary quiver,—during the scenes with Lady

Lambert,—were all finely present, and formed a highly-finished study of a sanctimonious, self-seeking, calculating hypocrite. We have seen Perlet, the French comedian, play the original counterpart of Cibber and Bickerstaff's Doctor Cantwell,—Molière's Tartuffe ; and .Perlet went so far as to paint additional vermilion round his mouth, so as to give the effect of the sensual, scarlet lip; but Dowton's alternated contraction and revealment of his naturally full lip gave even more vital effect to the characteristically suggestive play of feature. The tone, too, in which Dowton first calls to his secretary, uttering his Christian name, " Charles ! " in silky, palavering voice, when he bids him " Bring me that writing I gave you to lay up this morning," as contrasted with his subsequent imperious utterance of the surname, " Seyward ! " when he summons his secretary to abet him in his assertion of supreme mastery in Sir John Lambert's house, formed two admirably telling points in this, his perhaps most renowned performance. At the same time, be it stated, that his tempest of fury, in Sir Anthony Absolute and characters of that class, with his delightfully tolerant good-humour and pleasant cordiality in the part ot Old Hardcastle in Goldsmith's charming comedy, " She Stoops to Conquer," were quite as perfect each in their several ways.

Of Macready's playing Virginius, Rob Roy,—and subsequently King John [one of his very best-conceived impersonations, for our detailed description of which see pages 340-1-2 of " Shakespeare-Characters "], Henry V., Prospero, Benedick, Richelieu, Walsingham, and a score of other admirably characteristic personifications, we will not allow ourselves to speak at length ; owing many private kindnesses and courtesies to the gentleman, while we enjoyed so frequently his varied excellences as an actor, and approved so heartily his judicious arrangements as a manager.

Of Potier's acting we had frequent opportunities of judging; since he, with several of his best brother comedians, at the time we are referring to, came to London in the successive French companies that then first, and subsequently, repaired thither to act French pieces. It was a novelty that took: for the majority of fashionable play-goers were sufficiently versed in the language to appreciate and enjoy the finished acting and entertaining pieces then produced. In the year 1830 Leigh Hunt started his *Tatler*, generally writing the Theatre, Opera, and Concert notices in it himself, under the heading of " The Play-goer ;" but occasionally he asked me (C. C. C.) to supply his place; and accordingly, several of the articles —such as those recording Lablache's initiative appearances in London, Paganini's, Donzelli's, charming Madame Albert's, Laporte's, and on the Philharmonic Society, bear witness to our enjoyment of some of the best performances going on during the few years that Leigh Hunt's *Tatler* existed. Afterwards, we witnessed in brilliant succession Mademoiselle Mars,—whose Célimène in Molière's " Misanthrope " was unrivalled, and whose playing of Valerie, a blind girl of sixteen, who recovers her lost sight, when Mars was nearly sixty years of age, was a marvel of dramatic success—Mdlle. Plessy, a consummate embodiment of French lady-like elegance ; Jenny Vertpré, whose portrayal of feline nature and bearing beneath feminine person and carriage, as the cat metamorphosed into a woman, was unique in clever peculiarity of achievement ; Cartigny, great in Molière's " Dépit Amoureux" as Gros René ; Perlet, exquisite in Molière's

"Tartuffe," "Bourgeois Gentilhomme," and "Malade Imaginaire;" Lemaitre, pre-eminent in "Robert Macaire," "Trente Ans de la Vie d'un Joueur," "Don César de Bazan," and "Le Docteur Noir;" and, finally, glorious Rachel, peerless among all tragic actresses ever beheld by M. C. C., who never saw Mrs. Siddons. But we will not permit ourselves to be lured away into the pleasant paths of acting reminiscences: return we to our more strictly requested recollections of literary people. In Leigh Hunt's *Tatler* appeared a clever series of papers signed "Junius Redivivus," which were written by a gentleman who had married Sarah Flower Adams, authoress of the noble dramatic poem "Vivia Perpetua,' and sister to Eliza Flower, composer of "Musical Illustrations of the Waverley Novels," and other productions that manifested unusual womanly amount of scientific attainment in music. The two sisters were singularly gifted : graceful-minded, accomplished, exceptionally skilled in their respective favourite pursuits. One evening before her marriage we were invited to the house of a friend of hers, where Sarah Flower gave a series of dramatic performances, enacted in a drawing-room, with folding-doors opened and closed between the select audience and herself during the successive presentment of Ophelia's and other of Shakespeare's heroines' chief scenes, dressed in character, and played with much zest of impassioned delivery.

Another contributor to Leigh Hunt's *Tatler* was Mrs. Leman Grimstone, whose papers appeared with the signature "M. L. G." She was one of the very first of those who modestly yet firmly advocated women's rights : a subject now almost worn threadbare and hackneyed by zealous partisans, but then put forth diffidently, sedately, with all due deference of appeal to manly justice, reason, and consideration. In the number of the *Tatler* for 22nd March, 1832, Leigh Hunt printed these lines, preceded by a few words from himself within brackets :—

The Poor Woman's Appeal to her Husband.

[We affix a note to the following verses, not from any doubt that their beautiful tenderness can escape the observation of our readers, but because we owe to the fair author an acknow-ledgment for the heartfelt gratification which this and other previous communications from her pen have afforded to ourselves.]

You took me, Colin, when a girl, unto your home and heart,
To bear in all your after fate a fond and faithful part ;
And tell me, have I ever tried that duty to forego—
Or pined there was not joy for me, when you were sunk in woe?
No—I would rather share *your* tear than any other's glee,
For though you're nothing to the world, you're all the world
    to me ;
You make a palace of my shed—this rough-hewn bench a
    throne—
There's sunlight for me in your smile, and music in your tone.
I look upon you when you sleep, my eyes with tears grow dim,
I cry, " O Parent of the poor, look down from Heaven on
    him—
Behold him toil from day to day, exhausting strength and
    soul—
Oh look with mercy on him, Lord, for *Thou* canst make him
    whole ! "
And when at last relieving sleep has on my eyelids smiled,
How oft are they forbade to close in slumber, by my child ;
I take the little murmurer that spoils my span of rest,
And feel it is a part of *thee* I lull upon my breast.
There's only one return I crave—I may not need it long,
And it may soothe thee when I'm where—the wretched feel
    no wrong !
I ask not for a kinder tone—for thou wert ever kind ;
I ask not for less frugal fare—my fare I do not mind ;

I ask not for attire more gay—if such as I have got
Suffice to make me fair to *thee*, for more I murmur not.
But I would ask some share of hours that you at clubs
        bestow—
Of knowledge that *you* prize so much, might *I* not something
        know ?
Subtract from meetings among men, each eve, an hour
        for me—
Make me companion of your *soul*, as I may surely be !
If you will read, I'll sit and work : then think, when you're
        away,
Less tedious I shall find the time, dear Colin, of your stay.
A meet companion soon I'll be for e'en your studious hours—
And teacher of those little ones you call your cottage flowers ;
And if we be not rich and great, we may be wise and kind ;
And as my heart can warm your heart, so may my mind your
        mind.

M. L. G.

Leigh Hunt's *Tatler* was followed early in 1834 by his
London Journal, to which my (C. C. C.'s) lamented sister,
Isabella Jane Towers, contributed some verses, entitled
" To Gathered Roses,' in imitation of Herrick, as previously, in the *Literary Examiner*, which he published
in 1823, he had inserted her " Stanzas to a Fly that had
survived the Winter of 1822."   She was the author of three
graceful books of juvenile tales,· " The Children's Fire-
side," " The Young Wanderer's Cave," and " The Wanderings of Tom Starboard."

In the spring of 1835 was brought out at the English
Opera House a drama entitled " The Shadow on the
Wall," and when it made its appearance in printed form
it was accompanied by the following dedication :—

The truest gratification felt by an Author, in laying his
work before the Public, is the hope to render it a memento of
private affection.   The Writer of

"The Shadow on the Wall"
can experience no higher pleasure of this kind
than in inscribing it to
C. N.

Kensington, 1st May, 1835.

The writer of " The Shadow on the Wall " was Thomas James Serle, and the initials represented Cecilia Novello, who was his affianced future wife. He had already been known to the theatrical world by his play of " The Merchant of London," his tragedy of " The House of Colberg," his drama of " The Yeoman's Daughter," and his play of " The Gamester of Milan." After his marriage with my (M. C. C.'s) sister Cecilia in 1836, we watched with enhanced interest the successive production of his dramas and plays, " A Ghost Story," " The Parole of Honour," "Joan of Arc," "Master Clarke," "The Widow Queen," and " Tender Precautions :" when he combined with the career of dramatist that of lecturer, and, subsequently, that of political writer, continuing for many years editor of one of our London newspapers. Ultimately he has returned to his first love of literary production, having of late years written several carefully-composed plays and dramas with the utmost maturity of thought and consideration. It was at his house, immediately after his marriage, that we met an entirely new and delightful circle of literary men, his valued friends and associates. It was there we first met Douglas Jerrold, learning that he had written his " Black-eyed Susan " when only eighteen, that it was rapidly followed b his " Devil's Ducat," " Sally in Our Alley," " Mutiny at the Nore," " Bride of Ludgate," " Rent Day," " Golden Calf," " Ambrose Gwinett," and " John Overy ;" while he himself, soon after our introduction to him gave us a highly-prized presentation volume, containing his " Nell Gwynne," " Housekeeper," " Wedding Gown," " Beau Nash," and " Hazard of the Die." It was our happy fortune to be subsequently present on most of the first nights of representation of his numerous˙ dramas, including " The Painter of Ghent," in which he himself acted the principal character when it was originally brought out at the Standard Theatre, under the manage ment of his brother-in-law, Mr. Hammond. As the piece proceeded, and came to the point where Ichabod the Jew, speaking of his lost son, has to say, " He was a healing jewel to mine eye—a staff of cedar in my hand —a fountain at my foot," the actor who was playing the character made a mistake in the words, and substituted something of his own, saying " a well-spring " instead of " a fountain." A pause ensued ; neither he nor Jerrold going on for some minutes. Afterwards, talking over the event of the night with him, he told us that when his interlocutor altered the words of the dialogue, he had turned towards him and whispered fiercely, " It's neither a well-spring nor a pump ; and till you give me the right cue, I shan't go on." A more significant proof that the author in Jerrold was far stronger than the actor could hardly be adduced. And yet we have seen him act finely, too. When Ben Jonson's " Every Man in his Humour " was first performed by the amateur company of Charles Dickens and his friends, Douglas Jerrold then playing the part of Master Stephen, he acted with excellent effect ; and, could he but have quenched the intellect in his eyes, he would have looked the part to perfection, so well was he " got up " for the fopling fool. Jerrold had a delightful way of making a disagreeable incident into a delight by the brilliant, cheery way in which he would utter a jest in the midst of a dilemma. It was while walking home together from Serle's house, one bleak night of English spring, that, in crossing Westminster Bridge, with an east wind blowing keenly through every fold of clothing we wore, Jerrold said to us, " I blame nobody ; but they call this May !"

Of him and his super-exquisite wit more will be found in his letters to us, and our comments thereon, which we shall subsequently give in another portion of these Recollections.

It was at Serle's hospitable board that we met that right "merry fellow," Richard Peake, author of the droll farce " Master's Rival," and who used to write the " Entertainments " and " At Homes " for the elder Mathews. Peake was the most humorous storyteller and narrator himself ; so much so that could he but have conquered his overwhelming native bashfulness he would have made as good an actor, or even monologuist, as the best. We remember hearing him tell a history of some visit he paid in the country, where he accompanied his entertainers to their village church, in which was a preacher afflicted with so utterly inarticulate an enunciation, made doubly indistinct by the vaulty resonance of the edifice, that though a cavernous monotone pervaded the air yet not a syllable was audible to the congregation. This wabbling, stentorian, portentously solemn, yet ludicrously inefficient voice resounding through the aisles of the village temple, seems even yet to ring in our ears ; as well as a certain discordant yell that he affirmed proceeded from the bill of a bereaved goose, pent up with some ducks in the area of a house near to one where he was staying, and which perpetually proclaimed its griefs of captivity and desolation in the single screech of execration—" Jeemes !"—while the ducks offered vain consolation in the shape of a clutter of dull, gurgling quack-quack-quacks that seemed to imply, " What a fool you must be ! Why don't you take it coolly and philosophically as we do ? "

It was Peake's *manner* and *tone* that gave peculiar comicality to such things as these when he told them.

He wrote a whimsical set of tales for a magazine, giving them the ridiculous punning name of " Dogs' Tales;" in which there was a man startled by a noise in a lone house that made him exclaim, " Ha! is that a rat?" and then added, " No! it's only a rat-tat," on discovering that it was somebody knocking at the door. Peake was odd, excessively odd, in his fun. He told us that when he married, his wife continuing much affected by the circle of weeping friends from whom she had just parted, he suddenly snatched her hand in his, gave it a smart tap, and said peremptorily, " Come, come, come, come ! we must have no more of this crying ; we are now in another parish, you belong to me, and I insist upon it, you leave off ! "

Once, when we were spending an evening at Serle's, he, Douglas Jerrold, and Egerton Webbe—who was an exceptionally clever young man in many ways, but who, alas ! died early—happened to be in earnest conversation about Talfourd's account of Charles Lamb, seeming to think that Talfourd overrated Lamb's generosity of character in money-matters. We had listened silently to the discussion for a time, but when the majority of opinion seemed to be settling down into a confirmed belief that there was nothing, after all, so remarkably generous in the traits that Lamb's biographer had recorded, we stated, what we knew to be the truth, that

Charles Lamb, out of his small income (barely sufficient for his own and his sister's comfortable maintenance), dedicated a yearly sum of thirty pounds as a stipend to help support his old schoolmistress, an act of generosity, which, as compared with his means, we considered to be a really munificent gift. Douglas Jerrold, in his hearty manner, instantly exclaimed, "You're right, Mrs. Cowden Clarke! you've made out your case completely for Lamb!" And then he went on to quote, with a tone of warmth that showed he did not utter the words lightly :—

> After my death I wish no other herald,
> No other speaker of my living actions,
> To keep mine honour from corruption,
> But such an honest chronicler as Griffith.

Dear Douglas Jerrold! By a strange chance, years after his death, the "honest chronicler" he had wished for actually had an opportunity of vindicating his fame upon a point in which she heard it impugned, in the light, casual way that people will repeat defamatory reports of those who have enjoyed public favour and renown. At an English dinner-table in Italy Douglas Jerrold was spoken of in our presence as one who indulged too freely in wine, and we were able to vindicate his memory from the unfounded charge by asserting positively our knowledge to the contrary. Like many men of social vivacity and brilliant imagination, Douglas Jerrold would join in conviviality with great gusto and with animatedly expressed consciousness of the festive exhilaration imparted by wine to friendly meetings ; but to say that he habitually suffered himself to be overtaken by wine is utterly false.

Having mentioned Egerton Webbe, reminds us to relate that a sister of his was married to our early admirable friend Edward Holmes, who, after enjoying scarcely more than two years of happy wedded life with her,—of which he sent us a charming account in his letters to us when we had quitted England,—passed from earth for ever towards the close of the year 1859.

To our brother-in-law Mr. Serle we owe the pleasure of having known yet another accomplished writer,—Mr. John Oxenford, whom we used frequently to see in the boxes at the theatres after his highly poetical and romantic melodrama, entitled "The Dice of Death," had interested us in it and him by its first performances. In wonderful contrast to the sombre Faustian grandeur of this piece came the out-and-out fun and frolic of his two farces, "A Day Well Spent" and "My Fellow Clerk," proving him to be a master of versatility in dramatic art.

CHAPTER VII.

Macready—Thomas Carlyle—Leigh Hunt—Richard Cobden
—John Bright—Charles Pelham Villiers—George Wilson
—W. J. Fox—Sir John Bowring—Colonel Perronet Thompson—Mrs. Cobden—Thomas Hood—Julia Kavanagh—
Mrs. Loudon—Rev. Edward Tagart—Edwin and Charles
Landseer—Martin—Miss Martin—Mr. and Mrs. Joseph
Bonomi—Owen Jones—Noel Humphreys—Mr. and Mrs.
Milner Gibson—Louis Blanc—William Jerdan—Ralph
Waldo Emerson—Mrs. Gaskell—Charles Dickens—John
Forster—Mark Lemon—John Leech—Augustus Egg—
George Cruikshank—Frank Stone—F. W. Topham—
George H. Lewes—Charles Knight—J. Payne Collier—
Sheriff Gordon — Robert Chambers—Lord and Lady
Ellesmere.

ONE of the proudest privileges among the many pleasures
we received from Macready was that of writing our name
on the free list at the London theatres where he was
manager; and we shall not readily forget the exultant
sense of distinction with which we wrote for the first time
in the huge tome,—that magic book,—which conferred
the right of entry upon those who might put their signatures there. Once, as we stood ready to pen the open-
sesame words, we heard a deep voice near to us, and saw
a lofty figure with a face that had something of un-
doubted authority and superiority in its marked lines.
Voice, figure, face, at once impressed us so potently that
we instinctively drew back and yielded him precedence;

and when he, with courteous inclination of the majestic head, accepted the priority, signed his name, and went on, we, advancing, saw traced on the line above the one where we were to write, the honoured syllables—" Thomas Carlyle." It may be imagined with what reverence we placed our names beneath his and followed him up the staircase into the theatre.

Not very long after that we met him on a superlatively interesting occasion. Leigh Hunt had invited a few friends with ourselves to hear him read his newly-written play of " A Legend of Florence ;" and Thomas Carlyle was among these friends. The hushed room, its general low light,—for a single well-shaded lamp close by the reader formed the sole point of illumination,—the scarcely-seen faces around, all bent in fixed attention upon the perusing figure ; the breathless presence of so many eager listeners, all remains indelibly stationed in the memory, never to be effaced or weakened. It was not surpassed in interest,—though strangely contrasted in dazzle and tumult,—when the play was brought out at Covent Garden Theatre, and Leigh Hunt was called on to the stage at its conclusion to receive the homage of a public who had long known him through his delightful writings, and now caught at this opportunity to let him feel and see and hear their admiration of those past works as well as of his present poetical play. A touching sight was it to see that honoured head, grown grey in the cause of letters and in the ceaseless promotion of all that is tasteful and graceful, good and noble, a head that we remembered jet black with thick, clustered hair, and held proudly up with youthful poet thought and patriot ardour, now silvered and gently inclined to receive the applause thus for the first time publicly and face to facedly showered upon it; the figure that had always held apart its quiet, studious course, devoted to patient, ardent composition, now standing there in sight of men and women the centre of a thousand grateful and admiring eyes. His face was pale, his manner staid and simple : as if striving for composure to bear an incense that profoundly stirred him, a kind of resolute calmness assumed to master the natural timidity of a man unaccustomed to numerous and overt testimony of approbation; and as if there were a struggle between his desire to show his affectionate sense of his fellow-men's liking, and his dread lest he should be overcome by it. As he withdrew from the ovation it was evident that the man of retired habits was both glad and sorry, both relieved and regretting, to leave this shouting, welcoming, hurraing crowd.

There was a public occasion that brought us into contact with several noteworthy men of the time,—the Anti-Corn-Law Meetings at Covent Garden Theatre, and the Anti-Corn-Law-League Bazaar, held there in aid of the funds needed for the promotion of their object. Richard Cobden, John Bright, Charles Pelham Villiers, George Wilson, W. J. Fox, John Bowring (afterwards Sir John), and Colonel Perronet Thompson (afterwards General) were among the chief of these eloquent and earnest speakers. An excellent hit was made by Mr. Fox one night, when dancing was proposed to be got up after the speeches, and some of the demure and over-righteous objected to it as indecorous. Instead of answering their objection he took a most ingenious course. He rose to address the audience, and said, " I understand that dancing is about to take place, and that some inconsiderate persons have insisted that everybody shall dance, myself among the number. Now any one who looks for a moment at me must perceive that my figure wholly disqualifies me for a dancer, and would render it entirely unbecoming in me to take part in an amusement that is charming for the young and the slender. I beg you will excuse me from joining you; but pray, all you who enjoy dancing and can dance have dancing at once." Fox had a neat, epigrammatic mode of expressing himself that told admirably in some of the Anti-Corn-Law-League speeches. In one of them, as an illustration that England depends upon France for many luxuries, he said, "A rich Englishman has a French cook that dresses his dinner for him, and a French valet that dresses him for his dinner.

Of Richard Cobden's delightful society we had the honour and pleasure of enjoying a few perfect days in familiar home intercourse, several years afterwards abroad; he and his wife coming over from Cannes and taking up their abode under our cottage roof at Nice in the most easy, friendly, unaffected way imaginable. Of one Christmas Eve especially we retain strong recollection: when Mrs. Cobden sat helping us women-folk to stone raisins, cut candied fruits, slice almonds, and otherwise to make housewifely preparation for the morrow's plum-pudding—a British institution never allowed to pass into desuetude in our family—while Cobden himself read aloud the English newspapers to us in his own peculiar, practical, perspicuous way—going through the Parliamentary debates line by line: and as he came to each member mentioned we observed that he invariably added in parenthesis the constituency as thus :—" Mr. Roebuck [Bath] observed that if Mr. Disraeli [Buckinghamshire] thought that Mr. Bright [Birmingham] intended to say," etc. It was as though Cobden had made this a set rule, so that he might well fix in his mind each individual and the constituency he represented.

With Colonel Perronet Thompson we subsequently met under very pathetic circumstances. It was by the bedside of a poor young lady in St. George's Hospital, whose friends had asked him to go and see her there while she was in London hoping for cure, and who had likewise been recommended to our occasional visitation during her stay in that excellent establishment. It was by her own brave wish that she had come up to town from a distant northern county, and the visits of the benevolent-hearted veteran were most cheering to her. His steel-grey hair, his ruddy complexion, his bright, intelligent eyes, his encouraging smile, his enlivening conversation, shed a reflection of fortitude and trust around her, and made her youthful face kindle into renewed expectation of recovery as he spoke. The expectation was ultimately and joyfully fulfilled; for she was so completely cured of her spinal complaint as to return to her home able to walk, to resume her active duties, and, finally, to marry happily and well.

It was not long before the last illness of Thomas Hood that I (C. C. C.) met him at the house of a mutual friend, when his worn, pallid look strangely belied the effect of jocularity and high spirits conveyed by his writings. He punned incessantly but languidly, almost as if unable to think in any other way than in play upon words. His smile was attractively sweet: it bespoke the affectionate-natured man which his serious verses— those especially addressed to his wife or to his children— show him to be; and it also revealed the depth of pathos in his soul that inspired his "Bridge of Sighs," "Song of the Shirt," and "Eugene Aram." The large-hearted feeling he had for his fellow-men and his prompt sympathy for them were testified by his including me—we having met but this once—in the list of friends to whom he sent on his death-bed a copy of the then recently engraved bust-portrait of himself, subscribed by a few words of "kind regard" in his own handwriting.

While we were living at Bayswater some friends came to see us, accompanied by a young lady who, with her mother, was a neighbour of theirs, and in whom they took much interest, from her intellectual superiority and her enthusiasm of nature. She had luminous, dark eyes, with an elevated and spiritual cast of countenance; and was gentle and deferential in manner to her mother, and very kind and companionable towards the children of our friends, who had a large family of boys and girls, eager in play, active in juvenile pursuits, after the wont of their race. She seemed ever at hand to attend upon her mother, ever ready to enter into the delights of the child neighbours; and yet she was devoted heart and soul to the ambition of becoming an authoress, and spent hours in qualifying herself for the high vocation. Some time afterwards we read her most charming novel of "Nathalie," and found that the young lady of the dark eyes and gentle, unassuming deportment, Julia Kavanagh, had commenced her career of popular novelist, which thenceforth never stinted or ceased in its· prosperous course.

Our pretty homestead, Craven-hill Cottage, Bayswater, was one of the last lingering remains of the old primitive simplicity of that neighbourhood, ere it became built upon with modern houses, squares, and terraces. Of our own particular nook in that parent-nest—the last that we dwelt in together with our loved father and mother, ere they migrated to the Continent for warmer winters— Leigh Hunt once said, " This is the most poetical room in a most poetical house." It was a very small abode, and required close packing ; but, for people loving each other as its inmates did, `it was a very snug and happy- home.

We had two houses close by us that contained very kindly and pleasant neighbour friends. One was the house of Mrs. Loudon and her daughter ; the other that of the Rev. Edward Tagart, his wife and his family. So near to us were they that we could at any time put on hat, hood, or shawl over evening-dress and walk to and from the pleasant parties that were given there. Nay, on one occasion, when Sheridan's " Rivals " was got up at Mrs. Loudon's by her daughter and some of their friends, the Mrs. Malaprop, the Lucy, and the David went on foot ready dressed for their respective parts from Craven- hill Cottage to No. 3, Porchester Terrace, with merely a cloak thrown over their stage costumes. The David also enacted Thomas the Coachman, " doubling the parts," as it is called ; so that he went in his many-caped driving-coat over his David's dress. It chanced that he arrived just as the gentleman who was to play Fag was drinking tea with Mrs. Loudon, and she gave a cup also to the new arrival. Afterwards she told us that she had been much amused by learning that one of her maids had been overheard to say, " It's very strange, but missus is taking tea with two livery servants."

At Mrs. Loudon's house we met several persons of note and name : the Landseers, Edwin and Charles ; Martin, the painter of " Belshazzar's Feast," &c. ; his clever-headed and amiable daughter, Miss Martin ;

Joseph Bonomi, and his wife, who was another daughter of Martin ; Owen Jones, Noel Humphreys, Mr. and Mrs. Milner Gibson, Louis Blanc, William Jerdan, and others.

On one occasion, when Mrs. Loudon gave a fancy ball, few costumes, among the many very handsome and characteristic ones that gave picturesque variety to the scene, were more strikingly beautiful and artistic—as might be expected—than those of Owen Jones and the Bonomis.

Under Mr. Tagart's roof we had the gratification of meeting one evening Ralph Waldo Emerson, who did one of the company the honour of requesting to be introduced to her, and paid her a kind compliment ; while she, be it now confessed, was so occupied with a passage in one of his Essays that she had that morning been perusing with delight, and so longed to quote it to him and thank him for it, yet was so confused with the mingled fear of not repeating it accurately and the dread of appearing mad if she did venture to give utterance to what was passing in her mind, that she has often since had a pang of doubt that, as it was, she must have struck Emerson as peculiarly dull and absent and unconscious of the pleasure he really gave her.

One forenoon Mrs. Tagart, in her usual amiable, thoughtful way, sent round to say that she expected Mrs. Gaskell to lunch, and would we come and meet her ? Joyfully did we accept ; and delightful was the meeting. We found a charming, brilliant-complexioned, but quiet-mannered woman ; thoroughly unaffected, thoroughly attractive—so modest that she blushed like a girl when we hazarded some expression of our ardent admiration of her " Mary Barton ; " so full of enthusiasm on general subjects of humanity and benevolence that she talked freely and vividly at once upon them ; and so young in look and demeanour that we could hardly believe her to be the mother of two daughters she mentioned in terms that showed them to be no longer children. In a correspondence that afterwards passed between her and ourselves, on the subject of an act of truly valuable kindness she was performing anonymously for a young lady anxious to become a public singer, Mrs. Gaskell showed herself to be actuated by the purest and noblest motives in all she did. She tried her utmost to prevent her agency in the affair from being discovered ; giving as her reason the dread that if it were known it might tend to "injure the freedom of the intercourse" between herself and the young lady in question ; adding, " for I want her to look upon me as a friend rather than as a benefactor."

It was at a party at the Tagarts' house that we were introduced by Leigh Hunt to Charles Dickens ; when an additional light and delight seemed brought into our life. He had been so long known to us in our own home as " Dear Dickens," or " Darling Dickens," as we eagerly read, month after month, the moment they came out, the successive numbers of his gloriously original and heart-stirring productions, that to be presented to " Mr. Charles Dickens," and to hear him spoken of as " Mr. Dickens," seemed quite strange. That very evening— immediately—we felt at home and at ease with him. Genial, bright, lively-spirited, pleasant-toned, he entered into conversacion with a grace and charm that made it feel perfectly natural to be chatting and laughing as if we had known each other from childhood. So hearty was his enjoyment of what we were talking of that it caught the attention of our hostess, and she came up to inquire what it could be that amused Mr. Dickens so much. It was no other than the successive pictures that had then lately appeared in *Punch* of Mr. Punch himself; two, in particular, we recollect made Dickens laugh, as we recalled them, till the tears glistened in his eyes with a keen sense of the fun and ridiculous absurdity in the attitudes. They were, Mr. Punch as Caius Marius seated amid the ruins of Carthage, and Mr. Punch swimming in the sea near to a bathing-machine. Charles Dickens had that acute perception of the comic side of things which causes irrepressible brimming of the eyes ; and what eyes his were ! Large, dark blue, exquisitely shaped, fringed with magnificently long and thick lashes—they now swam in liquid, limpid suffusion, when tears started into them from a sense of humour or a sense of pathos, and now darted quick flashes of fire when some generous indignation at injustice, or some high-wrought feeling of admiration at magnanimity, or some sudden emotion of interest and excitement touched him. Swift-glancing, appreciative, rapidly observant, truly superb orbits they were, worthy of the other features in his manly, handsome face. The mouth was singularly mobile, full-lipped, well-shaped, and expressive ; sensitive, nay restless, in its susceptibility to impression that swayed him, or sentiment that moved him. He, who saw into apparently slightest trifles that were fraught to his perception with deepest significance ; he, who beheld human nature with insight almost superhuman, and who revered good and abhorred evil with intensity, showed instantaneously by his expressive countenance the kind of idea that possessed him. This made his conversation enthralling, his acting first-rate, and his reading superlative.

All three it has been our good-hap to enjoy completely ;

and that we have had this enjoyment will last us as a source of blest consciousness so long as we live.

His having heard of the recent private performance of " The Rivals " caused Charles Dickens that very evening of our first seeing him to allude in obliging terms to the " golden opinions " he understood my Mrs. Malaprop had won ; and this led to my telling him that I understood he was organizing an amateur company to play Shakespeare's " Merry Wives of Windsor," and that I should be only too delighted if he would have me for his Dame Quickly. He at first took this for a playfully-made offer ; but afterwards, finding I made it seriously and in all good faith, he accepted : the details of this enchanting episode in my life I reserve till we come to our Letters and Recollections of Charles Dickens ; but meanwhile I may mention that it brought us into most pleasant acquaintance with John Forster, Mark Lemon, John Leech, Augustus Egg, George Cruikshank, Frank Stone, F. W. Topham, George H. Lewes, and, correlatively, with Charles Knight, J. Payne Collier, Sheriff Gordon, and Robert Chambers. Of those who were fellow-actors in the glorious amateur company further will be said in the place above pre-referred to ; but of the four last-named men it is pleasant to speak at once. Both Charles Knight and J. Payne Collier in their conduct towards us thoroughly reversed the more usual behaviour of Shakespearian editors and commentators among each other : for Charles Knight was marked in his courtesy and kindness, while Payne Collier went so far as to entrust the concluding volume of his 1842-4 edition of Shakespeare, which was then still in manuscript, to Mary Cowden Clarke, that she might collate his readings and incorporate them in her " Concordance " before publication, though she was then personally unknown to him. And when in 1848 she played Mistress Quickly at the Haymarket Theatre, on the evening of the 15th of May, Payne Collier came round to the green-room, introduced himself to her, told her he had just come from the box of Lord and Lady Ellesmere, charged with their compliments on her mode of acting the character, and then—with a chivalrous air of gallantry that well became one whose knighthood had been won in Shakespearian fields—added that before taking leave he wished to kiss the hand that had written the " Concordance." This gave her the opportunity she had long wished for, of thanking him for the act of confidence he had performed in previous years, of entrusting one unknown to him with his unprinted manuscript. It is pleasant to record incidents that so completely refute the alleged hostility of feeling that exists between authors ; and to show them, on the contrary, as they mostly are, mutually regardful and respectful.

John T. Gordon, Sheriff of Mid-Lothian, was one of the most genial, frank-mannered, hearty-spoken men that ever lived. His sociality and hospitality were of the most engaging kind ; and his personal intercourse was as inspiriting as his expressions of friendliness in his letters were cordial.

Of Robert Chambers's friendly, open-armed reception to those who went to Edinburgh and needed introduction to the beauties of this Queen City of North Britain, no terms can be too strong or too high. He placed himself at the disposal of such visitors with the utmost unreserve and the most unwearied kindness ; and no man was better fitted to act cicerone by the most interesting among the numerous noteworthy objects there to be seen. He shone to great advantage himself while indicating them; for his talk was intelligent, clear, well-informed, and extremely pleasant. He seemed to enjoy afresh the things he was discussing and displaying for the thousandth time; and to be as much interested in them himself, as he made them doubly and trebly interesting to the person he was guiding.

CHAPTER VIII.

Lord Murray—John Hunter—Mrs. Stirling—Mrs. Catherine Crowe—Alexander Christie—Professor Pillans—William Smith—R. Mackay Smith—Henry Bowie—Robert Cox—Dr. and Mrs. Hodgson — Samuel Timmins — George Dawson—Mr. and Mrs. Follett Osler—Arthur Ryland—Francis Clark—Mathew Davenport Hill—Rowland Hill—John Adamson—Henry Barry Peacock—Beddoes Peacock—Robert Ferguson—Westland Marston—Robert Charles Leslie—Clarkson Stanfield—Sydney Dobell—Henry Chorley—Mrs. Newton Crosland—Miss Mulock—John Rolt—John Varley—William Etty—Leslie—William Havell.

DURING the twenty-one years that I (C. C. C.) lectured in London and the provinces scarcely any place surpassed Edinburgh in the warmth and cordiality with which I was not only received in the lecture-room, but welcomed into private homes by kindly hospitable men and women. The two men just named; Lord Murray; John Hunter of Craig Cook (the "friend of Leigh Hunt's verse," to whom was inscribed his lovely verse-story of "Godiva"); John Hunter's talented sister, Mrs. Stirling (authoress of two gracefully moral novels, "Fanny Hervey" and "Sedgely Court"); Mrs. Catherine Crowe (one of the earliest and perhaps most forcible of the sensational school of romancists); Alexander Christie (whose fine painting of "Othello's Despair" was presented, while

still personally unknown, to M. C. C., and which still is
daily before our eyes in the picture gallery at Villa
Novello); Professor Pillans, William Smith, R. Mackay
Smith, Henry Bowie, and Robert Cox,—are all names
associated with many a brilliant and jovial hour spent
in " canny Edinburgh."   With Liverpool come thronging
pleasant hospitable reminiscences of Mr. and Mrs. Richard
Yates (linked in delightful memory as co-travellers with
Harriet Martineau in her admirable book of " Eastern
Life Past and Present "); and of Dr. (erudite as kindly
and kindly as erudite) and Mrs. Hodgson (worthy help-
meet, but, alas ! now lost to him).   With Birmingham
troop to mind visions of friendliest and constantest
Samuel Timmins ; of George Dawson, as we first beheld
him there, a youth gifted with extraordinary oratorical
eloquence ; of hospitable Mr. and Mrs. Follett Osler ; of
obliging and agreeably-epistolary Arthur Ryland ; and of
Francis Clark and his numerous family, who subsequently
sought health in the milder-climed region of Australia.
A copy of the *Adelaide Observer*, containing a very
pleasant and broadly humorous Anglicised iteration of
the old French romance poem of " The Grey Palfrey "
(from which Leigh Hunt took the ground-work for his
poetical tale called " The Palfrey "), written by Howard
Clark, one of the sons of Francis Clark (who is himself
no longer living), reached me lately and brought the
whole family to my pleased recollection.   The Clarks are
related to the Hills of Birmingham, the proprietors and
conductors of their eminent scholastic establishment of
Hazlewood, so eminent as to have attracted the favour-
able opinion of so avowed an authority as the Edinburgh
Reviewers.   The widow of Francis Clark, and mother of
the many children who survive him, is sister to the

Hills,—to the eminently intellectual and quite as delightful late excellent Recorder of Birmingham, Mathew Davenport Hill; and to the man among the blessedest benefactors of the human race,—the illustrious and adored re-creator of the postal delivery—Rowland Hill; who has brought socialism—affectionate and commercial —to humane perfection all over the world; who enabled the labourer at Stoke Pogis to communicate with a brother or friend

> In Borneo's isle, where lives the strange ape,
> The ourang-outang almost human in shape.

At Newcastle I met with the scholarly John Adamson, author of " Lusitania Illustrata ;" and on my way thither I encountered a being of whom I cannot do other now than linger a few moments to speak. My most amiable and earliest northern friend, Henry Barry Peacock, of Manchester, hearing that I was engaged at Newcastle-on-Tyne, recommended me to pause on my journey thither at Darlington, where he would introduce me to his cousin, Beddoes Peacock, the medical professor of the district. This was one of the most interesting events of my social intercourse in life. In the first instance, I was introduced to a pale, bland, most cheerful-looking, and somewhat young man, lying out upon a sofa, from which he did not rise to greet me. His manner and tone of reception were so graceful, and so remarkable was the expression of an un-commonplace pair of eyes, that I felt suddenly released from the natural suspension of an immediate familiarity. He first of all explained the cause of his not rising to receive me. It was, that he could only move the upper part of his frame. His coachman and " total-help " lifted him from sofa to dinner-table; and, finally to his night-couch, which was a regular hospital water-bed. This is the most indefinite outline (for the moment) that I can give of the daily course of action of this most intensely—most attractively engrossing being, who fulfilled a constant series of medical, and (if requisite) of even surgical practice. With all his impedimental difficulties, so thoroughly, so profoundly esteemed was Dr. Peacock that his patients—lady-patients included—submitted to his being brought by his coachman to their bedside. This is a bare glance at his then course of life; with equal brevity I inform my readers that in his younger days he was a very active and athletic sportsman, ready for every action required, from the chase of the otter to the stag-hunt. One day, by some accident—the particulars of which (for evident reason) I would not require of himself—two men were in danger of drowning—one trying to save the other, and both being unable to swim—Dr. Peacock darted into the water, bade them be quiet, and hold back their heads. They were fortunately near enough to the bank for him to pull them within their depth, and he saved both. Whether from the noble service he then performed, or whether from some indescribable cause unknown to himself and his scientific brethren, he, shortly after this heroic act, was seized with the calamitous affection above described. My own opinion is, that the attack was indigenous; for his sister was prostrated with the same complaint; and every day, when he went out professionally, he always drove by her house; and she, expecting him, was always lying by her window, when they *cheerfully* nodded to each other. I have known very few individuals—not exclusively devoted to literary studies—who possessed so decided an accomplishment in high-class conversation : he was, of course, in education a classic; and for poetic reading he had a passionate fondness. Upon receiving a presentation copy of "The Riches of Chaucer," he acknowledged the gift with a sonnet, which I feel no appreciator of poetical composition will read without a sympathetic feeling :—

Full many a year, to ease the baleful stound
    Of blows by Fortune given, in mood unkind,
    No greater balm or solace could I find
Than wand'ring o'er the sweet oblivious ground
Where Poets dwell.   The gardens perfumed round
    Of modern Bards first kept me long in thrall :
On Shakespeare's breezy heights at length I found
    Freshness eterne—trees, flowers that never pall,
Nor farther wish'd to search.   A friendly voice
    Whisper'd, " Still onward ! much remains unsung ;
Old England's youthful days shall thee rejoice,
    When her strong-hearted Muse first found a tongue :
'Mongst Chaucer's groves that pathless seem and dark
Wealth is in store for thee."—God bless you, Clarke !
4th June, 1846.   BEDDOES PEACOCK.

When I was at Carlisle nothing could exceed the frank hospitality of Robert Ferguson, then Mayor of that ancient city and fine border town ; and he subsequently gratified me by a presentation copy of each of his valuable and interesting books—"The Shadow of the Pyramid," "The Pipe of Repose," "Swiss Men and Swiss Mountains," and "The Northmen of Cumberland and Westmoreland."

If it were only for the sterling sound-headed and sound-hearted people with whom my lecture career brought me into delightful connexion, I should always look back upon that portion of my life with a sense of gratification and gratitude.

We were never able to indulge much in what is called
" Society," or to go to many parties ; but at the few to
which we were able to accept invitations, we met more
than one person whom it was pleasure and privilege to
have seen. Westland Marston, Robert Charles Leslie,
Clarkson Stanfield, Sydney Dobell, Henry Chorley, Mrs.
Newton Crosland (with whom our acquaintance then
formed has since ripened into highly-valued letter
friendship), and Miss Mulock, we found ourselves in
company with ; while at John Rolt's dinners we encountered some of the first men in his profession. It had
been our joy to watch the rapid rise of this most
interesting and most intellectual man, from his youthful
commencement as a barrister, through his promotion as
Queen's Counsel, his honours as Solicitor-General
Attorney-General, Judge, Sir John Rolt ; and always to
know him the same kindly, cordial, warm-hearted friend,
and simple-mannered, true gentleman, from first to last.
Whether, as the young rising barrister, with his modest
suburban home,—where we have many times supped
with him, and been from thence accompanied by him on
our way home in the small hours after midnight, lured
into lengthened sittings by his enchanting conversation
and taste for literary subjects, — or whether seated at the
head of his brilliant dinner circle at his town-house in
Harley Street,—or when he was master of Ozleworth
Park, possessed of all the wealth and dignity that his
own sole individual exertions had won for him,—Rolt
was an impersonation of all that is noble and admirable
in English manhood. With a singularly handsome face,
eyes that were at once penetrating and sweet, and a
mouth that for chiselled beauty of shape was worthy of
belonging to one of the sculptured heads of Grecian

antique art, he was as winning in exterior as he was attractive from mental superiority; and when we have sometimes sat over the fire, late at night, after the majority of his guests had departed, and lingered on, talking of Purcell's music, or Goethe's "Wilhelm Meister," or any topic that chanced for the moment to engage his thoughts, we have felt John Rolt's fascination of appearance and talk to be irresistibly alluring.

The mention of two great artist names reminds us of the exceptional pleasure we have had from what intercourse we have enjoyed with celebrated artists. While one of us was still in her childhood, John Varley was known to her father and mother; and one or two of his choicest water-colour pictures are still in careful preservation with us. There is one little piece—a view of Cader Idris—on a small square of drawing-paper, that might easily be covered by the spread palms of two hands, which is so exquisite in subdued colouring and effect of light on a mountain-side, that William Etty used to say of it that it made him wish he had been a water-colour painter instead of a painter in oils. Once, when John Varley came to see his friend Vincent Novello, he told of a circumstance that had happened which excited the strongest sympathy and bitterest wrath in the hearers. It appeared that a new maid-servant had taken for kindling her fires a whole drawer-full of his water-colour sketches, fancying they were waste-paper! He was very eccentric; and at one time had a whim for astrology, believing himself to be an adept in casting nativities. He inquired the date of birth, &c., of Vincent Novello's eldest child; and after making several abstruse calculations of "born under this star," and when that planet was "in conjunction with t'other," &c., he assured Mrs.

Novello that her daughter would marry late, and have a numerous family of children, all of whom would die young. The daughter in question married early, and never had a single child !

Another charming water-colour artist known to the Novellos was William Havell; one of whose woody landscapes is still in treasured existence, as well as a sketch he took of M. C. C. in Dame Quickly's costume. Holland, too, the landscape painter, was pleasantly known to me (C. C. C.); and on one occasion, when I met him at the house of a mutual friend, he showed me an exquisite collection of remarkable sunsets that he had sketched from time to time as studies for future use and introduction into pictures.

At one time we knew William Etty well. It was soon after his return from Italy, where he went to study; and we recollect a certain afternoon, when we called upon him in his studio at his chambers in one of the streets leading off from the Strand down to the Thames, and found him at his easel, whereon stood the picture he was then engaged upon, "The Bevy of Fair Women," from Milton's "Paradise Lost." We remember the rich reflection of colour from the garland of orange lilies round the waist of one fair creature thrown upon the white creamy skin of the figure next to her, and Etty's pleasure when we rapturized over the effect produced. He was a worshipper of colour effects, and we recollect the enthusiasm with which he noticed the harmony of blended tints produced by a certain goldy-brown silk dress and a canary-coloured crape kerchief worn by one of his visitors, as she stood talking to him. It was on that same afternoon that he made us laugh by telling us of an order he had to paint a picture for some society, or board, or company, who gave him for his subject a range of line-of-battle ships giving fire in a full broadside ! Etty roared with laughter as he exclaimed, " *Me !* fancy giving *me* such a subject ! !   Fancy *my* painting a battle-piece ! ! ! " He said that the English, generally speaking, had little general taste or knowledge in art, adding, "You must always take an Englishman by the hand and lead him up to a painting, and say, 'That's a good picture,' before he can really perceive its merits."

Of Leslie we entertain the liveliest recollection on an evening when we met him at a party and he fell into conversation about Shakespeare's women as suited for painting, and asked us to give him a Shakespearian subject for his next picture. We suggested the meeting between Viola and Olivia, with Maria standing by ; seeing in imagination the charming way in which Leslie would have given the just-withdrawn veil from Olivia's half-disdainful, half-melting, wholly beautiful face, Viola's womanly loveliness in her page's attire, and Maria's mischievous roguery of look as she watches them both.

Clarkson Stanfield lives vividly in our memory, as we last saw him, when we were in England in 1862, in his pretty garden-surrounded house at Hampstead. He showed us a portfolio of gorgeous sketches made during a tour in Italy, two of which remain especially impressed upon our mind. One was a bit taken on Mount Vesuvius about daybreak, with volumes of volcanic smoke rolling from the near crater, touched by the beams of the rising sun ; the other was a view of Esa, a picturesque sea-side village perched on the summit of a little rocky hill, bosomed among the olive-clad crags and cliffs of the Cornice road between Nice and Turbia.

CHAPTER IX.

Publishers—Critics—George James De Wilde—James Lamb
—Thomas Pickering—Thomas Latimer—Isaac Latimer—
Alexander Ireland—Samuel Timmins—Mary Balmanno
—Austin Allibone—Dr. Charles Stearns—Rev. Dr. Scadd-
ing—Mr. and Mrs. Horace Howard Furness—John Watson
Dalby—Mr. and Mrs. Townshend Mayer—Edmund Ollier
—Gerald Massey—William Lowes Rushton—Frederick
Rule—Dr. C. M. Ingleby—Alexander Main—His Excel-
lency George Perkins Marsh—Mrs. John Farrar—Mrs.
Somerville—Mr. and Mrs. Pulszky——Miss Thackeray—
Mrs. William Grey—Miss Shirreff—John Bell—Edward
Novello—Barbara Guschl—(Mme. Gleitsman)—Clara
Angela Macirone—Mme. Henrietta Moritz—Herbert New
—Rev. Alexander Gordon—Rev. John Gordon—Mrs.
Stirling—Bryan Waller Procter—James T. Fields—Celia
Thaxter.

THE present compliance with the wish expressed that we
should record our Recollections of pleasant people we
have known, leads us to include our personal experience
of publishers—generally supposed, by an absurd popular
fallacy, to be anything but "pleasant people" to authors.
We, on the contrary, have found them to be invariably
obliging, considerate, and liberal. Besides, without publishers where would authors be? Evermore in manuscript! worst of limbos to a writer!

There is another class of men connected with authors,

and themselves writers, against whom an unfounded prejudice has existed which we are well qualified to refute.
We allude to critics ; generally supposed to be sour, acri-
monious, spiteful, even—venomous. Cruelly are they
maligned by such an imputation; for the most part inclined
to say an encouraging word, if possible ; and rather given
to pat a young author on the head than to quell him by
a sneer or a knock-down blow. At least this is OUR experience of literary reviewers. Who that knew thee, dear
lost George James De Wilde, will accuse criticism of as-
perity ? Who that saw thy bland, benign countenance,
beaming with a look of universal good-will, as though it
expressed affectionate fraternity of feeling toward all
human kind, could imagine thee other than the gentle and
lenient critic on moderately good attempts, and the largely,
keenly appreciative critic on excellent productions that
thou really wert ? What shall replace to us thy ever elegant
and eloquent pen ? What may console us for the vacancy
left in our life from missing thy hearty sympathy with
whatever we wrote, or thy loving comment upon whatever
we published, making thy circle of readers in the columns
of the *Northampton Mercury* take interest in us and our
writings from the sheer influence of thy genial, hearty
discriminative notices ? Another kindly critic whose loss
we have to deplore is James Lamb, of Paisley, warm-
hearted, generous in praise, unfailing in prompt greeting
for everything we produced. These men are lost, alas !
to friends on earth, though not to their ever-grateful
remembrance.

Among those still alive, thank Heaven, to encourage
in print our endeavours, and to interchange charities of
affectionate correspondence with us, are others, who,
amid active public and professional work, have found

time to write admirable critiques on literature or music in their local journals. Forgive us for openly naming thee —Thomas Pickering,[1] of Royston, one of the earliest to promote our lecture views, to cause us to deliver our maiden lecture (on Chaucer) in the Mechanics' Institute of thy town ; to receive us into thine own house ; to let thy young daughters vie with each other who should be the privileged bearer of the MS. Lecture-book to the Lecture Hall ; to incite re-engagement year after year ; to write pleasant notices of each successive lecture ; to pen kindly reviews of every fresh-written work ; and, in short, to combine friend and critic with indefatigable zeal and spirit. Excellent listener to music ! Excellent en-joyer of all things good and beautiful and tasteful and artistic ! Ever full of energy on behalf of those once loved and esteemed by thee, whom we playfully dubbed Thomas Pickering, Esq., F.A. (meaning " Frightful Activity "), take not amiss these our publicly expressed acknowledgments of thy unceasing goodness ; but remem-ber the title by which thou best lovest to call thyself— " Vincent Novello's pupil in musical appreciation and culture "—and take the mention in a tender spirit of pleasure for his sake.

We beg kindred indulgence from thee, Thomas Lati-mer, of Exeter, whose delicious gift of dainty Devonshire cream, sent by the hands of her husband to thy personally unknown " Concordantia," as thou styledst her, still lingers in delicate suavity of remembered taste on the memory-palate of its recipient ; together with the manifold creamy and most welcome eulogiums of her literary efforts that have flowed from thy friendly-partial

[1] 1878. Now, alas ! dead. M. C. C.

pen. Like thanks to thee, Isaac Latimer, of Plymouth, for like critical and kindly services ; and to thee, Samuel Timmins, of Birmingham, for a long series of courtesies, thoughtful, constant, cordial, as various in nature as gracefully rendered. Lastly, what may we say to thee, Alexander Ireland, of Manchester, warm friend, racy correspondent ? In Shakespeare's words, "We'll speak to thee in silence ;" for we have so lately had the supreme pleasure of seeing thee eye to eye, of shaking hands with thee, of welcoming thee and thy "other self" in this Italy of ours, that here on paper we may well deny ourselves the gratification of putting more down than thy mere deeply loved name.

Another set of friends from whom we have derived large gratification, and to whom we owe special thanks, are our unknown correspondents ; personally unknown, but whose persons are well known to our imagination, and whose hearts and minds are patent to our knowledge in their spontaneous outpourings by letter. Of one— now, alas, no more !—we knew as much through a long series of many-paged letters, sent during a period of several years, as we could have done had we met him at dinner-party after dinner-party for a similar length of time. He introduced himself by a quaint and original mode of procedure, which will be described when we come to Douglas Jerrold's letters ; he took delight in making an idol and ideal of his correspondent, calling her his "daughter in love," and his "Shakespearian daughter ;" and he scarcely let many weeks pass by without sending her a letter of two sheets closely covered with very small handwriting across the Atlantic from Brooklyn to Bayswater, Nice, or Genoa. Since we lost him, his dear widow follows his affectionate course of keeping up correspondence with his chosen "daughter in love;" writing the most spirited, clever descriptive letters of people, iucidents, and local scenes. Mary Balmanno[*] is the authoress of a pleasant volume entitled "Pen and Pencil;" and she wrote the "Pocahontas" for M. C. C. in her "World-noted Women." She is as skilful artistically as literarily, for she sent over two beautiful water-colour groups she painted of all the Fruits and all the Flowers mentioned by Shakespeare, as a gift to M. C. C., which now adorn the library where the present recollections are being written.

Austin Allibone, author of that grand monument of literary industry, the "Critical Dictionary of English Literature;" Dr. Charles Stearns, author of "The Shakespeare Treasury," and of "Shakespeare's Medical Knowledge;" the Rev. Dr. Scadding, author of "Shakespeare, the Seer, the Interpreter;" and the admirable Shakespearian couple, Mr. and Mrs. Horace Howard Furness—he devoting himself to indefatigable labours in producing the completest Variorum Edition of the world's great poet dramat.st ever yet brought out; and she dedicating several years to the compilation of a "Concordance to Shakespeare's Poems"—are all visible to our mind's eye, in their own individual personalities, through their friendly, delightful, familiarly-affectionate letters, sent over the wide waters of the ocean from America to England; making us feel towards them as intimates, and to think of them and ourselves in Camillo's words:—"They have seemed to be together, though absent; shook hands, as over a vast; and embraced, as it were, from the ends of opposed winds."

[*] 1878. Now also dead. M. C. C.

Among our cherished unknown correspondents of long standing in kindliness of quietly-felt yet earnestly-shown regard, is John Watson Dalby, author of " Tales, Songs, and Sonnets ;" also his accomplished son-in-law and daughter, Mr. and Mrs. Townshend Mayer, of whom (in her childhood) Leigh Hunt spoke affectionately as "mad-cap," and with whom (in her matronhood) Procter confessed in one of his letters to us that he had fallen secretly in love when he was eighty years of age.

Another pleasant feature in our unknown correspondentship has been the renewal in a second generation of friendships commenced in a first. Thus we have derived double delight from letter intercourse with the author of " Poems from the Greek Mythology; and Miscellaneous Poems. By Edmund Ollier."

In Shakespearian correspondents—personally unknown yet familiarly acquainted by means of the " one touch of Shakespeare " (or " Nature " almost synonymous !) that "makes the whole world kin"—we have been, and still are, most rich. Gerald Massey, that true poet, and author of the interesting book " Shakespeare's Sonnets and his Private Friends;" William Lowes Rushton, who commenced a series of several valuable pamphlets on Shakespearian subjects by his excellent one " Shakespeare a Lawyer ;" Frederick Rule, a frequent and intelligent contributor on Shakespearian subjects to *Notes and Queries*, and Dr. C. M. Ingleby, whose elaborate and erudite Shakespeare Commentaries scarcely more interest us than his graphic accounts, in his most agreeable letters, of his pleasantly-named country residence, " Valentines," with its chief ornament, his equally-pleasantly-named daughter, " Rose."

A delightful correspondent, that we owed to the loving

brotherhood in affection for Shakespeare which makes fast friends of people in all parts of the world and inspires attachments between persons dwelling at remotest distance from each other, is Alexander Main, who formed into a choice volume "The Wise, Witty, and Tender Sayings, in Prose and Verse, of George Eliot," and produced another entitled "The Life and Conversations of Dr. Samuel Johnson (founded chiefly upon Boswell)." For a full decade have we continued to receive from him frank, spontaneous, effusive letters, fraught with tokens of a young, enthusiastic, earnest nature, deeply imbued with the glories of poetry and the inmost workings of human nature – more especially, as legibly evolved in the pages of William Shakespeare.

To the same link of association we are indebted for another eminent correspondent—His Excellency, George Perkins Marsh—also personally unknown to us; yet who favours us, from his elevation as a distinguished philologist and as a man of high position, with interchange of letters, and even by entrusting us for more than two years with a rare work of the Elizabethan era which we wanted to consult during our task. of editing the greatest writer of that or any other period. The above is stated i no vaunting spirit, but in purest desire to show how happy such kind friendships, impersonal but solidly firm, make those who have never beheld more than the mere handwriting of their unknown (but well-known) correspondents.

Although we left our beloved native England in 1856 to live abroad, we ceased not occasionally to become acquainted with persons whom it is honour and delight to know. While we were living at Nice we learned to know, esteem, and love Mrs. John Farrar, of Springfield, Massachusetts, authoress of a charming little volume entitled, "The Young Lady's Friend," and "Recollections of Seventy Years." She passed one or two winters at Nice, and continued her correspondence with us after she returned to America, giving us animated descriptions of the civil war there as it progressed. To Mrs. Somerville we were first introduced at Turin; she afterwards visited us in Genoa; and latterly interchanged letters with us from Naples. She was as mild "and of 'her' porte as meek as is a maid;" utterly free from pretension or assumption of any sort; she might have been a perfect *ignorama*, for anything of didactic or dictatorial that appeared in her mode of speech : nay, 'tis ten to one that an ignoramus would have talked flippantly and pertly while Mary Somerville sat silent ; or given an opinion with gratuitous impertinence and intrepidity when Mrs. Somerville could have given hers with modesty and pertinent ability : for, mostly, Mrs. Somerville refrained from speaking upon subjects that involved opinion or knowledge, or science; rather seeming to prefer the most simple, ordinary, every-day topics. On one occasion we were having some music when she came to see us, and she begged my brother, Alfred Novello, to continue the song he was singing, which chanced to be Samuel Lover's pretty Irish ballad, "Molly Bawn." At its conclusion Mrs. Somerville was sportively asked whether she agreed with the astronomical theory propounded in the passage,—

> The Stars above are brightly shining,
> Because they've nothing else to do.

And she replied, with the Scottish accent that gave characteristic inflection to her utterance, "Well—I'm not just prepared to say they don't do so."

Mr. and Mrs. Pulszky, in passing through Genoa on their way to Florence, were introduced to us, and afterwards made welcome my youngest sister, Sabilla Novello, at their house there, while a concert and some *tableaux vivants* were got up by the Pulszkys to buy off a promising young violinist from conscription ; showing—in their own home circle with their boys and girls about them—what plain " family people" and unaffected domestic pair the most celebrated personages can often be.

Not very long ago a lady friend brought to our house the authoress of " The Story of Elizabeth," " The Village on the Cliff," " Old Kensington," and " Bluebeard's Keys," giving us fresh cause to feel how charmingly simple-mannered, quiet, and unostentatious the cleverest persons usually are. While we looked at Miss Thackeray's soft eyes, and listened to her gentle, musical voice, we felt this truth ever more and more impressed upon us, and thanked her in our heart for confirming us in our long-held belief on the point.

Letters of introduction bringing us the pleasure of knowing Mrs. William Grey, authoress of " Idols of Society," and numerous pamphlets on the Education of Women, with her sister Miss Shirreff, editress of the " Journal of the Women's Educational Union," afforded additional evidence of this peculiar modesty and unpretendingness in superiorly-gifted women; for they are both living instances of this noteworthy fact.

A welcome advent was that of John Bell, the eminent sculptor, who produced the exquisite statue of Shakespeare in the attitude of reflection, and several most graceful tercentenary tributes in relievo to the Poet-Dramatist : especially beautiful the one embodying the charming invention of making the rays of glory round the head consist of the titles of his immortal dramas. Beyond John Bell's artistic merit, he possesses peculiar interest for us in having been a fellow-student with our lost artist brother Edward Novello, at Mr. Sass's academy for design in early years.

Three enchanting visits we had from super-excellent lady pianists : Barbara Guschl (now Madame Gleitsmann), Clara Angela Macirone, and Madame Henrietta Moritz, Hummel's niece; all three indulging us to our hearts' content with the divine art of music during the whole time of their stay.

A pleasant afternoon was spent here in receiving delightful Herbert New, author of some sonnets on Keats, to which we can sincerely give the high praise of saying they are worthy of their subject, and also author of some charming little books upon the picturesque English locality in which he lives, the Vale of Evesham. To this single day's knowledge of him and to his fresh, graphically-written letters, we owe many a pleasant thought.

The Rev. Alexander Gordon, too, brought us news here of our long-esteemed friend, his father, the Rev. John Gordon, of Kenilworth ; both men of real talent and literary accomplishment. Mrs. Stirling, of Edinburgh, renewed acquaintance with us here in a foreign land, when she and her husband visited Genoa. Dear Alexander Ireland, author of a valuable chronological and critical list of Lamb's, Hazlitt's, and Leigh Hunt's writings, brought over the wife who has made the happiness of his latter years to make our acquaintance, and give, by the enchanting talk pressed into a few days' stay, endless matter for enlivening memories. Honoured Bryan Waller Procter wrote us a sprightly graceful letter

as late as 1868 ; the sprightliness and the grace touched
with tender earnestness, as in the course of the letter he
makes allusion to Vincent Novello and to Leigh Hunt.
Last, not least among the pleasures of communion with
distinguished people that we have enjoyed since we have
been domiciled in Italy, we rejoice in the renewal of
intercourse with James T. Fields, of Boston; to whom
we were introduced while in England several years ago.
His bright, genial, vivacious letters bring animation and
excitement to our breakfast-table whenever they arrive :
for the post is generally delivered during that fresh, cheery
meal : the reports of his spirited lectures " On Charles
Lamb," " On Longfellow," " On Masters of the Situation," and on many attractive subjects besides, come
with the delightful effect of evening-delivered discourses
shedding added brilliancy on the morning hour : while
his " Yesterdays with Authors" afforded several happy
readings-aloud by one of us to the other, as she
indulged in her favourite needle-work. To cordial,
friendliest Mr. Fields we owe our knowledge of a most
original, most poetical, most unique little volume, called
" Among the Isles of Shoals ;" and likewise sweet, ingenu-
ous, characteristic letters from its author, Celia Thaxter :
who seems to us to be a pearl among women-writers.

In coming to a close of this portion of our Recollections of Writers known to us, we look back relieved
from the sense of anxiety that beset us at its outset, when
we contemplated the almost bewildering task of selection
and arrangement amid such heaps of material as lay
stored in unsorted mingledom within the cells of our
brain : and now we can take some pleasure in hoping
that it is put into at least readable form. To us, this
gallery of memory-portraits is substantial ; and its figures,

while they presented themselves to our remembrance in succession, arose vivid and individual and distinct as any of those immortal portraits limned by Titian, Vandyck, Velasquez, or our own Reynolds, Gainsborough, Romney, and Lawrence. To have succeeded in giving even a faint shadow of our own clearly-seen images will be something to reward us for the pains it has cost us; for it has been a task at once painful and pleasurable. Painful in recalling so many dearly loved and daily seen that can never again be embraced or beheld on earth; pleasurable in remembering so many still spared to cheer and bless our life. Sometimes, when lying awake during those long night-watches, stretched on a bed the very opposite to that described by the wise old friar—

> But where unbruisèd youth, with unstuff'd brain,
> Doth couch his limbs, there golden sleep doth reign;

—we, unable to enjoy that lulling vacancy of thought, are fain to occupy many a sleepless hour by calling up these mind-portraits, and passing in review those who in themselves and in their memories have been a true beatitude to us. We behold them in almost material shape, and in spiritual vision, hoping to meet them where we trust to have fully solved those many forms of the "Great Why and Wherefore" that have so often and so achingly perplexed us in this beautiful but imperfect state of existence.

By day, our eyes feasting on the magnitude and magnificence of the unrivalled scene around us—blue expanse of sea, vast stretch of coast crowned by mountain ranges softened by olive woods and orange groves, with above all the cloudless sky, sun-lighted and sparkling, we often find ourselves ejaculating, "Ah, if Jerrold could have seen this!" "Ah, how Holmes would have enjoyed this!"—and ardently wishing for those we have known to be with us upon this beautiful Genoese promontory; making them still, as well as we can, companions in our pleasurable emotions, and feeling, through all, that indeed

A "loving friendship" is a joy for ever.

.

RECOLLECTIONS OF JOHN KEATS.

BY CHARLES COWDEN CLARKE.

IN the village of Enfield, in Middlesex, ten miles on the North road from London, my father, John Clarke, kept a school. The house had been built by a West India merchant in the latter end of the seventeenth or beginning of the eighteenth century. It was of the better character of the domestic architecture of that period, the whole front being of the purest red brick, wrought by means of moulds into rich designs of flowers and pomegranates, with heads of cherubim over niches in the centre of the building. The elegance of the design and the perfect finish of the structure were such as to secure its protection when a branch railway was brought from the Ware and Cambridge line to Enfield. The old school-house was converted into the station-house, and the railway company had the good taste to leave intact one of the few remaining specimens of the graceful English architecture of long-gone days.

Here it was that John Keats all but commenced and did complete his school education. He was born on the 29th of October, 1795; and he was one of the little fellows who had not wholly emerged from the child's costume upon being placed under my father's care. It will be readily conceived that it is difficult to recall from

the " dark backward and abysm " of seventy odd years
the general acts of perhaps the youngest individual in a
corporation of between seventy and eighty youngsters ;
and very little more of Keats's child-life can I remember
than that he had a brisk, winning face, and was a favourite with all, particularly my mother.   His maternal grand-
father, Jennings, was proprietor of a large livery-stable,
called the "Swan and Hoop," on the pavement in
Moorfields, opposite the entrance into Finsbury Circus.
He had two sons at my father's school : the elder was
an officer in Duncan's ship off Camperdown.   After the
battle, the Dutch admiral, De Winter, pointing to young
Jennings, told Duncan that he had fired several shots at
that young man, and always missed his mark ;—no credit to
his steadiness of aim, for Jennings, like his own admiral, was
considerably above the ordinary dimensions of stature.

Keats's father was the principal servant at the Swan and
Hoop stables—a man of so remarkably fine a common-
sense, and native respectability, that I perfectly remember
the warm terms in which his demeanour used to be canvassed by my parents after he had been to visit his boys.
John was the only one resembling him in person and
feature, with brown hair and dark hazel eyes. The
father was killed by a fall from his horse in returning
from a visit to the school.   This detail may be deemed
requisite when we see in the last memoir of the poet the
statement that "John Keats was born on the 29th of
October, 1795, in the upper rank of the middle class."
His two brothers—George, older, and Thomas, younger
than himself—were like the mother, who was tall, of good
figure, with large, oval face, and sensible deportment.
The last of the family was a sister—Fanny, I think, much
younger than all, and I hope still living—of whom I

remember, when once walking in the garden with her brothers, my mother speaking of her with much fondness for her pretty and simple manners. She married Mr. Llanos, a Spanish refugee, the author of " Don Esteban," and " Sandoval, the Freemason." He was a man of liberal principles, very attractive bearing, and of more than ordinary accomplishments.

In the early part of his school-life John gave no extra-ordinary indications of intellectual character; but it was remembered of him afterwards, that there was ever present a determined and steady spirit in all his under-takings : I never knew it misdirected in his required pursuit of study. He was a most orderly scholar. The future ramifications of that noble genius were then closely shut in the seed, which was greedily drinking in the moisture which made it afterwards burst forth so kindly into luxuriance and beauty.

My father was in the habit, at each half-year's vacation of bestowing prizes upon those pupils who had performed the greatest quantity of voluntary work ; and such was Keats's indefatigable energy for the last two or three successive half-years of his remaining at school, that, upon each occasion, he took the first prize by a considerable distance. He was at work before the first school-hour began, and that was at seven o'clock ; almost all the intervening times of recreation were so devoted ; and during the afternoon holidays, when all were at play, he would be in the school—almost the only one—at his Latin or French translation ; and so unconscious and regardless was he of the consequences of so close and persevering an application, that he never would have taken the necessary exercise had he not been sometimes driven out for the purpose by one of the masters.

It has just been said that he was a favourite with all. Not the less beloved was he for having a highly pugnacious spirit, which, when roused, was one of the most picturesque exhibitions—off the stage—I ever saw. One of the transports of that marvellous actor, Edmund Kean —whom, by the way, he idolized—was its nearest resemblance; and the two were not very dissimilar in face and figure. Upon one occasion, when an usher, on account of some impertinent behaviour, had boxed his brother Tom's ears, John rushed up, put himself in the received posture of offence, and, it was said, struck the usher— who could, so to say, have put him into his pocket. His passion at times was almost ungovernable; and his brother George, being considerably the taller and stronger, used frequently to hold him down by main force, laughing when John was in " one of his moods," and was endeavouring to beat him. It was all, however, a wisp-of-straw conflagration ; for he had an intensely tender affection for his brothers, and proved it upon the most trying occasions. He was not merely the " favourite of all," like a pet prize-fighter, for his terrier courage ; but his high-mindedness, his utter unconsciousness of a mean motive, his placability, his generosity, wrought so general a feeling in his behalf, that I never heard a word of disapproval from any one, superior or equal, who had known him.

In the latter part of the time—perhaps eighteen months —that he remained at school, he occupied the hours during meals in reading. Thus, his *whole* time was engrossed. He had a tolerably retentive memory, and the quantity that he read was surprising. He must in those last months have exhausted the school library, which consisted principally of abridgments of all the voyages and travels of any note ; Mavor's collection, also his "Universal History ;" Robertson's histories of Scotland, America, and Charles the Fifth ; all Miss Edgeworth's productions, together with many other works equally well calculated for youth. The books, however, that were his constantly recurrent sources of attraction were Tooke's "Pantheon," Lemprière's "Classical Dictionary," which he appeared to *learn*, and Spence's "Polymetis." This was the store whence he acquired his intimacy with the Greek mythology ; here was he "suckled in that creed outworn ;" for his amount of classical attainment extended no farther than the "Æneid ;" with which epic, indeed, he was so fascinated that before leaving school he had *voluntarily* translated in writing a considerable portion. And yet I remember that at that early age—mayhap under fourteen - notwithstanding, and through all its incidental attractiveness, he hazarded the opinion to me (and the expression riveted my surprise), that there was feebleness in the structure of the work. He must have gone through all the better publications in the school library, for he asked me to lend him some of my own books ; and, in my "mind's eye," I now see him at supper (we had our meals in the schoolroom), sitting back on the form, from the table, holding the folio volume of Burnet's "History of his Own Time" between himself and the table, eating his meal from beyond it. This work, and Leigh Hunt's *Examiner*— which my father took in, and I used to lend to Keats— no doubt laid the foundation of his love of civil and religious liberty. He once told me, smiling, that one of his guardians, being informed what books I had lent him to read, declared that if he had fifty children he would not send one of them to that school. Bless his patriot head !

When he left Enfield, at fourteen years of age, he was apprenticed to Mr. Thomas Hammond, a medical man, residing in Church Street, Edmonton, and exactly two miles from Enfield. This arrangement evidently gave him satisfaction, and I fear that it was the most placid period of his painful life; for now, with the exception of the duty he had to perform in the surgery—by no means an onerous one— his whole leisure hours were employed in indulging his passion for reading and translating. During his apprenticeship he finished the " Æneid."

The distance between our residences being so short, I gladly encouraged his inclination to come over when he could claim a leisure hour; and in consequence I saw him about five or six times a month on my own leisure afternoons. He rarely came empty-handed; either he had a book to read, or brought one to be exchanged. When the weather permitted, we always sat in an arbour at the end of a spacious garden, and—in Boswellian dialect—" we had good talk."

It were difficult, at this lapse of time, to note the spark that fired the train of his pöetical tendencies; but he must have given unmistakable tokens of his mental bent; otherwise, at that early stage of his career, I never could have read to him the " Epithalamion " of Spenser; and this I remember having done, and in that hallowed old arbour, the scene of many bland and graceful associations —the substances having passed away. At that time he may have been sixteen years old ; and at that period of life he certainly appreciated the general beauty of the composition, and felt the more passionate passages; for his features and exclamations were ecstatic. How often, in after-times, have I heard him quote these lines :—

Behold, while she before the altar stands,
Hearing the holy priest that to her speaks,
And blesses her with his two happy hands,
How the red roses flush up to her cheeks !
And the pure snow, with goodly vermeil stain,
Like crimson dyed in grain,
That even the angels, which continually
About the sacred altar do remain,
Forget their service, and about her fly,
Oft peeping in her face, that seems more fair,
The more they on it stare;
But her sad eyes, still fasten'd on the ground,
Are governèd with goodly modesty,
That suffers not one look to glance awry,
Which may let in a little thought unsound.

That night he took away with him the first volume of the " Faerie Queene," and he went through it, as I formerly told his noble biographer, " as a young horse would through a spring meadow—ramping !" Like a true poet, too—a poet " born, not manufactured," a poet in grain, he especially singled out epithets, for that felicity and power in which Spenser is so eminent. He *hoisted* himself up, and looked burly and dominant, as he said, " what an image that is—' *sea-shouldering whales!* '" It was a treat to see as well as hear him read a pathetic passage. Once, when reading the " Cymbeline " aloud, I saw his eyes fill with tears, and his voice faltered when he came to the departure of Posthumus, and Imogen saying she would have watched him—

'Till the diminution
Of space had pointed him sharp as my needle ;
Nay follow'd him till he had *melted from*
The smallness of a gnat to air; and then
Have turn'd mine eye and wept.

I cannot remember the precise time of our separating at this stage of Keats's career, or which of us first went to London; but it was upon an occasion, when walking thither to see Leigh Hunt, who had just fulfilled his penalty of confinement in Horsemonger Lane Prison for the unwise libel upon the Prince Regent, that Keats met me ; and, turning, accompanied me back part of the way.   At the last field-gate, when taking leave, he gave me the sonnet entitled, " Written on the day that Mr. Leigh Hunt left Prison."   This I feel to be the first proof I had received of his having committed himself in verse ; and how clearly do I recall the conscious look and hesitation with which he offered it !   There are some momentary glances by beloved friends that fade only with life. His biographer has stated that " The Lines in Imitation of Spenser "—

> Now Morning from her orient chamber came,
> And her first footsteps touch'd a verdant hill, &c.,

are the earliest known verses of his composition ; a probable circumstance, from their subject being the inspiration of his first love, in poetry—and such a love ! —but Keats's first *published* poem was the sonnet—

> O Solitude ! if I must with thee dwell,
>   Let it not be among the jumbled heap
>   Of murky buildings ; climb with me the steep—
> Nature's observatory—whence the dell,
> In flowery slopes, its river's crystal swell
>   May seem a span ; let me thy vigils keep
>   'Mongst boughs pavilion'd, where the deer's swift leap
> Startles the wild bee from the foxglove bell.
>   But though I'll gladly trace these scenes with thee,
> Yet the sweet converse of an innocent mind,
> Whose words are images of thoughts refined,

> Is my soul's pleasure ; and it sure must be
> Almost the highest bliss of human kind,
> When to thy haunts two kindred spirits flee.

This sonnet appeared in the *Examiner*, some time, I think, in 1816.

When we both had come to London—Keats to enter as a student of St. Thomas's Hospital—he was not long in discovering my abode, which was with a brother-in-law in Clerkenwell ; and at that time being housekeeper, and solitary, he would come and renew his loved gossip ; till, as the author of the " Urn Burial " says, " we were acting our antipodes—the huntsmen were up in America, and they already were past their first sleep in Persia." At the close of a letter which preceded my appointing him to come and lighten my darkness in Clerkenwell, is his first address upon coming to London. He says,— " Although the Borough is a beastly place in dirt, turnings, and windings, yet No. 8, Dean Street, is not difficult to find ; and if you would run the gauntlet over London Bridge, take the first turning to the right, and, moreover, knock at my door, which is nearly opposite a meeting, you would do me a charity, which, as St. Paul saith, is the father of all the virtues. At all events, let me hear from you soon : I say, at all events, not excepting the gout in your fingers." This letter, having no date but the week's day, and no postmark, preceded our first symposium ; and a memorable night it was in my life's career.

A beautiful copy of the folio edition of Chapman's translation of Homer had been lent me. It was the property of Mr. Alsager, the gentleman who for years had contributed no small share of celebrity to the great reputation of the *Times* newspaper by the masterly manner in which he conducted the money-market department of that journal. Upon my first introduction to Mr. Alsager he lived opposite to Horsemonger Lane Prison, and upon Mr. Leigh Hunt's being sentenced for the libel, his first day's dinner was sent over by Mr. Alsager.

Well, then, we were put in possession of the Homer of Chapman, and to work we went, turning to some of the "famousest" passages, as we had scrappily known them in Pope's version. There was, for instance, that perfect scene of the conversation on Troy wall of the old Senators with Helen, who is pointing out to them the several Greek Captains; with the Senator Antenor's vivid portrait of an orator in Ulysses, beginning at the 237th line of the third book :—

But when the prudent Ithacus did to his counsels rise,
He stood a little still, and fix'd upon the earth his eyes,
His sceptre moving neither way, but held it formally,
Like one that vainly doth affect. Of wrathful quality,
And frantic (rashly judging), you would have said he was ;
But when out of his ample breast he gave his great voice
    pass,
And words that flew about our ears like drifts of winter's
    snow,
None thenceforth might contend with him, though naught
    admired for show.

The shield and helmet of Diomed, with the accompanying simile, in the opening of the third book ; and the prodigious description of Neptune's passage to the Achive ships, in the thirteenth book :—

The woods and all the great hills near trembled beneath the
    weight
Of his immortal-moving feet. Three steps he only took, '
Before he far-off Ægas reach'd, but with the fourth, it shook
With his dread entry.

One scene I could not fail to introduce to him—the shipwreck of Ulysses, in the fifth book of the "Odysseis," and I had the reward of one of his delighted stares, upon reading the following lines :—

> Then forth he came, his both knees falt'ring, both
> His strong hands hanging down, and all with froth
> His cheeks and nostrils flowing, voice and breath
> Spent to all use, and down he sank to death.
> *The sea had soak'd his heart through;* all his veins
> His toils had rack'd t' a labouring woman's pains.
> Dead-weary was he.

On an after-occasion I showed him the couplet, in Pope's translation, upon the same passage :—

> From mouth and nose the briny torrent ran,
> And *lost in lassitude lay all the man.* [!!!]

Chapman [1] supplied us with many an after-treat; but it was in the teeming wonderment of this his first introduction, that, when I came down to breakfast the next morning, I found upon my table a letter with no other enclosure than his famous sonnet, "On First Looking into Chapman's Homer." We had parted, as I have already said, at day-spring, yet he contrived that I should receive the poem from a distance of, may be, two miles by ten o'clock. In the published copy of this sonnet he made an alteration in the seventh line :—

> Yet did I never breathe its pure serene.

The original which he sent me had the phrase—

> Yet could I never tell what men could mean ;

which he said was bald, and too simply wondering.   No

[1] With what joy would Keats have welcomed Mr. Richard Hooper's admirable edition of our old version !

one could more earnestly chastise his thoughts than Keats. His favourite among Chapman's "Hymns of Homer" was the one to Pan, which he himself rivalled in the "Endymion :"—

O thou whose mighty palace-roof doth hang, &c.

It appears early in the first book of the poem ; the first line in which has passed into a proverb, and become a motto to Exhibition catalogues of Fine Art :—

> A thing of beauty is a joy for ever :
> Its loveliness increases ; it will never
> Pass into nothingness ; but still will keep
> A bower quiet for us, and a sleep
> Full of sweet dreams, &c.

The "Hymn to Pan" alone should have rescued th's young and vigorous poem –this youngest epic—from the savage injustice with which it was assailed.

In one of our conversations, about this period, I alluded to his position at St. Thomas's Hospital, coasting and reconnoitring, as it were, for the purpose of discovering what progress he was making in his profession ; which I had taken for granted had been his own selection, and not one chosen for him. The total absorption, therefore, of every other mood of his mind than that of imaginative composition, which had now evidently encompassed him, induced me, from a kind motive, to inquire what was his bias of action for the future ; and with that transparent candour which formed the mainspring of his rule of conduct, he at once made no secret of his inability to sympathize with the science of anatomy, as a main pursuit in life ; for one of the expressions that he used, in describing his unfitness for its mastery, was perfectly characteristic. He said, in illustration of his argument,

"The other day, for instance, during the lecture, there came a sunbeam into the room, and with it a whole troop of creatures floating in the ray; and I was off with them to Oberon and fairyland." And yet, with all his self-styled unfitness for the pursuit, I was afterwards informed that at his subsequent examination he displayed an amount of acquirement which surprised his fellow-students, who had scarcely any other association with him than that of a cheerful, crotchety rhymester. He once talked with me, upon my complaining of stomachic derangement, with a remarkable decision of opinion, describing the functions and actions of the organ with the clearness and, as I presume, technical precision of an adult practitioner; casually illustrating the comment, in his characteristic way, with poetical imagery: the stomach, he said, being like a brood of callow nestlings (opening his capacious mouth) yearning and gaping for sustenance; and, indeed, he merely exemplified what should be, if possible, the "stock in trade" of every poet, viz, to *know* all that is to be known, "in the heaven above, or in the earth beneath, or in the waters under the earth."

It was about this period that, going to call upon Mr. Leigh Hunt, who then occupied a pretty little cottage in the Vale of Health, on Hampstead Heath, I took with me two or three of the poems I had received from Keats. I could not but anticipate that Hunt would speak encouragingly, and indeed approvingly, of the compositions —written, too, by a youth under age; but my partial spirit was not prepared for the unhesitating and prompt admiration which broke forth before he had read twenty lines of the first poem. Horace Smith happened to be there on the occasion, and he was not less demonstrative n his appreciation of their merits. The piece which he read out was the sonnet, " How many Bards gild the Lapses of Time !" marking with particulai emphasis and approval the last six lines :—

> So the unnumber'd sounds that evening store,
>   The songs of birds, the whisp'ring of the leaves,
>   The voice of waters, the great bell that heaves
> With solemn sound, and thousand others more,
>   *That distance of recognizance bereaves,*
> Make pleasing music, and not wild uproar.

Smith repeated with applause the line in italics, sayin*, " What a well-condensed expression for a youth so young ! " After making numerous and eager inquiries about him personally, and with reference to any peculiarities of mind and manner, the visit ended in my being requested to bring him over to the Vale of Health.

That was a " red-letter day " in the young poet's life, and one which will never fade with me while memory lasts.

The character and expression of Keats's features would arrest even the casual passenger in the street ; and now they were wrought to a tone of animation that I could not but watch with interest, knowing what was in store for him from the bland encouragement, and Spartan deference in attention, with fascinating conversational eloquence, that he was to encounter and receive. As we approached the Heath, there was the rising and accelerated step, with the gradual subsidence of all talk. The interview, which stretched into three " morning calls," was the prelude to many after-scenes and saunterings about Caen Wood and its neighbourhood ; for Keats was suddenly made a familiar of the household, and was always welcomed.

It was in the library at Hunt's cottage, where an

extemporary bed had been made up for him on the sofa,
that he composed the frame-work and many lines of the
poem on " Sleep and Poetry "—the last sixty or seventy
being an inventory of the art garniture of the room, commencing,—

> It was a poet's house who keeps the keys
> Of Pleasure's temple.   *   *   *

In this composition is the lovely and favourite little
cluster of images upon the fleeting transit of life—a
pathetic anticipation of his own brief career :—

> Stop and consider! Life is but a day;
> A fragile dew-drop on its perilous way
> From a tree's summit; a poor Indian's sleep
> While his boat hastens to the monstrous steep
> Of Montmorenci. Why so sad a moan?
> Life is the rose's hope while yet unblown;
> The reading of an ever-changing tale;
> The light uplifting of a maiden's veil;
> A pigeon tumbling in the summer air;
> A laughing school-boy, without grief or care,
> Riding the springy branches of an elm.

Very shortly after his installation at the cottage, and on
the day after one of our visits, he gave in the following
sonnet, a characteristic appreciation of the spirit in
which he had been received :—

> Keen fitful gusts are whispering here and there
>   Among the bushes half leafless and dry;
>   The stars look very cold about the sky,
>   And I have many miles on foot to fare;
>   Yet I feel little of the cool bleak air,
>   Or of the dead leaves rustling drearily,
>   Or of those silver lamps that burn on high,
>   Or of the distance from home's pleasant lair:
>   For I am brimful of the friendliness

> That in a little cottage I have found;
> Of fair-hair'd Milton's eloquent distress,
>   And all his love for gentle Lycid' drown'd;
> Of lovely Laura in her light green dress,
>   And faithful Petrarch gloriously crown'd.

The glowing sonnet upon being compelled to "Leave Friends at an Early Hour"—

> Give me a golden pen, and let me lean, &c.,

followed shortly after the former. But the occasion that recurs with the liveliest interest was one evening when – some observations having been made upon the character, habits, and pleasant associations with that reverend denizen of the hearth, the cheerful little grasshopper of the fireside— Hunt proposed to Keats the challenge of writing then, there, and to time, a sonnet "On the Grasshopper and Cricket." No one was present but myself, and they accordingly set to. I, apart, with a book at the end of the sofa, could not avoid furtive glances every now and then at the emulants. I cannot say how long the trial lasted. I was not proposed umpire; and had no stop-watch for the occasion. The time, however, was short for such a performance, and Keats won as to time. But the event of the after-scrutiny was one of many such occurrences which have riveted the memory of Leigh Hunt in my affectionate regard and admiration for unaffected generosity and perfectly unpretentious encouragement. His sincere look of pleasure at the first line—

> The poetry of earth is never dead.

"Such a prosperous opening!" he said; and when he came to the tenth and eleventh lines :—

> On a lone winter evening, *when the frost*
> *Has wrought a silence—*

"Ah! that's perfect! Bravo Keats!" And then he went on in a dilatation upon the dumbness of Nature during the season's suspension and torpidity. With all the kind and gratifying things that were said to him, Keats protested to me, as we were afterwards walking home, that he preferred Hunt's treatment of the subject to his own. As neighbour Dogberry would have rejoined, "'Fore God, they are both in a tale!" It has occurred to me, upon so remarkable an occasion as the one here recorded, that a reunion of the two sonnets will be gladly hailed by the reader.

ON THE GRASSHOPPER AND CRICKET.

The poetry of earth is never dead:
  When all the birds are faint with the hot sun,
  And hide in cooling trees, a voice will run
From hedge to hedge about the new-mown mead;
That is the Grasshopper's,—he takes the lead
  In summer luxury,—he has never done
  With his delights, for when tired out with fun
He rests at ease beneath some pleasant weed.
The poetry of earth is ceasing never;
  On a lone winter evening, when the frost
Has wrought a silence; from the stove there thrills
The Cricket's song, in warmth increasing ever,
  And seems to one in drowsiness half lost,
The Grasshopper's among some grassy hills.

Dec. 30, 1816.   JOHN KEATS.

ON THE GRASSHOPPER AND THE CRICKET.

Green little vaulter in the sunny grass
  Catching your heart up at the feel of June,
  Sole voice that's heard amidst the lazy noon,
When ev'n the bees lag at the summoning brass;
And you, warm little housekeeper, who class

With those who think the candles come too soon,
  Loving the fire, and with your tricksome tune
Nick the glad silent moments as they pass :
Oh sweet and tiny cousins, that belong,
  One to the fields, the other to the hearth,
Both have your sunshine; both though small are strong
  At your clear hearts; and both were sent on earth
To sing in thoughtful ears this natural song,—
  In doors and out, Summer and Winter, Mirth !

Dec. 30, 1816.   LEIGH HUNT.

Keats had left the neighbourhood of the Borough, and was now living with his brothers in apartments on the second floor of a house in the Poultry, over the passage leading to the Queen's Head Tavern, and opposite to one of the City Companies' halls—the Ironmongers', if I mistake not. I have the associating reminiscence of many happy hours spent in this abode. Here was determined upon, in great part written, and sent forth to the world, the first little, but vigorous, offspring of his brain :—

POEMS
By
JOHN KEATS.

" What more felicity can fall to creature
Than to enjoy delight with liberty ! "
Fate of the Butterfly: Spenser.

London :
Printed for C. and J. Ollier,
3, Welbeck Street, Cavendish Square.
1817.

And here, on the evening when the last proof-sheet was brought from the printer, it was accompanied by the information that if a " dedication to the book was intended it must be sent forthwith." Whereupon he withdrew to a side-table, and in the buzz of a mixed conversation (for there were several friends in the room) he composed and brought to Charles Ollier, the publisher, the Dedication Sonnet to Leigh Hunt. If the original manuscript of that poem — a legitimate sonnet, with every restriction of rhyme and metre — could now be produced, and the time recorded in which it was written, it would be pronounced an extraordinary performance : added to which the non-alteration of a single word in the poem (a circumstance that was noted at the time) claims for it a merit with a very rare parallel. The remark may be here subjoined that, had the composition been previously prepared for the occasion, the mere writing it out would have occupied fourteen minutes; and lastly, when I refer to the time occupied in composing the sonnet -on " The Grasshopper and the Cricket," I can have no hesitation in believing the one in question to have been extempore.

" The poem which commences the volume," says Lord Houghton in his first memoir of the poet, " was suggested to Keats by a delightful summer's day, as he stood beside the gate that leads from the battery on Hampstead Heath into a field by Caen Wood ;" and the following lovely passage he himself told me was the recollection of our having frequently loitered over the rail of a footbridge that spanned (probably still spans, notwithstanding the intrusive and shouldering railroad) a little brook in the last field upon entering Edmonton :—

> Linger awhile upon some bending planks
> That lean against a streamlet's rushy banks,
> And watch intently Nature's gentle doings;
> They will be found softer than ring-dove's cooings.
> How silent comes the water round that bend !
> Not the minutest whisper does it send

To the o'er-hanging sallows ; blades of grass
Slowly across the chequer'd shadows pass.
Why, you might read two sonnets, ere they reach
To where the hurrying freshnesses aye preach
A natural sermon o'er their pebbly beds ;
Where swarms of minnows show their little heads,
Staying their wavy bodies 'gainst the streams,
To taste the luxury of sunny beams
Temper'd with coolness. *How they wrestle*
With their own delight, and ever nestle
Their silver bellies on the pebbly sand !
If you but scantily hold out the hand,
That very instant not one will remain ;
But turn your eye and they are there again.

He himself thought the picture correct, and acknowledged to a partiality for it.

Another example of his promptly suggestive imagination, and uncommon facility in giving it utterance,
occurred one day upon returning home and finding me
asleep on the sofa, with a volume of Chaucer open at the
"Flower and the Leaf." After expressing to me his admiration of the poem, which he had been reading, he gave
me the fine testimony of that opinion in pointing to the
sonnet he had written at the close of it, which was an
extempore effusion, and without the alteration of a single
word.   It lies before me now, signed " J. K., Feb., 1817.
If my memory do not betray me, this charming out-door
fancy scene was Keats's first introduction to Chaucer.
The " Troilus and Cresseide" was certainly an after acquaintance with him ; and clearly do I recall his approbation of the favourite passages that had been marked in
my own copy.   Upon being requested, he retraced the
poem, and with his pen confirmed and denoted those
which were congenial with his own feeling and judgment.

These two circumstances, associated with the literary career of this cherished object of his friend's esteem and love, have stamped a priceless value upon that friend's miniature 18mo. copy of Chaucer.

The first volume of Keats's minor muse was launched amid the cheers and fond anticipations of all his circle. Every one of us expected (and not unreasonably) that it would create a sensation in the literary world ; for such a first production (and a considerable portion of it from a minor) has rarely occurred. The three Epistles and the seventeen sonnets (that upon "first looking into Chapman's Homer" one of them) would have ensured a rousing welcome from our modern-day reviewers. Alas ! the book might have emerged in Timbuctoo with far stronger chance of fame and approbation. It never passed to a second edition ; the first was but a small one, and that was never sold off. The whole community, as if by compact, seemed determined to know nothing about it. The word had been passed that its author was a Radical ; and in those days of "Bible-Crown-and-Constitution" supremacy, he might have had better chance of success had he been an Anti-Jacobin. Keats had not made the slightest demonstration of political opinion ; but with a conscious feeling of gratitude for kindly encouragement, he had dedicated his book to Leigh Hunt, Editor of the *Examiner*, a Radical and a dubbed partisan of the first Napoleon ; because when alluding to him, Hunt did not always subjoin the fashionable cognomen of "Corsican Monster." Such an association was motive enough with the dictators of that day to thwart the endeavours of a young aspirant who should presume to assert for himself an unrestricted course of opinion. Verily, " the former times were *not* better than these." Men may now utter a word in favour of " civil liberty" without being chalked on the back and hounded out.

Poor Keats ! he little anticipated, and as little merited, the cowardly treatment that was in store for him upon the publishing of his second composition—the " Endymion." It was in the interval of the two productions that he had moved from the Poultry, and had taken a lodging in Well Walk, Hampstead—in the first or second house on the right hand, going up to the Heath. I have an impression that he had been some weeks absent at the seaside before settling in this district ; for the " Endymion " had been begun, and he had made considerable advances in his plan. He came to me one Sunday, and we passed the greater part of the day walking in the neighbourhood. His constant and enviable friend, Severn, I remember, was present upon the occasion, by a little circumstance of our exchanging looks upon Keats reading to us portions of his new poem with which he himself had been pleased ; and never will his expression of face depart from me ; if I were a Reynolds or a Gainsborough I could now stamp it for ever. One of his selections was the *now* celebrated " Hymn to Pan " in the first book :—

> O thou whose mighty palace-roof doth hang
> From jagged roofs ;

which alone ought to have preserved the poem from unkindness ; and which would have received an awarding smile from the " deep-brow'd " himself. And the other selections were the descriptions in the second book of the " bower of Adonis," and the ascent and descent of the silver car of Venus, air-borne :—

Whose silent wheels, fresh wet from clouds of morn,
Spun off a drizzling dew.

Keats was indebted for his introduction to Mr. Severn to his schoolfellow Edward Holmes, who also had been one of the child scholars at Enfield ; for he came there in the frock-dress.

Holmes ought to have been an educated musician from his first childhood, for the passion was in him. I used to amuse myself with the pianoforte after supper, when all had gone to bed. Upon some sudden occasion, leaving the parlour, I heard a scuffle on the stairs, and discovered that my young gentleman had left his bed, to hear the music. At other times, during the day, in the intervals of school-hours, he would stand under the window listening. At length he entrusted to me his heart's secret, that he should like to learn music, when I taught him his tonic alphabet, and he soon knew and could do as much as his tutor. Upon leaving school, he was apprenticed to the elder Seeley, the bookseller ; but, disliking his occupation, he left it, I think, before he was of age. He did not lose sight of his old master, and I introduced him to Mr. Vincent Novello, who had made himself a friend to me ; and who, not merely with rare profusion of bounty gave Holmes instruction, but received him into his house and made him one of his family. With them he resided some years. I was also the fortunate means of recommending him to the chief proprietor of the *Atlas* newspaper ; and to that journal during a long period he contributed a series of essays and critiques upon the science and practice of music, which raised the journal into a reference and an authority in the art. He wrote for the proprietors of the *Atlas* an elegant little book of dilettante criticism, " A

Ramble among the Musicians in Germany." And in the
later period of his career he contributed to the *Musical
Times* a whole series of masterly essays and analyses upon
the masses of Haydn, Mozart, and Beethoven. His own
favourite production was a " Life of Mozart," in which
he performed his task with considerable skill and equal
modesty, contriving by means of the great musician's
own letters to convert the work into an autobiography.

I have said that Holmes used to listen on the stairs.
In after-years, when Keats was reading to me the manuscript of "The Eve of St. Agnes," upon the repeating of
the passage when Porphyro is listening to the midnight
music in the hall below,—

> The boisterous midnight festive clarion,
> The kettle-drum and far-heard clarionet,
> Affray his ears, though but in dying tone :
> *The hall door shuts again, and all the noise is gone ;—*

"that line," said he, "came into my head when I remembered how I used to listen in bed to your music at
school." How enchanting would be a record of the
germs and first causes of all the greatest artists' con-
ceptions ! The elder Brunel's first hint for his " shield "
in constructing the tunnel under the Thames was taken
from watching the labour of a sea insect, which, having
a projecting hood, could bore into the ship's timber
unmolested by the waves.

It may have been about this time that Keats gave a
signal example of his courage and stamina, in the recorded
instance of his pugilistic contest with a butcher boy. He
told me, and in his characteristic manner, of their
" passage of arms." The brute, he said, was tormenting
a kitten, and he interfered ; when a threat offered was
enough for his mettle, and they " set to." He thought

he should be beaten, for the fellow was the taller and stronger; but like an authentic pugilist, my young poet found that he had planted a blow which "told" upon his antagonist; in every succeeding round, therefore (for they fought nearly an hour), he never failed of returning to the weak point, and the contest ended in the hulk being led home.

In my knowledge of fellow-beings, I never knew one who so thoroughly combined the sweetness with the power of gentleness, and the irresistible sway of anger, as Keats. His indignation would have made the boldest grave; and they who had seen him under the influence of injustice and meanness of soul would not forget the expression of his features—"the form of his visage was changed." Upon one occasion, when some local tyranny was being discussed, he amused the party by shouting, "Why is there not a human dust-hole, into which to tumble such fellows?"

Keats had a strong sense of humour, although he was not, in the strict sense of the term, a humorist, still less a farcist. His comic fancy lurked in the outermost and most unlooked-for images of association; which, indeed, may be said to form the components of humour; nevertheless, they did not extend beyond the *quaint* in fulfilment and success. But his perception of humour, with the power of transmitting it by imitation, was both vivid and irresistibly amusing. He once described to me his having gone to see a bear-baiting, the animal the property of a Mr. Tom Oliver. The performance not having begun, Keats was near to, and watched, a young aspirant, who had brought a younger under his wing to witness the solemnity, and whom he oppressively patronized, instructing him in the names and qualities of all the magnates present. Now and then, in his zeal to manifest and impart his knowledge, he would forget himself, and stray beyond the prescribed bounds into the ring, to the lashing resentment of its comptroller, Mr. William Soames, who, after some hints of a practical nature to " keep back," began laying about him with indiscriminate and unmitigable vivacity, the Peripatetic signifying to his pupil, " My eyes ! Bill Soames giv' me sich a licker !" evidently grateful, and considering himself complimented upon being included in the general dispensation. Keats's entertainment with and appreciation of this minor scene of low life has often recurred to me. But his concurrent personification of the baiting, with his position—his legs and arms bent and shortened till he looked like Bruin on his hind legs, dabbing his fore paws hither and thither, as the dogs snapped at him, and now and then acting the gasp of one that had been suddenly caught and hugged —his own capacious mouth adding force to the personation, was a remarkable and as memorable a display. I am never reminded of this amusing relation but it is associated with that forcible picture in Shakespeare, in " Henry VI.:"—

> . . . . As a bear encompass'd round with dogs,
> Who having *pinch'd* a few and *made them cry*,
> The rest stand all aloof and bark at him.

Keats also attended a prize fight between the two most skilful " light weights " of the day, Randal and Turner ; and in describing the rapidity of the blows of the one, while the other was falling, he tapped his fingers on the window-pane.

I make no apology for recording these events in his life ; they are characteristics of the natural man, and prove, moreover, that the partaking in such exhibitions did not for one moment blunt the gentler emotions of his heart, or vulgarize his inborn love of all that was beautiful and true.   He would never have been a "slang gent," because he had other and better accomplishments to make him conspicuous.   His own line was the axiom of his moral existence, his civil creed : "A thing of beauty is a joy for ever," and I can fancy no coarser association able to win him from his faith.   Had he been born in squalor he would have emerged a gentleman.   Keats was not an easily swayable man ; in differing with those he loved his firmness kept equal pace with the sweetness of his persuasion, but with the rough and the unlovable he kept no terms—within the conventional precincts, of course, of social order.

From Well Walk he moved to another quarter of the Heath, Wentworth Place, I think, the name.   Here he became a sharing inmate with Charles Armitage Brown, a retired Russia merchant upon an independence and literary leisure.   With this introduction their acquaintance commenced, and Keats never had a more zealous, a firmer, or more practical friend and adviser than Armitage Brown.   Mr. Brown brought out a work entitled, "Shakespeare's Autobiographical Poems.   Being his Sonnets clearly developed ; with his Character drawn chiefly from his Works."   It cannot be said that the author has clearly educed his theory ; but, in the face of his failure upon the main point, the book is interesting for the heart-whole zeal and homage with which he has gone into his subject.   Brown accompanied Keats in his tour in the Hebrides, a worthy event in the poet's career, seeing that it led to the production of that magnificent sonnet to "Ailsa Rock."   As a passing observation, and to show how the minutest circumstance did not escape him, he told me that when he first came upon the view of Loch Lomond the sun was setting, the lake was in shade, and of a deep blue, and at the further end was "*a slash across it* of deep orange." The description of the traceried window in the "Eve of St. Agnes" gives proof of the intensity of his feeling for colour.

It was during his abode in Wentworth Place, that unsurpassedly savage attacks upon the "Endymion" appeared in some of the principal reviews—savage attacks, and *personally* abusive ; and which would damage the sale of any magazine in the present day.

The style of the articles directed against the writers whom the party had nicknamed the "Cockney School" of poetry, may be conceived from its producing the following speech I heard from Hazlitt : "To pay those fellows *in their own coin,* the way would be to begin with Walter Scott, and *have at his clump foot.*" "Verily, the former times were not better than these."

To say that these disgusting misrepresentations did not affect the consciousness and self-respect ot Keats would be to underrate the sensitiveness of his nature. He did feel and resent the insult, but far more the *injustice* of the treatment he had received ; and he told me so. They no doubt had injured him in the most wanton manner ; but if they, or my Lord Byron, ever for one moment supposed that he was crushed or even cowed in spirit by the treatment he had received, never were they more deluded. "Snuffed out by an article," indeed ! He had infinitely more magnanimity, in its fullest sense, than that very spoiled, self-willed, and mean-souled man—and I have unquestionable authority for the last term. To say nothing of personal and private transactions, Lord Houghton's observations, in his life of our poet, will be full authority for my estimate of Lord Byron. "Johnny Keats" had indeed "a little body with a mighty heart," and he showed it in the best way ; not by fighting the "bush-rangers" in their own style—though he could have done that—but by the resolve that he would produce brain work which not one of their party could exceed ; and he did, for in the year 1820 appeared the "Lamia," "Isabella," "Eve of St. Agnes," and the "Hyperion"—that illustrious fragment, which Shelley said "had the character of one of the antique desert fragments;" which Leigh Hunt called a "gigantic fragment, like a ruin in the desert, or the bones of the Mastodon ;" and Lord Byron confessed that "it seemed actually inspired by the Titans, and as sublime as Æschylus."

All this wonderful work was produced in scarcely more than one year, manifesting—with health—what his brain could achieve ; but, alas ! the insidious disease which carried him off had made its approach, and he was preparing to go to, or had already departed for, Italy, attended by his constant and self-sacrificing friend Severn. Keats's mother died of consumption ; and he nursed his younger brother, in the same disease, to the last ; and, by so doing, in all probability hastened his own summons.

Upon the publication of the last volume of poems, Charles Lamb wrote one of his finely appreciative and cordial critiques in the *Morning Chronicle.* At that period I had been absent for some weeks from London, and had not heard of the dangerous state of Keats's health, only that he and Severn were going to Italy : it was, therefore, an unprepared-for shock which brought me the news of his death in Rome.

Lord Houghton, in his 1848 and first "Biography of Keats," has related the anecdote of the young poet's introduction to Wordsworth, with the latter's appreciation of the " Hymn to Pan " (in the " Endymion "), which the author had been desired to repeat, and the Rydal-Mount poet's snow-capped comment upon it—" H'm ! a pretty piece of Paganism ! " The lordly biographer, with his genial and placable nature, has made an amiable apology for the apparent coldness of Wordsworth's appreciation, " that it was probably intended for some slight rebuke to his youthful compeer, whom he saw absorbed in an order of ideas that to him appeared merely sensuous, and would have desired that the bright traits of Greek mythology should be sobered down by a graver faith." Keats, like Shakespeare, and every other real poet, put his whole soul into what he had imagined, portrayed, or embodied ; and hence he appeared the true young Greek. The wonder is that Wordsworth should have forgotten the quotation that might have been made from one of his own deservedly illustrious sonnets :—

> The world is too much with us.
> .   .   Great God ! I'd rather be
> A pagan suckled in a creed outworn ;
> So might I, standing on this pleasant lea,
> Have glimpses that would make me less forlorn ;
> Have sight of Proteus rising from the sea ;
> Or hear old Triton blow his wreathèd horn.

From Keats's description of his mentor's manner, as well as behaviour that evening, it would seem to have been one of the usual ebullitions of egoism, not to say of the uneasiness known to those who were accustomed to hear the great moral philosopher discourse upon his own productions, and descant upon those of a contemporary. During that same interview, some one having observed that the next Waverley novel was to be " Rob Roy," Wordsworth took down his volume of

Ballads, and read to the company "Rob Roy's Grave;" then, returning it to the shelf, observed, "I do not know what more Mr. Scott can have to say upon the subject." Leigh Hunt, upon his first interview with Wordsworth, described his having lectured very finely upon his own writings, repeating the entire noble sonnet, "Great men have been among us"—"in a grand and earnest tone:" that rogue, Christopher North, added, "Catch him repeating any other than his own." Upon another and similar occasion, one of the party had quoted that celebrated passage from the play of "Henry V.," "So work the honey-bees;" and each proceeded to pick out his "pet plum" from that perfect piece of natural history; when Wordsworth objected to the line, "The singing masons building roofs of gold," because, he said, of the unpleasant repetition of "*ing*" in it! Why, where were his poetical ears and judgment? But more than once it has been said that Wordsworth had not a genuine love of Shakespeare: that, when he could, he always accompanied a "*pro*" with his "*con.*," and, Atticus-like, would "just hint a fault and hesitate dislike." Mr James T. Fields, in his delightful volume of "Yesterdays with Authors," has an amiable record of his interview with Wordsworth; yet he has the following casual remark, "I thought he did not praise easily those whose names are indissolubly connected with his own in the history of literature. It was languid praise, at least, and I observed he hesitated for mild terms which he could apply to names almost as great as his own." Even Crabb Robinson more than once mildly hints at the same infirmity. "Truly are we *all* of a mingled yarn, good and ill together."

When Shelley left England for Italy, Keats told me that he had received from him an invitation to become his guest, and, in short, to make one of his household. It was upon the purest principle that Keats declined his noble proffer, for he entertained an exalted opinion of Shelley's genius—in itself an inducement ; he also knew of his deeds of bounty, and, from their frequent social intercourse, he had full faith in the sincerity of his proposal ; for a more crystalline heart than Shelley's has rarely throbbed in human bosom. He was incapable of an untruth, or of deceit in any form. Keats said that in declining the invitation his sole motive was the consciousness, which would be ever prevalent with him, of his being, in its utter extent, not a free agent, even within such a circle as Shelley's—he himself, nevertheless, being the most unrestricted of beings. Mr. Trelawney, a familiar of the family, has confirmed the unwavering testimony to Shelley's bounty of nature, where he says, "Shelley was a being absolutely without selfishness." The poorest cottagers knew and benefited by his thoroughly *practical* and unselfish nature during his residence at Marlow, when he would visit them, and, having gone through a course of medical study in order that he might assist them with advice, would commonly administer the tonic, which such systems usually require, of a good basin of broth or pea-soup. And I believe that I am infringing on no private domestic delicacy when repeating that he has been known upon an immediate urgency to purloin —"*Convey* the wise it call "—a portion of the warmest of Mrs. Shelley's wardrobe to protect some poor starving sister. One of the richer residents of Marlow told me that "they all considered him a madman." I wish he had bitten the whole squad.

> No settled senses of the world can match
> The "wisdom" of that madness.

Shelley's figure was a little above the middle height, slender, and of delicate construction, which appeared the rather from a lounging or waving manner in his gait, as though his frame was compounded barely of muscle and tendon; and that the power of walking was an achievement with him and not a natural habit.   Yet I should suppose that he was not a valetudinarian, although that has been said of him on account of his spare and vegetable diet : for I have the remembrance of his scampering and bounding over the gorse-bushes on Hampstead Heath late one night,—now close upon us, and now shouting from the height like a wild school-boy.   He was both an active and an enduring walker—feats which do not accompany an ailing and feeble constitution.   His face was round, flat, pale, with small features ; mouth beautifully shaped ; hair bright brown and wavy ; and such a pair of eyes as are rarely in the human or any other head,—intensely blue, with a gentle and lambent expression, yet wonderfully alert and engrossing ; nothing appeared to escape his knowledge.

Whatever peculiarity there might have been in Shelley's religious faith, I have the best authority for believing that it was confined to the early period of his life.   The *practical* result of its course of *action*, I am sure, had its source from the " Sermon on the Mount."   There is not one clause in that Divine code which his conduct towards his fellow mortals did not confirm and substantiate him to be—in action a follower of Christ.   Yet, when the news arrived in London of the death of Shelley and Captain Williams by drowning near Spezzia, an evening journal of that day capped the intelligence with the following remark :—" He will now know whether there is a Hell or not."   I hope there is not one journalist of the present day who would dare to utter that surmise in his record. So much for the progress of freedom and the power of opinion.

At page 100, vol. i., of his first "Life of Keats," Lord Houghton has quoted a literary portrait which he received from a lady who used to see him at Hazlitt's lectures at the Surrey Institution. The building was on the south, right-hand side, and close to Blackfriars Bridge. I believe that the whole of Hazlitt's lectures on the British poets and the writers of the time of Elizabeth were delivered in that institution during the years 1817 and 1818; shortly after which the establishment appears to have been broken up. The lady's remark upon the character and expression of Keats's features is both happy and true. She says, " His countenance lives in my mind as one of singular beauty and brightness ; it had an expression *as if he had been looking on some glorious sight.*" That's excellent. " His mouth was full, and less intellectual than his other features." True again. But when our artist pronounces that "his eyes were large and *blue,*" and that "his hair was *auburn,*" I am naturally reminded of the "Chameleon" fable :—"They were *brown,* ma'am—*brown,* I assure you !" The fact is, the lady was enchanted—and I cannot wonder at it—with the whole character of that beaming face ; and "blue" and "auburn" being the favourite tints of the front divine in the lords of the creation, the poet's eyes consequently became "blue" and his hair "auburn." Colours, however, vary with the prejudice or partiality of the spectator ; and, moreover, people do not agree upon the most palpable prismatic tint. A writing-master whom we had at Enfield was an artist of more than ordinary merit, but he had one dominant defect, he could not distinguish between true blue and true green. So that, upon one occasion, when he was exhibiting to us a landscape he had just completed, I hazarded the critical question, why he painted his trees so *blue?* " Blue ! " he replied, " What do you call green ? " Reader, alter in your copy of the " Life of Keats," vol. i., page 103, " eyes " *light hazel,* " hair " *lightish brown and wavy.*

The most perfect and favourite portrait of him was the one—the first—by Severn, published in Leigh Hunt's " Lord Byron and his Contemporaries," which I remember the artist sketching in a few minutes, one evening, when several of Keats's friends were at his apartments in the Poultry. The portrait prefixed to the " Life" (also by Severn) is a most excellent one-look-and-expression likeness—an every-day and of " the earth, earthy" one ; and the last, which the same artist painted, and which is now in the possession of Mr. John Hunter, of Craig Crook, Edinburgh, may be an equally felicitous rendering of one look and manner ; but I do not intimately recognize it. There is another and a curiously unconscious likeness of him in the charming Dulwich Gallery of Pictures. It is in the portrait of Wouvermans, by Rembrandt. It is just so much of a resemblance as to remind the friends of the poet, although not such a one as the immortal Dutchman would have made had the poet been his sister. It has a plaintive and melancholy expression which, I rejoice to say, I do not associate with Keats.

There is one of his attitudes during familiar conversation which at times (with the whole earnest manner and sweet expression of the man) ever presents itself to me as though I had seen him only last week. How gracious is the boon that the benedictions and the blessings in our life careers last longer, and recur with stronger influences

than the ill-deeds and the curses ! The attitude I speak
of was that of cherishing one leg over the knee of the
other, smoothing the instep with the palm of his hand.
In this action I mostly associate him in an eager parley
with Leigh Hunt in his little Vale of Health cottage.
This position, if I mistake not, is in the last portrait of
him at Craig Crook ; if not, it is a reminiscent one,
painted after his death. His stature could have been
very little more than five feet ; but he was, withal, com-
pactly made and well-proportioned ; and before the
hereditary disorder which carried him off began to show
itself, he was active, athletic, and enduringly strong—as
the fight with the butcher gave full attestation.

His perfect friend, Joseph Severn, writes of him,
" Here in Rome, as I write, I look back through forty
years of worldly changes, and behold Keats's dear image
again in memory. It seems as if he should be living with
me now, inasmuch as I never could understand his
strange and contradictory death, his falling away so
suddenly from health and strength. He had a fine
compactness of person, which we regard as the promise
of longevity, and no mind was ever more exultant in
youthful feeling."

The critical world —by which term I mean the censor-
ious portion of it, for many have no other idea of
criticism than that of censure and objection—the critical
world have so gloated over the feebler, or, if they will,
the defective side of Keats's genius, and his friends have
so amply justified him, that I feel inclined to add no more
to the category of opinions than to say that the only
fault in his poetry I could discover was a redundancy of
imagery—that exuberance, by the way, being a quality of
the greatest promise, seeing that it is the constant accom-

paniment of a young and teeming genius. But his steady friend, Leigh Hunt, has rendered the amplest and truest record of his mental accomplishment in the preface to his " Foliage," quoted at page 150 of the first volume of the " Life of Keats ;" and his biographer has so zealously, and, I would say, so amiably, summed up his character and intellectual qualities, that I can add no more than my assent.

With regard to Keats's political opinions I have little doubt that his whole civil creed was comprised in the master principle of " universal liberty"—viz. " Equal and stern justice to all, from the duke to the dustman."

There are constant indications through the memoirs and in the letters of Keats of his profound reverence for Shakespeare. His own intensity of thought and expression visibly strengthened with the study of his idol; and he knew but little of him till he had himself become an author. A marginal note by him in a folio copy of the plays is an example of the complete absorption his mind had undergone during the process of his matriculation ; and, through life, however long with any of us, we are all in progress of matriculation, as we study the " myriad-minded's " system of philosophy. The note that Keats made was this :—" The genius of Shakespeare was an *innate universality ;* wherefore he laid the achievements of human intellect prostrate beneath his indolent and kingly gaze ; *he could do easily men's utmost.* His plan of tasks to come was not of this world. If what he proposed to do hereafter would not in the idea answer the aim, how tremendous must have been his conception of ultimates !" I question whether any one of the recognized high priests of the temple has uttered a loftier homily in honour of the world's intellectual homage and renown.

A passage in one of Keats's letters to me evidences that he had a " firm belief in the immortality of the soul," and, as he adds, " so had Tom," whose eyes he had just closed. I once heard him launch into a rhapsody on the genius of Moses, who, he said, deserved the benediction of the whole world, were it only for his institution of the " Sabbath." But Keats was no " Sabbatarian" in the modern conventional acceptation of the term. " Every day," he once said, was " Sabbath" to him, as it is to every grateful mind, for blessings momentarily bestowed upon us. This recalls Wordsworth's lines where he tells us that Nature,—

> Still constant in her worship, still
> Conforming to th' Eternal will,
> Whether men sow or reap the fields,
> Divine admonishments she yields,
> That not by hand alone we live,
> Or what a hand of flesh can give ;
> That every day should have some part
> Free for a Sabbath of the heart :
> So shall the seventh be truly blest,
> From morn to eve with hallow'd rest.

Sunday was indeed Keats's " day of rest," and I may add, too, of untainted mirth and gladness ; as I believe, too, of unprofessing, unostentatious gratitude. His whole course of life, to its very last act, was one routine of unselfishness and of consideration for others' feelings. The approaches of death having come on, he said to his untiring nurse-friend,—" Severn —I—lift me up. I am dying. *I shall die easy ; don't be frightened ;* be firm, and thank God it has come."

> Now burning through the inmost veil of heaven,
> The soul of Adonais, like a star,
> Beams from the abode where the Eternal are.

SOME LETTERS OF CHARLES LAMB;

WITH

REMINISCENCES OF HIMSELF AWAKENED THEREBY.

BY MARY COWDEN CLARKE.

THE other day, in looking over some long-hoarded papers, I came across the following letters, which struck me as being too intrinsically delightful to be any longer withheld from general enjoyment. The time when they were written—while they had all the warm life ot affectionate intercourse that refers to current personal events, inspiring the wish to treasure them in privacy— has faded into the shadow of the past. Some of the persons addressed or referred to have left this earth; others have survived to look back upon their young former selves with the same kindliness of consideration with which Charles Lamb himself confessed to looking back upon " the child Elia—that ' other me,' there, in the background," and cherishing its remembrance. Even the girl, then known among her friends by the second of her baptismal names, before and not long after she had exchanged her maiden name of Mary Victoria Novello for the married ·one with which she signs her present communication, can feel willing to share with her more recent friends and readers the pleasure derived from dear and honoured Charles Lamb's sometimes playful, sometimes earnest allusions to her identity.

The first letter is, according to his frequent wont, undated; and the post-mark is so much blurred as to be undecipherable; but it is addressed "V. Novello, Esqre., for C. C. Clarke, Esqre. :"—

MY DEAR SIR,—Your letter has lain in a drawer of my desk, upbraiding me every time I open the said drawer, but it is almost impossible to answer such a letter in such a place, and I am out of the habit of replying to epistles otherwhere than at office. You express yourself concerning H. like a true friend, and have made me feel that I have somehow neglected him, but without knowing very well how to rectify it. I live so remote from him—by Hackney—that he is almost out of the pale of visitation at Hampstead. And I come but seldom to Cov* Gard" this summer time—and when I do, am sure to pay for the late hours and pleasant Novello suppers which I incur. I also am an invalid. But I will hit upon some way, that you shall not have cause for your reproof in future. But do not think I take the hint unkindly. When I shall be brought low by any sickness or untoward circumstance, write just such a letter to some tardy friend of mine—or come up yourself with your friendly Henshaw face—and that will be better. I shall not forget in haste our casual day at Margate. May we have many such there or elsewhere! God bless you for your kindness to H., which I will remember. But do not show N. this, for the flouting infidel doth mock when Christians cry God bless us. Yours and *his, too,* and all our little circle's most affect^e   C. LAMB.

Mary's love included.

"H." in the above letter refers to Leigh Hunt; but the initials and abbreviated forms of words used by Charles Lamb in these letters are here preserved verbatim.

The second letter is addressed "C. C. Clarke, Esqre.," and has for post-mark "Fe. 26, 1828 :"—

Enfield, 25 Feb.

MY DEAR CLARKE,—You have been accumulating on me such a heap of pleasant obligations that I feel uneasy in writing as to a Benefactor. Your smaller contributions, the little weekly rills, are refreshments in the Desart, but your large books were feasts. I hope Mrs. Hazlitt, to whom I encharged it, has taken Hunt's Lord B. to the Novellos. His picture of Literary Lordship is as pleasant as a disagreeable subject can be made, his own poor man's Education at dear Christ's is as good and hearty as the subject. Hazlitt's speculative episodes are capital; I skip the Battles. But how did I deserve to have the Book? The *Companion* has too much of Madam Pasta. Theatricals have ceased to be popular attractions. His walk home after the Play is as good as the best of the old Indicators. The watchmen are emboxed in a niche of fame, save the skaiting one that must be still fugitive. I wish I could send a scrap for good will. But I have been most seriously unwell and nervous a long long time. I have scarce mustered courage to begin this short note, but conscience duns me.

I had a pleasant letter from your sister, greatly over acknowledging my poor sonnet. I think I should have replied to it, but tell her I think so. Alas for sonnetting, 'tis as the nerves are ; all the summer I was dawdling among green lanes, and verses came as thick as fancies. I am sunk winterly below prose and zero.

But I trust the vital principle is only as under snow. That I shall yet laugh again.

I suppose the great change of place affects me, but I could not have lived in Town, I could not bear company.

I see Novello flourishes in the Del Capo line, and dedications are not forgotten. I read the *Atlas*. When I pitched on the Ded" I looked for the Broom of " *Cowden* knows " to be harmonized, but 'twas summat of Rossini's.

I want to hear about Hone, does he stand above water, how is his son? I have delay'd writing to him, till it seems impossible. Break the ice for me.

The wet ground here is intolerable, the sky above clear and delusive, but under foot quagmires from night showers, and I am cold-footed and moisture-abhorring as a cat; nevertheless I yesterday tramped to Waltham Cross; perhaps the poor bit of exertion necessary to scribble this was owing to that unusual bracing.

If I get out, I shall get stout, and then something will out—I mean for the *Companion*—you see I rhyme insensibly.

Traditions are rife here of one Clarke a schoolmaster, and a runaway pickle named Holmes, but much obscurity hangs over it. Is it possible they can be any relations?

'Tis worth the research, when you can find a sunny day, with ground firm, &c. Master Sexton is intelligent, and for half-a-crown he'll pick you up a Father.

In truth we shall be most glad to see any of the Novellian circle, middle of the week such as can come, or Sunday, as can't. But Spring will burgeon out quickly, and then, we'll talk more.

You'd like to see the improvements on the Chase, the new Cross in the market-place, the Chandler's shop from whence the rods were fetch'd. They are raised a farthing since the spread of Education. But perhaps you don't care to be reminded of the Holofernes' days, and nothing remains of the old laudable profession, but the clear, firm, impossible-to-be-mistaken schoolmaster text hand with which is subscribed the ever-welcome name of Chas. Cowden C. Let me crowd in both our loves to all.—C. L. [Added on the fold-down of the letter :] Let me never be forgotten to include in my rememb⁰ᵉ my good friend and whilom correspondent Master Stephen.

How, especially, is Victoria?

I try to remember all I used to meet at Shacklewell. The little household, cake-producing, wine-bringing out Emma— the old servant, that didn't stay, and ought to have staid, and was always very dirty and friendly, and Miss H., the counter-tenor with a fine voice, whose sister married Thurtell. They all live in my mind's eye, and Mr. N.'s and Holmes's walks with us half back after supper. Troja fuit!

His hearty yet modestly-rendered thanks for lent and

given books; his ever-affectionate mention of Christ's Hospital; his enjoyment of Hazlitt's " Life of Napoleon," minus "the battles ;" his cordial commendation of Leigh Hunt's periodical, the *Companion* (with the witty play on the word " fugitive "), and his wish that he could send the work a contribution from his own pen; his touching reference to the susceptibility of his nervous system; the sportive misuse of musical terms when alluding to his musician friend Vincent Novello, immortalized in Elia's celebrated "Chapter on Ears ;" his excellent pun in the word "insensibly;" his humorous mode of touching upon the professional avocation of his clerkly correspondent's father and self—the latter having been usher in the school kept some years previously at Enfield by the former—while conveying a genuine compliment to the handwriting which at eighty-five is still the " clear, firm, impossible-to-be-mistaken schoolmaster text hand " that it was at forty-one, when Lamb wrote these words; the genial mention of the hospitable children; the whimsically wrong-circumstanced recollection of the "counter-tenor " lady; the allusion to the night walks " half back " home; and the classically-quoted words of regret—are all wonderfully characteristic of beautiful-minded Charles Lamb. In connexion with the juvenile hospitality may be recorded an incident that illustrates his words. When William Etty returned as a young artist student from Rome, and called at the Novellos' house, it chanced that the parents were from home; but the children, who were busily employed in fabricating a treat of home-made hard-bake (or toffy), made the visitor welcome by offering him a piece of their just-finished sweetmeat, as an appropriate refection after his long walk; and he declared that it was the most veritable piece of spontaneous hospitality he had ever met with, since the children gave him what they thought most delicious and best worthy of acceptance. Charles Lamb so heartily shared this opinion of the subsequently renowned painter that he brought a choice condiment in the shape of a jar of preserved ginger for the little Novellos' delectation ; and when some officious elder suggested that it was lost upon children, therefore had better be reserved for the grown-up people, Lamb would not hear of the transfer, but insisted that children were excellent judges of good things, and that they must and should have the cate in question. He was right, for long did the remembrance remain in the family of that delicious rarity, and of the mode in which " Mr. Lamb " stalked up and down the passage with a mysterious harberingering look and stride, muttering something that sounded like conjuration, holding the precious jar under his arm, and feigning to have found it stowed away in a dark chimney somewhere near.

Another characteristic point is recalled by a concluding sentence of this letter. On one occasion—when Charles Lamb and his admirable sister Mary Lamb had been accompanied "half back after supper" by Mr. and Mrs. Novello, Edward Holmes, and Charles Cowden Clarke, between Shacklewell Green and Colebrooke Cottage, beside the New River at Islington, where the Lambs then lived, the whole party interchanging lively, brightest talk as they passed along the road that they had all to themselves at that late hour—he, as usual, was the noblest of the talkers. Arrived at the usual parting-place, Lamb and his sister walked on a few steps ; then, suddenly turning, he shouted out after his late companions in a tone that startled the midnight silence, " You're very nice people ! " sending them on their way home in happy laughter at his friendly oddity.

M 2

The third is addressed to " C. C. Clarke. Esqre.," without date; but it must have been written in 1828 :—

DEAR CLARKE,—We did expect to see you with Victoria and the Novellos before this, and do not quite understand why we have not. Mrs. N. and V. [Vincent] promised us after the York expedition ; a day being named before, which fail'd. 'Tis not too late. The autumn leaves drop gold, and Enfield is beautifuller—to a common eye—than when you lurked at the Greyhound. Benedicks are close, but how I so totally missed you at that time, going for my morning cup of ale duly, is a mystery. 'Twas stealing a match before one's face in earnest. But certainly we had not a dream of your appropinquity. I instantly prepared an Epithalamium, in the form of a Sonata—which I was sending to Novello to compose—but Mary forbid it me, as too light for the occasion—as if the subject required anything heavy— —so in a tiff with her, I sent no congratulation at all. Tho' I promise you the wedding was very pleasant news to me indeed. Let your reply name a day this next week, when you will come as many as a coach will hold ; such a day as we had at Dulwich. My very kindest love and Mary's to Victoria and the Novellos. The enclosed is from a friend nameless, but highish in office, and a man whose accuracy of statement may be relied on with implicit confidence. He wants the *exposé* to appear in a newspaper as the " greatest piece of legal and Parliamentary villainy he ever remembd," and he has had experience in both ; and thinks it would answer afterwards in a cheap pamphlet printed at Lambeth in 8° sheet, as 16,000 families in that parish are interested. I know not whether the present *Examiner* keeps up the character of exposing abuses, for I scarce see a paper now. If so, you may ascertain Mr. Hunt of the strictest truth of the statement, at the peril of my head. But if this won't do, transmit it me back, I beg, per coach, or better, bring it with you. Yours unaltered,

C. LAMB.

This letter quaintly rebukes, yet, at the same time, most affectionately congratulates, the friend addressed for silently making honeymoon quarters of the spot where Charles Lamb then resided. But lovely Enfield—a very beau-ideal of an English village—was the birthplace of Charles Cowden Clarke ; and the Greyhound was a simple hostelry kept by an old man and his daughter, where there was a pretty white-curtained, quiet room, with a window made green by bowering vine leaves ; combining much that was tempting as an unpretending retirement for a town-dweller to take his young new-made wife to. The invitation to "name a day this next week" was cordially responded to by a speedy visit ; and very likely it was on that occasion Charles Lamb told the wedded pair of another bridal couple who, he said, when they arrived at the first stage of their marriage tour, found each other's company so tedious that they called the landlord upstairs to enliven them by his conversation. The "Epithalamium," here called a "Sonata," is the "Serenata" contained in the next letter, addressed to "Vincent Novello, Esqre.:"—

My dear Novello,—I am afraid I shall appear rather tardy in offering my congratulations, however sincere, upon your daughter's marriage.[1] The truth is, I had put together a little Serenata upon the occasion, but was prevented from sending it by my sister, to whose judgment I am apt to defer too much in these kind of things ; so that, now I have her consent, the offering, I am afraid, will have lost the grace of seasonableness. Such as it is, I send it. She thinks it a little too old-fashioned in the manner, too much like what they wrote a century back. But I cannot write in the modern style, if I try ever so hard. I have attended to the proper divisions for the music, and you will have little difficulty in composing it. If I may advise, make Pepusch your model, or Blow. It will be necessary to have a good second voice, as the stress of the melody lies there :—

---

[1] Which marriage took place 5th July, 1828.

SERENATA, FOR TWO VOICES,

*On the Marriage of Charles Cowden Clarke, Esqre., to
Victoria, eldest daughter of Vincent Novello, Esqre.*

DUETTO.

Wake th' harmonious voice and string,
Love and Hymen's triumph sing,
Sounds with secret charms combining,
In melodious union joining,
Best the wondrous joys can tell,
That in hearts united dwell.

RECITATIVE.

First Voice.

To young Victoria's happy fame
   Well may the Arts a trophy raise,
   Music grows sweeter in her praise,
And, own'd by her, with rapture speaks hei
     name.
To touch the brave Cowdenio's heart,
   The Graces all in her conspire ;
Love arms her with his surest dait,
   Apollo with his lyre.

AIR.

The list'ning Muses all around her
   Think 'tis Phœbus' strain they hear ;
And Cupid, drawing near to wound her,
   Drops his bow, and stands to hear.

RECITATIVE.

Second Voice.

While crowds of rivals with despair
Silent admire, or vainly court the Fair,
Behold the happy conquest of her eyes,
A Hero is the glorious prize !
In courts, in camps, thro' distant realms
    renown'd,
   Cowdenio comes !—Victoria, see,
He comes with British honour crown'd,
   Love leads his eager steps to thee.

AIR.

In tender sighs he silence breaks,
 The Fair his flame approves,
Consenting blushes warm her cheeks,
 She smiles, she yields, she loves.

RECITATIVE.

First Voice. Now Hymen at the altar stands,
And while he joins their faithful hands,
 Behold! by ardent vows brought down,
Immortal Concord, heavenly bright,
Array'd in robes of purest light,
 Descends, th' auspicious rites to crown.
Her golden harp the goddess brings;
 Its magic sound
Commands a sudden silence all around,
And strains prophetic thus attune the
 strings.

DUETTO.

First Voice. The Swain his Nymph possessing,
Second Voice. The Nymph her swain caressing,
First & Second. Shall still improve the blessing,
 For ever kind and true.
Both. While rolling years are flying
Love, Hymen's lamp supplying,
With fuel never dying,
Shall still the flame renew.

To so great a master as yourself I have no need to suggest that the peculiar tone of the composition demands sprightliness, occasionally checked by tenderness, as in the second air,—

 She smiles,—she yields,—she loves.

Again, you need not be told that each fifth line of the two first recitatives requires a crescendo.

And your exquisite taste will prevent your falling into the error of Purcell, who at a passage similar to *that* in my first air,

Drops his bow, and stands to hear,

directed the first violin thus :—

Here the first violin must drop his *bow*.

But, besides the absurdity of disarming his principal performer of so necessary an adjunct to his instrument, in such
an emphatic part of the composition too, which must have
had a droll effect at the time, all such minutiæ of adaptation
are at this time of day very properly exploded, and Jackson
of Exeter very fairly ranks them under the head of puns.

Should you succeed in the setting of it, we propose having
it performed (we have one very tolerable second voice here,
and Mr. Holmes, I dare say, would supply the minor parts)
at the Greyhound. But it must be a secret to the young
couple till we can get the band in readiness.

Believe me, dear Novello,
Yours truly,

Enfield, 6 Nov., '29.　　　　　　　　　　　　　C. LAMB.

Peculiarly *Elian* is the humour throughout this last
letter. The advice to "make Pepusch your model, or
Blow;" the affected "divisions" or "Duetto," "Reci-
tative," "Air," "First Voice," "Second Voice," "First
and Second," "Both," &c.; the antiquated stiffness of
the lines themselves, the burlesque "Love and Hymen's
triumph sing;" the grotesque stiltedness of "the brave
Cowdenio's heart," and "a Hero is the glorious prize;"
the ludicrous absurdity of hailing a peaceful man of letters (who, by the way, adopted as his crest and motto an
oak-branch with Algernon Sydney's words, "*Placidam
sub libertate quietem*") by "In courts, in camps, thro'
distant realms renown'd, Cowdenio comes !"; the adula-
tory pomp of styling a young girl, nowise distinguished
for anything but homeliest simplicity, as "the Fair,"
"the Nymph," in whom "the Graces all conspire;" the
droll, illustrative instructions, suggesting "sprightliness,

occasionally checked by tenderness," in setting lines purposedly dull and heavy with old-fashioned mythological
trappings ; the grave assumption of technicality in the introduction of the word "crescendo;" the pretended
citation of "Purcell" and "Jackson of Exeter;" the
comic prohibition as to the too literal "minutiæ of adaptation" in such passages as "*Drops his bow*, and stands
to hear;" the pleasant play on the word in "the minor
parts ;" the mock earnestness as to keeping the proposed
performance "a secret to the young couple ;" are all in
the very spirit of fun that swayed Elia when a sportive
vein ran through his Essays.

The next letter is to Charles Cowden Clarke ; though
it has neither address, signature, date, nor postmark :—

MY DEAR THREE C's,—The way from Southgate to Colney
Hatch thro' the unfrequentedest Blackberry paths that ever
concealed their coy bunches from a truant Citizen, we have
accidentally fallen upon—the giant Tree by Cheshunt we have
missed, but keep your chart to go by, unless you will be our
conduct—at present I am disabled from further flights than
just to skirt round Clay Hill, with a peep at the fine back
woods, by strained tendons, got by skipping a skipping-rope
at 53—hei m hi non sum qualis—but do you know, now you
come to talk of walks, a ramble of four hours or so—there
and back—to the willow and lavender plantations at the
south corner of Northaw Church by a well dedicated to Saint
Claridge, with the clumps of finest moss rising hillock fashion,
which I counted to the number of two hundred and sixty, and
are called "Claridge's covers"—the tradition being that that
saint entertained so many angels or hermits there, upon occasion of blessing the waters ?   The legends have set down the
fruits spread upon that occasion, and in the Black Book of St.
Alban's some are named which are not supposed to have been
introduced into this island till a century later.   But waiving
the miracle, a sweeter spot is not in ten counties round ;

you are knee deep in clover, that is to say, if you are not above a middling man's height—from this paradise, making a day of it, you go to see the ruins of an old convent at March Hall, where some of the painted glass is yet whole and fresh.

If you do not know this, you do not know the capabilities of this country, you may be said to be a stranger to Enfield. 1 found it out one morning in October, and so delighted was I that I did not get home before dark, well a-paid.

I shall long to show you the clump meadows, as they are called ; we might do that, without reaching March Hall— when the days are longer, we might take both, and come home by Forest Cross, so skirt ver Pennington and the cheerful little village of Churchley to Forty Hill.

But these are dreams till summer ; meanwhile we should be most glad to see you for a lesser excursion—say, Sunday next, you and *another*, or if more, best on a weekday with a notice, but o' Sundays, as far as a leg of mutton goes, most welcome. We can squeeze out a bed. Edmonton coaches run every hour, and my pen has run out its quarter. Heartily farewell.

Charles Lamb's enjoyment of a long ramble, and his (usually) excellent powers of walking are here denoted. He was so proud of his pedestrian feats and indefatig- ability, that he once told the Cowden Clarkes a story of a dog possessed by a pertinacious determination to follow him day by day when he went forth to wander in the Enfield lanes and fields ; until, unendurably teased by the pertinacity of this obtrusive animal, he determined to get rid of him by fairly *tiring him out !* So he took him a circuit of many miles, including several of the loveliest spots round Enfield, coming at last to a by-road with an interminable vista of up-hill distance, where the dog turned tail, gave the matter up, and laid down beneath a hedge, panting, exhausted, thoroughly worn out and dead beat ; while his defeater walked freshly home, smiling and triumphant.

Knowing Lamb's fashion of twisting facts to his own humorous view of them, those who heard the story well understood that it might easily have been wryed to represent the narrator's real potency in walking, while serving to cover his equally real liking for animals under the semblance of vanquishing a dog in a contested foot-race. Far more probable that he encouraged its volunteered companionship, amusing his imagination the while by picturing the wild impossibility of any human creature attempting to tire out a dog—of all animals! As an instance of Charles Lamb's sympathy with dumb beasts, his two friends here named once saw him get up from table, while they were dining with him and his sister at Enfield, open the street-door, and give admittance to a stray donkey into the front strip of garden, where there was a glass-plot, which he said seemed to possess more attraction for the creature than the short turf of the common on Chase-side, opposite to the house where the Lambs then dwelt. This mixture of the humorous in manner and the sympathetic in feeling always more or less tinged the sayings and the doings of beloved Charles Lamb ; there was a constant blending of the overtly whimsical expression or act with betrayed inner kindliness and even pathos of sentiment. Beneath this sudden opening of his gate to a stray donkey that it might feast on his garden grass while he himself ate his dinner, possibly lurked some stung sense of wanderers unable to get a meal they hungered for when others revelled in plenty,— a kind of pained fancy finding vent in playful deed or speech, that frequently might be traced by those who enjoyed his society.

The next letter is addressed "C. C. Clarke, Esqre.," with the postmark (much defaced) "Edmonton, Fe. 2, 1829:"—

DEAR COWDEN,—Your books are as the gushing of streams in a desert. By the way, you have sent no autobiographies. Your letter seems to imply you had. Nor do I want any. Cowden, they are of the books which I give away. What damn'd Unitarian skewer-soul'd things the general biographies turn out. Rank and Talent you shall have when Mrs. May has done with 'em. Mary likes Mrs. Bedinfield much. For me I read nothing but Astrea—it has turn'd my brain—I go about with a switch turn'd up at the end for a crook; and Lambs being too old, the butcher tells me, my cat follows me in a green ribband. Becky and her cousin are getting pastoral dresses, and then we shall all four go about Arcadizing. O cruel Shepherdess! Inconstant yet fair, and more inconstant for being fair! Her gold ringlets fell in a disorder superior to order!

Come and join us.

I am called the Black Shepherd—you shall be Cowden with the Tuft.

Prosaically, we shall be glad to have you both,—or any two of you—drop in by surprise some Saturday night.

This must go off.

Loves to Vittoria.

C. L.

The book he refers to as " Astrea " was one of those tall folio romances of the Sir Philip Sidney or Mdme. de Scudéry order, inspiring him with the amusing rhapsody that follows its mention; the ingeniously equivocal "*Lambs* being too old;" the familiar mingling of "Becky" (their maid) " and her cousin " with himself and sister in " pastoral dresses," to " go about Arcadizing; " the abrupt bursting forth into the Philip-Sidneyan style of antithetical rapturizing and euphuism; the invented Arcadian titles of " the Black Shepherd " and " Cowden with the Tuft "—are all in the tone of mad-cap spirits which were occasionally Lamb's. The latter name (" Cowden with the Tuft ") slyly implies the smooth

baldness with scant curly hair distinguishing the head of
the friend addressed, and which seemed to strike Charles
Lamb so forcibly, that one evening, after gazing at it for
some time, he suddenly broke forth with the exclamation,
"'Gad, Clarke! what whiskers you have behind your
head!"

He was fond of trying the dispositions of those with
whom he associated by an odd speech such as this; and
if they stood the test pleasantly, and took it in good part,
he liked them the better ever after. One time that the
Novellos and Cowden Clarkes went down to see the
Lambs at Enfield, and he was standing by his book-
shelves, talking with them in his usual delightful, cordia
way, showing them some precious volume lately added
to his store, a neighbour chancing to come in to remind
Charles Lamb of an appointed ramble, he excused himself by saying, "You see I have some troublesome
people just come down from town, and I must stay and entertain them; so we'll take our walk together to-morrow."
Another time, when the Cowden Clarkes were staying a
few days at Enfield with Charles Lamb and his sister,
they, having accepted an invitation to spend the evening
and have a game of whist at a lady-schoolmistress's house
there, took their guests with them. Charles Lamb, giving
his arm to "Victoria," left her husband to escort Mary
Lamb, who walked rather more slowly than her brother.
On arriving first at the house of the somewhat prim and
formal hostess, Charles Lamb, bringing his young visitor
into the room, introduced her by saying, "Mrs.——,
I've brought you the wife of the man who mortally hates
your husband;" and when the lady replied by a polite
inquiry after "Miss Lamb," hoping she was quite well,
Charles Lamb said, "She has a terrible fit o' toothache,

and was obliged to stay at home this evening ; so Mr. Cowden Clarke remained there to keep her company." Then, the lingerers entering, he went on to say, " Mrs. Cowden Clarke has been telling me, as we came along, that she hopes you have sprats for supper this evening." The bewildered glance of the lady of the house at Mary Lamb and her walking-companion, her politely stifled dismay at the mention of so vulgar a dish, contrasted with Victoria's smile of enjoyment at his whimsical words, were precisely the kind of things that Charles Lamb liked and chuckled over. On another occasion he was charmed by the equanimity and even gratification with which the same guests and Miss Fanny Kelly (the skilled actress whose combined artistic and feminine attractions inspired him with the beautiful sonnet beginning

> You are not, Kelly, of the common strain,

and whose performance of " The Blind Boy " caused him to address her in that other sonnet beginning

> Rare artist ! who with half thy tools or none
> Canst execute with ease thy curious art,
> And press thy powerful'st meanings on the heart
> Unaided by the eye, expression's throne !)

found themselves one sunny day, after a long walk through the green Enfield meadows, seated with Charles Lamb and his sister on a rustic bench in the shade, outside a small roadside inn, quaffing draughts of his favourite porter with him from the unsophisticated pewter, supremely indifferent to the strangeness of the situation ; nay, heartily enjoying it *with him*. The umbrageous elm, the water-trough, the dip in the road where there was a ford and foot bridge, the rough wooden table at which the little party were seated, the pleasant voices

of Charles and Mary Lamb and Fanny Kelly,—all are
vividly present to the imagination of her who now writes
these few memorial lines, inadequately describing the
ineffaceable impression of that happy time, when Lamb
so cordially delighted in the responsive ease and enjoyment of his surrounders.

The last letter is addressed " V. Novello, Esqre.," with
post-mark " No. 8, 1830 :"—

> Tears are for lighter griefs.   Man weeps the doom
> That seals a single victim to the tomb.
> But when Death riots, when with whelming sway
> Destruction sweeps a family away ;
> When Infancy and Youth, a huddled mass,
> All in an instant to oblivion pass,
> And Parents' hopes are crush'd ; what lamentation
> Can reach the depth of such a desolation ?
> Look upward, Feeble Ones ! look up, and trust
> That He, who lays this mortal frame in dust,
> Still hath the immortal Spirit in His keeping.
> In Jesus' sight they are not dead, but sleeping.

Dear N., will these lines do ? I despair of better. Poor
Mary is in a deplorable state here at Enfield.

Love to all,
C. LAMB.

These tenderly pathetic elegiac lines were written at
the request of Vincent Novello, in memory of four sons
and two daughters of John and Ann Rigg, of York.
All six—respectively aged 19, 18, 17, 16, 7, and 6—were
drowned at once by their boat being run down on the
river Ouse, near York, August 19, 1830. The unhappy
surviving parents had begged to have lines for an epitaph
from the best poetical hand ; but, owing to some local
authority's interference, another than Charles Lamb's
verse was ultimately placed on the monument raised to
the lost children.

MARY LAMB

THOSE belonging to a great man—his immediate family connexions, who are, as it were, a part of himself—-are always reflectively interesting to his admirers. His female relatives especially, who form so integral a portion of his home existence, possess this interest, perhaps, beyond all others. In a more than usual degree was Charles Lamb's sister, Mary Lamb, blended with his life, with himself—consociated as she was with his every act, word, and thought, through his own noble act of self-consecration to her. The solemn story of this admirable brother-and-sister couple is told in all its pathetic circumstances by Thomas Noon Talfourd, in his "Final Memorials of Charles Lamb;" and there Miss Lamb is pictured with esteeming eloquence of description. To that account of her are here appended a few remembered touches, by one who enjoyed the privilege of personal communion with "the Lambs," as they were affectionately styled by those who knew them in what Wordsworth calls their beautiful "dual loneliness" of life together. So simple, so holy a sobriety was there in all their ways, that to the unperceiving eyes of youth they scarce appeared so great as they really were ; and yet less did any idea of the profoundly tragic secret attaching to their early years present itself to the imagination of her who knew them as

' Mr. and Miss Lamb," prized friends of her father and mother, taking kindly notice of a young girl for her parents' sake.

Miss Lamb bore a strong personal resemblance to her brother; being in stature under middle height, possessing well-cut features, and a countenance of singular sweetness, with intelligence. Her brown eyes were soft, yet penetrating; her nose and mouth very shapely; while the general expression was mildness itself. She had a speaking-voice, gentle and persuasive; and her smile was her brother's own—winning in the extreme. There was a certain catch, or emotional breathingness, in her utterance, which gave an inexpressible charm to her reading of poetry, and which lent a captivating earnestness to her mode of speech when addressing those she liked. This slight check, with its yearning, eager effect in her voice, had something softenedly akin to her brother Charles's impediment of articulation: in him it scarcely amounted to a stammer; in her it merely imparted additional stress to the fine-sensed suggestions she made to those whom she counselled or consoled. She had a mind at once nobly-toned and practical, making her ever a chosen source of confidence among her friends, who turned to her for consolation, confirmation, and advice, in matters of nicest moment, always secure of deriving from her both aid and solace. Her manner was easy, almost homely, so quiet, unaffected, and perfectly unpretending was it. Beneath the sparing talk and retired carriage, few casual observers would have suspected the ample information and large intelligence that lay comprised there. She was oftener a listener than a speaker. In the modest-havioured woman simply sitting there, taking small share in general conversation, few who did not know her would have imagined the accomplished classical scholar, the excellent understanding, the altogether rarely-gifted being, morally and mentally, that Mary Lamb was. Her apparel was always of the plainest kind ; a black stuff or silk gown, made and worn in the simplest fashion. She took snuff liberally—a habit that had evidently grown out of her propensity to sympathize with and share all her brother's tastes ; and it certainly had the effect of enhancing her likeness to him. She had a small, white, and delicately-formed hand ; and as it hovered above the tortoise-shell box containing the powder so strongly approved by them both, in search of the stimulating pinch, the act seemed yet another link of association between the brother and sister, when hanging together over their favourite books and studies.

As may be gathered from the books which Miss Lamb wrote, in conjunction with her brother—" Poetry for Children," " Tales from Shakespeare," and " Mrs. Leicester's School,"—she had a most tender sympathy with the young. She was encouraging and affectionate towards them, and won them to regard her with a familiarity and fondness rarely felt by them for grown people who are not their relations. She entered into their juvenile ideas with a tact and skill quite surprising. She threw herself so entirely into their way of thinking, and contrived to take an estimat of things so completely from *their* point of view, that she made them rejoice to have her fcr their co-mate in affairs that interested them. While thus lending herself to their notions, she, with a judiciousness peculiar to her, imbued her words with the wisdom and experience that belonged to her maturer years ; so that, while she seemed but the listening, concurring friend, she was also the helping, guiding friend. Her valuable monitions never took the form of reproof, but were always dropped in with the air of agreed propositions, as if they grew out of the subject in question, and presented themselves as matters of course to both her young companions and herself.

One of these instances resulted from the kind permission which Mary Lamb gave to the young girl above alluded to—Victoria Novello—that she should come to her on certain mornings, when Miss Lamb promised to hear her repeat her Latin grammar, and hear her read poetry with the due musically-rhythmical intonation. Even now the breathing murmur of the voice in which Mary Lamb gave low but melodious utterance to those opening lines of the " Paradise Lost,"—

> " Of man's first disobedience, and the fruit
> Of that forbidden tree, whose mortal taste
> Brought death into the world, and all our woe,"—

sounding full and rounded and harmonious, though so subdued in tone, rings clear and distinct in the memory of her who heard the reader. The echo of that gentle voice vibrates through the lapse of many a revolving year, true and unbroken, in the heart where the low-breathed sound first awoke response ; teaching, together with the fine appreciation of verse music, the finer love of intellect conjoined with goodness and kindness. The instance of wise precept couched in playful speech pertained to the Latin lessons. One morning, just as Victoria was about to repeat her allotted task, in rushed a young boy, who, like herself enjoyed the privilege of Miss Lamb's instruction in the Latin language. His mode of entrance— hasty and abrupt—sufficiently denoted his eagerness to have his lesson heard at once and done with, that he might be gone again; accordingly, Miss Lamb, asking Victoria to give up her turn, desired the youth—Hazlitt's son—to repeat his pages of grammar first. Off he set; rattled through the first conjugation post-haste; darted through the second without drawing breath; and so on, right through in no time. The rapidity, the volubility, the triumphant slap-dash of the feat perfectly dazzled the imagination of poor Victoria, who stood admiring by, an amazed witness of the boy's proficiency. She herself,—a quiet, plodding little girl—had only by dint of diligent study, and patient, persevering poring, been able to achieve a slow learning, and as slow a repetition of her lessons. This brilliant, off-hand method of despatching the Latin grammar was a glory she had never dreamed of. Her ambition was fired: and the next time she presented herself, book in hand, before Miss Lamb, she had no sooner delivered it into her hearer's, than she attempted to scour through her verb at the same rattling pace which had so excited her emulative admiration. Scarce a moment, and her stumbling scamper was checked. "Stay, stay! how's this? What are you about, little Vicky?" asked the laughing voice of Mary Lamb. "Oh, I see. Well, go on: but gently, gently: no need of hurry." She heard her to an end, and then said, "I see what we have been doing—trying to be as quick and clever as William, fancying it vastly grand to get on at a great rate as he does. But there's this difference: it's natural in him, while it's imitation in you. Now, far better go on in your old, staid way—which is your own way—than try to take up a way that may become him but can never become you, even were you to succeed in acquiring it. We'll each of us keep to our own natural ways, and then we shall be sure to do our best."

On one of these occasions of the Latin lessons in Russell Street, Covent Garden, where Mr. and Miss Lamb then lived, Victoria saw a lady come in, who appeared to her strikingly intellectual-looking, and still young; she was surprised, therefore, to hear the lady say, in the course of conversation, "Oh, as for me, my dear Miss Lamb, I'm nothing now but a stocking-mending old woman." When the lady's visit came to an end, and she was gone, Mary Lamb took occasion to tell Victoria who she was, and to explain her curious speech. The lady was no other than Miss Kelly; and Mary Lamb, while describing to the young girl the eminent merits of the admirable actress, showed her how a temporary depression of spirits in an artistic nature sometimes takes refuge in a half-playful, half-bitter irony of speech.

At the house in Russell Street Victoria met Emma Isola; and among her pleasantest juvenile recollections is the way in which Mary Lamb thought for the natural pleasure the two young girls took in each other's society, by bringing them together; and when, upon one occasion, there was a large company assembled, Miss Lamb allowed Emma and Victoria to go together into a room by themselves, if they preferred their mutual chat to the conversation of the elder people. In the not too spacious London lodging, Mary Lamb let them go into her own bedroom to have their girlish talk out, rather than let them feel restrained. Most, most kind, too, was the meeting she planned for them, when Emma was about to repair to school, at the pleasant village of Dulwich. Miss

Lamb made a charming little dinner : a dinner for three, herself and the two girls,—a dinner most toothsome to young feminine appetite ; roast fowls and a custard-pudding.   Savoury is the recollection of those embrowned and engravied birds ! sweet the remembrance of that creamy cate ! but pleasant, above all, is the memory of the cordial voice which said, in a way to put the little party at its fullest ease, " Now, remember, we all pick our bones.   It isn't considered vulgar here to pick bones."

Once, when some visitors chanced to drop in unexpectedly upon her and her brother, just as they were going to sit down to their plain dinner of a bit of roast mutton, with her usual frank hospitality she pressed them to stay and partake, cutting up the small joint into five equal portions, and saying in her simple, easy way, so truly her own, " There's a chop a-piece for us, and we can make up with bread and cheese if we want more." With such a woman to carve for you and eat with you, neck of mutton was better than venison, while bread and cheese more than replaced varied courses of richest or daintiest dishes.

Mary Lamb, ever thoughtful to procure a pleasure for young people, finding that one of her and her brother's acquaintances—Howard Payne—was going to France, she requested him, on his way to Paris, to call at Boulogne and see Victoria Novello, who had been placed by her parents in a family there for a time to learn the language.   Knowing how welcome a visit from any one who had lately seen her friends in England would be to the young girl, Miss Lamb urged Howard Payne not to omit this ; her brother Charles seconding her by adding, in his usual sportive style, "Do ; you needn't be afraid of Miss Novello, she speaks only a little coast French."

At "the Lambs' house," Victoria several times saw Colonel Phillips (the man who shot the savage that killed Captain Cook), and heard him describe Madame de Staël's manner in society, saying that he remembered she had a habit while she discoursed of taking a scrap of paper and a pair of scissors, and snipping it to bits, as an employment for her fingers; that once he observed her to be at a loss for this her usual mechanical resource, and he quietly placed near her the back of a letter from his pocket: afterwards she earnestly thanked him for this timely supply of the means she desired as a needful aid to thought and speech. He also mentioned his reminiscence of Gibbon the historian, and related the way in which the great man held a pinch of snuff between his finger and thumb while he recounted an anecdote, invariably dropping the pinch at the point of the story. The colonel once spoke of Garrick, telling how, as a raw youth, coming to town, he had determined to go and see the great actor, and how, being but slenderly provided in pocket, he had pawned one of his shirts ("and shirts were of value in those days, with their fine linen and ruffles," he said), to enable him to pay his entrance at the theatre. Miss Lamb being referred to, and asked if she remembered Garrick, replied, in her simple-speeched way, "I saw him once, but I was too young to understand much about his acting. I only know I thought it was mighty fine."

There was a certain old-world fashion in Mary Lamb's diction which gave it a most natural and quaintly pleasant effect, and which heightened rather than detracted from the more heartfelt or important things she uttered. She had a way of repeating her brother's words assentingly when he spoke to her. He once said (with his peculiar mode of tenderness, beneath blunt, abrupt speech), "You must die first, Mary." She nodded, with her little quiet nod and sweet smile, "Yes, I must die first, Charles."

At another time, he said in his whimsical way, plucking out the words in gasps, as it were, between the smiles with which he looked at her, "I call my sister 'Moll,' before the servants; 'Mary,' in presence of friends; and 'Maria,' when I am alone with her."

When the inimitable comic actor Munden took his farewell of the stage, Miss Lamb and her brother failed not to attend the last appearance of their favourite, and it was upon this occasion that Mary made that admirable pun, which has sometimes been attributed to Charles— "Sic transit gloria *Munden !*" During the few final performances of the veteran comedian, Victoria was taken by her father and mother to see him, when he played Old Dornton in "The Road to Ruin," and Crack in "The Turnpike Gate." Miss Lamb, hearing of the promised treat, with her usual kindly thought and wisdom, urged the young girl to give her utmost attention to the actor's style. "When you are an old woman like me, people will ask you about Munden's acting, as they now ask me about Garrick's, so take particular care to observe all he does, and *how* he does it." Owing to this considerate reminder, the very look, the very gesture, the whole bearing of Munden—first in the pathetic character of the gentleman-father, next in the farce-character of the village cobbler—remain impressed upon the brain of her who witnessed them as if beheld but yesterday. The tipsy lunge with which he rolled up to the table whereon stood that tempting brown jug ; the leer of mingled slyness and attempted unconcernedness with which he slid out his furtive thought to the audience—" Some gentleman has left his ale ! " then, with an unctuous smack of his lips, jovial and anticipative, adding, " And some other gentleman will drink it ! "—all stand present to fancy, vivid and unforgotten.

Still more valuable was Mary Lamb's kindness at a period when she thought she perceived symptoms of an unexplained dejection in her young friend. How gentle was her sedate mode of reasoning the matter, after delicately touching upon the subject, and endeavouring to draw forth its avowal ! more as if mutually discussing and consulting than as if questioning, she endeavoured to ascertain whether uncertainties or scruples of faith had arisen in the young girl's mind, and had caused her pre-occupied, abstracted manner. If it were any such source of disturbance, how wisely and feelingly she suggested reading, reflecting, weighing; if but a less deeply-seated depression, how sensibly she advised adopting some object to rouse energy and interest ! She pointed out the efficacy of studying a language (she herself at upwards of fifty years of age began the acquirement of French and Italian) as a remedial measure ; and advised Victoria to devote herself to a younger brother she had, in the same way that she had attended to her own brother Charles in his infancy, as the wholesomest and surest means of all for cure.

For the way in which Mary Lamb could minister to a

stricken mind, witness a letter of hers addressed to a
friend—a mother into whose home death had for the
first time come, taking away her last-born child of barely
two months old.   This letter, sacredly kept in the family
of her to whom it was written, is here given to the eyes
of the world.   Miss Lamb wrote few letters, and fewer
still have been published.   But the rareness of her effusions
enhance their intrinsic worth, and render it doubly impera-
tive that their gentle beauty of sense and wisdom should
not be withheld from general knowledge.   The letter bears
date merely " Monday, Newington," and the post-mark is
undecipherable ; but it was written in the spring of 1820,
and was directed to Mrs. Vincent Novello :—

My dear Friend,—Since we heard of your sad sorrow,
you have been perpetually in our thoughts ; therefore, you
may well imagine how welcome your kind remembrance of
us must be.   I know not how enough to thank you for it.
You bid me write you a long letter ; but my mind is so possessed with the idea that you must be occupied with one
only thought, that all trivial matters seem impertinent.   I
have just been reading again Mr. Hunt's delicious Essay,[1]
which I am sure must have come so home to your hearts, I
shall always love him for it.   I feel that it is all that one can
think, but which none but he could have done so prettily.
May he lose the memory of his own babies in seeing them all
grow old around him !   Together with the recollection of your
dear baby, the image of a little sister I once had comes as
fresh into my mind as if I had seen her as lately.   A little
cap with white satin ribbon, grown yellow with long keeping,

---

[1] Entitled " Deaths of Little Children," which appeared in
the *Indicator* for   5th April, 1820, and which had its
origin in the sorrowful event that occasioned Miss Lamb's
letter.

and a lock of light hair, were the only relics left of her.   The
sight of them always brought her pretty, fair face to my view,
that to this day I seem to have a perfect recollection of her
features.   I long to see you, and I hope to do so on Tuesday
or Wednesday in next week.   Percy Street ![2]   I love to
write the word: what comfortable ideas it brings with it !   We
have been pleasing ourselves ever since we heard this piece
of unexpected good news with the anticipation of frequent
drop-in visits, and all the social comfort of what seems almost
next-door neighbourhood.

Our solitary confinement has answered its purpose even
better than I expected.   It is so many years since I have
been out of town in the Spring, that I scarcely knew of the
existence of such a season.   I see every day some new flower
peeping out of the ground, and watch its growth ; so that I
have a sort of an intimate friendship with each.   I know the
effect of every change of weather upon them—have learned
all their names, the duration of their lives, and the whole
progress of their domestic economy.   My landlady, a nice,
active old soul that wants but one year of eighty, and her
daughter, a rather aged young gentlewoman, are the only
labourers in a pretty large garden ; for it is a double house,
and two long strips of ground are laid into one, well stored
with fruit-trees, which will be in full blossom the week after
I am gone, and flowers, as many as can be crammed in, of
all sorts and kinds.   But flowers are flowers still ; and I
must confess I would rather live in Russell Street all my life,
and never set my foot but on the London pavement, than be
doomed always to enjoy the silent pleasures I now do.   We
go to bed at ten o'clock.   Late hours are life-shortening
things ; but I would rather run all risks, and sit every night
—at some places I could name—wishing in vain at eleven
o'clock for the entrance of the supper tray, than be always
up and alive at eight o'clock breakfast as I am here.   We have

---

[2] Whither Miss Lamb's friend was about to remove her
residence from the farther (west) end of Oxford Street.

a scheme to reconcile these things. We have an offer of a very low-rented lodging a mile nearer town than this. Our notion is, to divide our time, in alternate weeks, between quiet rest and dear London weariness. We give an answer to-morrow ; but what that will be, at this present writing, I am unable to say. In the present state of our undecided opinion, a very heavy rain that is now falling may turn the scale. " Dear rain, do go away," and let us have a fine cheerful sunset to argue the matter fairly in. My brother walked seventeen miles yesterday before dinner. And not-withstanding his long walk to and from the office, we walk every evening ; but I by no means perform in this way so well as I used to do. A twelve-mile walk one hot Sunday morning made my feet blister, and they are hardly well now. Charles is not yet come home ; but he bid me, with many thanks, to present his *love* to you and all yours, to all whom and to each individually, and to Mr. Novello in particular, I beg to add mine. With the sincerest wishes for the health and happiness of all, believe me, ever, dear Mary Sabilla, your most affectionate friend,

MARY ANN LAMB.

Many a salutary influence through youth, and many a cherished memory through after-years, did Victoria owe to her early knowledge of Charles Lamb's sister. This revered friend entered so genuinely and sympathetically into the young girl's feelings and interests, that the great condescension in the intercourse was scarcely compre-hended by the latter at the time ; but as age and experience brought their teaching, she learned to look back upon the gracious kindness shown her in its true light, and she became keenly aware of the high privilege she had once enjoyed. Actuated by this consciousness, she has felt impelled to record her grateful sense of Mary Lamb's generous genial goodness and noble qualities

by relating her own individual recollections of them, and
by sharing with others the gratification arising out of their
treasured reminiscences.

This Victoria Novello was a namesake of honoured
Mary Lamb, having been christened " Mary " Victoria.
When she married, she abided by her first and simpler
baptismal name, as being more in consonance with the
good old English (plain but *clerkly*) surname of her
husband, and became known to her readers as their
faithful servant,

MARY COWDEN CLARKE.

LEIGH HUNT AND HIS LETTERS.

WE have said that Leigh Hunt's conversation even surpassed his writing, and that his mode of telling a story in speech was still better than his mode of narrating it with his pen. His letters and friendly notes have something of both his conversation and his style of composition—they are easy, spirited, genial, and most kindly. To receive a letter from him was a pleasure that rendered the day brighter and cheerier; that seemed to touch London smoke with a golden gleam; that made prosaic surroundings take a poetical form; that caused common occurrences to assume a grace of romance and refinement, as the seal was broken and the contents were perused. The very sight of his well-known handwriting, with its delicate characters of elegant and upright slenderness, sent the spirits on tip-toe with expectation at what was in store.

At intervals, through a long course of years, it was our good fortune to be the receivers of such letters and notes, a selection from which we place before our readers, that they may guess at our delight when the originals reached us. Inasmuch as many of them are undated, it has been difficult to assign each its particular period; and therefore we give them not exactly in chronological order; though as nearly according to the sequence of time in which they were probably written and received as may be. The first five belong to the commencement of the acquaintance between Leigh Hunt and C. C. C., and to the " Dear Sir" stage of addressing each other; yet are quite in the writer's charming cordiality of tone, and make allusion in his own graceful manner to the basket of fresh flowers, fruit, and vegetables sent weekly from the garden at Enfield :—

To Mr. C. C. Clarke.

Surrey Jail, Tuesday, July 13th, 1813.

DEAR SIR,—I shall be truly happy to see yourself and your friend to dinner next Thursday,•and can answer for the mutton, if not for the " cordials " of which you speak.   However, when you and I are together there can be no want, I trust, of cordial hearts, and those are much better.   Remember, we dine at three !   Mrs. Hunt begs her respects, but will hear of no introduction, as she has reckoned you an old acquaintance ever since you made your appearance before us by proxy in a basket.—Very sincerely yours,

LEIGH HUNT.

To C. C. C.

Surrey Jail, January 5th, 1814.

DEAR SIR,—. . . . The last time I saw your friend P., he put into my hands a letter he had received from your father at the time of our going to prison—a letter full of kindness and cordiality.   Pray will you give my respects to Mr. Clarke, and tell him that had I been aware of his good wishes towards my brother and myself, I should have been anxious to say so before this ; but I know the differences of opinion that sometimes exist in families, and something like a feeling to that effect kept me silent.   I should quarrel with this rogue P. about it if, in the first place, I could afford to quarrel with anybody, and if I did not believe him to be one of the best-natured men in the world.

Should your father be coming this way, I hope he will do me the pleasure of looking in.   I should have sent to yourself some weeks ago, or at least before this, to come and see how we enjoy your vegetables, only 1 was afraid that, like most people at this season of the year, you might be involved in a round of family engagements with aunts, cousins, and second cousins, and all the list at the end of the Prayer-book. As soon as you can snatch a little leisure, pray let us see you. You know our dinner-hour, and can hardly have to learn, at this time of day, how sincerely 1 am, my dear sir, your friend and servant, LEIGH HUNT.

To C. C. C., Enfield.

Surrey Jail, May 17th, 1814.

MY DEAR SIR,—. . . . I am much obliged to Mr. Holt White for his communication. Your new-laid eggs were exceedingly welcome to me at the time they came, as 1 had just then begun once more to try an egg every morning ; but 1 have been obliged to give it up. Perhaps I shall please you by telling you that 1 am writing a Mask[1] in allusion to the late events. It will go to press, I hope, in the course of next week, and this must be one of my excuses both for having delayed the letter before me, and for now abruptly concluding it. I shall beg the favour of your accepting a copy when it comes out, as 1 should have done with my last little publication,[2] except for a resolution to which some of my most intimate friends had come for a particular reason, and which induced me to regard you as one of those to whom I could pay the compliment of *not* sending a copy. This reason is now no longer in force, and therefore you will oblige me by waiting to hear from myself instead of your bookseller.— Yours, my dear sir, most sincerely, LEIGH HUNT.

To C. C. C.

Surrey Jail, November 2nd, 1814.

MY DEAR SIR,—I hope you have not been accusing your friends Ollier and Robertson of forgetting you—or, at least, thinking so—for all the fault is at my own door. The truth is, that when I received your request relative to the songs of

---

[1] "The Descent of Liberty."   [2] "The Feast of the Poets."

Mozart, I had resolved to answer it myself, and did not say a word on the subject to either one or the other ; so that I am afraid I have been hindering two good things—your own enjoyment of the songs, and an opportunity on the part of Messrs. O. and R. of showing you that they were readier correspondents than myself. After all, perhaps a little of the fault is attributable to yourself, for how can you expect a man rolling in hebdomadal luxuries—pears, apples, and pig—should think of anything? By the way, now I am speaking of luxuries, let me thank you for your very acceptable present of apples to my brother John. If you had ransacked the garden of the Hesperides, you could not have made him, I am sure, a more welcome one. I believe his notion of the highest point of the sensual in eating is an apple, hard, juicy, and fresh. . . . . The printers have got about half through with my Mask. You will be pleased to hear that I have been better for some days than ever I have felt during my imprisonment—and in spite too of rains and east winds.

To C. C. C., Enfield.

Vale of Health, Hampstead,
Tuesday, Nov. 7th, 1815.

MY DEAR SIR,—You have left a picture for me, I understand, at Paddington, where the rogues are savagely withholding it from me. I shall have it, I suppose, in the course of the day, and conjecture it to be some poet's or politician's head that you have picked up in turning over some old engravings. I beg you to laugh very heartily, by the bye, if I am anticipating a present, where there is none. I am apt, from old remembrances, to fall into this extravagance respecting the Enfield quarter, and do it with the less scruple, inasmuch as you are obliging enough to consult my taste in this particular—which is, small gifts from large hearts. I am glad, however, in the present instance that I have been made to wait a little, since it enables me, for *once*, to be beforehand with you, and I can at least send you your long-promised books. The binder, notwithstanding my particular injunctions, and not having seen, I suppose, the colour of the fields lately enough to remember it, has made the

O

covers red instead of green. You must fancy the books are blushing for having been so long before they came.—Yours most sincerely,   LEIGH HUNT.

The books here referred to were "The Descent of Liberty" and "The Feast of the Poets, with other pieces in verse." The binder to whom I (C. C. C.) subsequently entrusted the task of putting Leigh Hunt's volume of poems entitled "Foliage" into an appropriately coloured cover of *green* played me a similar trick to the one above recorded, by sending the book home encased in bright *blue!*

The next letter alludes to John Keats, by the playful appellation that Leigh Hunt gave him of "Junkets," and commences by a pleasanter and more familiar form of address to C. C. C. than the previously used "Dear Sir:"—

To C. C. C.

Maida Hill, Paddington, July 1st, 1817.

MY DEAR FRIEND,— .... I saw Mr. Hazlitt here last night, and he apologizes to me, as I doubt not he will to you, for having delayed till he cannot send it [the opera-ticket] at all. You shall have it without fail if you send for it to the office on Thursday, though with still greater pleasure if you come and fetch it yourself in the meantime. You shall read "Hero and Leander" with me, and riot also in a translation or two from Theocritus, which are, or ought to be, all that is fine, floral, and fruity, and any other *f* that you can find to furnish out a finished festivity. But you have not left off your lectures, I trust, on punctuality. Pray do not, for I am very willing to take, and even to profit by them ; and *ecce signum!* I answer your letter by return of post. You began this reformation in me ; my friend Shelley followed it up nobly ; and you must know that friendship can do just as much with me as enmity can do little. What has become of Junkets I know not. I suppose Queen Mab has eaten him.

. . . I came to town last Wednesday, spent Saturday evening with Henry Robertson, who has been unwell, and supped yesterday with Novello. Harry tells me that there is news ot the arrival of *Havell;* and so we are conspiring to get all together again, and have one of our old evenings, joco-serio-musico-pictorio-poetical.—Most sincerely yours,

LEIGH HUNT.

The next three letters bear date in the same year. "Ave Maria" and "Salve Regina" were names sportively given by Leigh Hunt to Mrs. Vincent Novello and her sister, in reference to their being dear to a composer of Catholic Motets. "Marlowe" was where Percy Bysshe Shelley then resided, and where Leigh Hunt and his family were then staying on a summer visit with his poet friend. The jest involved in the repeated recurrence to "Booth" is now forgotten :—

To Vincent Novello, 240, Oxford Street.

Hampstead, April 9th, 1817.

MY DEAR NOVELLO,—Pray pardon—in the midst of our hurry—this delay in answering your note. My vanity had already told me that you would not have stayed away on Wednesday for nothing ; but 1 was sorry to find the cause was so painful a one. I believe you take exercise ; but are you sure that you always take enough, and stout enough? All arts that involve sedentary enjoyment are great affecters of the stomach and causers of indigestion ; and I have a right to hint a little advice on the occasion, having been a great sufferer as well as sinner on the score myself. If you do not need it, you must pardon my impertinence. We set off at eleven to-morrow morning, and are in all the chaos of packed trunks, lumber, litter, dust, dirty dry fingers, &c. But Booth is still true to the fair, so my service to them, both Ave Maria and Salve Regina. The ladies join with me in these devoirs, and so does Mr Keats, as in poetry bound.

Ever my dear Novello most heartily yours,

LEIGH HUNT.

P.S.—I will write to you from the country.

To Vincent Novello.

Marlowe, April 17th, 1817.

MY DEAR NOVELLO,—One of Mr. Shelley's great objects is to have a pianoforte *as quickly as possible*, so that though he cannot alter his ultimatum with regard to a *grand* one, he wishes me to say that, if Mr. Kirkman has no objection, he will give him the security requested, and of the same date of years, for a cabinet piano from fifty to seventy guineas. Of course he would like to have it as good as possible, and under your auspices. Will you put this to the builder of harmonies? I have been delighted to see in the *Chronicle* an advertisement of Birchall's, announcing editions of all Mozart's works; and shall take an early opportunity of expressing it and extending the notice. I would have Mozart as common in good libraries[3] as Shakespeare and Spenser, and prints from Raphael. Most of us here envy you the power of seeing "Don Giovanni;" yet we still muster up virtue enough to wish you all well, and to send our best remembrances in return to Ave and Salve, to whom I am as good a Boothite as I can be, considering that I am also very truly yours, LEIGH HUNT.

To Vincent Novello, 240, Oxford Street.

Albion House, Marlowe, Bucks,
June 24th, 1817.

MY DEAR NOVELLO,—You must not think ill of me for having omitted to write to you before, except, indeed, as far as concerned an old bad habit of delay in these matters, which all my friends have reproved in turn, and which all help to spoil me by excusing. I begged Mr. Clarke to let you know how much we liked the piano here; but when you wrote about poor Wesley, I happened myself to be suffering under a pretty strong fever, which lasted me from one Friday to the next, and from which I did not quickly recover. I have since got well again, however, and yet I have not written; nay, I am going to make an excuse out of my very

---

[3] [Thanks to Vincent Novello, this is now the case. C.C.C., 1875.]

impudence (1 hope the ladies are present), and plainly tell you, that the worse my reason is for writing at last, the better you will be pleased with it, for we are coming home to-morrow. If that will not do, I have another piece of presumption, which 1 shall double my thrust with, and fairly run you through the *heart;* and this is, that we are coming to live near you, towards the end of the new road, Paddington.

1 am sorry 1 can tell you nothing about the music of this place, except as far as the birds make it. I say *the* music, because it seems there are a party of the inhabitants who are fond of it. At least, 1 was invited the other day in a very worshipful manner to one, and regret I was not able to go, as I fear it might have been misconstrued into pride. There are other things, however, which you are fond of—beautiful walks, uplands, valleys, wood, water, steeples issuing out of clumps of trees, most luxuriant hedges, meads, cornfields, brooks, nooks, and pretty looks. (Here a giggle, and a shake of the head from the ladies. *Ave* and *Salve*, be quiet.) The other day a party of us dined in a boat under the hanging woods of Cleveden—mentioned, you know, by Pope :—

> Cleveden's proud alcove
> The bower of wanton Shrewsbury and Love.

(Giggle and shake) and a day or two before we spent a most beautiful day, dining, talking, wining, spruce-beering, and walking, in and about Medmenham Abbey, where strangers are allowed to take this liberty in memory of a set of "lay friars" who are said to have taken many more,—I mean Wilkes and his club, who feasted and slept here occasionally, performing profane ceremonies, and others perhaps which the monks would have held to be not quite so. (Giggle and shake.)—If these people were the gross libertines they were said to be, the cause of kindly virtue was indeed in bad hands,—hands but just better than the damnatory and selfish ones to which the world has usually committed it ;—but there is little reason to doubt that the stories of them (such as the supposed account for instance in "Crysal, or the

Adventures of a Guinea ") have been much exaggerated. If men of the most heartfelt principle do not escape, although they contradict in theory only the vile customs of the world, what can be expected from more libertine departers from them?—It is curious that the people at Medmenham itself do not seem to think so ill of the club as others. To be sure, it is not easy to say how far some *family* feelings may not be concerned in the matter; but so it is; and together with their charity, they have a great deal of health and beauty. It was said with equal *naïveté* and shrewdness, the other day, by a very excellent person that "faith and charity are incompatible," and so the [*illegible, torn by seal*] seem resolved to maintain; but hope and charity are excellent companions, and seem [*illegible*] of St. Paul's reading, I would have the three Graces completed thus,—Charity, Hope, and Nature. I have done nothing to my proposed *Play* here :— I do not know how it is; but I love things essentially dramatic, and yet I feel less inclination for dramatic writing than any other,—I mean my own, of course. Considering also what the taste of the day has been,—what it is to run the gauntlet through managers, actors, and singers,—and what a hobgoblin I have been in my time to the playwrights themselves, I cannot help modestly repeating to myself some lines out of your favourite Address of Beaumont to Fletcher about the Faithful Shepherdess,—upon which, by the bye, I am writing this letter, seated on a turfy mound in my friend's garden, a little place with a rustic seat in it, shrouded and covered with trees, with a delightful field of sheep on one side, a white cottage among the leaves in a set of fields on the other, and the haymakers mowing and singing in the fields behind me. On the side towards the lawn and house, it is as completely shut in, as Chaucer's "pretty parlour" in the "Flower and the Leafe."—Mrs. Hunt in the meantime is revenging the cause of all uninspired fiddlers,—namely, scraping Apollo. Pray let the ladies remain out of the secret of this as long as the suspense shall give them any pleasure; and then tell them that the said Apollo, whatever they may think or even hope to the contrary, is no gentleman, but a plaster statue, which Marianne is putting into a proper condition for Mr. Shelley's library. A Venus is already scraped, to my infinite relief, who sympathized extremely with her ribs,—a sentiment which the ladies nevertheless are not very quick to show towards *theirs.* I beg pardon of *Ave*,—I mean *are* very,—"nevertheless" being a shocking and involuntary intrusion, suggested by my unjustifiable forget‑fulness of Mr. Booth.

I will let you know where I am when I return. If I have written no play, I have not been idle with other verses, and am in all things the same as I was when I left town, so that I need not say I am sincerely yours,

LEIGH HUNT.

The following letter has no date; but its postscript explanation of the verse-signatures in the "Literary Pocket-Book" shows it to have been written in 1819, which was the first year in which that publication appeared. It begins without set form of address, plunging at once, in sportive fashion, into a whimsically-worded yet most kindly rebuke to C. C. C. for having been impatient at his friend's delay in answering a communication. The reference to the actor Fawcett and his grating laugh comes in with as pleasant an effect as the reference to John Keats's loss of his brother Tom strikes with pain‑fully vivid impression after this long lapse of years :—

To C. C. C. [No date.]

And so Charles Clarke is very angry with me for not sooner answering his two letters, and talks to my friends about my "regal scorn." Well,—I have been guilty cer‑tainly of not sooner answering said two ;—I have not answered them, even though they pleased me infinitely :—Charles Clarke also sent me some verses, the goodness of which (if he will not be very angry) even surprised me, yet I answered not :—he sent me them again, yet I answered not :—undoubtedly I have been extremely unresponsive ; I have seemed to neglect him,—I have been silent, dilatory, unepistolary, strange, distant (miles), and (if the phrase " regal scorn " be true) without an excuse.

C. C. C. (meditative, but quick)—Ho, not without an excuse, I dare say. Come, come, I ought to have thought of that, before I used the words " regal scorn." I did not mean them in fact, and therefore I thought they would touch him. Bless my soul, I ought to have thought of an excuse for him, now I think of it ;—let me see ;—he must have been very busy ;—yes, yes, he was very busy, depend upon it :—I should not wonder if he had some particular reason for being busy just now ;—I warrant you he has been writing like the Devil ;—I'll stake my life on't,—he has almost set his tingling head asleep like my foot, with writing ;—and then too, you may be certain he reproached himself every day nevertheless with not writing to me ;—I'll be bound to say that he said : I *will* write to Charles Clarke to-day, and I will not forget to give another notice to him in the *Examiner* (for he did give one), and above all, he will see his verses there, and then he will guess all ;—then one day he is busy till it is too late to write by the post, and in some cursed hurry he forgets me on Saturday, and then—and what then ? Am I not one of his real friends ? Have I not a *right* to be forgotten or rather unwritten to by him, for weeks, if by turning his looks, not his heart, away from me, he can snatch repose upon the confidence of my good opinion of him ? I think I see him asking me this ; and curse me (I beg your pardon, Miss Jones), but confound me, I should say—no, I should not say,—but the deuce take—in short, here's the beginning of his letter, and so there's an end of my vagaries.

My dear friend, you are right. I *have* been very busy,—so busy both summer and winter, that summer has scarcely been any to me ; and my head at times has almost grown benumbed over my writing. I have been intending everything and anything, except loyal anti-constitutionalism and Christian want of charity. I have written prose, I have written poetry, I have written levities and gravities, I have written two acts of a Tragedy, and (*oh Diva pecunia*) I have written a Pocket-Book ! Let my Morocco blushes speak for e ; for with this packet comes a copy. When you read my

Calendar of Nature, you will *feel* that I did not forget you ; for you are one of those in whose company I always seem to be writing these things. Had your poetry arrived soon enough, I should have said " Oh, ho ! " and clapped it among my Pocket-Book prisoners. As it is, it must go at large in the *Examiner*, where it will accordingly be found in a week or two. And here let me say, that bad as I have been, I begged Mr. Holmes to explain why I had not written ; so that if he has been a negligent epistolian as well as myself, why—there are two good fellows who have done as they ought not to have done, and there is no epistle in us. (Here Charles Clarke gives a laugh, which socially speaking is very musical ; but abstractedly, resembles fifty Fawcetts, or ten rusty iron gates scraping along gravel.) You must know that you must keep my tragic drama a secret, unless you have *one* female ear into which you can own for me the rough impeachment. (Here ten gates.) It is on the same subject as the " Cid " of Corneille ; and I mean it to be ready by the middle of January for the so *theatre ;* if you will get your hands in training meantime, I trust, God willing, the groundlings will have their ears split. If not, I shall make up my mind, like a *damned* vain fellow, that they are too large and tough ; and so with this new pun in your throat, go you along with me in as many things as you did before, my dear friend, for I am ever the same, most truly yours,

LEIGH HUNT.

P.S —The verses marked Φ in the Pocket-Book are mine, Δ Mr. Shelley's, P.R. a Mr. Procter's, and I. Keats's, who has just lost his brother Tom after a most exemplary attendance on him. The close of such lingering illness, however, can hardly be lamented. Mr. Richards, who has just dropped in upon me, begs to be remembered to you.

The following letter alludes to a project for a work which was to be published by Power, was to be entitled " Musical Evenings," and was to consist of poetry, original or selected, by Leigh Hunt, adapted to melodies, original or selected, by Vincent Novello. The work, most tasteful in conception and most tastefully carried out by the poet and musician in concert (so far as it proceeded towards execution), was ultimately given up, as being much too far in advance of the then existing public taste for music, and from the conviction that not enough copies would be sold to make the enterprise profitable to either publisher, poet, or musician :—

To V. N.

13, Mortimer Terrace, Kentish Town,
Feb. 15th, 1820.

MY DEAR NOVELLO,—Unless you should avail yourself of the holiday to-morrow to transact any unprofessional business elsewhere, will you oblige me by coming and taking your chop or your tea here to-morrow, to talk over a proposal which *Power* has made me, and which I think you will consider a good one ?   The truth is, I want you, if you have no objection, to negotiate the money part of the business between him and me ; as I have no face in these matters but a mediating one, like your own.   I will chop at half-past three. At all events, in case you go to Hampstead, and can come after your schooling.   Hampstead is now in my eye, hill, trees, church and all, from the slopes near Caen wood to my right, and Primrose and Haverstock Hills with Steele's cottage to my left.   I trust I shall have an early opportunity of introducing Mrs. Novello to Pan—both in his frying and sylvan character. When I add that we have been in great confusion (it is not great now), I do it to bar all objections from you on that score, and to say that I expect you the more confidently on that very account, if you can come at all.   The house is most convenient and cheerful, and considered by us as quite a bargain.

P.S.—Power is half prepared to welcome you, if you have no objection.   He speaks of *your* power (I must call him fondly my Power) in the highest terms ; but this, I suppose, is no new thing to your lyrical ears.

If you can come early, we will make a whole holiday, which will be a great refreshment to me.

The "original" manuscript copy of Leigh Hunt's translation of Tasso's "Amyntas," alluded to in the next letter, Vincent Novello caused to be bound in green and gold, together with the printed presentation copy of the first edition ; and the volume is still in excellent preservation.   On the title-page is written in Leigh Hunt's hand, "To Vincent Novello, from his affectionate friend the translator;" and inside the cover is written in Vincent Novello's hand, beneath his own name and address, "I prize this volume, which was so kindly presented to me by my dear friend Leigh Hunt, as one of the most valuable books in my library; and I particularly request that it may be carefully preserved as an heirloom in my family when I am no more.—V. N." The "sorrows" to which Leigh Hunt sympathizingly refers were those of losing a beautiful boy of four years old, Sydney Vincent Novello :—

To V. N. (8, Percy Street.)

Kentish Town, Wednesday,
July, 1820.

MY DEAR NOVELLO,—In addition to the "Morgante," I send you the first volume of "Montaigne," which I have marked (so that I shall be in a manner in your company if you read any of it), and also the promised copy of "Amyntas," with the original to compare it with in any passage, as you seem to like those awful confrontings. Pray get an "Ariosto," if you have time. I am sure his natural touches and lively variety will delight you. The edition I spoke of is Boschini's, a little duodecimo or eighteens, printed by Schulze and Dean, Poland Street, where I believe it is to be bought. But you could get it at any foreign bookseller's. Be good enough to leave the Cenci MS. out for me with the Gliddons. I should not care about it, but the Gisbornes are about to return to Italy, and I am not sure whether they have given or lent it me. God bless you. You know how I respect sorrow :—you know also how I respect the wisdom and kindness that try to be cheerful again.   I need not add how much the feelings of you and Mrs. Novello (to whom give our kindest good wishes in case we do not see you to-morrow) are respected, and sympathized with, by your ever affectionate friend,

LEIGH HUNT.

P.S.—Do not trouble yourself to answer this note.   Go out instead and buy the "Ariosto."   It is the pleasantest little pocket-rogue in the world.   The translation of "Montaigne" is an excellent one, by Cotton the poet, old Izaak Walton's friend.

The next letter is superscribed after the pleasant fashion that Leigh Hunt occasionally adopted, in directing his letters to his friends, of putting some gay jest *outside*, as if he must add a last word or two in sending off a communication with those he loved, and as if he could not bear to conclude his chat or take leave of them :—

> To C. C. C.
> Bellevue House, Ramsgate.
> By favour of Mrs. Gliddon—post *unpaid*.

Percy Street, August 31st, 1821.

MY DEAR

Si si si

Mr. and Mrs. Novello tell me that you will be gratified at having a word from me, however short   What word shall I send you, equally short and sweet ?   I believe I must refer you to the postwoman ; for the ladies understand these beatic brevities best.   However, if I cannot prevail on myself to send you a mere word or a short one, I will send you a true one, which is, that in spite of all my non-epistolary offences—(come, it is a short one too, after all)—I am, my dear Clarke, very truly and heartily *yours*,

LEIGH HUNT.

P.S.—Novello and I are just putting the finishing touch to

our first Musical Evening, which I hope *Power* will put it into *my* ditto to send you a copy of.

It is difficult to ascertain the period when the following note was written, but it appears to belong to an early one :—

To C. C. C.

[No date.]

MY DEAR FRIEND,—. . . . I send you on the opposite side some verses which my Summer Party sing on the grass after dinner. I forgot, by-the-bye, to tell you yesterday a piece of news which has flattered me much—that Stothard told an acquaintance of mine the other day he had been painting a subject from " Rimini :"—

> To the Spirit great and good,
> Felt, although not understood,—
> By whose breath, and in whose eyes,
> The green earth rolls in the blue skies,— .
> Who we know, from things that bless,
> Must delight in loveliness;
> And who, therefore, we believe,
> Means us well in things that grieve,—
>   Gratitude ! Gratitude !
> Heav'n be praised as heavenly should,
> Not with slavery, or with fears,
> But with a face as towards a friend, and with thin sparkling
>   [tears.

The next five letters were written while Leigh Hunt and his family were on their way to Italy. The allusion to " Fanchon" refers to an arrangement of Himmel's so-named opera, which Vincent Novello had brought out in four books of Pianoforte duets.

" Wilful Woman" was an affectionate nickname of Leigh Hunt's for Mrs. Vincent Novello, in recognition of her having a decided "will" in matters right and good. A woman less " wilful" in the unreasonable sense of the term, or more full of will in the noblest sense of the term, could not be cited than herself :—

To V. N. [*in pencil.*]

2, High Street, Ramsgate,
Monday, December 3rd, 1821.

MY DEAR NOVELLO,—Here we are in absolute quiet, with a real flat place to sit upon, and several foot square of parlour to walk about when one pleases : in short, in lodgings — the rudder of the vessel having been so broken that she cannot set sail, fair wind or foul, till Wednesday evening.

We now, with a rascally selfishness, wish that the wind may not change for a whole week, though the 200 sail in the harbours should be groaning every timber ; for though we were much alarmed at first in moving my wife, she already seems wonderfully refreshed by this little taste of shore ; and at all events while we do remain at Ramsgate, I am sure it is much better for both of us that we should be here. Only think ! we shall have a quiet bed at night, and even air ! If we were moving *on* at sea, it would be another matter ; but I confess the idea of lying and lingering in that manner in a muddy harbour was to me, in my state of health, like rotting alive.

When I say, we can go on Wednesday, I do not mean that we shall do so, or that I think we shall ; for the wind is still in the west, and I suspect after all these winds, we shall have a good mass of rain to fall, of which they are generally the *avant-couriers*. What say you then ? Will you come and beatify us again ? And will Mrs. Novello come with you ? Why not give the baby a dip in a warm bath, if they must be still one and indivisible. I think we can get you a bed in the house ; if not, there are plenty in the neighbourhood. Pray remember me cordially to the Gliddons, and tell the fair one that her sugar-plums have been a shower of aids and assistance to us with the children. I shall see if I can't send her something as sweet from Italy. In the meantime I send her and Mrs. Novello, and all of you, the best salutations you can couple with the idea of

L. H.

To Mr. and Mrs. Novello, and Mr. and Mrs. G.
 (Percy Street.)
     Dartmouth, December 24th, 1821.

DEAR FRIENDS,—Here we are again in England, after beating twice up and down the Channel, and getting as far as the Atlantic. What we have suffered I will leave you to imagine, till you see my account of the voyage ; but we were never more inclined to think that "All's well that ends well," and what we hoped we still hope, and are still prepared to venture for. We arrived on Saturday, which was no post-day. Next day I wrote to my brother and Miss Kent, and begged the latter to send you news of our safety ; for I was still exhausted with the fatigue and anxiety, and I knew well that you would willingly wait another day for my handwriting when you were sure of our welfare. I had hoped that this letter would reach you in the middle of what *I* would reach in vain—your Christmas festivities ; so that a bit of my soul if not of my body, of my handwriting if not my grasping hand, might come in at your parlour door and seem to join you as my representative ; but a horrid matter-of-fact woman at the Castle Inn here, who proclaims the most unwelcome things in a voice hideously clear and indisputable, says that a post takes two nights and a day. I hope, however, to hear from you, and to write again, for the vessel has been strained by the bad weather, and must be repaired a little, and the captain vows he will not go to sea again till the wind is exquisitely fair. Above all, Dartmouth is his native place, and who shall say to him, "Get up from your old friends and fireside, and quench yourself in a sea fog?" Not I, by St. Vincent and St. Sabilla, and King Arthur and Queen Anastasia. I am sorry to say that the alarms which it is impossible not to help feeling on such occasions have done no good to Mrs. Hunt's malady, though when she was in repose the sea air was evidently beneficial. For my part, I confess I was as rank a coward many times as a father and husband who has seven of the best reasons for cowardice can be ; but Hope and *Mutuality* you know are my mottoes. And so, with all sorts of blessings upon your heads, farewell, dear friends, till we hear from each other again.—Stop ! Here is

a Christmas Carol in which perhaps some of you will pay me
a visit—Mistletoe and Holly! Mistletoe and Holly!

L. H.

Remember me to the Lambs, to Mr. Clarke, to the Robert-
sons, etc.

To V. N.

Stonehouse, near Plymouth, Feb. 11th, 1822.

Oh Novello! what a disappointing, wearisome, vexatious,
billowy, up-and-downy, unbearable, beautiful world it is! I
cannot tell you all I have gone through since I wrote to you;
but I believe, after all, that all has been for the best, bad as
it is. The first stoppage, unavoidable as it was, almost put
me beside myself. Those sunshiny days and moonlight
nights! And the idea of running merrily to Gibraltar! I
used to shake in my bed at night with bilious impatience,
and feel ready to rise up and cry out. But knowing what I
since know, I have not only reason to believe that my wife
would have suffered almost as terribly afterwards as she did
at the time, but I am even happy that we underwent the
second stoppage at this place,—at least as happy as a man
can be whose very relief arises from the illness of one dear to
him. Marianne fell so ill the day on which the new vessel
we had engaged sailed from Plymouth, that she was obliged
to lose forty-six ounces of blood in twenty-four hours, to
prevent inflammatory fever on the lungs. With the exception
of a few hours she has been in bed ever since, sometimes
improving, sometimes relapsing and obliged to lose more
blood, but always so weak and so ailing that, especially
during the return of these obstinate S.W. winds, I have con-
grátulated myself almost every hour that circumstances conspired with my fears for her to hinder us from proceeding.
Indeed I should never have thought of doing so after her
Dartmouth illness, had she not, as she now confesses, in her
eagerness not to be the means of detaining me again, mis-
represented to me her power of bearing the voyage. I shall
now set myself down contentedly till spring, when we shall
have shorter nights, and she will be able to be upon deck in the
daytime. She will then receive benefit from the sea, as she

ought to do, instead of being shaken by it ; and as to gunpowder ! be sure I shall always make inquiries enough about that. She starts sometimes to this hour in the middle of the night, with the horror of it, out of her sleep. It gave a sort of horrible sting to my feet sometimes as I walked the deck, and fancied we might all be sent shattered up in the air in the twinkling of an eye ; but I seldom thought of this danger, and do not believe there was any to be seriously alarmed at, though the precautions and penalties connected with the carriage of such an article were undoubtedly sufficient to startle a freshwater imagination, to say nothing of that of a sick mother with six children. The worst feeling it gave me was when it came over me down in the cabin while we were comparatively comfortable,—especially when little baby was playing his innocent tricks. I used to ask myself what right I had to bring so much innocent flesh and blood into such an atrocious possibility of danger. But what used chiefly to rouse my horrors was the actual danger of shipwreck during the gales; and of these, as you may guess from my being imaginative, I had my full share. Oh the feelings with which I have gone out from the cabin to get *news*, and have stood at the top of that little staircase down which you all came to bid me goodbye ! How I have thought of you in your safe, warm rooms, now merrily laughing, now " stopping the career of laughter with a sigh " to wonder how the " sailors " might be going on! My worst sensation of all was the impossibility I felt of dividing myself into seven different persons in case anything happened to my wife and children. But as the voyage is not yet over—remember, however, that the worst part, the winter part, *is* over. You shall have an account of that as well as the rest when I get to Italy and write it for the new work. Remember in the meantime what I tell you, and that we mean to be very safe, very cowardly, and vernal all the rest of the way. It was a little hard upon me,—was it not? that I could not have the [qu ? reward—illegible] of finishing the voyage boldly at once, especially as it was such fine weather when they set off again, and I can go through any danger as stubbornly as most persons, provided you allow me a pale face and a considerable quantity of internal poltroonery : —

P

but my old reconciling philosophy, such as it is, has not forsaken me ; and well it may remain, for God only knows what I should have done, had my wife been seized with this illness during the late return of the winds. I am very uneasy about her at all times : but in that case, considering too I might have avoided bringing her into such a situation, I should have been almost out of my wits. The vessel in which we intended to resume our journey (besides being more ornamental than solid, and never yet tried by a winter passage, except three days of one, which shattered it grievously) must have had a bad time of it ; and it is the opinion of everybody here, both doctors and seamen, that her life was not to be answered for had we encountered such weather. So I look at her in her snug, unmoving bed, and hope and trust she is getting strength enough from repose to renew her journey in the spring. We set off in April.—As to myself, my health is not at its best, but it is not at its worst. I manage to write a little, though the weather has been against me. I read more, and sometimes go to the Plymouth public library, where a gentleman has got me admission, and receive infinite homage from Examinerions in these parts, who have found me out. They want me to meet a "hundred admirers" at a public dinner : but this, you know, is not to my taste. I tell them I prefer a cup of tea with one of them now and then in private, and so they take me at my word, and I find them such readers as I like,—good-natured, cordial men, with a smack of literature.—I saw the announcement of the 4th part of your " Fanchon " in the *London Magazine*. You cannot imagine how the look of your name delighted me. You must know I had a design upon you for *our new Italian work* when I bore away your "Fanchon." So, say nothing about it (I mean to myself), but wait for an increase of your laurel from a hand you love. I think it will come with a good and profitable effect from such a quarter.—Tell Mrs. Gliddon, albeit she retains a piece of them, that I have found the cheeks which she and her sister left in Devonshire. There is a profusion of such,—faces that look built up of cream and roses, and as good-natured as health can make them. In looking for lodgings I lit also upon a namesake of hers, no relation, who spelt her name with a Y. I suppose a hundred and fiftieth cousin. She was a pleasant, chattering old woman with a young spirit, who, not being able to accommodate us herself, recommended her neighbours all round, and told me millions of things in a breath.—Dear Novello, I cannot tell you how I feel the kindness of my friends,—kindness, of which I know that you and Mrs. Novello, together with Bessie Kent, have been the souls. God bless you all. I will say more to you all from Italy. You will see my hand in the *Examiner* again in a week or two (about the time I could have written on the subject from abroad) with a few touches for Southey and the *Quarterly*.—It delights me to see the intimacy there is between you and Miss K.; she speaks in the most affectionate terms of you and your wife, and receives all the solace from your intercourse which I expected. Take a dozen hearty shakes of the hand from me, dear Novello, and give (you see how much I can ask of you) as many kisses of the same description to Mrs. Novello, unless "dear Mr. Arthur" is present and will do it for us. Convey also as many kisses to Mrs. Gliddon as the said dear Mr. Arthur could have given my wife had she been at your Christmas festivities, taking care (as in the former instance) that they be in high taste and most long and loud.—And so, Heaven bless you all and make us to send many good wishes to and from Italy to each other till we meet again face to face.—Your affectionate friend,   LEIGH HUNT.

P.S.—I can tell you nothing of the Plymouth neighbourhood, being generally occupied with my wife's bedside; but the town is a nice clean one; and after being at Dartmouth I felt all the price of Mirabeau's gratitude, who when he came into England, and saw streets paved, fell on his knees and thanked God there was a country in the world where some regard was had for foot-passengers. Dartmouth is a kind of sublime Wapping, being a set of narrow muddy streets in a picturesque situation on the side of a hill. The people too, poor creatures, are as dirty there as can be, having lost all their trade; whereas at Plymouth they are all fat and flourishing.—Stonehouse is a kind of separate suburb to Plymouth on the seashore.—My wife's kindest remembrances.—And mine to all rememberers.

To M. S. N.   Percy Street.

March 2nd, 1822.

DEAR MARY NOVELLO,—Your letter was a very great pleasure to us indeed, though it made us very impatient to be in the midst of our friends. We are like Mahomet's coffin at present, suspended between our two attractions ; but the ship will carry us off in April, and turn us again into living creatures. No : it is you and Novello who must revive us meanwhile. Do you know, I was going to ask you to come down here, and see us once more before we go ; but I was afraid you would think there was no end of my presuming upon your regards. Guess, however, what pleasure your own intimation gave us. You *must* fulfil it, now you have given it. No excuse—no *sort* of excuse. Novello must tear himself from all the boarding-school ladies, let them lay hold of the flaps of his coat never so Potipharically. There *are*, as you say, stages, waggons. carts, trucks, wheelbarrows, &c. : —there are also kind hearts in stout bodies : and finally, our direction is, *Mrs. L'Amoureux, Devil's Point*, Stonehouse, Plymouth, Devonshire.

You see the way we are in, in this *Devon* of a county. Then there are the Devonshire creams, *too* good ; Mount Edgecombe here close at our elbow looking like a Hampstead in the sea ; boats and smooth harbours to sail about in ; the finest air in England, with a little bit of the South of Europe in it ; all sorts of naval curiosities ; sunshine every day, and moonlight too, just now, every night ; and finally, dear friends, who want the society of dear friends to strengthen them through their cares and delays. I must not forget, that the road between London and Plymouth is said to be excellent, and that there is a safety-coach just set up, which boasts itself to be worthy of the road. *So we shall expect you in the course of the week*,—mind that I shall expect a letter too, to arrive just before you. You must send it off on Monday evening, and follow it with all your might and muscles. At least Novello must do so. I forgot, that ladies have no

muscles. They have only eyes and limbs. You must not
talk of your music, till Novello is here to inspire a pianoforte
which I have just hired for a month. It is the only pleasure
to which I have treated myself, and without him I find it but
a pain. There is a regiment stationed here, who have a band
that plays morning and evening. It plays Mozart too, and
pretty well, only I longed to jog their elbows the other day,
when they came to the 2nd part of " Batti, batti." However,
it was so beautiful, that I could not stand it out ; it reminded
me of so many pleasures, that between you and me and two
or three others, the tears came into my eyes, and I was
obliged to go out of the place to hide them. . . .

Your truly affectionate friend,

L. H.

Stonehouse, near Plymouth, March 26th, 1822.

DEAR MARY NOVELLO,—Your last letter was a great disappointment to me, but I have been so accustomed to dis-
appointments of late, that I looked out for the pleasant points
it contained to console me, and for these I am very thankful.
I should have written before, but I have been both ill and
rakish, which is a very bad way of making oneself better, at
least anywhere but in old places with old friends, and there
it does not always do. Remember me affectionately to the
Lambs. There are no Lambs here, nor Martin Burneys
neither ; "though by your smiling you don't seem to think
so." Smile as you may, I find I cannot comfortably give up
anybody whom I have been accustomed to associate with the
idea of friends in London ; and besides, there are some men,
like Collins's music, " by distance made more sweet ;" which
is a sentiment I beg you will not turn to ill account. How
cheerful I find myself getting, when fancying myself in Percy
Street ! I hope Mr. Clarke will find himself quite healthy
again in Somersetshire. He ought to be so, considering the
prudence, and the good nature, and the stout legs, and the
pleasant little *bookeries* which he carries about with him; but
then he must renounce those devils and all their works, the
cheesemonger and pieman. Perhaps he has ; but his complexion is like mine, and I remember what a world of back-

sliding and nightmare I went through before I could deliver myself from the crumbling *un*-crumblingness of Cheshire cheese, and that profound attraction, the under-crust of a veal or mutton pie. . . .

It is kind of you to tell me of the gratification which Mr. Holmes says I have been the means of giving him.   Tell him I hope to give him more with my crotchets before I die, and receive as much from *his* crotchets.   How much pleasure have you all given me!   And this reminds me that I must talk a little to Novello; so no more at present, dear black-headed, good-hearted, wilful woman, from yours most sincerely,   L. H.

The next two letters explain themselves:—

To V. N. and M. S. N.

Genoa, June 17th, 1822.

Amici veri e costanti,—Miss Kent will have told you the reason why I did not write on Saturday.   The boatman was waiting to snatch the letters out of my hand ; and besides hers, I was compelled to write three—one to my brother John, one to Mr. Shelley, and another to Lord B.—Neither can I undertake to write you a long letter at present, and I must communicate with my other friends by driblets, one after the other ; for my head is yet very tender, though I promise to get more health, and you know I have a great deal of writing to think about and to do.   Be good enough therefore to show this letter to the Gliddons, the Lambs, Mr. Coulson, and Mr. Hogg, whom I also request to show you theirs, or such parts, of them as contain news of Italy and nothing private.   Need I add, that of whatever length my letters may be, my heart is still the same towards you ?   I wish you could know how often we have thought and talked of you.   You know my taste for travelling.   I should like to take all my friends with me, like an Arabian caravan.   Fond as I am of home, my home is dog-like, in the persons—not cat-like, in the place ; and I should desire no better Paradise, to all eternity, than gipsyizing with those I love all over the world.   But I must tell you news, instead of *olds*.   I wrote the preceding page, seated

upon some boxes on deck, surrounded by the shipping and
beautiful houses of Genoa; an awning over my head, a fine
air in my face, and only comfortably warm, though the natives
themselves are complaining of the heat. (I have not forgotten, by the bye, that your family, Novello, came from
Piedmont, so that I am nearer to your old original country,
and to England too, than I was two or three weeks ago.) I
was called down from deck to Mrs. Hunt, who is very weak;
a winter passage would certainly have killed her. The
" Placidia " had a long passage for winter with rough winds;
and even the agitations of summer travelling are almost too
much for my wife; nor has that miserable spitting of blood
ceased at all. But we hope much from rest at Pisa.. As for
the " Jane," she encountered a violent storm in the Gulf of
Lyons which laid her on her side, and did her great injury.
Only think—as the young ladies say. Captain Whitney was
destined after all to *land* me in Italy, for the " Jane " is here,
and he accompanied me yesterday evening when I first went
on shore. I found him a capital *cicerone*, and he seemed pleased
to perform the office. My sensations on first touching the
shore I cannot express to you. Genoa is truly *la superba*.
Imagine a dozen Hampsteads one over the other, intermingled
with trees, rock, and white streets, houses, and palaces.
The harbour lies at the foot in a semicircle, with a quay full
of good houses and public buildings. Bathers, both male
and female, are constantly going by our vessel of a morning
in boats with awnings, both to a floating bath, and to swim
(*i. e.*, the male) in the open sea. They return dressing themselves as they go, with an indelicacy, or else delicacy, very
startling to us Papalengis. The ladies think it judicious to
conceal their absolute ribs; but a man (whether gentleman
or not I cannot say) makes nothing of putting on his shirt,
as he returns; or even of alfrescoing it without one, as he
goes; and people, great and small, are swimming about us in
all directions. The servant, a jolly Plymouth damsel (for
Elizabeth was afraid to go on), thinks it necessary to let us
know that she takes no manner of interest in such spectacles.
I had not gone through a street or two on shore before I had
the luck to meet a religious procession, the last this season.

Good God ! what a thing ! It consisted, *imprimis*, of soldiers; secondly, of John the Baptist, four years of age, in a sheep-skin ; thirdly, of the Virgin, five or six ditto, with a crown on her head, led by two ladies ; fourthly, friars—the young ones (with some fine faces among them) looking as if they were in earnest, and rather melancholy—the others apparently getting worldly, sceptical, and laughing in proportion as they grew old ; fifthly, a painting of St. Antonio ; sixthly, monks with hideous black cowls all over their faces, with holes to look through ; seventhly, a crucifix as large as life, well done (indeed, every work of art here has an *air* of that sort if nothing else) ; eighthly, more friars, holding large wax-lights, the ends of which were supported, or rather pulled down, by the rag-gedest and dirtiest boys in the city, who collect the dropping wax in paper and sell it for its virtues; ninthly, music, with violins ; tenthly and lastly, a large piece of waxwork, carried on a bier by a large number of friars, who were occasionally encouraged by others to trot stoutly (for a shuffling trot is their pace), and representing St. Antonio paying homage to the Virgin, both as large as life, surrounded with lights and artificial flowers, and seated on wax clouds and cherubim. It would have made me melancholy had not the novelty of everything and the enormous quantity of women of all ranks diverted my thoughts. The women are in general very plain, and the men too, though less so ; but when you do meet with fine faces, they are fine indeed ; and the ladies are apt to have a shape and air very consoling for the want of better features. But my trembling hands, as well as the paper, tell me that I must leave off, and that I have gone, like Gilpin, "farther than I intended." God bless you, dear friends. La Sposa and you must get me up a good long letter. My wife sends her best remembrances. Your ever affectionate friend,

L. H.

To V. N. and M. S. N. (By favour of Mrs. Williams.)

Pisa, September 9th, 1822.

DEAR, KIND FRIENDS,—The lady who brings you this is the widow of Lieutenant Williams. You know the dreadful calamity we have sustained here—an unspeakable one to me

as well as to her ; but we are on every account obliged and
bound to be as patient as possible under it. The nature of
the friends we have lost at once demands it and renders it
hard. I have reason to be thankful that I have suffered so
much in my life, since the habit renders endurance more
tolerable in the present instance. Think of me as of one
going on altogether very well, and who still finds a reason in
everything for reposing on those who love him.

Mrs. Williams wishes to know you, and from what I have
seen and heard of her is worthy to do so. My departed
friend had a great regard for her. She is said to be an
elegant musician, but she has not had the heart to touch an
instrument since I have known her. Distance and other
scenes will doubtless show her the necessity of breaking
through this tender dread. There is something peculiar in
her history which she will one day perhaps inform you of, but
I do not feel myself at liberty to disclose it, though it does her
honour. When she relates it, you will do justice to my
reasons for keeping silence. I envy her the sight of you, the
hearing of the piano, the sharing of your sofa, the bookcase
on the right hand, the stares of my young old acquaintances,
&c. But I still hope to see the best part of these movables
in Italy. I dare not dwell upon the break-up that was given
here to all the delights I had anticipated. Lord B. is very
kind, and I *may* possibly find a new acquaintance or two that
will be pleasant ; but what can fill up the place that such a
man as S. occupied in my heart ? Thank God it has places
still occupied by other friends, or it would be well content to
break at once against the hardness of this toiling world. But
let me hold on. It is a good world still while it is capable of
producing such friends. I must also tell you, to comfort you
for all this dreary talking, that we have abundance of materials for our new work, the last packet for the first number of
which goes to England this week.

I can also work in this climate better than in England, and
my brother and I are such correspondents again as we ought
to be. This is much. My wife also is much better, and I
hear good accounts of her sister and other dear friends. I
had heard of the Lambs and their ultra voyages, with what

pleasure at first and with what melancholy at last, you may guess. Remember me to all the kind friends who send me *their* remembrances—Mr Clarke, Mr. Holmes, and particularly the Gliddons, whom I recollect with a tenderness which they will give me credit for when they see—what they shall see, to wit, the letter which accompanies the present one, and which I beg you will give them.

The work will very speedily be out now, entirely made up by Lord B., dear S., and myself. I refer you to it for some account of Pisa.

God bless you. A kiss for you, Mary, and a shake of the hand for you, Vincent.—Your affectionate friend,

L. H.

P.S.—We drank Novello's health on his birthday. Be sure that we always drink healths on birthdays.

The next seven are still from Italy, the concluding one showing how strong was his yearning to be back in dear old England.

To V. N.   (By favour of Mrs. Shelley.)

Albaro, July 24th, 1823.

MY DEAR NOVELLO,—Mary Wollstonecraft's daughter brings you this letter. I know you would receive her with all your kindness and respect for that designation alone; but there are a hundred other reasons why you will do so, including her own extraordinary talents (which, at the same time, no woman can be less obtrusive with), the pleasure you will find in her society, and last not least, her love of music and regard for a certain professor of ditto—but I have spoken of this introduction already. I do not send you a long letter, for reasons given in the same place ; but I trust it will be as good as a long letter in its returns to *me*, because it sets you the example of writing a short one when you cannot do more. How I envy Mary Shelley the power of taking you all by the hands and joining your kind-hearted circle ! But I am there very often myself, I assure you ; invisible, it is true, and behind the curtain ; but it is possible, you know, to be behind a curtain and yet be very intensely present besides. But do not let any one consider Mary S. in the light of a Blue, of which she has a great horror, but as an unaffected person, with her faults and good qualities like the rest of us ; the former extremely corrected by all she has seen and endured, the latter inclining her, like a wise and kind being, to receive all the consolation which the good and the kind can give her. She will be grave with your gravities and laugh as much as you please with your merriments. For the rest, she is as quiet as a mouse, and will drink in as much Mozart and Paesiello as you choose to afford her, with an enjoyment that you might take for a Quaker's, unless you could contrive some day to put her into a state of pain, when she will immediately grow as eloquent and say as many fine pleasurable things as she can discourse in a novel.

God bless you, dear Novello. From Florence I shall send you some music, especially what you wanted in Rome.

From this place I can send you nothing except a ring of my hair, which you must wear for the sake of your affectionate friend,

L. H.

To Mr. and Mrs. Novello and Mr. and Mrs. Gliddon, *imprimis:* secondly, to Mrs. Novello alone. (Favoured by Mrs. Shelley.)

Albaro, July 25th, 1823.

DEAR FRIENDS,—I send you these modicums of distributive justice - first because, though now getting well again, I have been unwell, and secondly, because I have so much to do with my pen just now that, as I wish to keep a head on my shoulders for all your sakes, I am sure you would not willingly let me tax it beyond my strength. I shall answer, however, whatever letters you have been kind enough to send me by the box separately and at proper length. But lo ! the box has not yet arrived, and when it will arrive *box* knows. Meanwhile let me introduce to you all in a body the dear friend who brings you this letter, and with whom you are already acquainted in some measure both privately and publicly. You will show her all the kindness and respect in your power, I am sure, for her husband's sake, and for her mother's sake, and for my sake, and for her own. I am getting grave here. So now we are all in company again I will rouse my spirits and attack you separately ; and first for " Wilful Woman :"—

> Mary Novello,
> I know not your fellow
> For having your way
> Both by night and by day.

It was thus I once began a letter in verse to the said Mary Novello, which happened not to be sent ; and it is thus I now begin a letter in prose to her because it is of course as applicable as ever—is it not, thou " wilful woman "? (Here I look full in the face of the same M. N., shaking my head at her : upon which she looks *ditta* at me—for we cannot say ditto of a lady—and shakes her head in return, imprudently denying the fact with her good-humoured, twinkling eyes and her laughing mouth, which, how it ever happened to become wilful, *odd* only knows—odd is to be read in a genteel Bond Street style, Novello knows how.) So I understand, Wilful, that you sometimes get up during the perusal of passages of these mine epistles and unthinkingly insist that tired ladies who have a regard for you should eat their dinners, as if the regard for me, Wilful, is not to swallow up everything—appetite, hunger, sickness, faintness, and all. Do you HEAR? The best passage in all Mr. Reynolds's plays is one that Mary Shelley has reminded me of. It is where a gentleman traveller and the governor of a citadel compliment each other in a duet, dancing, I believe, at the same time :—

> *Dancing* Governor !
> *Pleasing* Traveller !

Now you must know that the Attorney-General once, in an indictment for libel, had the temerity to designate me as " a yeoman "—" Leigh Hunt, yeoman." However, the word rhymes to " Woman," which is a pleasing response : so I shall end my present epistle with imagining you and me on a Twelfth Night harmoniously playing at cross purposes, and singing to one another—

Wilful Woman !
Revengeful Yeoman !

God bless the hearts of you both.—Your affectionate friend,

LEIGH HUNT.

P.S.—I send you a ring of my hair, value 2*s.* 8*d*. When I can afford another such splendid sum I will try and get some little inscription engraved on it, and would have done so indeed already had I thought of it in time. I'd have you to know, at the same time, that the gold is "right earnest," which, if you mention the sum, I'd be glad you'll also let the curious inquirers understand. So don't be ashamed, now, but wear it. If you don't I'll *pinch back*.

The ring *was* worn by " Mary Novello," and the name of " Leigh Hunt" was engraved upon the small piece of " gold" as an " inscription." It is now in our possession, mounted on a card, bearing these memorial lines :—

SONNET ON A RING OF LEIGH HUNT'S HAIR.

Nor coal, nor jet, nor raven's wing more black
  Than this small crispy plait of ebon hair :
  And well I can remember when the rare
Young poet-head, in eager thought thrown back,
Bore just such clusters ; ere the whitening rack
  Of years and toil, devoted to the care
  For human weal, had blanch'd and given an air
Of snow-bright halo to the mass once black.
In public service, in high contemplations,
  In poesy's excitement, in the earnest
Culture of divinest aspirations,
Thy sable curls grew grey ; and now thou turnest
Them to radiant lustre, silver-golden,
Touch'd by that Light no eye hath yet beholden.

To M. S. N.

Albaro, August 21st, 1823.

WILFUL WOMAN !—And so you have got a great, large,

big Shacklewell house, and a garden, and good-natured trees in it (like those in my Choice)—

> And Clarke and Mr. Holmes are seen
> Peeping from forth their alleys green ;

and you are looking after the " things," and you are all to be gay and merry, and I am not to be there. Well, I don't deserve it, whatever Fate may say, and it shall go hard but I'll have my revenge, and *my* house, and *my* garden and things, all at Florence ; and friends, fair and brown too, will come to see me there, though you won't ; and I'll peep, *without* being seen, from forth *my* alleys green.

We go off to-morrow, and I shall send you such accounts as shall make you ready to ask Clara's help (she being the bigger) to toss you all, as she threatened, " out of the windows." There is nobody that will do it with so proper and grave a face.   So there's for your Shacklewell house and your never-not-coming-at-all to Italy.   And now you shan't get a word more out of me for the present, excepting that I am your old, grateful, and affectionate friend,

LEIGH HUNT.

Mrs. Hunt joins in love to all the old circle.

To V. N. (favoured by Mrs. Payne.)

Florence, Sept. 9th, 1823.

MY DEAR NOVELLO,—You must not imagine I am going to send you all the pleasant people I may happen to meet with ; but I could not resist the chance of introducing you to the grand-daughter of Dr. Burney, daughter of Captain Cooke's Burney, niece of Evelina's and Camilla's Burney, friend of Charles and Mary Lamb, and a most lively, refreshing, intelligent, good-humoured person to boot, who is also a singer and pianoforte-player.   All this, at least, she seems to me, in my gratitude for having met with a countrywoman who could talk to me of my old friends.   I cannot write farther, for I hear the voices of gentlemen who have come to go with me, to take leave of her and her husband : but whether she happens to bring this letter or not, I could not help giving you the chance I speak of, nor her that of know-

ing you and yours, your music, &c., which is the best return
I can make her for the recreation she has afforded me : and,
besides, this will show you we were going on well.   Florence,
besides its other goods, has libraries, bookstalls, and Cockney meadows ; and we begin to breathe again.   I hope by
this time you and Mrs. Shelley have shaken cordial hands.

Your affectionate friend,
L. H.

To V. N. and M. S. N.
Florence, January 9th, 1824.

Happy New Years for all of us : and may we all, as we do
now, help to make them happier to one another.

Vincenzo mio, I have at length found out the secret of
making you write a whole letter.   It is to set you upon some
painful task for your friends ; so having the prospect now
before me of getting out of my troubles, I think I must contrive to fall into some others, purely in order that you may be
epistolary.   Dear Novello, how heartily I thank you !   I
must tell you that I had written a long letter to my brother
in answer to his second one, in which I had agreed to submit
the whole matter to arbitration, and had called upon your
friendship to enter into it, especially in case you had any
fears that you should be obliged in impartiality to be less for
me than you wished.   His third letter has done away with
the necessity of sending this, and he will show you the letter
I have written to him instead.   All will now proceed amicably ;
but if you think me a little too inordinate and haggling, I beg
you first of all to count the heads of seven of your children
with their mother besides them.   I have no other arithmetic
in my calculations.   But I will not return to my melancholy
now that you have helped to brighten life for me again.   I
assure you it was new-burnished on New Year's Day, for then
I received all your letters at once. . . . But enough.   Judge
only from what a load of care you have helped to relieve me,
and take your pride and pleasure accordingly, you, you—you
Vincent, you.   Observe, however :—all this is not to hinder from
the absolute necessity and sworn duty o coming to see us as
you promised.   *It will be sheer inhumanity if you do not;*

always excepting it would make you ill to be away from home (Mary Shelley will laugh to hear this) ; but then you are to have companions, who will also be very inhuman to all of us, if they do not do *their* duty. The cheating of the Italians in conjunction with all the other circumstances have made us frightened, or rather agreeably economical (a little difference !). We have taken wood, oil, and every possible thing out of the hands of the servants, locking it up and doling it out, and even (oh, new and odd paradise of sensation !) chuckling over the *crazie and quattrini* that we save. I tell you this to show you how well we prepare for visitors. But wine, and very pleasant wine too, and wholesome, is as cheap in this country as small beer ; and then there will be ourselves, and *your* selves, and beautiful walks and weather, and novelty, and God knows how many pleasures besides, for all are comprised in the thought of seeing friends from *England*. So mind—I will not hear of the least shadow of the remotest approach to the smallest possible distant hint of a put-off. All the "Gods in Council" would rise up and say, "This is a shame !" So in your next tell me when you are coming. I must only premise that it must be when the snows are well off the mountain road. You see by this how early, as well as how certainly, I expect you. I must leave off and rest a little ; for I have had much letter-writing after much other writing, and I am going to have much *other* writing. But my head and spirits have both bettered with my prospects ; at least the latter have, and I have every reason to believe the former will, though I shall have more original composition to do than of late. But I shall work with *certainties* upon me, in my old paper, and not be tied down to particular dimensions. As you have seen all my infirmities, I must tell you of a virtue of mine, which is, that having no pianoforte at present, I lent, with rage and benevolence in my heart, all the new music you sent me to a lady who is going to Rome. It is very safe, or you may believe my benevolence would not have gone so far. Besides, it was to be played and sung by the Pope's own musicians. Think of that, thou chorister. I shall have it back before you come, and shall lay aside a particular hoard to hire an instrument for your playing it.

Thank Charles Clarke for his letter, and tell him that he will be as welcome in Italy as he was in my less romantic prison of Horsemonger Gaol. I am truly obliged to him, also, for his kindness to Miss Kent's book, and shall write to tell him so after I have despatched a few articles for the *Examiner*— all which articles, observe also, are written to my friends.

Your affectionate friend,
LEIGH HUNT.

To Mrs. Novello.

Oh thou wilful—for art thou not wilful? Charles Clarke says no, and that your name is Brougham; "but I, Mr., calls him Bruffam"—but art thou not always wilful woman, and oughtest thou not for ever to remain so, seeing that thy will is bent upon "inditing a good matter," and that thou sittest up at midnight with an infinitely virtuous profligacy to write long and kind and delightful letters to exiles on their birthdays? Do not think me ungrateful for not having answered it sooner. It is not, as you might suppose, my troubles that have hindered me, saving and except that the quantity of writing that I have had, or rather the effect which writing day after day has upon me, made me put off an answer which I wished to be a very long one. Had I not wished that, I should have written sooner; and wishing it or not, I ought to have done so; but your last letter shows that you can afford to forgive me. Latterly, I will confess that the pitch of trouble to which my feelings had been wrought made it more difficult for me than usual to come into the company of my friends, with the air they have always inspired me with; but I bring as well as receive a pleasure now, and wish I could find some means of showing you how grateful I am for all your sendings, those in the box included. Good God! I have never yet thanked you even for that. But you know how late it must have come. My wife has been brilliant ever since in the steel bracelets, which she finds equally useful and ornamental. They were the joy and amazement of an American artist (now in Rome), who had never been in England, and who is wise enough to be proud of the superior workmanship of his cousins the English,

Q

though a sturdy Republican. (Speaking of Rome, pray tell Novello to send me the name of the musical work which he wanted there, which I have put away in some place so very safe that it is undiscoverable.) The needles also were more than welcome. As to the pencils, I made a legitimate use of my despotic right as a father of a family, and appropriated them almost all to myself. "Consider the value of such timber here." Here the needles don't prick, and the pencils do : and as to elastic bracelets, you may go to a ball, if you please, in a couple of rusty iron hoops made to fit. Do you know that I had half a mind to accept your offer of coming over to take us to England, purely that you might go back without us—including your stay in the meantime. You must not raise such images to exiles without realizing them. I hope some day or other to be able to take some opportunity of running over during a summer, though Mary Shelley will laugh at this, and I know not what Marianne Hunt would say to it. Profligate fellow that I am ! I never slept out of my bed ever since I was married, but two nights at Sydenham. As to coming to England to stay, it is quite out of the question for either of us at present. The winters would kill her side and my head. On the other hand, the vessel in her side is absolutely closing again here in winter-time, and our happier prospects in other respects render the prospect happier in this. Cannot you as well as C. C. come with Novello? Bring some of the children with you. Why cannot you all come—you and Statia, and Mrs. Williams, and Mary S., and Miss Kent, and Holmes (to study), and every other possible and impossible body? Write me another good, kind, long letter, to show that you forgive me heartily for not writing myself, and tell me all these and a thousand other things. I think of you all every day more or less, but particularly on such days as birthdays and Twelfthdays. We drank your health the other night sitting in our country solitude, and longing *infinitely*, as we often do, for a larger party—but always a party from home. What a birthnight you gave me ! These are laurels indeed ! Tell me in your next how all the children are, not forgetting Clara, who threatened in a voice of tender acquiescence to throw us all out of the window, herself included. All our children continue extremely well, little Vincent among them, who is one of the liveliest yet gentlest creatures in the world.

Pray remember me to Mr. and Mrs. B. H. I would give anything at present to hear one of her songs ; and I suppose she would give anything to have a little of my sunshine. Such is the world ! But it makes one love and help one another too. So love me and help me still, dear friends all.

L. H.

To M. S. N.

Florence, November 13th, 1824.

OH, WILFUL !—Am I to expect another birthday letter ? If so (but two such birthdays can hardly come together), I will do my best to be grateful, and send you a *mirth*-day letter. Do you know that however differently-shaped you may regard yourself at present at Shacklewell, here at Florence you are a *square?* and that I am writing at present in one of your second stories at Mrs. Brown's lodgings, who can only find me this half-sheet of paper to write upon ? I should have thought better of you, considering you have the literary interest so much at heart. ·Your name is *Sancta Maria Novella*, and there is a church in a corner of you, which makes a figure in the opening of Boccaccio's " Decameron." So adieu, dear Sancta.—Ever yours, sick or merry,

L. H.

To Mrs. Novello, to Mrs. Gliddon, to " dear Arthur."

Florence, September 7th, 1825.

The Ladies first—To Mrs. Novello.

MADAM,—My patience is not so easily worn out as your Wilfulship imagines. I allow you have seen me impatient of late on one subject ; but I beg you to believe I confine my want of philosophy to that single point. That is the wolf in my harmony. On all other matters (a three-years-and-a-half's dilapidation excepted) you will find me the same man I was ever—half melancholy and half mirth—and gratefully ready to forego the one whenever in the company of my friends.

Q

So, madam, I'd have you to know that I am extremely patient, and that if I do not *take* courage it is because I have it already; and you must farther know, madam, that we do not mean to live at Plymouth, but at a reasonable distance from town; and also that if we cannot get a cottage to go into immediately we shall go for a month or two into metropolitan lodgings: *item*, that we shall all be glad to hear of any cottage twenty or twenty-five miles off, or any lodgings in any quiet and cheap street in London; farthermore, that, besides taking courage, we have taken the coach from Florence to Calais; and finally, that we set off next Saturday, the 10th instant, and by the time you receive this shall be at the foot of the Alps. "I think here be proofs." We go by Parma, Turin, Mont Cenis, Lyons, and Paris. Mrs. Shelley will be better able to tell you where a letter can reach us than I can—yet a calculation, too, might be made, for we travel forty miles a day, and stop four days out of the thirty-one allotted to us: one at Modena, one at Turin, one at Lyons, one at Paris. Can we do anything for you? I wish I could bring you some bottled sunshine for your fruit-trees. It is a drug we are tired of here. Mud—mud—is our object; cold weather out of doors, and warm hearts within. By the way, as you know nothing about it, I must tell you that somebody has been dedicating a book to me under the title of "A Day in Stowe Gardens" (send and buy it for my sake), and it is a very pretty book, though with the airs natural to a dedicatee, I have picked some verbal faults with it here and there. What I like least is the story larded with French cookery. Some of the others made me shed tears, which is very hard upon me, from an Old Boy (for such on inspection you will find the author to be); I should not have minded it had it been a woman. The Spanish Tale ends with a truly dramatic surprise; and the Magdalen Story made me long to hug all the parties concerned, the writer included. So get the book, and like it, as you regard the sympathies and honours of yours, ever cordially,

L. H.

To Mrs. Gliddon.

Well, madam. and as to you. They tell me you are getting rich : so you are to suppose that during my silence I have been standing upon the dignity of my character, as a poor patriot, and not chosen to risk a suspicion of my independence. Being " Peach-Face," and " Nice-One," and missing your sister's children, I might have ventured to express my regard ; but how am I to appear before the rich lady and the Sultana ? I suppose you never go out but in a covered litter, forty blacks clearing the way. Then you enter the bath, all of perfumed water, and beautiful attendant slaves, like full moons : after which you retire into a delicious apartment, walled with trellis-work of mother-of-pearl, covered with myrtle and roses, and whistling with a fountain ; and clapping your hands, ten slaves more beautiful than the last serve up an unheard-of dinner : after which, twenty slaves, much more beautiful than those, play to you upon lutes ; after which the Sultan comes in, upon which thirty slaves, infinitely more beautiful than the preceding, sing the most exquisite compliments out of the Eastern poets, and a pipe, forty yards long, and fresh from the Divan, is served up, burning with the Sultan's mixture, and the tonquin bean. However, I shall come for a chop.

DEAR MR. ARTHUR,—I am called off in the midst of my oriental description. and have only time to say that I thank you heartily for your zeal and kindness in my behalf, and am sure Novello could not have chosen a second more agreeable to myself, whatever the persons concerned may resolve upon. I hope soon to shake you by the hand.

The following one affords a specimen of the manful way in which Leigh Hunt dealt with depression, and strove to be cheery for his friends' sake, in acknowledgment of their friendship for him :—

To V. N. and M. S. N.

Paris, October 8th, 1825.

DEAR FRIENDS,—I can write you but a word. We shall

be in London next Thursday, provided there is room in the steamboat, as we understand there certainly will be ; but we are not certain of the hour of arrival.   They talk here at the agency office of the boats leaving Calais at two in the morning (night-time).   If so, we ought to be in town at one.   This, however, is not to be depended on ; and there will not be time to write to you again.   The best way, I think, would be to send a note for us (by the night post) to the place where the boat puts up, stating where the lodgings are.   The lodgings you will be kind enough to take for us (if there is time) in the quietest and airiest situation you have met with.   We prefer, for instance, the street in the Hampstead Road, or thereabouts, to the one in London Street, to which said street I happen to have a particular objection ; said particular objection, however, being of no account, if it cannot be helped.   Should any circumstance prevent our having a note at the boat-office we shall put up in the neighbourhood for the night, and communicate with you as fast as possible. . . . . I write in ill spirits, which the sight of your faces, and the firm work I have to set about, will do away. I feel that the only way to settle these things is to meet and get through them, sword in hand, as stoutly as I may.   If I delayed 1 might be pinned for ever to a distance, like a fluttering bird to a wall, and so die in that helpless yearning. I have been mistaken.   During my strength my weakness, perhaps, only was apparent ; now that 1 am weaker, indignation has given a fillip to my strength.   But how am I digressing !   I said 1 should only write a word, and I certainly did not intend that that word should be upon any less agreeable subject than a steamboat.   Yet I must add, that I remember the memorandum you allude to about the balance. 1 laid it to a very different account !   Lord ! Lord !   Well, my dear Vincent, you have a considerable fool for your friend, but one who is nevertheless wise enough to be, very truly yours,

L. H.

P.S.—Thanks to the two Marys for their kind letters.   I must bring them the answers myself.   This is what women ought to do. They ought to be very kind and write, and read books, and go about through the mud for their friends.

The three next give an excellent idea of Leigh Hunt's manner of writing to a friend suffering from nervous illness: by turns remonstrating, rallying, urging, humouring, consoling, and strengthening —all done tenderly, and with true affection for the friend addressed :—

To V. N.

30, Hadlow Street, Dec. 6th, 1825.

MY DEAR NOVELLO,—I expected you at Harry Robertson's, and I looked for you last fine Wednesday at Highgate, and I have been to seek you to-day at Shacklewell. I thought we were sometimes to have two Sabbaths, always one, and I find we have none. How is this? If you are not well enough to meet me at Highgate, and will not make yourself better by coming and living near your friends somewhere, why I must come to you at Shacklewell on a Wednesday, that's all; and come I will, unless you will have none of me. I should begin to have fears on that score, when I hear that you are in town twice a week, and yet never come near me; but in truth, coxcomb as I have been called, and as I sometimes fear I show myself when I talk of prevailing on my friends to do this and that, *this* is a blow which would really be too hard for the vanity of, and let me add, the affection of your ever true friend,

LEIGH HUNT.

Will you not give us a call this evening, and at what time? Have I not a chop for a friend? And is there not Souchong in the town of Somers?

To Vincent Novello.

[No date.]

MY DEAR NOVELLO,—As I am not sure that you were at Mrs. Shelley's last night, I write this to let you know that a violent cold, which I am afraid of tampering with any longer, has kept me at home the two last evenings, and will do the same on this. I defied it for some nights, but found myself under the necessity, on every account, of doing so no longer. You know how bad it was on Wednesday ; but Wednesday night's return home made it worse. I repent this the more, because I wish to see you very much. I want to chat with you on the musical and other matters, and to assent to my privilege of a friend in doing all I can to make you adopt certain measures I have in view equally useful to both of us, for the recovery of your health. I said equally pleasant, and I trust and feel certain they would be so in the long-run ; but undoubtedly in the first instance you might find them painful. However, as I never yet found an obstacle like this stand in your way when a friend was to be obliged, I give you notice that you have spoilt me in that matter, and that I shall not expect it now.

" Hunt, you are very kind, but—" Novello, so are you ; and therefore I do not expect to be put off with words. Besides, did I not have a long conversation the other evening with Mary ? And did she not promise me, like a good wife as she was, not to listen to a word you had to say ? I mean, against putting yourself in the best possible position for recovering your health. Or rather, did she not say, with good wifely tears in her eyes, that she would let you do all you pleased, which of course ties up your hands—only she hoped you would think as I did, if it was really as much for your good as I supposed—which of course ties them up more ? And does not all that she has said, and all that I have said, and all that I mean to say, (which is quite convincing, I assure you, in case you are not convinced already, as you ought to be,) prove to you that you must leave that dirty Shacklewell, that wet Shacklewell, that flat, floundering and foggy Shacklewell, that distant, out-of-the-way, dreary, unfriendly, unheard-of, melancholy, moping, unsocial, unmusical, un-meeting, uneveningy, un-Hunt-helping, unimproper, un-Glid-dony, un-Kentish-towny, un-Hampsteady, un-Hadlowincial, far, foolish, faint, fantastical, sloppy, hoppy, moppy, brick-fieldy, bothery, mothery, misty, muddling, meagre, megrim, Muggletonian, dim, dosy, booty, cold-arboury, plashy, mashy, squashy, Old-Street-Roady, Balls-Pondy, Hoxtony, hurtful, horrid, lowering, lax, languid, musty, sepulchral, shameful, washy, dim, cold, sulky, subterraneous, sub-and-supra-lapsarian, whity-brown, clammy, sick, silent, cheap, expensive, blameable, gritty, hot, cold, wheezy, vapourish, inconsequential, what-next?-y, go-to-beddy, lumpish, glumpish, mumpish, frumpish, pumpish, odd, thievish, coining, close-keeping, chandlering, drizzling, mizzling, duck-weedy, rotting, perjured, forsaking, flitting, bad, objected-to, false, cold-potatoey, inoperative, dabby, draggle-tailed, shambling, huddling, indifferent, spiteful, meek, milk-and-watery, inconvenient, lopsided, dull, doleful, damnable Shacklewell. Come, "I think here be proofs."

Ever dear N.'s affectionate

L. H.

P.S.—I know not what Holmes thinks of Shacklewell; but he can hardly have an opinion in favour of it after this Rabelais argument. Clarke is bound to side with all friends at a distance.

To V. N.

Hadlow Street, 19th January, 1826.

MY DEAR NOVELLO,—Pray do not think that I did, or shall, or ever can feel angry at my friend's ill-health. I have suffered bitterly from ill-health myself; and know too well, even now, what it is. If I have plagued you at all about Shacklewell, or anything else, I can do so no more when you talk to me thus; especially when I see you doing what you so much dislike, to gratify your friends. I recognize there my old friend triumphant, however he may suffer for a time. That you suffer extremely I doubt not, being in the agony of the passage from one mode of diet and living to another—a voyage enough to shake the most Ancient Mariner. But believe one who speaks from experience—that these things have an end. A little medicine will, I doubt not, do you good, especially if you follow it up with some appeals to natural remedies—such as walking, early rising, etc. Upon early rising (always speaking from experience) I think the very greatest stress ought to be laid, and I reserve this one subject to plague you upon—always provided that you get up to a warm fire and speedy and good breakfast. Do not plague yourself till you are better about coming to me. I will, in the meantime, come to you on your own Sundays as well as mine, and I am sorry I cannot do so on Sunday next. Suffer not a moment's uneasiness about the Lambs. They will set all down to the very best account, depend upon it; and, besides, you were as cheerful, and more so, than anybody could reasonably expect from a sick man ; and your going away was no more than what Lamb does himself.

The necessity of being heroical under nervousness, tensions of the head, and "other gentilities" (as Metastasio has it) is, says he, a great nuisance. But he got over them : so have I, and so will you; so have hundreds of others. The thing is common when people come to compare notes. Lady Suffolk, who had a head of this sort, and lived to see a tranquil old age, said she never knew a head without them "that was worth anything." Think of that ; and she knew the wits and poets of two generations. Love to dear Mary and dear Vincent.

From their truly affectionate friend,
LEIGH HUNT.

The following was addressed to Mrs. Vincent Novello, when her husband and she and three of their children went to the seaside near Hastings :—

To the Queen of Little Bohemia.

Highgate, 1st August, 1826

GYPSY,—I know not what there is in this word gypsy, but somehow or other it makes me very tender, and if I were near you, I should be obliged to turn round and ask Vincent's permission to give you a considerable thump on the blade-bone. I believe it is the association of ideas with tents, green fields, and black eyes—a sort of Mahomedan heaven upon earth—very touching to my unsophisticated notions. I wish we were all of us gypsies ; I mean all of us who have a value for one another ; and that we could go seeking health and happiness without a care up all the green lanes in England, half gypsy and half gentry, with books instead of pedlary. I should prefer working for three or four hours of a morning, if it were only to give the rest of the day a greater zest ; then we would dine early, chat or read under the trees, tea early (I think we must have some tea), and so to stray about by starlight if it is fine, and sit and hug ourselves with the thought of being well sheltered from the rain on a dripping night. I don't think we would have candles. Our hours should be too good. Up with the lark, fresh air, green bowers, russetin-apple cheeks—why the devil doesn't the world live in this manner, or allow honest people to do so that would? Oh, but we must wait a long while first, if ever; and meanwhile we must have a great number of children ("Leigh Hunt for instance—just so"), purely to worry our-selves about more than will ever do them any good ; and we must have a vast number of fine clothes, and visitors, and cooks (to provide us with all the fever we have not got already), and Doctors, and gossips, and tabernacle , and cheese-cakes, and other calamities; and we must all sacrifice ourselves for our children, and they must all sacrifice them-selves for theirs, and they for theirs, and so on to the third and fourth generation of them that worry us, wondering all the while (poor devils ! both we and they) how it is that so much good love and good will (for there the sting lies, that the unhappiness should arise out of the very love on all sides) does not hit upon modes of existence a little discreeter. Only let the world *come to me*—leave me alone with him, as the lady said ; and *I'd* teach him how to make his children grateful, what pleasures to substitute for his cookery, and how he should cultivate mind and muscle by a pleasing alterna-tion. But I am getting moral, and I am sure I didn't intend to be so. Don't think ill of me. I intended in this letter to be all full of pleasure, as I should be if we could do as I say. As to the cookery and all that, I sometimes fear that the theories of Vincent's friends (which, between you and my conscience, are much better than their practice) set him upon an extreme of diet which has done him no good, and which it might be to his advantage to contradict a little more. He did himself harm by great sudden gulps of dinner and tea (no man being less of a gourmand than he was), rendered more hurtful by long fasting and overwork ; and I sometimes fear he too suddenly went counter to all this. Well, patience is a rascally necessity, as the poet said, and he has enough of it ; but patience is rewarded at last. We have such miraculous accounts in the newspapers of cures of the spirits as well as body effected by the gymnastic exercises now spreading abroad, that I cannot help wishing Vincent would give them a trial when he returns ; especially as in spite of the fat he had, I remember he used to be very active, and a vaulter over gates. So now, gypsy, stand in awe of me and my knowledge (which is what I like on the part of the sex), and then, sus-pecting me nevertheless to be not a jot more awful than yourself (rather the reverse, if you knew all), give me the most insolent pinch of the cheek you can think of (which is what I like much better), and in spite of all my airs and assumptions, keep for me one of the little corners that a large heart like yours possesses, and there let me occupy it when I please, with " dear Mr. Arthur," and dearer Statia, and one or two others who would willingly hold the rest of it, and its inmate among them, in their affectionate arms, till he got well and made us all happy again.

Ever most truly yours,
Leigh Hunt.

P.S.—Pray write again speedily, and we will be better boys and girls, and rewrite instantly. . . . Oh, the letters of Lady Suffolk and the Genlis which you ought to have had long ago. I send them now, with one or two other works which I think may amuse you, and a proof sheet of an article of mine (the Dictionary of Love and Beauty), which you must take with all its mistakes of the press on its head. . . . Marianne begs her kindest remembrances. She is very well and in excellent spirits, with the exception of a swollen eye, given her by that mysterious personage called a Blight. I tell her it looks very conjugal ; and yet I am sure I ought not to tell her so, but I may tell her that it is " all *my* eye." Do you remember the Merry Wives of Tavistock ? Statia and she are at present the Merry Wives of Highgate. We only want the other Tavistock one in good spirits again to beat the Windsor ones hollow.

The next is a very characteristic example of one of his playful notes of invitation :—

To V. N., Great Queen Street.

Sunday morning, 27th Dec. [Query 1828].

MY DEAR VINCENT,—Tho' it is very proper that people should go out in cold weather to see their friends, it does not appear to me quite so proper that they should go out after dinner as before ; *ergo*, this comes to say that I hope, in consideration of the frost and snow, you will come at three to-morrow instead of five. I will treat you *exactly* as you treated me, therefore there is to be no excuse on that score. If anybody prefers it, I will not treat them so well; they shall have a cold potatoe at a sideboard, with their feet in a pail of water. So pray come. Our meeting will be two hours the earlier ; and not to dine with me, under all the circumstances, would be indecent.

Ever truly yours,
LEIGH HUNT.

COME AT 3 (a placard *yell*, or Clarke whisper).

P.S.—l find that my *exactly* is not quite exact. There is to be a piece of boiled beef to-morrow ; but then we have mutton to-day, which will be conveniently cold for those who prefer the worse fare. By the way I hope you all like boiled beef. I think I recollect that you and Mary do, but not so sure of the Clarkes. I must presume, with them, upon the ground of its being generally liked.

The three following, being sent from " Cromwell Lane," are grouped together ; but no date being affixed to them, it is difficult to trace the period when they were written :—

To M. S. N. (66, Queen Street.)

Cromwell Lane, Dec. 23rd, Wednesday.

DEAR MARY,—By a miraculous chance I slept from home on Monday night, and did not get your letter till the night following ; so that you must consider this as an answer by return of post. I shall come with the greatest pleasure to-morrow at three and pay my respects to you all, and to my old friend Bacchus senior. Is there any Septuor? However, that is not necessary. There will at all events be a Quatuor (you and Vincent, Charles Clarke and Victorinella), and any two of you would make a good duet, to say nothing of a *soul-o*. I am glad you like my verses so well. Marianne begs her love and hopes to see you soon. It is lucky that I had not time to be tempted into the Requiem, for besides what you say, there are too many thoughts on certain subjects pass thro' my mind on these occasions, and put me into a state unsuitable both to the dignity of my philosophy and the cheerfulness of my hopes; so there is a pretty sound period for you. I shall compliment myself by saying that I should have felt the Requiem too much as Mozart did himself; and greatly for the same reason; to wit, that my liver is not in good condition. If it be thought too vain to have even a liver in common with Mozart, tell Vincent it is owing to his flattery of me in the postscript. To be serious I never see his hand but it seems to come with a blessing upon me, like that of one of your Catholic priests,—only sincere:—a Thais, only not vicious. You remember, I suppose, whose pleasant passage this last sentence alludes to.

Dear Wilful (for I cannot part with any of my old ways) I am heartily thine.

LEIGH HUNT.

To M. S. N.

Cromwell Lane, Feb. 18.

DEAR MARY,—You have seen by the *Tatler* how acceptable your critical epistle was; but how you must have wondered, with all your breakfast-table, at the signature "Manthele"! I have fancied you have been saying fifty times in your heart, "What the devil does he mean by 'Manthele'"?—for ladies, you know, do say "what the devil" in their hearts, though it may not be quite bad enough for their tongues. (There; that is a dramatic surprise for you, very ingenious; for you thought I was going to say "not quite good enough," which I own would have been less proper.) Well, Manthele should have been Melanthe (dark flower): I tbought "an amateur" not so well, because it is pretty to see ladies' letters distinguished by ladies' names, and so I thought I would give you a nice horticultural one, such as you would like ; and I wrote or rather printed it in capitals, that there might be no mistake ; and Mr. Reynolds tells me that he saw it right in the proof. He says the letters must have subsequently fallen out, when going to press, and been huddled back loosely. Never apologize, dear Mary, about books : for then what am *I* to do ? Keep them, an you love me, and I shall think I am obliging somebody. Do you know there is somebody in the world, who owes me tenpence ? It is a woman at Finchley. I bought two-pennyworth of milk of her one day, to give a draught to Marianne ; and she hadn't change ; so I left a shilling with her, and cunningly said I should call. Now I never *shall* call, improvident as you may think it : so that upon the principle of compound interest, her great-great-grandchildren or *their* great-great, or whichever great it is, will owe my posterity several millions of money. This, I hope, will give you a lively sense of the shrewdness which experience has taught me. Love, love, and ten times love, to dear Vincent.

Ever sincerely yours,
LEIGH HUNT.

To Mary Cowden Clarke
Thursday night, Cromwell Lane.

DEAR VICTORIA,—(For I have been used to call you so, Mary being your name in heaven, but Victoria that upon earth—

In heaven yclept "my own Mary,"
But on earth heart-easing Vic.)

I conclude from Charles' letter and your own searching eyes, that you saw the announcement of the verses in the *Tatler*. Be good enough therefore to inspire your husband, if you please, with some of his best rhymes on the spot, for a reason which he will tell you ; and believe me,

For your kind words and attentions,

Your truly obliged friend,
LEIGH HUNT.

The two next short notes are given as specimens of Leigh Hunt's affectionate, bright, off-hand style of writing a mere few lines to his friends :—

To M. S. N.

Wednesday, July 11.

DEAR NOVELLA,—Many thanks for your lemons, and many more for your inquiries and kind attentions. We have had some heart-tugging work since I saw Novello in the streets. Both Mary and baby have been in danger, the former for a short time, the latter moaning for two nights and a day with the anguish of acute inflammatory fever :—but you know all this sort of trouble, and more : nor would I say anything to bring any more tears into your eyes, but that I owe you a true account how we go on; and even tears are good things in this world, after a time :—they help to melt us all into one heart. God bless you and all our friends. I hope to enjoy them again shortly, and still reckon myself getting better.

Your affectionate friend,
LEIGH HUNT.

P.S.—The danger is now over.

To Charles Cowden Clarke.

Saturday, Dec. 29, 66, Great Queen Street.

THOU COWDEN,—Will you vouchsafe to step down here, and confer with me half an hour or so respecting a certain unborn acquaintance of yours yclept the Companion?—and if you cannot come directly, will you say at what hour before 8 o'clock you can come ; or whether you can or cannot come at all this afternoon ?—for time presses upon a project I have in my head, because of the New Year.

Truly yours,
L. H.

The next is a notelet that drolly mimics the flourishing and superlative style used in Italian letter-writing, and gives a whimsically literal translation of "Cowden" into "*Spelonca delle Vacche :*"—

To. C. C. C.

[No date.]

(Address :)   All 'ornatissimo Signore il Signor
Carlo *Spelonca delle Vacche.*

Signor Carlo,

Amico mio osservantissimo,

Have you heard anything of this confounded quarterly payment? (Don't you like this plunge out of the Italian amenity into Damme-by-G-d English?)

Very sincerely yours,

L. H.

The following is an exquisite example of a poet-friend's candour in criticism and even objection, combined with the most refined and affectionate praise, when sent a MS. copy of some of the verses that subsequently were printed in a small volume entitled " Carmina minima :"—

To C. C. C.

5, York Buildings, New Road, Dec. 13th.

MY DEAR CLARKE,—I beg your acceptance of a copy of my book. I do not send one to Vincent, because tho' he is one of the few friends to whom one of my few copies, sent in this manner, would otherwise have gone, he is among its patrons and purchasers, and therefore, I must, even out of my sense of his kindness, omit him. But tho' it is not altogether out of his power to stretch a point for me in this way with his purse, I dare to tell you that I know it to be yours and that your generosity, equally real with his but unequal to show itself in the same manner, will give me credit for understanding you thoroughly and believing that you understand *me.* I appeal to it also, with hand on heart, for giving me entire credit when I say, that the sonnet in which you were mentioned, and the one mentioning himself, were omitted solely in consequence of the severe law I had laid down for myself in selecting my verses (as you will see in the Preface), and which, much against my will, forced me to throw out others

R

relating to a variety of my friends.   I am still, however, to be inspired with better ones, if they insist upon overwhelming me with amiableness and being illustrious.   Pray tell him all this.

Now let me tell you that there is real poetry in some of the verses you have sent me, and that I have read them over and over again.   There are one or two points which might be amended perhaps, in point of construction, and it is a pity, I think, that you have made the Fairy so entirely *serious* at the close of his song,[1] as to say " Oh, misery ! " He should have

---

[1] We append the following copy of this " Song."

THE LAST OF THE FAIRIES.

Gone are all the merry band !   Gone
Is my Lord—my Oberon !
Gone is Titania !   Moonlight song
And roundel now no more
Shall patter on the grassy floor.
And Robin too ! the wild bee of our throng,
Has wound his last recheat—
    Oh fate unmeet !
The roosted cock, with answering crow,
No longer starts to his " Ho ! ho ! ho ! "
    For'low he lies in death,
    With violet, and muskrose breath
    Woven into his winding-sheet.
And now I wander through the night,
An old and solitary sprite !
No laughing sister meets me ;
No friendly chirping greets me ;
But the glow-worm shuns me,
And the mouse outruns me.
    And every hare-bell
    Rings my knell ;
    For I am old,
    And my heart is cold.
    Oh misery !
    Alone to die !

died like Suet, between sorrow, astonishment, and jest, and he might have perished of frost, because there was no longer any fireside for him.   But the idea of a "*Last* of the fairies," is excellent, and the treatment of it too, especially down to the words I have quoted, from the line beginning "the roosted cock."

"Robin Goodfellow's winding-sheet" is worthy of Keats. I admire also the first eight lines of the sonnet beginning " I feel my spirit humbled," only you should not have said " *small* as is the love I bear you :" you want to say such as is the value of it ; and this is not what the other words can be made to imply.   At least I think so.   The allusion to the " room" is good.   How good is truth, and how sure it is to tell !   I have always admired, my dear Clarke, the way in which you took your fortunes, and the wiseheartedness with which you found out the jewel of good at the core of them, and known how to cherish it.   It has made you superior to them, and gives you an advantage which many richer persons might envy.   God bless you both, and all of you, and believe me,

Your affectionate friend,
LEIGH HUNT.

Next come two delightful Chaucerian discussions ; together with a kindly criticism of an early-written story, by M. C. C. called "First Love ;" and an amusing imitation of Johnsonian talk :—

To C. C. C. & Vincent Novello, Frith Street.

Chelsea, Feb. 11th.

EVER DEAR CLARKE AND VINCENT,—I have been going to write to Frith St. not only for the last ten days, but for the last ten weeks ; but my health is so unceasingly tried by my pen, that when necessity allows me to lay it down, it costs me such efforts to resume it, as must throw themselves on the indulgence of kind friends.   I rejoiced to hear of the intention about Chaucer, but so far from wondering at your leaving out the passages you speak of, I may perhaps bespeak,

R 2

your astonishment in return when I tell you, that I am not sure I have ever entirely *read* even the stories in question; I mean those in which *Swift* is horribly mixed up with ˙La Fontaine; so much do I revolt from those kind of degrading impertinences, in proportion to the voluptuousness I am prepared to license. And yet I ought to beg pardon of divine Chaucer for using such words; for his sociality condescended to the grossness of the time, and was doubtless superior to it, in a certain sense, at the moment it included it in his good-natured universality. They may even have been salutary, for what I know, by reason of certain subtle meetings of extremes between grossness and refinement, which I cannot now speak of.

What good things they were, Clarke, in some of those verses you sent me; and yet what a strange fellow you are, who with such a feeling of the poetical, and a nice sense of music, can never write a dozen lines together without committing a false quantity—leaving out some crotchets of your bar. You almost make me begin to think that Chaucer wrote in the same manner, and not, as I have fondly imagined, with syllabical perfection. I am glad you did not dislike my criticism; and you too, dear Vincent. I send Clarke one or two more, which I have cut out of periodicals. *Item*, another True Sun, merely because it contains a mention of him, and may amuse him in the rest. He will see by it that Christianity is getting on, and that Blackwood and I, poetically, are becoming the best friends in the world. The other day, there was an Ode in Blackwood in *honour of the memory of Shelley;* and I look for one to Keats. I hope this will give you faith in glimpses of the golden age.

You may have seen a *popular* edition of the " Indicator " advertised; I mean with omissions. It is not mine, but Colburn's, or I should have had copies to load my friends with, whereas I have been obliged to be silent about it to some of my oldest and nearest. What am I then to do in your house? I must, for the present (for I still hope to do better), cut the gentlemen, and confine myself, with a pleasing narrowness, to the lady—I beg pardon, to Mary, to whom I beg kindest remembrances, and her acceptance of the book she *christened.* Dear Vin, I think of you all, be assured, quite as often as you think of me. What have I to do, sitting, as I do, evening after evening by myself in my study, but to think of old times and friends, and attempt the con- solation of a verse? May you all be very happy is the constant wish of

Your affectionate friend,
LEIGH HUNT.

To C. C. C.

4, Upper Cheyne Row, July 18th.

I was much obliged to you for your letter, and rejoice to see that you continue to like the journal ; but as to prejudice, thou Cowden, against "the Siddons," I disclaim it, and do accuse thee (proof not being brought) of prejudice thyself in the accusation. The prejudice is nature's ;—what think you of that ?—for I have no pique against the Kembles, excepting that they were an artificial generation, and their sister, with all her superiority, a sort of "mankind woman" as the old writers phrase it.

But now to better things,—Chaucer and first love ; and first of the first ; for love forbid that love should not go before Chaucer, seeing that love made Chaucer himself, or ought to have done so, and certainly made him a poet. I have read it twice, and both times with emotion. The only fault I find is that the uncle, under the circumstances, would not have stuck to his vow. He would at the utmost have gone to his rector or bishop with a case of conscience, and the bishop would have told him it was a wicked thing to stick to such a vow. As to the rest, all I say is, that the writer deserves to be a man's first love and his last.

What you say about Lyonnet makes me "pause and wonder ;" yet I cannot help thinking that it was unworthy of "his greatness" to put himself into such a state of fume and energy for such an object. What need had he to prove his energy, and by rope-dancing? Conceive the time it must have taken, and the grave daily joltering practice, an immortal soul (as an old divine or Johnson might have phrased it) bobbing up and down every day, with a grave face, and with nothing better before it to warrant its saliences than the hope of beating a fellow at a fair !   Sir, he had much better have taken Mrs. Lyonnet by the hand, and danced a *pas-de-deux* with her.

Boswell. There is a grace in that dance, sir.

Johnson. Yes, sir, and it promotes benevolence.

Boswell. And yet you would not have it danced every day, sir,—not with so formal a recurrence,—not as a matter of course.

Johnson. Why, no, sir; not *ex-officio;* not professionally; not like the clock, sir.   Sir, I would not have a man horo-logically saltatory.   An impulse should be an impulse, and circumstances should be considered besides.

Boswell. You have danced yourself, sir ?

Johnson (with complacency). Yes, sir; (*then with a shrewd look*) though people would not easily suppose it.   (*Then rising with a noble indignation.*)   But, sir, I did not dance on the rope, like this Lyonnet, I left that to the paltry egotism of Frenchmen, fellows that think nothing too small to be made mighty by their patronage, that go and write the lives of caterpillars. . . .

I will come on Sunday week, if you will be good enough to let me know the hour.

Can you lend me for a day or two your copy of " Adam the Gardener " ?   I want to extract the description of the rainstorm for next Wednesday week.

Ever truly yours,
Leigh Hunt.

P.S.—I have omitted to speak of the Chaucer MS. after all.   But you will see I had not forgotten him, either in MS. or letter.   I need not repeat how I like your project, and as little, I am sure, need I apologize for the little corrections suggested in the preface.

The following is one of his courageous struggles against ill-health and its consequent feeling of dejection ; determining to take comfort from friendship and his own power of cheerful rallying :—

To M. S. N.

4, Upper Cheyne Row, Chelsea, April 15th.

What shall I say to dear Mary for being so long before I reply to her kind letter? What but that I have a bruised head, and am always full of work and trouble, and always desiring to write such very long answers to kind letters, that I seem as if I should never write any. I once heard Hobhouse say a good thing—much better than any he ever said in Parliament—to wit, that the only real thing in life was to be always doing wrong, and always be forgiven for it. Is not that pretty and Christian? For my part I cannot always be doing wrong; I have no such luck; on the contrary, I am obliged to waste a great deal of time in doing much which is absolutely right,—nay, I am generally occupied with it all day, so strange and unpardonable is my existence. And yet this putting off of letters is a very bad thing; I grant my friends have much to forgive in it, so I hope they will forgive me accordingly, and think I am not so very bad and virtuous after all. As to being "venerable," however, I defy anybody to accuse me of that, and they will find some difficulty in persuading me that you are so. Venerable! why it's an Archdeacon that's venerable, or Bede, the oldest historian— "Venerable Bede"—or the oldest Duke or Viscount living, whoever he is, the "venerable Duke" of the newspapers. What time may do with me I cannot say, but it shall at any rate be with no consent of mine that I become even aged, much less venerable, and therefore I have resolved not to fear being so, lest fear make me what I fear. Alas! I fear I am not wholly without misgivings while I say it, for white hairs are fast and fearfully mingling with my black, and I fear that my juvenility is all brag. I have told Clarke that I have none remaining, and I fear that is more like the truth than these ostentations, that is to say, in point of matter of fact, for as to matter of fancy I love and desire just the same things as I did of old, read the same books, long for the same fields, love the same friends (whatever some of these may think), and will come and hear dear little Clara sing (great Clara now) whenever you give me notice that you have an evening for me; for here I sit, work, work, work, and headache, headache, headache, at the mercy of "Copy" and Printer's Devils, and am not blissful enough to be able to risk the loss of an evening by finding you from home. With love to dear Vincent,

Ever your affectionate,
LEIGH HUNT.

The allusion in the postscript of the next letter refers to an Italian gentleman's having told M. C. C. that he rather liked a London fog than not, inasmuch as it allowed of two dawns a day,—one at sunrise, the other when the fog lifted off and cleared away from the sky :—

To M. C. C.

Chelsea, December 15th.

MY DEAR VICTORIA,—Though my head is so beaten with work just at this instant as to be no better than a mashed turnip, and though I am not aware that I have any thorough right to make you pay threepence because I am grateful, yet being apt to obey impulses to that effect, I am unable to forbear thanking you for your very nice and kind letter, so well written because you have a brain, and so warmly felt because you have a heart. I love your love of your mother, and of your husband, and of all other loveable things, and as a lover of them all myself shall think it no impertinence, especially as they give me leave, to beg you to continue to keep a little corner in your heart for the love of

Your affectionate friend,
LEIGH HUNT.

P.S.—I enjoy heartily your Italian's "perfection of playful sophistry." Happily do you describe it ; and yet see what a *really* different thing he makes a fog from those who do nothing but grumble at it, for everything is nothing but a *result of our sensations*, and the more pleasant we can make this, how lucky we ! There is a poor hand-pianoforte playing at my window this moment the song of "Jenny Jones," and *now* "The Light of Other Days," I believe it is called. But I have got such a delicious abstract idea of a "Jenny Jones" of my own (which I intend to embody in words), and there is something which falls so sweetly on some part of my feelings from the other air too, that tears between sadness and pleasure come into my eyes. God bless you nice hearty people, you Clarkes ; and so no more at present from yours till death.

The next two refer to the " Legend of Florence :" the interesting evening of its "second reading" having been described at page 86. The sentence respecting the " MS." refers to the fifth Act of the " Legend of Florence " as originally written by its author, which gave a different close to the play from the one given in the acted and printed versions. The copy of this original fifth Act, which Leigh Hunt permitted M. C. C. to make from his own manuscript, is still in our possession, appended to his presentation copy of the first printed edition of the play.

To C. C. C. and M. C. C., Dean Street.

Thursday.

MY DEAR CLARKE,—I want you both particularly to-night to stand by me in my readings to some *new* friends (very cordial people nevertheless). This is my *second* reading of my play, and I am to have a third, and I mix up new and old friends together when I read, though indeed of dear old friends I retain very few out of the claws of Death or distance, and those in Dean Street, despite of the perplexities of this beautiful world (which keep apart sometimes those who sympathize most), have ever been among the dearest to your affectionate friend,

Dear Charles and " Molly,"
L. H.

To M. C. C., Dean Street.

Chelsea, Feb. 20th, 1840.

MY DEAR VICTORIA—Do not think me ungrateful for

either of your kind and most welcome notes in having thus
hitherto delayed to answer them.   The conclusion of the
first brought the tears into my eyes, which, I assure you, the
exclamations it speaks of, delightful as they were, did *not;*
such a difference is there between a public idea and the
distinct and ascertained affection of a private one.   But I
have not even yet recovered from the hurry and perplexity of
an exquisitely overwhelming correspondence, and I delayed
copies of the play to your father and you two (for I am not
yet rich enough to offer it the only desirable divorce between
you, that of giving you a book apiece) till I could send the
second edition, which contains the proper acknowledgment
of the music he was so kind as to send me, and which I
expect to be out every day, and the MS. of the act you so
naturally prefer shall come at the same time.   Meanwhile
(with Charles' leave) pray let me give you in imagination the
half dozen kisses which you would certainly have had to
undergo, as others did, had you been near me on that
occasion.   I suppose your mother does not care for them, or
for me, as she does not send me a word.   Well, never mind,
I'll sulk and try to do without her.   And yet, somehow, give
her my love to vex her ; and to everybody else that is loving,
and grasp Charles' hand for me till he cries out.

Your affectionate friend,
L. H.

The following seven afford samples of Leigh Hunt's
fascinating mode of implying complimentary things in
what he said to those honoured by his regard.   He had
a perfectly charming mode of paying a compliment; a
mode that inspired the ambition to *be* all he imputed,
and that tended to exalt and improve the object of his
praise.   A remark that I (M. C. C.) once overheard him
make at a dance of young people upon my dancing was
such as to call forth a proud feeling quite other than that
of mere gratified vanity : it caused me to dance with
better grace and spirit ever after.   On another occasion,

he said :—"I always know how to call the light into
Victorinella's face,—by speaking of her husband."   I may
here cite a specimen of the playful kind of direction to
which I have previously alluded, as one that he sometimes
put outside a letter.   This I now speak of contained a
press-order for the theatre ; and the direction ran thus :—
"To Mrs. Clarke, Mr. Novello's, Frith Street, Soho."
(Then, written in minute characters) :—"Private, especially the outside.   Written suddenly out of a loving
and not a petulant impulse.   Why don't female friends,
and other friends, take walks to see their sick friends,—
especially when they live near the Hampstead fields
again ? I hope this question won't be considered base
from one who sends orders for theatres, which, it seems,
are considered favours out in the world.   I know nothing
of what is out in the world, but it is not my fault if I wish
to see the pleasant people in it.   Hallo, though ! I forgot
I have not been lately to Frith Street.   The above therefore, has not been written.   ' There's no such thing !'"

To M. C. C.

Kensington, April 27tb.

COWDENIA MIA,—I am afraid you must have thought it
very strange, my not sooner answering your kind and most
welcome letter with its good news about the Concordance ;
but we have all been in such a state here with influenza and
measles, etc., that a sort of *cordon sanitaire* was drawn round
us, and even the people in Church St. (naturally enough,
Heaven knows, considering how they have suffered) were
afraid of having anything to do with us, or receiving even a
book from us at their doors; so it made us take ourselves for a
set of the most *plaguey* invalids possible, people wholly to be
eschewed and eschewing.   The girls, however, being at length
about and Vincent himself, who has been longest in bed of any,
I think we may venture to think of a remote knock at some
person's door ; and the consequence is, that here comes to you

and Carlo mio a little book, which has been waiting for you these three weeks. It does not contain quite all that even *I* would have had inserted ; and most unluckily the Nile, and the song which your father set, have got out of it purely by an accident of delay arising out of my wish to improve them. *Au reste*, I have always regretted that I could not retain that Sonnet to Keats in which Charles was mentioned, because it really was unworthy of both of them ; so I have taken an opportunity of mentioning *en passant* your dear good husband in the Preface. Tell him, if he never saw my Sonnet on the Fish and Man before, I bespeak his regard for it. How rejoiced I was to see the specimen of the Concordance ! *Item*, to hear of the admirable impulse felt by the lady when she heard the Sonnet about the lock of hair. *Vide* the Rondeau at page 155, for the impulse turned into fact,—a very pretty example, let me tell you, for all honest female friends, especially Cowdenians. I say no more. *Verbum sat.;* which means a word to the womanly.

Ever dear Charles and Victoria's
Affectionate friend, LEIGH.

To M. C. C.

Kensington, February 17th.

VITTORIA MIA,—(For you know I always claim a little bit of right in you, Caroli gratiâ) I· think I have repeated the remark you speak of more than once, and yet I cannot remember anything more like it at present than in some passages in the accompanying " Recollections of a dead body " in the *Monthly Repository*, pages 218, 219; which book I accordingly send you. I still think, however, there must be a passage somewhere else, and I will look for it, and if I find it, send it off directly. With love to dear Clarke,

Believe me, ever affectionately yours,

LEIGH HUNT.

To M. C. C.

Kensington, February 18th.

MY DEAR VICTORIA,—I send you overleaf the manifest passage. Your clue (" the end of a paragraph ") enabled me

to find it almost instantly at p. 20 of the *London Journal.*
Sempre Clarke-issimo.

L. H.

" We see in the news from Scotland, that at the interment of
the venerable widow of Burns (Bonnie Jeannie Armour, who
we believe made him a very kind and considerate wife) the
poet's body was for a short time exposed to view, and his
aspect found in singular preservation. An awful and affecting sight ! We should have felt, if we had been among the
bye-standers, as if we had found him in some bed, in the
night of Time and space, and as if he might have said something ! grave but kind words of course, befitting his spirit and
that of the wise placidity of Death, for so the aspect of death
looks. *A corpse seems as if it suddenly knew everything, and
was profoundly at peace in consequence.*"

To M. C. C. (*with vignette of Burns's House*).

VICTORIANINA DIAVOLINA,—*Friday* by all means. I will
be with you all on ditto at 2 o'clock. Greatly pleased am I
at hearing that Charles is to be at home, for I began to think
I should never see him till this time next century. Herewith come the woodcuts I spoke of. We will talk farther of
the subject when we meet, and then I will put down, on the
spot, any memorandums you like. I shall quite look forward
to Friday.

Ever, you devilish good people,
Most truly yours,

LEIGH HUNT.

To M. C. C.

Kensington, September 27th.

CARA VITTORIA MIA,—I address this to you, because I
conclude it is more likely to find you at home, and because
being so much of a *one*-ness with your husband I suppose
you could act for him as well as if he were on the spot, and
send me the little book I ask for in case he happens to possess
a copy. It is the Literary Pocket-book (if you remember
such a thing) containing the collection of the sayings of

poor Beau Brummel, under the title of "Brummelliana." A gentleman who is writing a life of him has sent to me to borrow it, and my own copy has disappeared. I need not say, that I should stipulate with the gentleman to take every care of it, and that at all events I would become personally responsible for its return. And so with best blessings to both of you (for tho' not a Papist I am Catholic in all benedictory articles) I am ever, dear Victoria,

Your and his faithful friend,

LEIGH HUNT.

To M. C. C.

Kensington, October 21st.

VICTORIANELLINA CARINA, BUONINA,—You must have thought me a strange dilatory monster all this while ; but in the first place, my Keatses (as usual) were all borrowed, so that I had to wait till I could get one of them back. In the second place, I did so, the fullest (Galignani's) ; when lo! and behold, there was *no* Nile Sonnet! ergo, in the third place we commenced a search amongst boxes and papers, Mrs. Hunt being pretty sure that she had got it "somewhere ;" but unfortunately, after long and repeated ransacking, the somewhere has proved a nowhere. Now what is to be done? I have an impression on my memory that all the three Sonnets were published in the *Examiner,* and as your father has got an *Examiner* (which I have not) perhaps you will find it there. I regret extremely that I cannot meet with it, particularly as I was to be so much honoured. Shelley's comes on the next page. Oh, what memories they recall! I am obliged to shut them up with a great sigh, and turn my thoughts elsewhere. The Brummelliana came back with many thanks. There is to be a book respecting the poor Beau, which doubtless we shall all see. Tell Charles I have been getting up a volume called " True Poetry," with a prefatory essay on the nature of ditto, and extracts, with comments, from Spenser, Marlow, Shakespeare, Beaumont and Fletcher, Milton, Coleridge, Shelley, and Keats. I know he will be glad to hear this. It is a book of veritable pickles and preserves ; rather say, nectar and ambrosia ; and there is not a man in England

who will relish or understand the Divine bill of fare better
than he.   With kindest love ever his and yours,

Madamina,

LEIGH HUNT.

To M. C. C.   Kensington, November 12th.

VICTORIANELLINUCCIA,—You would have heard from me
earlier in the week than this, had I not been suffering under
a cold and cough of such severity, that it affected the very
muscles of my neck to a degree which rendered it painful for
me to do anything with my head but to let it lie back on the
top of an armchair, and so direct its eyes on a book and read.
Of all kinds of approbations of my scribblements—nay, I will
call them writings in consideration of their sincerity and their
approvers—there is none that ever pleases me so much as those
like Mr. Peacock's; and I beg you to make him my grateful
acknowledgments, as well as to accept them yourself for
sending them to me in a letter so delightful.   As to any
violation of modesty in your showing me what he says of you,
in the first place there is no such violation ; and secondly, if
there could be, it is the privilege of women so really modest
(and the wicked exquisites know it) to be able to set this
modesty aside on occasions gloriously appropriate, and so
make us love it the more on all others.   With cordial remembrances to your traveller,

Your ever affectionate

LEIGH HUNT.

The next two are charmingly characteristic of the
writer.

To V. N.

Kensington, 25th February, 1843.

MY DEAR VINCENT,—Lēmŭrĕs sometimes called Lēmŭrs
(as in Milton, Ode to Nativity,—

"The Lārs and Lēmurs moan with midnight plaint") is
accented on the first syllable   The Lemurs were the departed
souls of the wicked, as the Lars or Lares were those of the
good ; so the former came and *bothered* people, while the
latter befriended them.   A fellow who leaves us his male-
diction, and does *not* leave us his money, is a Lemur.   An

old lady, who was tiresome in her life, and who says that her spirit will watch over the premises to see we behave properly is a sort of fair Lemur; for she candidly gives us notice to quit.

I have been going to write to you every day to thank you for your kind present of the music, *before* hearing it, and in despair, just now, of hearing it properly. You recollect you asked me to give you my opinion *after* hearing it. How can I doubt, however, that it will be very delightful, considering who selected and harmonized it? The next time I see you I hope to be able to speak from the particular experience.

Ever, my dear Vincent,
Your affectionate old friend,
LEIGH HUNT.

To V. N.

32, Edwardes Square, 2nd July.

MY DEAR VINCENT,—I am so hard driven just at this moment, that I can but afford a hasty word of thanks even for such presents as yours and dear Mary's (to whom pray give an *embracing* word for me); but I need not entreat you to believe, that that word contains a thousand kind thoughts. As to coming to see you, it is what I long for; but with the exception of one unavoidable engagement for next Saturday week, I have been obliged to "*cut*" all my friends, as far as visiting *them* goes, till my new play is finished (don't you feel a particularly great gash? for the "cutting" is of necessity proportioned to the love). On the other hand, I take it particularly kind of them, if *they* in the meantime come to see *me*, while resting of an evening after my work (for the going out to visit after dinner knocks me up for the next day). Impudently, nay lovingly then, let me request you to do so, and Clarke also, and dear Vic, if they, or she, or all of you, or each, or either, will come (I have two loves of the name of "Vic" now, Clarke and Prince Albert permitting!) Tea will be always ready for you any time between six and eight, and hearty thanks,　　　From your affectionate friend,

L. H.

P.S. The moment my play is finished, I will come, and

come again, as fast as possible. Tell Clarke my new study is very snug and nice, and that I have a bit of vine over my window. Bid him make haste and see it.

The following breathes all his old affectionate spirit of friendship and hope for the best :—

To M. S. N.

Phillimore Terrace, Kensington,
August 4th (probably 1851).

MY DEAR MARY,—Your letter, full of warm and most welcome old friendship, to say nothing (which means much) of the box of my favourite sweetmeats, came like a beam of sunshine upon a house full of trouble; for your husband's namesake had been taken suddenly ill. . . . . But we have all experienced these sorrows in the course of our lives, so I will say no more of them.

Truly, in spite of anxiety, did I rejoice to think of your southern rest, and our patient's condition has made us doubly desirous to hear more of a place, where you so naturally wish to have more old friends near you, and where we should be so willing to find ourselves. . . . We might pass some months perhaps at Nice, or some longer time, as cheaply as we live in this neighbourhood (where, by the way, I have not yet seen the exhibition, so anxious have I been !) . . . . . A thousand recollections of past times often spring up in my mind, connected with yourselves and other friends, all loving, and wishing I could have made them all happy for ever. But some day I believe we shall be so, in some Heavenly and kindly place. Meantime, just now, I shall dry my eyes, and fancy myself with you at Nice, imitating some happy old evening in Percy Street. We would have a little supper, precisely of the old sort, and fancy ourselves not a bit older in years ; and " Victoria " if she were there, should put on a pinafore to help the illusion ; and we would repeat the old jokes, and at all events love one another and so deserve to have all the happiness we could. Now is not this a thing to look forward to, in case I can take the journey ? Marianne, who sends cordialest greetings, looks up with a bright eye at what

s

you say about rheumatism, and asks me if it is possible we could go? "Possible." I do not know whether it is, till I hear and see further ; but I will seriously hope it not otherwise ; and at all events it is a thought with too many good things in it to give up before we must. Kindest remembrances to all around you, and a happy meeting somewhere still on earth, should Nice not allow it. What charming things are in your daughter's Shakespearian books.

Your ever affectionate friend,
LEIGH HUNT.

The two next felicitously hit off a combination of business seriousness with old-acquaintance kindliness :—

To J. Alfred Novello.

Hammersmith, May 8th,
Monday morning, 10 o'clock.

DEAR ALFRED,—Your letter has only this moment reached me. You will find the parody on the next leaf ; at least it is all which I recollect, and to the best of my recollection there was really nothing more. It is not masterly, tho' not unamusing. I don't know the author.

Yours ever,
L. H.

GENTLY STIR AND BLOW THE FIRE.

Gently stir and blow the fire,
  Lay the mutton down to roast ;
Dress it quickly, I desire ;
  In the dripping put a toast ;
    Hunger that I may remove ;
    Mutton is the meat I love.

On the dresser see it lie ;
  Oh, the charming white and red !
Finer meat ne'er met my eye ;
  On the sweetest grass it fed.
    Let the jack go swiftly round ;
    Let me have it nicely brown'd.

To J. A. N.

7, Cornwall Road, Hammersmith,
Decr. 13th.

MY DEAR ALFRED—(For, notwithstanding your jovial proportions and fine bass voice, I have danced you on my knee when a child, and Christmas topics and dear old memories will not allow me, out of very regard, to call you "sir") I enjoyed exceedingly your kind recollection of me and the place which you gave that Christmas effusion of mine in the midst of all those harmonious advertisements. I seemed to be made the centre of some great musical party. I see also my dear old friend "C. C. C." as touching and cordial as ever.

I need not say how heartily I return your Christmas wishes. I have had a great sorrow to endure of late years—one that often seemed all but unbearable—but it is softening, and I never, thank God, wished any other person's happiness to be less during it, but greater. How desirable then to me must be the happiness of my friends.

I take this opportunity of asking a question which I have often been going to put to some one acquainted with musico-commercial affairs, of which I am totally ignorant; will you tell me at one of your leisure moments (if such things there be) whether a man of letters like myself could purchase a musical instrument with his pen, instead of his purse; that is to say, for such and such an amount of literary matter, verse or prose, or both, as might be agreed upon? and if so, what sort of matter would be likeliest to be required of him?

Should you be ever wandering this way, and would give me a look in (I have tea and bread and cheese ready for anybody from 6 o'clock onwards), I have long had a musico-literary project or two in my head which possibly you might not be unwilling to hear of.

Ever sincerely yours,
LEIGH HUNT.

In the following two there are traces of the cordia sincerity with which Leigh Hunt praised and encouraged

S 2

the attempts of other writers.   The MS. " Lecture "
was lent to him for perusal, and he returned it scored
with approval marks and valuable marginal remarks.
This was a delightful mode he had of manifesting his interest in and careful reading through of such works as his
friends had written; and so precious were his pencilled
notes of this kind to the writer of " Kit Bam's Adventures,"
and " The Iron Cousin," that she asked him to follow the
plan suggested by the crafty magician in " Aladdin," and to
" exchange old lamps for new ones," sending her back
his well-worn presentation copies of the two books in
question, for which she sent him fresh copies.   In consequence of his kind compliance with her wish, we now
possess the first-sent copy of " Kit Bam," inscribed "to
the grown-up boy, Leigh Hunt," which contains numerous marginal pencilled comments; one of which
(playfully written on the page where is described a
vision of the dead Felix Morton with his wife and child
wafted to the sky), runs thus :— " A mistake.   The
'father' of the winged child is still alive; and for that
matter, the rogue of a charming writer who *brought him
forth ;* I shall not say who, as we happen not to be
married.   F. M. sen."   This was Leigh Hunt's pleasant mode of referring to a confession I (M. C. C.) had
made him when I sent him the book, that I once upon
a time had heard him say a pretty idea for a story would
be that of a child born with wings, owing to the strong
yearning of his mother to reach a distant place constantly
within her view but beyond her attainment, and that I
had adopted the idea and had ventured to work it out
in this story.   We also possess the copy of " The Iron
Cousin " scored repeatedly by Leigh Hunt, and on the
blank pages at the end of which he has written in pencil :

—" There is no story (so to speak) in this book; the
explanation to which the lovers come, they might have
come to much sooner (the fault most common perhaps
to novels in general), and the illiterate persons in it, not
excepting the Squire, often make use of language too
literate. Nevertheless, to a reader like myself, who
prefers character and passion out and out to plot or to a
thorough consistency on those minor points, the book is
very interesting. Its descriptive power is of a kind the
liveliest and most comprehensive; its powers of expression
are still rarer,—very rare indeed either with man or
woman, the latter particularly; so well has the authoress
profited by her long and loving abode in the house (for
'School' does not express the thing) of Shakespeare;
and what is rarest of all, there is some of the daintiest
and noblest love-making (and love-*taking*) in it, which I
can recollect in any book." The reader will, we trust,
forgive the seeming egoism of giving this transcription,
for the sake of the genuine thought of Leigh Hunt himself and his generous commendation which filled our
heart as we copied out the faint pencilled traces, so
precious to us that when we first received them we passed
them through milk to prevent their being rubbed out by
time;—

To C. C. C.

Hammersmith, Novr. 19th, 1854.

My dear Clarke,—I have been thinking of the Hamlet
and Midsummer Night's Dream, hoping the lecture is going
to be delivered at some reachable place, fearing I might not
be able (owing to a cough and catarrh) and wondering
whether it would be possible to hear it *here* some evening, in
this my hut, between tea and supper, I being the sole poor,
but grateful audience. Such things you must know have
been, though I don't at all assume that they can be in this

instance, however great the good will. But if not, might I read it? I need not tell you that it would be perused in strictest confidence, except as far as you might allow me to speak of it.

Nothing is more just, though I say it who *should* (one likes to give impudent baulks sometimes to prudish old sayings), than what you think in regard to my critical sincerity. I love too much to praise where I can, not to preserve the acceptability of the praise by qualifying when I must.

Besides, half my life has been, and is, a martyrdom to truth, and I should be absurd indeed to stultify it with the other half. My faults have enough to answer for without being under the necessity of owning to any responsibility in the lying and cheating direction ; but where am I running to ? I always, as far as I had the means of judging, took your wife to be a thoroughly loving woman (if I may so speak) in every particle of her nature ; and I hold it for an axiom, though exclusives in either the material or spiritual would count it a paradox, that it is only such persons who can have thoroughly fine perceptions into any nature whatsoever. In other words, incompleteness cannot possibly judge completeness. So with this fine peremptory sentence I complete this very complete letter of four sides down to the cover, and with all loving respect,

My dear Clarke,

Am hers and yours,

LEIGH HUNT.

To M. C. C.

Hammersmith, January 8th, 1855.

VICTORIANELLINA AMABILE E CARINA,—Very pleasant to me was the sight of your handwriting, yet so much the more unpleasant it is to be forced to write to you briefly. The address of the London Library is 12, St. James' Square. Circumstances have conspired to hamper me with three books at once, the " Kensington " aforesaid, a collection of my " Stories in verse " with revisals, new Preface and a continuation of my autobiography. The consequence is that

I have been overworked in the midst of severe cold and cough (the latter the longer and rather severest I have yet had, for cough I always have) and thus I am able only to continue the reading of Charles' lecture, attractive as it is, by driblets (availing myself of the additional time he gave me, though not *all* of it), and am forced still to postpone writing to Alfred. Give, pray, my kindest remembrances to him. Tell him I tried hard to write an article for the *Musical Times* by the 20th of December, but could not do it; that I wished very much to begin the New Year with him; that I still purpose to go on (having more than one special object in so doing); that I will recommence the very first moment I can; and that meantime I rejoice to see the honour done to my Christmas verses by Mr. Macfarren's music. I have not heard it, for I have heard nothing but the voice of booksellers and the sound of my pen and my lungs; but I shall make the first acquaintance with it feasible, and look to it as a greeting at the close of some toilsome vista.

Dear Victoria, Mary, or whatsoever title best please thine ear, I am ever the sincere old friend of you and yours,

LEIGH HUNT.

I need not say how heartily I reciprocate your Christmas wishes.

In the Autumn of 1856, when we were going abroad, to live in the milder climate of Nice, we went to take leave of dear Leigh Hunt at his pretty little cottage in Cornwall Road, Hammersmith. We found him, as of old, with simple but tasteful environments, his books and papers about him, engravings and plaster-casts around his room; while he himself was full of his wonted cordiality and cheerful warmth of reception for old friends. The silvered hair, the thin pale cheek, the wondrous eyes, were no less beautiful in their aged aspect than in their youthful one; while his charm of manner was, if anything enhanced by the tender softening of years. We,—who could well remember the brilliancy and fascination of his bearing in youthful manhood, the effect of bright expectant pleasure attending his entrance into a company, the influence of his general handsomeness with refined bearing and beauty of countenance, especially the vivacity and sparkling expression of his eyes, still so dark and fine, though with a melancholy depth in them now,—felt as though he were even more than ever beautiful to look upon. It was perhaps an unconscious consciousness (if the expression may be allowed) of this personal attractiveness on his own part, which lent that ease and grace and self-possession to his demeanour which was always so inexpressibly winning : it arose not from self-complacency so much as from imagination and instinctive feeling of its giving him a pleasant ascendancy over those whom he addressed. This ascendancy it was that inspired the childish impulse (previously recorded) to creep round the back of the sofa and lay a loving cheek on his resting hand,—that hand so slender, so white, so true a poet's hand. It was this ascendancy that often thrilled the little girl's heart with a fancy for wishing to nurse his foot, as she watched its shapely look, and lithe tossing to and fro in the earnestness of his talk. It was this innate personal ascendancy peculiar to Leigh Hunt that exercised its amplest sway when we went to bid him good-bye in 1856. The ring of his hair was worn on this occasion, and shown to him between two hoops of pearl as the " black diamond " treasured in our family ; he, taking the incident in his own tenderly gracious way and with his own gift of tenderly recognizant words.

After we left England we received several letters from him, among which were the two following :—

To C. C. C.

7, Cornwall Road, Hammersmith,
July 7th, 1857.

MY DEAR FRIENDS—DEAR CLARKE AND DEAR MARY VICTORIA,—(for you know I don't like to part with the old word) the first letter from Nice came duly to hand ; but for the reason kindly contemplated by itself, I could not answer it at the moment, and the same reason made me delay the answer, and now still makes me say almost equally little on that particular point, except that I sigh as I am wont to do from the bottom of my heart, and thank you with tears for the privilege of silence accorded me.

Were it not for dear friends and connexions still living, I should now feel as if I belonged wholly to the next world ; but while they remain to me, or I to them, I must still do my best to make the most of the world I am in, in order to deserve their comfort of me during the remainder of my progress to that other ; where I do believe that all the wants which hearts and natures yearn to be lovingly made up, *will* be made up, as surely as in this world fruits are sounded and perfected (final short-comings of any kind being not to be thought possible in God's works) and where " all tears will be wiped from all faces." Why was any text inconsistent with that, ever suffered to remain in the book that contains it ? But I am talking when I thought to become mute. Be you mute for me. I shall take your silence for dumb and loving squeezes of the hand. Winter here has been as severe with us, after its severer kind, as it has been with you in the midst of its lemon-blossoms and green peas. I hope your summer has turned out as proportionately excellent, and then you will have had a summer indeed ; for we have been astonished at our June without fires, and our continuously blue weather. Your walks are noble truly, and would be wonderful if you had not a companion ; a thing which always makes me feel as if I could walk anywhere and for ever ; that is to say, if anything like such a companion as yours, but doubtless stoppings would occasionally be found desirable, especially at inns, or where "*si vende birra.*" "*Strada Smollett*" is delightful. By-and-by there will be

such streets all over the world. People will know, not only
the name of a street, but the reason for it, "and by the
visions splendid," be " on their way attended." Let who
else will live in " Smollett Street," Matthew Brambles, and
Randoms, and Bowlings will be met there by passengers, as
long as the name endures. I see the last, turning a corner
with little Roderick in his hand, hitching up his respectable,
bad-fitting trousers, and jerking the tobacco out of his mouth
at the thought of unfeeling old hunkses of grandfathers.
Your finale respecting Burns was to good final purpose ; and
I do not wonder at its exciting the applause of the genial
portion of his countrymen ; for such only would be the portion to come to your lectures. They must have felt it like
an utterance of their own hearts, let free for the first time ;
at least, thus publicly. To find fault with Burns is to find
fault with the excess of geniality of, Nature, herself ; which,
tho' like the sun it may do harm here and there, or seem to
do it in its hottest places, is a universal beneficence, and
could not be perhaps what it is without them. Nor are
those irremediable to such as are in Nature's secrets, or " to
the matter born." The life of Burns by Robert Chambers, a
serene and sweet-minded philosophic kind of man, is undoubtedly, as you say, the best of all the lives of him. . . . .
I long to see the fifteen famous women,[1] and am truly obliged
by the desire expressed to the publisher to send it me. It is
impossible they should be in better hands than in those of
the bringer-up of the women of Shakespeare ; people, that
make a Mormon of me ; and, with your leave, a *Molly*—as
well as a *Poly*gamist. Indeed with the help of another *l*, the
latter word might express both. You see you have made me
a little wild, with the compliment paid to my portrait. But
I am no less respectful at heart ; as in truth you know ;
otherwise I should not be where you have put me. So I feel
new times and old mingled beautifully together, with the
champagne once more over my hair, and all kindly nights and
mornings, and outpourings of heart as well as wine, and

---

[1] In allusion to "World-noted Women," written by M. C. C.
for Messrs. Appleton, of New York, in 1857.

laughters and tears too, that make such extremes meet as veritably seem to join heaven and earth and render the most transient joys foretastes of those that are to last for ever.

Ah me! Thus preach I my first sermon to loving eyes from my wall in *Maison Quaglia*, at Nice.

The other day I got news at last of the safe arrival of my box of books and manuscripts (for the American press) at Washington, Pennsylvania, which it had reached by a circuitous progress thro' other Washingtons, caused by my ignorance of there being any other Washington than one, and so having omitted the Pennsylvania. One London, I thought, one Washington; forgetting that London is a word of unknown meaning, therefore who cares to repeat it? Whereas Washington was a man, of whom men are proud; and hence it seems, there are 70 Washingtons! All goes well with my " works " (grand sound !) and they are to come out, both in verse and prose, the former forthwith; and special direction shall be sent to Boston for all being forwarded duty free to Maison Quaglia, in return for my " fifteen women " (strange, impossible sound of payment !) so I do not send you the list you speak of, meantime; only I should be glad to know what prose works of mine you may happen to possess at present, in case, if the publication of them in America be comparatively delayed, I may be able to send you some of them, such as I think you would best like; for there is a talk of republishing those in England. Besides, I need room for an extract which I had got to make for Victoria from my friend Craik's " English of Shakespeare." I must not even stop to enjoy with you some quotations from Drayton and Jonson, but I must *not* omit to congratulate you both, and everybody else, on the new edition of Shakespeare, especially as I reckon upon her turning her unique knowledge of him to dainty account in her Preface, and would suggest to that end (if it be not already in her head) that she would let us know what particular flowers, feelings, pursuits, readings, and other things great and small he appears to have liked best. Other people might gather this from her Concordance, but who so well as she that made it? Therefore

pray let her forestall those who might take it into their heads
to avail themselves of the information afforded them by that
marvellous piece of love and industry. But to the extract :
. . . . Shall I send my copy of it to Nice ? It would interest
editorship and occasion would be found to say a grateful and
deserved word for it in the introduction to Julius Cæsar. I
lend the " Iron Cousin " to all understanding persons, and
they are unanimous in their praises. *Item.*—I trust to read
and mark it again, myself, shortly. Loving friends, both, I
am your *ever loving* friend,

LEIGH HUNT.

To " Mr. and Mrs Cowden Clarke " as men call them.
To Charles and Mary-Victoria among the Gods.

Feb. 4th, 1858, Hammersmith.

MY DEAR FRIENDS,—Tho' it was a very delightful moment
to me when I was again received by the house in that manner—far more delightful, for reasons which you may guess,
than when I was first received, (with such strange memories
sometimes will the brain of a poor humanist be haunted) yet
the crown of the crown of congratulation is, after all that
which one receives from families and old friends ; terrible
nevertheless, as the absence is of that which one misses. Bitter
was the moment, after that other moment, when on returning
home, I could not go first of all, and swiftly, into one particular
room. But I ought to give you none but glad thoughts, in
return for the gladness which you have added to mine. I
had several times reproached myself for not writing to thank
certain most kind remembrances of me in *Musical Times*,
and then (as always seems to be the retributive case) comes
this loving congratulation, before I have spoken. But work
is mine, you must know, still and ever, and must be so till
my dying day, only leaving me too happy at last, if I do but
render it as impossible for any one individual in private to
mistake me, as it seems to be with the blessed public, for
whom, as I sometimes feared, might be the case, I have not
gone through my martyrdoms (such as they are) in vain.
Great, great indeed was my joy when they seemed as it
were, at that moment, to take me again, and in a special

manner, into their arms, the warm arms of my fellow-creatures. And now come yours, my dear friends, about me as warmly. Imagine me returning them with an ardour of heart, which no snows on my head can extinguish.

A few weeks ago there came to me from a certain pleasant-named house in New York a most magnificent book, full of handsome ladies, and better comments upon them, which till this moment I have thanked neither publishers nor authoress for, having wished to read it thro' first in order to thank properly. My acknowledgments for it go accordingly to Nice and New York at the same time. The ladies are somewhat too much of a family, and of a drawing-room family, especially in the instances of the divine peasant, Joan of Arc, of lovely-hearted Pocahontas, who must still have been a Cherokee or Chickasaw beauty, and of what ought to have been the "beautiful plain" face of your Sappho. What a pity the artist had not genius enough in him to anticipate the happy audacity of that praise! The finery of her company I think, (for she seems to have guessed what sort of a book the publishers would make of it) has seduced our dear *Mary-Victoria* into a style florider and more elaborate than when she poured her undressed heart out in the charming "Iron Cousin" (my copy of which by the way, has just come home to me again in beautiful relaxed and dignified condition from its many perusals) ; but still the heart as well as head is there, and I have read every bit of the book with interest ; unbribed, I cannot add, seeing what abundant warm-hearted reminiscences of me it contains ; too many for it, I should have feared a little while ago ; but not just now, for the promised edition of my "poetical works" has come out at Boston, and being welcomed with as universal cordiality in America, as my play has been by the press in London (for such you must know in addition to my reception on the stage, is the fact : at least so I am told, and have reason to believe ; for I possess upwards of twenty eulogies from daily and weekly newspapers and reviews, and I hear there are half as many more, which I am yet to see). What think you of this unexpected (for indeed I never looked for it) winter-flowering, and in the two

hemispheres at once?   An American friend of mine, who is
one of the Secretaries of legation here, tells me, that there is
but one exception to the applause in his country, and this in
a penny paper ; so at all events that amount of drawback is
not worth twopence.   No : it is not he who tells me,—first
tho' he was to give me the good news.   I learn it from my
other American friend, the editor of the " Works" who is
going to feast the transatlantic half of my vanity with a collection of the praises ; some of which, he adds, will make
my " very heart leap within me."   Heaven be thanked for it.

And now you have seen a certain " Tapiser's Tale,"
which accompanies this letter—oh, but my vanity must not
forget to add,—nay, my hope of solid good must not forget to add,—and unspeakable joys hanging thereon, that
the manager anticipates a " long run " for the play, and says
also, that he will, " carry it in triumph thro' all the provinces." *Item*, I have reason to hope, that he will bring out
one, perhaps more, of certain MS. plays which I have by me,
and for which I never expected any such chance; and
furthermore I think there is playable stuff in them—and so
—and then—why, it is not impossible, verily, that I may
have a whole golden year of it ; alas ! that any sighs should
mix with that thought, but it is wholesome that they should
do so, to prepare me for disappointment.   There would even
be a certain sweet in them then.   There are faces that in
that case would not be so much missed.

But to return to the Tapiser.   Here is a bold venture ;
bold to send to anybody and anywhere, but boldest of all to
such Chaucerophilists as live at Nice.   Luckily their love is
equal to their knowledge ; so extremes will meet in this as
in other cases ; and positively I trust to fare best where
under less loving circumstances I might have had least
reason to expect it.   Besides, the subject is so beautiful in
itself that a devout Chaucer student could not well take all
interest out of it with the sympathetic.

So I shan't fear that you will make any very heavy retalia-
tions for what I have ventured to object up above ; especially
as in reference to the great poet, I am prepared to bow to
any speeches of shortcoming that may be objected, saving

something in behalf of the wet eyes with which the tale was written .... It has appeared in Fraser's Magazine, and prospered.

Dear friends, imagine me blessing you both from the place which I occupy in your house, *my* house, you know, as well as your own. What if I should be able to see it some day, with eyes not of spirit only?

Your ever loving friend,
LEIGH HUNT.

Little more than a twelvemonth elapsed after the above words had been written ere we heard of Leigh Hunt's death. We felt that one of the most salutary and pleasurable sources of influence upon our life was withdrawn, and a sense of darkness seemed to fall around us. Our regret at his loss inspired us with the following verse tribute to his memory :—

TWO SONNETS

On hearing of Leigh Hunt's Death.

I.

The world grows empty : fadingly and fast
   The dear ones and the great ones of my life
   Melt forth, and leave me but the shadows rife
Of those who blissful made my peopled past ;
Shadows that in their numerousness cast
   A sense of desolation sharp as knife
   Upon the soul, perplexing it with strife
Against the vacancy, the void, the vast
Unfruitful desert which the earth becomes
   To one who loses thus the cherished friends
   Of youth. The loss of each beloved sends
An aching consciousness of want that dumbs
The voice to silence,—akin to the dead blank
All things became, when down the sad heart sank.

II.

And yet not so would thou thyself have view'd
  Affliction : thy true poet soul knew how
  The sorest thwartings patiently to bow
To wisest teachings; that they still renew'd
In thee strong hope, firm trust, or faith imbued
  With cheerful spirit,—constant to avow
  The " good of e'en things evil," and allow
All things to pass with courage unsubdued.
Philosophy like thine turns to pure gold
  Earth's dross; imprisonment assumed a grace,
A dignity, as borne by thee, in bold
  Defence of liberty and right ; thy face
Reflected thy heart's sun 'mid sickness, pain,
And grief; nay, loss itself thou mad'st a gain.

DOUGLAS JERROLD AND HIS LETTERS.

THE leading characteristic of Douglas Jerrold's nature was earnestness. He was earnest in his abhorrence of all things mean and interested; earnest in his noble indignation at wrong and oppression; earnest in the very wit with which he vented his sense of detestation for evil-doing. He was deeply earnest in all serious things; and very much in earnest when dealing with less apparently important matters, which he thought needed the scourge of a sarcasm. Any one who could doubt the earnestness of Jerrold should have seen him when a child was the topic; the fire of his eye, the quiver of his lip, bore witness to the truth of the phrase he himself uses in his charming drama of " The Schoolfellows," showing that to him indeed "children are sacred things." We once received a letter from him expressing in pungent terms his bitter disgust at an existing evil, and concluding with a light turn serving to throw off the load that oppresses him :—

Putney, Oct. 21st, 1849.

MY DEAR MRS. CLARKE,—The wisdom of the law is about to preach from the scaffold on the sacredness of life ; and, to illustiate its sanctity, will straightway strangle a woman as soon as she have strength renewed from childbirth. I would fain believe, despite the threat oi Sir G——— G——— to hang this wretched creature as soon as restorations shall have had their benign effect, that the Government only need pressure from without to commute the sentence. A

T

petition—a woman's petition—is in course of signature. You are, I believe, not a reader of that mixture of good and evil, a newspaper ; hence, may be unaware of the fact. I need not ask you, Will you sign it? The document lies at Gilpin's—a noble fellow—the bookseller, Bishopsgate. Should her Majesty run down the list of names, I think her bettered taste in Shakespeare would dwell complacently on the name of Mary Cowden Clarke.

I don't know when they pay dividends at the Bank, but if this be the time, you can in the same journey fill your pocket, and lighten your conscience. Regards to Clarke.

Yours ever truly,
D. JERROLD.

Jerrold took a hearty interest in an attempted reform, in a matter which affected him as a literary man, a reform since accomplished—the Repeal of all Taxes on Knowledge. He had been invited to take the chair at a meeting for the consideration of the subject; and he sent the following witty letter to be read instead of a speech from him, being unable to attend :—

West Lodge Putney, Lower Common.
Feb. 25th, 1852.

DEAR SIR,—Disabled by an accident from personal attendance at your meeting, I trust I may herein be permitted to express my heartiest sympathy with its great social purpose. That the fabric, paper, newspapers, and advertisements should be taxed by any Government possessing paternal yearnings for the education of a people, defies the argument of reason. Why not, to help the lame and to aid the short-sighted, lay a tax upon crutches, and enforce a duty upon spectacles ?

I am not aware of the number of professional writers—of men who live from pen to mouth—flourishing this day in merry England ; but it appears to me, and the notion, to a new Chancellor of the Exchequer (I am happy to say one of *my* order—of the cosequill, not of the heron's plume) may have some significance; why not enforce a duty upon the very source and origin of letters? Why not have a literary poll-tax, a duty upon books and "articles" in their rawest materials? Let every author pay for his licence, poetic or otherwise. This would give a wholeness of contradiction to a professed desire for knowledge, when existing with taxation of its material elements. Thus, the exciseman, beginning with authors' brains, would descend through rags, and duly end with paper. This tax upon news is captious and arbitrary; arbitrary, I say, for what is *not* news? A noble lord makes a speech : his rays of intelligence compressed like Milton's fallen angels, are in a few black rows of this type ; and this is news. And is not a new book "news"? Let Ovid first tell us how Midas first laid himself down, and—private and confidential—whispered to the reeds, "I have ears ;" and is not that news? Do many noble lords, even in Parliament, tell us anything newer?

The tax on advertisements is — it is patent—a tax even upon the industry of the very hardest workers. Why should the Exchequer waylay the errand boy and oppress the maid-of-all-work? Wherefore should Mary Ann be made to disburse her eighteenpence at the Stamp Office ere she can show her face in print, wanting a place, although to the discomfiture of those first-created Chancellors of the Exchequer—the spiders?

In conclusion, I must congratulate the meeting on the advent of the new Chancellor of the Exchequer. The Right Honourable Benjamin D'Israeli is the successful man of letters. He has ink in his veins. The goosequill—let gold and silver-sticks twinkle as they may—leads the House of Commons. Thus, I feel confident that the literary instincts of the right honourable gentleman will give new animation to the coldness of statesmanship, apt to be numbed by tightness of red-tape. We are, I know, early taught to despair of the right honourable gentleman, because he is allowed to be that smallest of things, "a wit." Is arithmetic for ever to be the monopoly of substantial respectable dulness? Must it be that a Chancellor of the Exchequer, like *Portia's* portrait, is only to be found in lead?

T 2

No, sir, I have a cheerful faith that our new fiscal minister will, to the confusion of obese dulness, show his potency over pounds, shillings, and pence. The Exchequer L.S.D. that have hitherto been as the three Witches—the weird sisters—stopping us, wherever we turned, the right honourable gentleman will at the least transform into the three Graces, making them in all their salutations, at home and abroad, welcome and agreeable. But with respect to the L.S.D. upon knowledge, he will, I feel confident, cause at once the weird sisterhood to melt into thin air; and thus—let the meeting take heart with the assurance—thus will fade and be dissolved the Penny News'-tax—the errand-boy and maid-of-all-work's tax—and the tax on that innocent white thing, the tax on paper. With this hope I remain, yours faithfully,

DOUGLAS JERROLD.

J. Alfred Novello, Esq.,
Sub-Treasurer of the Association for the Repeal
of all Taxes upon Knowledge.

Another letter, excusing his attendance at a meeting, serves to show his lively interest in the Whittington Club, of which he was the Founder and President; and also demonstrates his sincere desire for the establishment of recognized social equality for women with men. This is the letter:—

To the Secretary of the Whittington Club.

West Lodge, Putney Lower Common, June 18th.

DEAR SIR,—It is to me a very great disappointment that I am denied the pleasure of being with you on the interesting occasion of to-day; when the club starts into vigorous existence, entering upon—I hope and believe—a long life of usefulness to present and succeeding generations. I have for some days been labouring with a violent cold, which, at the last hour, leaves me no hope of being with you. This to me is especially discomfiting upon the high occasion the council meet to celebrate; for we should have but very little to boast of by the establishment of the club, had we only

founded a sort of monster chop-house ; no great addition
this to London, where chop-houses are certainly not among
the rarer monuments of British civilization.

We therefore recognize a higher purpose in the Whittington Club ; namely, a triumphant refutation of a very old,
respectable, but no less foolish fallacy—for folly and respectability are somehow sometimes found together—that female
society in such an institution is incompatible with female
domestic dignity. Hitherto, Englishmen have made their
club-houses as Mahomet made his Paradise—a place where
women are not admitted on any pretext whatever. Thus
considered, the Englishman may be a very good Christian
sort of a person at home, and at the same time little better
than a Turk at his club.

It is for us, however, to change this. And as we are the
first to assert what may be considered a great social principle,
so it is most onerous upon us that it should be watched with
the most jealous suspicion of whatever might in the most
remote degree tend to retard its very fullest success. Again
lamenting the cause that denies me the gratification of being
with you on so auspicious a day,

Believe me, yours faithfully,
DOUGLAS JERROLD.

That Jerrold felt the misinterpretation with which his
satirical hits at women's foibles had been sometimes
received is evident in the following letter, which he wrote
to thank our sister, Sabilla Novello, who had knitted him
a purse :—

Putney Green, June 9th.

DEAR MISS NOVELLO,—I thank you very sincerely for
your present, though I cannot but fear its fatal effect upon
my limited fortunes, for it is so very handsome that whenever
I produce it I feel that I have thousands a year, and, as in
duty bound, am inclined to pay accordingly. I shall go
about, to the astonishment of all omni*bii* men, insisting upon
paying sovereigns for sixpences Happily, however, this

amiable insanity will cure itself (or I may always bear my wife with me as a keeper).

About this comedy. I am writing it under the most significant warnings. As the Eastern king—name unknown, to me at least—kept a crier to warn him that he was but mortal and must die, and so to behave himself as decently as it is possible for any poor king to do, so do I keep a flock of eloquent geese that continually, within ear-shot, cackle of the British public. Hence, I trust to defeat the birds of the Haymarket by the birds of Putney.

But in this comedy I *do* contemplate *such* a heroine, as a set-off to the many sins imputed to me as committed against woman, whom I have always considered to be an admirable idea imperfectly worked out. Poor soul! she can't help that. Well, this heroine shall be woven of moon-beams—a perfect angel, with one wing cut to keep her among us. She shall be all devotion. She shall hand over her lover (never mind *his* heart, poor wretch!) to her grandmother, who she suspects is very fond of him, and then, disguising herself as a youth, she shall enter the British navy, and return in six years, say, with epaulets on her shoulders, and her name in the Navy List, rated Post-Captain. You will perceive that I have Madame Celeste in my eye—am measuring her for the uniform. And young ladies will sit in the boxes, and with tearful eyes, and noses like rose-buds, say, " What magnanimity !" And when this great work is done—this monument of the very best gilt gingerbread to woman set up on the Haymarket stage—you shall, if you will, go and see it, and make one to cry for the " Author," rewarding him with a crown of tin-foil, and a shower of sugar-plums.

In lively hope of that ecstatic moment, I remain, yours truly,

DOUGLAS JERROLD.

The following is one of his playful notes, also addressed to Sabilla Novello :—

Putney Common, June 18th.

MY DEAR MISS NOVELLO,—I ought ere this to have thanked you for the prospectus. I shall certainly avail myself of its proffered advantages, and, on the close of the vacation, send my girl.

I presume, ere that time, you will have returned to the purer shades of Bayswater from all the pleasant iniquities of Paris. I am unexpectedly deprived of every chance of leaving home, at least for some time, if at all this season, by a literary projection that I thought would have been deferred until late in the autumn ; otherwise, how willingly would I black the seams and elbows of my coat with my ink, and elevating my quill into a *cure-dent*, hie me to the " *Trois-Frères* " ! But this must not be for God knows when—or the Devil (my devil, mind) better. I am indeed " nailed to the dead wood," as Lamb says ; or rather, in this glorious weather, I feel as somehow a butterfly, or, since I am getting fat, a June fly, impaled on iron pin, or pen, must feel fixed to one place, with every virtuous wish to go anywhere and everywhere, with anybody and almost *every* body. I am not an independent spinster, but—" I won't weep." Not one unmanly tear shall stain this sheet

With desperate calmness I subscribe myself, yours faithfully,

DOUGLAS JERROLD.

The next enclosed tickets of admission to the performance of Ben Jonson's comedy of " Every Man in his Humour," at Miss Kelly's little theatre in Dean Street, Soho, when Jerrold played Master Stephen ; Charles Dickens, Bobadil ; Mark Lemon, Brainworm ; John Forster, Kitely ; and John Leech, Master Mathew. It was the first attempt of that subsequently famous amateur company, and a glorious beginning it was. Douglas Jerrold's Master Stephen,—that strong mongrel likeness of Abraham Slender and Andrew Aguecheek,—was excellently facetious in the conceited coxcombry of the part, and in its occasional smart retorts was only *too good*—that is to say, he showed just too keen a consciousness of the aptness and point in reply for the blunt perceptions of such an

oaf as Master Stephen.   For instance, when Bobadil,
disarmed and beaten by Downwright, exclaims, "Sure I
was struck with a planet thence," and Stephen rejoins
"No, you were *struck with a stick*," the words were
uttered with that peculiar Jerroldian twinkle of the eye
and humorously dry inflection of the voice that accompanied the speaker's own repartees, and made one behold
Douglas Jerrold himself beneath the garb of Master
Stephen.

Thursday, Sept., 1845.

MY DEAR MRS. CLARKE,—In haste I send you accompanying. "Call no man happy till he is dead," says the
sage.   Never give thanks for tickets for an amateur play till
the show is *over*. You don't know what may be in store for
you—and for *us!*

> Alas, regardless of their doom,
> The little victims play—(or try to play).

Yours faithfully,
D. JERROLD.

Jerrold would perceive the germ of a retort before you
had well begun to form your sentence, and would bring
it forth in full blossom the instant you had done speaking.
He had a way of looking straight in the face of one to
whom he dealt a repartee, and with an expression of eye
that seemed to ask appreciation of the point of the thing
he was going to say, thus depriving it of personality or
ill-nature.   It was as if he called upon its object to enjoy
it with him, rather than to resent its sharpness.   There
was a peculiar compression with a sudden curve or lift
up of the lip that showed his own sense of the fun of
the thing he was uttering, while his glance met his
interlocutor's with a firm, unflinching roguery and an

unfaltering drollery of tone that had none of the sidelong, furtive look and irritating tone of usual utterers of mere rough retorts. When an acquaintance came up to him and said, " Why, Jerrold, I hear you said my nose was like the ace of clubs ! " Jerrold returned, " No, I didn't ; but now I look at it, I see it is very like." The question of the actual resemblance was far less present to his mind than the neatness of his own turn upon the complainant. So with a repartee, which he repeated to us himself as having made on a particular occasion, evidently relishing the comic audacity, and without intending a spark of insolence. When the publisher of *Bentley's Miscellany* said to Jerrold, " I had some doubts about the name I should give the magazine ; 1 thought at one time of calling it 'The Wits' Miscellany ; '" " Well," was the rejoinder, " but you needn't have gone to the other extremity." Knowing Jerrold, we feel that had the speaker been the most brilliant genius that ever lived the retort would have been the same, the patness having once entered his brain. He would drop his witticisms like strewed flowers, as he went on talking, lavishly, as one who possessed countless store ; yet always with that glance of enjoyment in them himself, and of challenging your sympathetic relish for them in return which acknowledges the truth of the Shakespearian axiom, " A jest's prosperity lies in the ear of him that hears it." He illustrated his conversation, as it were, by these wit-blossoms cast in by the way. Speaking of a savage biting critic, Jerrold said, " Oh yes, he'll review the book, as an east wind reviews an apple-tree." Of an actress who thought inordinately well of herself, he said, " She's a perfect whitlow of vanity." And of a young writer who brought out his first raw specimen of authorship, Jerrold said, "He is like a man taking down his shop-shutters before he has any goods to sell."

One of the pleasant occasions on which we met Douglas Jerrold was at a house where a dance was going on as we entered the room; and in a corner, near to the dancers, we saw him sitting, and made our way to his side. With her back towards where he and we sat was a pretty little shapely figure in pink silk, standing ready to begin the next portion of the quadrille; and he pointed towards it, saying,—

"Mrs. Jerrold is here to-night; there she is.

"Not like the figure of a *grandmamma*," was the laughing reply, for we had heard that a grandchild had just been born to them, and we thought of what we had once heard recounted of the first time he had seen her,— he, an impetuous lad of eighteen, just returned from sea,—and she, a girl with so neat and graceful a figure that as he beheld it he exclaimed, "That girl shall be my wife!" So mere a stripling was he when he married that he told us the clergyman who joined their hands, seeing the almost boyishly youthful look of the bride-groom, addressed a few kind and fatherly words to him after the ceremony, bidding him remember the serious duty he had undertaken of providing for a young girl's welfare, and that he must remember her future happiness in life depended henceforth mainly upon him as her husband.

It was on that same evening that we are speaking of that Jerrold said, "I want to introduce you to a young poetess only nineteen years of age;" and took us into the next room, where was a young lady robed in simple white muslin, with light brown hair smoothly coiled round a well-formed head, and an air of grave and queenly quiet dignity. She sat down to the piano at request, and accompanied herself in Tennyson's song of " Mariana in the Moated Grange," singing with much expression and with a deep contralto voice. It was before she was known to the world as a prose writer, before she had put forth to the world her first novel of " The Ogilvies."

Another introduction to a distinguished writer we owe to Douglas Jerrold. We had been to call upon him at his pretty residence, West Lodge, Putney Common, when we found him just going to drive himself into town in a little pony carriage he at that time kept. He made us accompany him ; and as we passed through a turnpike on the road back to London we saw a gentleman approaching on horseback. Jerrold and he saluted each other, and then we were presented to him, and heard his name, —William Makepeace Thackeray. Many years after that his daughter, paying her first visit to Italy, was brought by a friend to see us in Genoa, and charmed us by the sweetness and unaffected simplicity of her manners.

That cottage at Putney—its garden, its mulberry-tree, its grass-plot, its cheery library, with Douglas Jerrold as the chief figure in the scene—remains as a bright and most pleasant picture in our memory. He had an almost reverential fondness for books—books themselves—and said he could not bear to treat them, or to see them treated, with disrespect. He told us it gave him pain to see them turned on their faces, stretched open, or dog's-eared, or carelessly flung down, or in any way misused. He told us this holding a volume in his hand with a caressing gesture, as though he tendered it affectionately and gratefully for the pleasure it had given him. He spoke like one who had known what it was in former years to buy a book when its purchase involved a sacrif.ce of some other object, from a not over-stored purse. We have often noticed this in book-lovers who, like ourselves, have had volumes come into cherished possession at times when their glad owners were not rich enough to easily afford book-purchases. Charles Lamb had this tenderness for books; caring nothing for their gaudy clothing, but hugging a rare folio all the nearer to his heart for its worn edges and shabby binding. Another peculiarity with regard to his books Jerrold had, which was, that he liked to have them thoroughly *within reach ;* so that, as he pointed out to us, he had the book-shelves which ran round his library walls at Putney carried no higher than would permit of easy access to the top shelf. Above this there was sufficient space for pictures, engravings, &c., and we had the pleasure of contributing two ornaments to this space, in the form of a bust of Shakespeare and one of Milton, on brackets after a design by Michael Angelo, which brought from dear Douglas Jerrold the following pleasant letter :—

Putney, August 8th.

MY DEAR MRS. CLARKE,—I know not how best to thank you for the surprise you and Clarke put upon me this morning. These casts, while demanding reverence for what they represent and typify, will always associate with the feeling that of sincerest regard and friendship for the donors. These things will be very precious to me, and, I hope, for many a long winter's night awaken frequent recollections of the thoughtful kindness that has made them my household gods. I well remembered the brackets, but had forgotten the master. But this is the gratitude of the world.

I hope that my girl will be able to be got ready for this quarter; but in a matter that involves the making, trimming, and fitting of gowns or frocks, it is not for one of my benighted sex to offer a decided opinion. I can only timidly venture to believe that the young lady's trunk will be ready in a few days.

Pandora's box was only a box of woman's clothes—with a Sunday gown at the bottom.—Yours truly,

DOUGLAS JERROLD.

It was while Jerrold was living at West Lodge that he not only founded the Whittington Club, but also the Museum Club, which, when he asked us to belong to it, he said he wanted to make a mart where literary men could congregate, become acquainted, form friendships, discuss their rights and privileges, be known to assemble, and therefore could be readily found when required. " I want to make it," he said, " *a house of call for writers.*" It was at Putney that Jerrold told us the amusing (and very characteristic) story of himself when he was at sea as a youngster. He and some officers on board had sent ashore a few men to fetch a supply of fresh fruit and vegetables, at some port into which the ship had put when she was on one of her voyages, and, on the boat's return alongside, it was found that one of the men had decamped. The ship sailed without the runaway, and on her return to England Jerrold quitted the service. Some years after he was walking in the Strand, and saw a man with a baker's basket on his shoulder staring in at a shop window, whom Jerrold immediately recognized as the deserter from the ship. He went up to the man, slapped him on the shoulder, and exclaimed, " I say ! what a long time you've been gone for those cherries !" The dramatic surprise of the exclamation was quite in Jerrold's way.

There was a delightful irony—an implied compliment beneath his sharp things—that made them exquisitely agreeable. They were said with a spice of slyness, yet with a fully evident confidence that they would not be misunderstood by the person who was their object. When we went over to West Lodge after the opening of the Whittington Club, to take him a cushion for his library arm-chair, with the head of a cat that might have been Dick Whittington's own embroidered upon it, Jerrold turned to his wife, saying, " My dear, they have brought me your portrait." And the smile that met his showed how well the woman who had been his devoted partner from youth comprehended the delicate force of the ironical jest which he could *afford* to address to *her*. In a similar spirit of pleasantry he wrote in the presentation copy of " Mrs. Caudle's Curtain Lectures" which he gave to M. C. C. : " Presented with great timidity, but equal regard, to Mrs. Cowden Clarke."

In 1848 was brought out a small pocket volume entitled "Shakespeare Proverbs ; or, The Wise Saws of our Wisest Poet collected into a Modern Instance ;" and its dedication ran thus : " To Douglas Jerrold, the first wit of the present age, these Proverbs of Shakespeare, the first wit of any age, are inscribed by Mary Cowden Clarke, of a certain age, and no wit at all." This brought the following playful letter of acknowledgment :—

West Lodge, Putney, December 31st.

MY DEAR MRS. CLARKE,—You must imagine that all this time I have been endeavouring to regain my breath, taken away by your too partial dedication. To find my name on such a page, and in such company, I feel like a sacrilegious knave who has broken into a church and is making off with the Communion plate. One thing is plain, Shakespeare *had* great obligations to you, but this last inconsiderate act has certainly cancelled them all. I feel that I ought never to speak or write again, but go down to the grave with my thumb in my mouth. It is the *only* chance I have of not betraying my pauper-like unworthiness to the association with which you have—to the utter wreck of your discretion—astounded me.

The old year is dying with the dying fire whereat this is penned. That, however, you may have many, many happy years (though they can only add to the remorse for what you have done) is the sincere wish of yours truly (if you will not show the word to Clarke, I will say affectionately),

DOUGLAS JERROLD.

When the "Concordance to Shakespeare" made its complete appearance, it was thus greeted :—

December 5th, West Lodge, Putney Common.

MY DEAR MRS. CLARKE,—I congratulate you and the world on the completion of your monumental work. May it make for you a huge bed of mixed laurels and bank-notes.

On your first arrival in Paradise you must expect a kiss from Shakespeare,—even though your husband should *happen* to be there.

That you and he, however, may long make for yourselves a Paradise here, is the sincere wish of—Yours truly,

DOUGLAS JERROLD.

P.S. I will certainly *hitch* in a notice of the work in *Punch*, making it a special case, as we eschew Reviews.

The kind promise contained in the postscript to the above letter was fulfilled in the most graceful and in-genious manner by its writer, in a brilliant article he wrote some time after on "The Shakespeare Night" at Covent Garden Theatre, that took place the 7th December, 1847. After describing in glowing terms the festive look of the overflowing house, Jerrold proceeded : —"At a few minutes to seven, and quite unexpectedly, William Shakespeare, with his wife, the late Anne Hathaway, drove up to the private box door, drawn by

Pegasus, for that night only appearing in harness. . . . .
Shakespeare was received – and afterwards lighted to his
box—by his editors, Charles Knight and Payne Collier,
upon both of whom the poet smiled benignly ; and saying some pleasant, commendable words to each, received
from their hands their two editions of his immortality.
And then from a corner Mrs. Cowden Clarke, timidly,
and all one big blush, presented a play-bill, with some
Hesperian fruit (of her own gathering).   Shakespeare
knew the lady at once; and, taking her two hands, and
looking a Shakespearian look in her now pale face, said,
in tones of unimaginable depth and sweetness, 'But
where is *your* book, Mistress Mary Clarke? Where is
your *Concordance ?'*   And, again, pressing her hands,
with a smile of sun-lighted Apollo, said, ' I pray you let
me take it home with me.'   And Mrs. Clarke, having no
words, dropped the profoundest 'Yes,' with knocking
knees.   'A very fair and cordial gentlewoman, Anne,'
said Shakespeare, aside to his wife ; but Anne merely
observed that 'It was just like him ; he was always seeing
something fair where nobody else saw anything.   The
woman –odds her life ! –was well enough.'   And Shakespeare smiled again !"

That sentence, of Shakespeare's " always seeing something fair where nobody else saw anything," is a profound
piece of truth as well as wit ; while the smile with which
the poet is made to listen to his wife's intolerance of
hearing her husband praise another woman is perfectly
Jerroldian in its sly hit at a supposed prevalent feminine
foible.

Jerrold had a keen sense of personal beauty in women.
In the very article above quoted he uses expressions in
speaking of Shakespeare's admiration for Mrs. Nesbitt's

charms that strikingly evidence this point : — " Then taking a *deep look—a very draught of a look*—at Mrs. Nesbitt as Katherine, the poet turned to his wife and said, *drawing his breath*, ' What *a peach of a woman !* ' Anne said nothing." Here, too, again, he concludes with the Jerroldian sarcastic touch. In confirmation of the powerful impression that loveliness in women had upon his imagination, we remember his telling us with enthusiasm of the merits in the Hon. Mrs. Norton's poem " The Child of the Islands," dilating on some of its best passages, and, adding that he had lately met her and spoken to her face to face ; he concluded with the words " She herself is beautiful—even *dangerously* beautiful !"

Four letters we received from him were in consequence of an application that is stated in the first of them. The second mentions the wish of " the correspondent ; " and this was that the letter in which the desired " two lines " were written should be sent without envelope, and on a sheet of paper that would bear the *post-mark*, as an evidence of genuineness. The third accepts the offer to share the promised " two ounces of Californian gold." And the fourth was written with one of the two gold pens, which were the shape in which the promised " two ounces " were sent to England by the " Enthusiast :"—

West Lodge, Putney, October 10th, 1849.

MY DEAR MRS. CLARKE,—I know a man who knows a man (in America) who says, "I would give two ounces of Californian gold for two lines written by Mrs. Cowden Clarke !" Will you write me two lines for the wise enthusiast? and, IF I get the gold, that will doubtless be paid with the Pennsylvanian Bonds, I will struggle with the angel Conscience that you may have it—that is, if the angel get the best of it. But against angels there are heavy odds.

I hope you left father and mother well, happy, and complacent, in the hope of a century at least. I am glad you stopped at Nice, and did not snuff the shambles of Rome. Mazzini, I hear, will be with us in a fortnight. European liberty is, I fear, manacled and gagged for many years. Nevertheless, in England, let us rejoice that beef is under a shilling a pound, and that next Christmas ginger will be hot i' the mouth.

Remember me to Clarke. I intend to go one of these nights and sit beneath him.—Yours faithfully,

DOUGLAS JERROLD.

October 19th, 1849, Putney.

MY DEAR MRS. CLARKE,—Will you comply with the wish of my correspondent? The Yankees, it appears, are suspicious folks. I thought them Arcadians.—Truly yours,

D. JERROLD.

West Lodge, Putney Common, February 22nd, 1850.

MY DEAR MRS. CLARKE,—I will share anything with you, and can only wish—at least for myself—that the matter to be shared came not in so pleasant a shape as that dirt in yellow gold. I have heard naught of the American, and would rather that his gift came brightened through you than from his own hand. The savage, with glimpses of civilization, is male.

Do you read the *Morning Chronicle?* Do you devour those marvellous revelations of the inferno of misery, of wretchedness that is smouldering under our feet? We live in a mockery of Christianity that, with the thought of its hypocrisy, makes me sick. We know nothing of this terrible life that is about us—us, in our smug respectability. To read of the sufferings of one class, and of the avarice, the tyranny, the pocket cannibalism of the other, makes one almost wonder that the world should go on, that the misery and wretchedness of the earth are not, by an Almighty fiat, ended. And when we see the spires of pleasant churches pointing to Heaven, and are told—paying thousands to bishops for the glad intelligence—that we are Christians! the cant of this country is enough to poison the atmosphere.

I send you the *Chronicle* of yesterday. You will therein read what I think you will agree to be one of the most beautiful records of the nobility of the poor: of those of whom our jaunty legislators know nothing ; of the things made in the statesman's mind, to be taxed—not venerated. I am very proud to say that these papers of "Labour and the Poor" were projected by Henry Mayhew, who married my girl. For comprehensiveness of purpose and minuteness of detail they have never been approached. He will cut his name deep. From these things I have still great hopes. A revival movement is at hand, and—you will see what you'll see. Remember me with best thoughts to Clarke, and believe me yours sincerely,

DOUGLAS JERROLD.

Putney, February 25th, 1850.

MY DEAR MRS. CLARKE,—Herewith I send you my "first copy," done in, I presume, American gold. Considering what American booksellers extract from English brains, even the smallest piece of the precious metal is, to literary eyes, refreshing. I doubt, however, whether these gold pens really work ; they are pretty holiday things, but to earn daily bread with, I have already my misgivings that I must go back to iron. To be sure, I *once* had a gold pen that seemed to write of itself, but this was stolen by a Cinderella who, of course, could *not* write even with that gold pen. Perhaps, however, *the* Policeman *could.*

That the *Chronicle* did not come was my blunder. I hope 'twill reach you with this, and with it my best wishes and affectionate regards to you and flesh and bone of you.

Truly ever,
DOUGLAS JERROLD.

The next note evinces how acutely Jerrold felt the death of excellent Lord George Nugent : the wording is solemn and earnest as a low-toned passing-bell :—

Putney, December 2nd, 1850.

MY DEAR CLARKE,—I have received book, for which

U 2

thanks, and best wishes for that and all followers. Over a sea-coal fire, this week—all dark and quiet outside—I shall enjoy its flavour. Best regards, I mean love, to the authoress. Poor dear Nugent! He and I became great friends : I've had many happy days with him at Lilies. A noble, cordial man ; and—the worst of it—his foolish carelessness of health has flung away some ten or fifteen years of genial winter—frosty, but kindly. God be with him, and all yours.   Truly yours,

D. JERROLD.

There was a talk at one time of his going into Parliament; and at a dinner-table where he was the subject was discussed, there chancing to be present several members of the house, some of them spoke of the very different thing it was to address a company under usual circumstances and to " address the House," observing what a peculiarly nervous thing it was to face *that assembly*, and that few men could picture to themselves the difficulty till they had actually encountered it. Jerrold averred that he did not think he should feel this particular terror : then turning to the Parliamentary men present round the dinner-table, he counted them all, and said, "There are ten of you members of Parliament before me ; I suppose you don't consider yourselves the greatest fools in the house, and yet I can't say that I feel particularly afraid of addressing you."

We have a portrait of Douglas Jerrold, which he himself sent to us ; and which we told him we knew must be an excellent likeness, for we always found ourselves smiling whenever we looked at it. A really good likeness of a friend we think invariably produces this effect. The smile may be glad, fond, tender—nay, even mournful : but a smile always comes to the lip in looking upon a truly close resemblance of a beloved face.

Jerrold was occasionally a great sufferer from rheumatic pains, which attacked him at intervals under various forms. The following letter adverts to one of these severe inflictions; at the same time that it is written in his best vein of animation and vigour of feeling :—

Friday, Putney.

MY DEAR CLARKE,—I have but a blind excuse to offer for my long silence to your last: but the miserable truth is, I have been in darkness with acute inflammation of the eye; something like toothache in the eye—and very fit to test a man's philosophy; when he can neither read nor write, and has no other consolation save first to discover his own virtues, and when caught to contemplate them. I assure you it's devilish difficult to put one's hand upon one's virtue in a dark room. As well try to catch fleas in "the blanket o' the dark." By this, however, you will perceive that I have returned to paper and ink. The doctor tells me that the inflammation fell upon me from an atmospheric blight, rife in these parts three weeks ago. *I* think I caught it at Hyde Park Corner, where for three minutes I paused to see the Queen pass after being fired at. She looked very well, and—as is not always the case with women—none the worse for powder. To be sure, considering they give princesses a salvo of artillery with their first pap—they ought to stand saltpetre better than folks who come into the world w'thout any charge to the State—without even blank charge.

Your friend of the beard is, I think, quite right. When God made Adam he did *not* present him with a razor, but a wife. 'Tis the d—d old clothesmen who have brought discredit upon a noble appendage of man. Thank God we've revenge for this. They'll make some of 'em members of Parliament.

I purpose to break in upon you some early Sunday, to kiss the hands of your wife, and to tell you delightful stories of the deaths of kings. How nobly Mazzini is behaving ! And what a cold, calico cur is John Bull, as—I fear—too truly rendered by the *Times*. The French are in a nice mess. Heaven in its infinite mercy confound them !—Truly yours,

DOUGLAS JERROLD.

And now we give the last letter, alas! that we ever received from him. It is comforting in its hearty valedictory words: yet how often did we—how often do we still—regret that his own yearning to visit the south could never be fulfilled! He is among those whom we most frequently find ourselves wishing could behold this Italian matchless view that lies now daily before our eyes. That his do behold it with some higher and diviner power of sight than belongs to earthly eyes is our constant, confident hope :—

26, Circus Road, St. John's Wood,
October 20th, 1856.

MY DEAR FRIENDS,—I have delayed an answer to your kind letter (for I cannot but see in it the hands and hearts of *both*) in the hope of being able to make my way to Bayswater. Yesterday I had determined, and was barred, and barred, and barred by droppers-in, the Sabbath-breakers! Lo, I delay no longer. But I only shake hands with you for a time, as it is my resolute determination to spend nine weeks at Nice next autumn with my wife and daughter. I shall give you due notice of the descent, that we may avail ourselves of your experience as to "*location,*" as those savages the Americans yell in their native war-whoop tongue.

Therefore, God speed ye safely to your abiding-place, where I hope long days of serenest peace may attend ye.

Believe me ever truly yours,
DOUGLAS JERROLD.

Charles Cowden } Clarke.
Mary Victoria }

It chanced, at one time of our lives, that we had frequently to pass along the New Road ; and as we drove by one particular house—a tall house, the upper windows of which were visible above the high wall that enclosed its front garden—we always looked at it with affectionate interest as long as it remained in sight. For in that house, No. 1, Devonshire Terrace, we knew lived the young author who had "witched the world with noble penmanship" in those finely original serials that put forth their "two green leaves" month by month. We then knew no more of his personal identity than what we had gathered from the vigorous youthful portrait of him by Samuel Lawrence as "Boz," and from having seen him and heard him speak at the "Farewell dinner" given to Macready in 1839. We little thought, as we gazed at the house where he dwelt, that we should ever come to sit within its walls, palm to palm in greeting, face to face in talk, side by side at table, with its fascinating master, who shone with especial charm of brilliancy and cordiality as host entertaining his guests. We knew him by his portrait to be superlatively handsome, with his rich, wavy locks of hair, and his magnificent eyes ; and we knew him by what we saw of him at the Macready dinner to be possessed of remarkably observant faculty, with perpetually discursive glances at those around him, taking note as it were of every slightest peculiarity in look, or manner, or speech, or tone that characterized each individual. No spoonful of soup seemed to reach his lips unaccompanied by a gathered oddity or whimsicality, no morsel to be raised on his fork unseasoned by a droll gesture or trick he had remarked in some one near. And when it came to his turn to speak, his after-dinner speech was one of the best in matter and style of delivery then given, —though there were present on that occasion some practised speakers. His speech was like himself,— genial, full of good spirit and good spirits, of kindly feeling and cheery vivacity.

At length came that never-to-be-forgotten day—or rather, evening—when we met him at a party, and were introduced to him by Leigh Hunt, who, after a cordial word or two, left us to make acquaintance together. At once, with his own inexpressible charm of graceful ease and animation, Charles Dickens fell into delightful chat and riveted for ever the chain of fascination that his mere distant image and enchanting writings had cast about M. C. C., drawing her towards him with a perfect spell of prepossession. The prepossession was confirmed into affectionate admiration and attachment that lasted faithfully strong throughout the happy friendship that ensued, and was not even destroyed by death; for she cherishes his memory still with as fond an idolatry as she felt during that joyous period of her life when in privileged holiday companionship with him.

Charles Dickens—beaming in look, alert in manner, radiant with good humour, genial-voiced, gay, the very soul of enjoyment, fun, good taste and good spirits, admirable in organizing details and suggesting novelty of entertainment,—was of all beings the very man for a holiday season; and in singularly exceptional holiday fashion was it my [1] fortunate hap to pass every hour that I spent in his society. First, at an evening party; secondly, during one of the most unusually festive series of theatrical performances ever given; thirdly, in delightful journeys to various places where we were to act; fourthly, in hilarious suppers after acting (notedly among the most jubilant of all meal-meetings!); fifthly, in one or two choice little dinner-parties at his own house; sixthly, in a few brilliant assemblages there, when artistic, musical, and literary talent were represented by some of the most eminent among artists, musicians, and people of letters of the day; seventhly, in a dress rehearsal at Devonshire House of Lytton Bulwer's drama of "Not so bad as we seem," played by Charles Dickens and some of his friends; and, eighthly, in a performance at Tavistock House (where he then lived) of a piece called "The Lighthouse," expressly written for the due display of Charles Dickens' and his friend Mark Lemon's supremely good powers of acting.

It has been before mentioned that when I first offered Charles Dickens to join his Amateur Company in 1848 and enact Dame Quickly in the performance of Shakespeare's "Merry Wives," which he was then proposing, he did not at first comprehend that my offer was made in earnest; but on my writing to tell him so, he sent me the following letter,--which, when I received it, threw me into such rapture as rarely falls to the lot of woman possessing a strong taste for acting, yet who could hardly have expected to find it thus suddenly gratified in a manner beyond her most sanguine hopes. I ran with it to my beloved mother (my husband was

---

[1] Mary Cowden Clarke.

in the North of England, on a Lecture tour), knowing her unfailing sympathy with my wildest flights of gladness, and re-read it with her :—

Devonshire Terrace, 14th April, 1848.

DEAR MRS. COWDEN CLARKE,—I did not understand, when I had the pleasure of conversing with you the other evening, that you had really considered the subject, and desired to play. But I am very glad to understand it now; and I am sure there will be a universal sense among us of the grace and appropriateness of such a proceeding. Falstaff (who depends very much on Mrs. Quickly) may have, in his modesty, some timidity about acting with an amateur actress. But I have no question, as you have studied the part, and long wished to play it, that you will put him completely at his ease on the first night of your rehearsal. Will you, towards that end, receive this as a solemn "call" to rehearsal of "The Merry Wives" at Miss Kelly's theatre, to-morrow, Saturday *week* at seven in the evening ?

And will you let me suggest another point for your consideration ? On the night when "The Merry Wives" will *not* be played, and when "Every man in his Humour" *will* be, Kenny's farce of "Love, Law, and Physic" will be acted. In that farce, there is a very good character (one Mrs. Hilary, which I have seen Mrs. Orger, I think, act to admiration) that would have been played by Mrs. C. Jones, if she had acted Dame Quickly, as we at first intended. If you find yourself quite comfortable and at ease among us, in Mrs. Quickly, would you like to take this other part too ? It is an excellent farce, and is safe, I hope, to be very well done.

We do not play to purchase the house [2] (which may be positively considered as paid for), but towards endowing a perpetual curatorship of it, for some eminent literary veteran. And I think you will recognize in this, even a higher and

---

[2] The house in which Shakespeare was born at Stratford-on-Avon.—M. C. C.

more gracious object than the securing, even, of the debt incurred for the house itself.

Believe me, very faithfully yours,
CHARLES DICKENS.

Amid my transport and excitement there mingled some natural trepidation when the evening of "the first rehearsal" arrived, and I repaired with my sister Emma—who accompanied me throughout my "Splendid Strolling"—to the appointed spot, and found myself among the brilliant group assembled on the stage of the miniature theatre in Dean Street, Soho, men whom I had long known by reputation as distinguished artists and journalists. John Forster, Editor of the *Examiner;* two of the main-stays of *Punch,* Mark Lemon, its Editor, and John Leech, its inimitable illustrator; Augustus Egg and Frank Stone, whose charming pictures floated before my vision while I looked at themselves for the first time: all turned their eyes upon the "amateur actress" as she entered the foot-lighted circle and joined their company. But the friendliness of their reception—as Charles Dickens, with his own ready grace and alacrity, successively presented her to them—soon relieved timidity on her part. Forster's gracious and somewhat stately bow was accompanied by an affable smile and a marked courtesy that were very winning; while Mark Lemon's fine open countenance, sweet-tempered look, and frank shake of the hand, at once placed Falstaff and Mistress Quickly "at ease" with each other. There was one thing that helped me well through that evening. I had previously resolved that I would "*speak out,*" and not rehearse in half-voice, as many amateur performers invariably do who are suffering from shyness; but I, who, though I did not feel shy in acting, felt a good deal of awe at my brother actors' presence, took refuge in maintaining as steady and duly raised a tone of voice as I could possibly muster. This stood me in doubly good stead; it proved to them that I was not liable to stage fright—for, the amateur-performer who can face the small, select audience of a few whom he knows (which is so infinitely more really trying to courage than the assembled sea of unknown faces in a theatre) runs little risk of failure in performance after success in rehearsal,—and it tested to myself my own powers of self-possession and capability of making myself heard in a public and larger assemblage.

I was rewarded by being told that in next Monday morning's *Times*, which gave an amiable paragraph about the rehearsal at Miss Kelly's, there were a few words to the effect that Dame Quickly, who was the only lady amateur among the troop, promised to be an acquisition to the company.

Then followed other rehearsals, delightful in the extreme; Charles Dickens ever present, superintending, directing, suggesting, with sleepless activity and vigilance: the essence of punctuality and methodical precision himself, he kept incessant watch that others should be unfailingly attentive and careful throughout. Unlike most professional rehearsals, where waiting about, dawdling, and losing time, seem to be the order of the day, the rehearsals under Charles Dickens' stage-managership were strictly devoted to work—serious, earnest, work; the consequence was, that when the evening of performance came, the pieces went off with a smoothness and polish that belong only to finished stage-business and practised performers. He was always there among the first arrivers at rehearsals, and remained in a conspicuous position during their progress till the very last moment of conclusion. He had a small table placed rather to one side of the stage, at which he generally sat, as the scenes went on in which he himself took no part. On this table rested a moderate-sized box ; its interior divided into convenient compartments for holding papers, letters, etc., and this interior was always the very pink of neatness and orderly arrangement. Occasionally he would leave his seat at the managerial table, and stand with his back to the foot-lights, in the very centre of the front of the stage, and view the whole effect of the re-hearsed performance as it proceeded, observing the attitudes and positions of those engaged in the dialogue, their mode of entrance, exit, etc., etc. He never seemed to overlook anything ; but to note the very slightest point that conduced to the "going well" of the whole performance. With all this supervision, however, it was pleasant to remark the utter absence of dictatorial-ness or arrogation of superiority that distinguished his mode of ruling his troop : he exerted his authority firmly and perpetually ; but in such a manner as to make it universally felt to be for no purpose of self-assertion or self-importance ; on the contrary, to be for the sole pur-pose of ensuring general success to their united efforts.

Some of these rehearsals were productive of incidents that gave additional zest to their intrinsic interest. I remember one evening, Miss Kelly—Charles Lamb's admired Fanny Kelly—standing at "the wing" while I went through my first scene with Falstaff, watching it keenly ; and afterwards, coming up to me, uttering many kind words of encouragement, approval, and lastly sug-gestion, ending with, " Mind you stand well forward on the stage while you speak to Sir John, and don't let that great big burly man hide you from the audience; you generally place yourself too near him, and rather in the rear of his elbow." I explained that my motive had been to denote the deference paid by the messenger of the " Merry Wives " to the fat Knight, and that it might be I unconsciously had the habit of usually standing anything but in advance of those with whom I talked; for it had often been observed by my friends that I did this, and also generally allowed others to pass before me in or out of a room. She laughed and said she too had observed these peculiarities in me; and then she gave me another good stage hint, saying, "Always keep your eyes looking well *up*, and try to fix them on the higher range of boxes, otherwise they are lost to the audience; and much depends on the audience getting a good sight of the eyes and their expression." I told her that I dreaded the glare of the chandelier and lights, as my eyes were not strong. She replied, " Look well *up*, and you'll find that the under eyelids will quite protect you from the glare of the foot-lights, the dazzle of which is the chief thing that perplexes the sight." On the night of the dress rehearsal at Miss Kelly's theatre of the " Merry Wives," William Macready came to see us play; and during one of the intervals between the acts, Charles Dickens brought him on to the stage and introduced him to me. The reader may imagine what a flutter of pleasure stirred my heart, as I stood with apparent calm talking to the great tragedian; at length plucking up sufficient bravery of ease to tell him how much I admired his late enacting of Benedick, and the artistic mode in which he held up the muscles of his face so as to give a light-comedy look to the visage accustomed to wear a stern aspect in Coriolanus, a sad one in Hamlet, a serious one in Macbeth, a worn one in Lear, etc. As I spoke, the "muscles of his face" visibly relaxed into the pleasant smile so exquisite on a countenance of such rugged strength and firmness as his ; and he looked thoroughly amused and not ungratified by my boldness. I was amused, and moreover amazed, at it myself, as we remained conversing on ; until the time for resuming the rehearsal came, and I had the honour of hearing the technical cry of " Clear the stage ! " addressed to *Macready and myself* (!) and having to hurry off the boards *together* (!) Then there were rehearsals on the Haymarket stage itself, that we might become acquainted with the exact locality on which we were to give the two nights of London public performance. The time fixed for one of these rehearsals was early in the afternoon of a day when there had been a morning rehearsal of the Haymarket company themselves ; and I was diverted to notice that several of its members remained lingering about the side scenes—the professionals interested to see how the amateurs would act. Among them was William Farren, who, when a young man of little more than twenty, was so excellent an impersonator of old men, and whose Lord Ogleby, Sir Peter Teazle, and other old-gentlemanly characters, will not readily be forgotten by those who saw him play them. There too, that afternoon, with the daylight streaming through an upper window upon her surpassingly beautiful face, was Mrs. Nesbitt ; and, to the dismay of one who knew herself to be well-nigh as plain and quiet-looking as Mrs. Nesbitt was handsome and brilliant, they both chanced to wear on that occasion precisely the same kind of grey chip bonnet, with pale pink tulle veil and trimmings, which was at that time "*the* fashion." This was a bit of secret feminine consciousness which it seems strange to be now revealing; but it occurred in that bright, keenly-felt time, when everything seemed especially vivid to its enjoyer, and is therefore worth while recording as lending vividness and reality to the impressions sought to be conveyed by the present writer in her fast advancing old age.

Besides a list of rehearsals and a copy of the "Rules for Rehearsals" (extracts from which are given in a Note at page 363-4, vol. ii., of Forster's "Life of Charles Dickens") signed by his own hand, I had received the following notelet in reply to my inquiry of what edition of Shakespeare's "Merry Wives" would be used; all giving token of his promptitude and business-like attention to the enterprise in hand. The "family usage" alluded to was that of always calling him at home by the familiar loving appellation of "Dear Dickens" or "Darling Dickens."   So scrupulously has been treasured every scrap of his writing addressed to me or penned for me, that the very brown paper cover in which the copy of "Love, Law, and Physic" was sent is still in existence; as is the card, bearing the words "Pass to the stage: Charles Dickens," with the emphatic scribble beneath his name, which formed the magic order for entrance through the stage-door of the Haymarket Theatre :—

Devonshire Terrace, Sunday morning,
16th April, 1848.

DEAR MRS. COWDEN CLARKE,—As I am the Stage manager, you could not have addressed your inquiry to a more fit and proper person. The *mode* of address would be unobjectionable, but for the knowledge you give me of that family usage,—which I think preferable, and indeed quite perfect.

Enclosed is Knight's cabinet edition of the "Merry Wives;"

from which the company study. I also send you a copy of " Love, Law, and Physic." Believe me always very faithfully yours, CHARLES DICKENS.

As the period for performance approached, I more and more regretted that my husband was still away lecturing ; but, as whenever he was absent from home we invariably wrote to each other once (sometimes twice) a day, he and I were able thoroughly to follow in spirit all that we were respectively engaged with and interested in.

The date of our first night at the Haymarket Theatre was the 15th of May,[1] 1848 ; when the entertainment consisted of " The Merry Wives of Windsor " and " Animal Magnetism." The " make up" of Charles Dickens as Justice Shallow was so complete, that his own identity was almost unrecognizable, when he came on to the stage, as the curtain rose, in company with Sir Hugh and Master Slender ; but after a moment's breathless pause, the whole house burst forth into a roar of applausive reception, which testified to the boundless delight of the assembled audience on beholding the literary idol of the day, actually before them. His impersonation was perfect : the old, stiff limbs, the senile stoop of the shoulders, the head bent with age, the feeble step, with a certain attempted smartness of carriage characteristic of the conceited Justice of the Peace,— were all assumed and maintained with wonderful accuracy ; while the articulation,—part lisp, part thickness of utterance, part a kind of impeded sibillation, like that of a voice that " pipes and whistles in the sound" through loss of teeth—

[1] In Forster's " Life of Charles Dickens " the month is erroneously stated to be April ; but I have the Haymarket Play-bill, beautifully printed in delicate colours, now before me.—M. C. C.

gave consummate effect to his mode of speech. The one in which Shallow says, " 'Tis the heart, Master Page ; 'tis here, 'tis here. I have seen the time with my long sword I would have made you four tall fellows skip like rats," was delivered with a humour of expression in effete energy of action and would-be fire of spirit that marvellously imaged fourscore years in its attempt to denote vigour long since extinct.

Mark Lemon's Sir John Falstaff was a fine embodiment of rich, unctuous, enjoying raciness ; no caricatured, rolling greasiness and grossness, no exaggerated vul- garization of Shakespeare's immortal "fat knight ;" but a florid, rotund, self-contented, self-indulgent voluptuary — thoroughly at his ease, thoroughly prepared to take advantage of all gratification that might come in his way ; and throughout preserving the manners of a gentleman, accustomed to the companionship of a prince, " the best king of good fellows." John Forster's Master Ford was a carefully finished performance. John Leech's Master Slender was picturesquely true to the gawky, flabby, booby squire : hanging about in various attitudes of limp ecstasy, limp embarrassment, limp disconsolateness. His mode of sitting on the stile, with his long, ungainly legs dangling down, during the duel scene between Sir Hugh and Dr. Caius, looking vacantly out across " the fields," as if in vapid expectation of seeing " Mistress Anne Page at a farm-house a-feasting,"—as promised him by that roguish wag mine Host of the Garter, ever and anon ejaculating his maudlin, cuckoo-cry of " Oh sweet Anne Page,"—was a delectable treat. Mr. G. H. Lewes's acting, and especially his dancing, as Sir Hugh Evans, were very dainty, with a peculiar drollery and quaintness, singularly befitting the peppery but kindly-natured Welsh

parson. I once heard Mr. Lewes wittily declare that his
were not so much "animal spirits," as "vegetable spirits;"
and these kind of ultra light good-humours shone to
great advantage in his conception and impersonation of
Sir Hugh. George Cruikshanks as mine Ancient Pistol,
was supremely artistic in "get up," costume, and attitude ;
fantastic, spasmodic, ranting, bullying. Though taking
the small part of Slender's servant, Simple, Augustus Egg
was conspicuous for good judgment and good taste in his
presentment of the character. Over his well-chosen
suit of sober-coloured doublet and hose he wore a leather
thong round his neck that hung loosely over his chest ;
and he told me he had added this to his dress, because
inasmuch as Master Slender was addicted to sport,
interested in coursing, and in Page's "fallow greyhound,"
it was likely that his retainer would carry a dog-leash
about him. Egg was a careful observer of costume ; and
expressed his admiration of mine for Dame Quickly,
remarking (like a true artist) that it looked "more toned
down" than the rest of the company's, and seemed as if
it might have been worn in Windsor streets, during the
daily trottings to and fro of the match-making busy-body.
It may well have looked thus ; for while the other members of the company had their dresses made expressly for
the occasion by a stage costume-maker, I had fabricated
Dame Quickly's from materials of my own, previously
used, in order that they might not look "*too new*," and
that they might be in strict consonance with my ideas of
correct dressing for the part. To this end, I had written
to ask the aid of Colonel Hamilton Smith, an authority
in costumes of all ages and countries. To my inquiry
respecting Dame Quickly's costume, he replied by sending
me two coloured sketches accompanied by a kind letter

from which I transcribe this extract, evincing his extreme care to ensure accuracy :—

"I find only one difficulty in producing a drawing for Mistress Quickly, and that is whether on the stage it is now a clear case as to the date to be assigned, not the writing of the play, but the period when Falstaff and the Merry Wives are to be supposed living. If you take the date of Henry IV. or Henry V., that is between 1400 and 1425, or the beginning of the seventeenth century, between 1600 and 1620. Shakespeare, I believe, had no image in his view but that of his own times, and I believe also the figures artists have given relating to the play are all, with some licence, of the times of Elizabeth and James I. My own opinion is likewise inclining to that period, because the humorous character of the play becomes more obvious when represented in dresses and scenery which we can better appreciate for that purpose than when we take the more recondite manners of the age when the red rose was in the ascendant. The special character of Mistress Quickly, with manners somewhat dashed with Puritanism, dresses admirably in the later period, and is not to be found in the early period of the Lollards. No dress of the time would tell the audience that it is the costume of a Mistress Quickly. It would only show a gentlewoman, a young lady, or a countrywoman.

This question being settled, I have now only to offer a dress, and I recommend that of a Dame Bonifant figured on a Devon brass of the year 1614. I think you will find it sufficiently *piquant;* demure though it be. I think it just the thing, and you may select the colours that will suit you best. The other is Champernoun Lady Slanning, from her monument dating 1583 If this period will not answer, pray let me know, and I will endeavour to select others of the times of Henry IV. and V."

In making my dress for Dame Quickly, I availed myself of Colonel Hamilton Smith's suggestions and sketches for some particulars ; but also copied from the effective costume given by Kenny Meadows to her at p. 91, vol. i.

of his " Illustrated Shakespeare," published by Tyas in
1843. To the very characteristic coif there depicted
(which I made in black velvet lined with scarlet silk) I
added a pinner and lappet of old point-lace, the latter of
which floated from the outside together with long ribbon
streamers of scarlet, so as to give an idea of "the ship-
tire" mentioned by Falstaff, as one of the fashionable
head-gears of the period. William Havell, the artist, a
short time afterwards made for my husband a water-
coloured sketch of me in my Quickly costume ; which
now hangs in the picture-gallery of our Italian home ; and
it gave me a strange feeling of suddenly-recalled past
times amid the present, when the other day I saw the
delicate point lappet and pinner,—worn by Dame
Quickly in 1848, and which had been given to my niece
Valeria,—figuring round the young throat as a modern
lace cravat in 1876.

As I stood at the side scene of the Haymarket Theatre
that memorable May night with Augustus Egg, waiting to
make our first entrance together upon the stage, and face
that sea of faces, he asked me whether I felt nervous.

"Not in the least," I replied ; "my heart beats fast ;
but it is with joyful excitement, not with alarm." And,
from first to last, "joyful excitement" was what I felt
during that enchanting episode in my life.

In Mrs. Inchbald's amusing farce of "Animal Magnetism," the two characters of the Doctor and La Fleur,
as played by Charles Dickens and Mark Lemon, formed
the chief points of drollery : but in the course of the
piece, an exquisitely ludicrous bit of what is technically
called "Gag" was introduced into the scene where George
Lewes, as the Marquis, pretends to fall into a fit of
rapturous delirium, exclaiming,—

"What thrilling transport rushes to my heart; Nature appears to my ravished eyes more beautiful than poets ever formed! Aurora dawns—the feathered songsters chant their most melodious strains—the gentle zephyrs breathe," etc.

At the words, "Aurora dawns," Dickens interrupted with "*Who* dawns?" And being answered with "Aurora," exclaimed "La!!" in such a tone of absurd wonderment, as if he thought anybody rather than Aurora might have been expected to dawn.

The first night's Haymarket performance was followed by my dining next evening at Charles Dickens' house in Devonshire Terrace, when Mrs. Dickens, having a box at the opera to see Jenny Lind in "La Sonnambula," invited me to go with her there; and immediately upon this ensued the second night's performance at the Haymarket Theatre, when the play-bill announced Ben Jonson's "Every Man in his Humour," and Kenny's farce of "Love, Law, and Physic."

The way in which Charles Dickens impersonated that arch braggart, Captain Bobadil, was a veritable piece of genius : from the moment when he is discovered lolling at full length on a bench in his lodging, calling for a "cup o' small beer" to cool down the remnants of excitement from last night's carouse with a set of roaring gallants, till his final boast of having "not so much as once offered to resist" the "coarse fellow" who set upon him in the open streets, he was capital. The mode in which he went to the back of the stage before he made his exit from the first scene of Act ii., uttering the last word of the taunt he flings at Downright with a bawl of stentorian loudness —"Scavenger!" and then darted off the stage at full speed; the insolent scorn of his exclamation, "This a Toledo? pish!" bending the sword into a curve as he spoke; the swaggering assumption of ease with which he leaned on the shoulder of his interlocutor, puffing away his tobacco smoke and puffing it off as "your right Trinidado;" the grand impudence of his lying when explaining how he would despatch scores of the enemy,— "challenge twenty more, kill them; twenty more, kill them; twenty more, kill them too;" ending by "twenty score, that's two hundred; two hundred a day, five days a thousand; forty thousand; forty times five, five times forty, two hundred days kills them all up by computation," rattling the words off while making an invisible sum of addition in the air, and scoring it conclusively with an invisible line underneath,—were all the very height of fun.

It was noteworthy, as an instance of the forethought as to effect given to even the slightest points, that he and Leech (who played Master Mathew) had their stage-wigs made, for the parts they played in Ben Jonson's comedy, of precisely opposite cut : Bobadil's being fuzzed out at the sides and extremely bushy, while Master Mathew's was flat at the ears and very highly peaked above his forehead. In the green-room, between the acts, after Bobadil has received his drubbing and been well cudgelled in the fourth act, and has to reappear in the first scene of the fifth act, I saw Charles Dickens wetting the plume of vari-coloured feathers in his hat, and taking some of them out, so as to give an utterly crest-fallen look to his general air and figure. "Don't take out the *white* feather !" I said; it was pleasant to see the quick glance up with which he recognized the point of my meaning. He had this delightful, bright, rapid glance of intelligence in his eye whenever anything was said to please him; and it was my good hap many times to see this sudden light flash forth.

The farce of " Love, Law, and Physic" was a large field, for the very hey-day of frolic and mirth. The opening scene, with its noisy bustle of arrival of the fellow-travellers in the stage coach at the Inn ; the dash and audacity of Lawyer Flexible (Dickens) ; the loutish conceit and nose-led dupedom of Lubin Log (Lemon) ; the crowning absurdity of the scene where they pay court to the supposed Spanish heiress ; which last—by the time we had played it four times, reached a perfect climax of uproarious " gag " and merriment on the fifth representation—always kindled the house into sympathetic uproar. Mark Lemon's lumpish approaches, stealthily kissing his hand to the stage diamonds worn profusely in my hair to fasten the Spanish veil, turning to Charles Dickens with a loud aside : " Eh ? All real, I suppose, eh ? " and between every speech looking to him for support or prompted inspiration of love-making ; extra ridiculous scraps introduced into the dialogue where the Spanish lady mentions her accomplishments, " Prosody, painting, poetry, music and phlebotomy"—at the word "music," Lemon used to turn to Dickens and say, " What ?—so ? " (*making signs of playing on the violoncello ;*) when the reply was, " No, no ;—so," (*making signs of playing on the pianoforte ;*) and on my adding, "poonah-painting—" Lemon used to turn to his friend and abettor with, " What ? Poney-painting ? Does she draw horses ? " till laughter among the audience was infectiously and irrepressibly met by laughter on the stage, in the side scenes, where the rest of the company used to cluster like bees (against all rule !) to see that portion of the farce.

In token of Charles Dickens's appropriateness of

gesture, and dramatic discrimination, I may instance his different mode of entrance on the stage with me as Dame Quickly and as Mrs. Hilary. Where Justice Shallow comes hurriedly in with the former, Act iii. Scene 4, saying to her, "Break their talk, Mistress Quickly;" he used to have hold of my arm, partly leaning on it, partly leading me on by it,—just like an old man with an inferior : but—as the curtain rose to the ringing of bells, the clattering of horses, the blowing of mail-coach horn, the voices of passengers calling to waiter, and chamber-maid, etc., at the opening of " Love, Law, and Physic,"— Charles Dickens used to tuck me under his arm with the free-and-easy familiarity of a lawyer patronizing an actress whom he chances to find his fellow-traveller in a stage coach, and step smartly on the stage, with—"Come, bustle, bustle ; tea and coffee for the ladies."—It is something to remember, having been tucked under the arm by Charles Dickens, and had one's hand hugged against his side ! One thinks better of one's hand ever after. He used to be in such a state of high spirits when he played Flexible, and so worked himself into hilarity and glee for the part, that he more than once said in those days, "Somehow, I never see Mrs. Cowden Clarke, but I feel impelled to address her with 'Exactly ; and thus have I learned from his own obliging communication, that he is the rival of my friend, Captain Danvers ; who, fortu-nately for the safety of Mr. Log's nose, happened to be taking the air on the box.'" And he actually did, more than once, utter these words (one of Flexible's first speeches to Mrs. Hilary) when we met. He was very fond of this kind of reiterated joke.

Next came our first set of provincial performances,— Manchester, 3rd June ; Liverpool, 5th June ; and Bir-

mingham, 6th June, 1848. What times those were!
What rapturous audiences a-tiptoe with expectation to
see, hear, and welcome those whom they had known and
loved through their written or delineated productions.
What a heap of flowers—exquisitely choice orchids and
rare blossoms—packed carefully in a box by a friend's
hand, awaited our arrival at the Manchester Hotel, and
furnished me with a special rose-bud for Charles Dickens'
acceptance, and button-hole nosegays for the other gentlemen of the company; besides a profusion for Mrs.
Charles Dickens, her sister, and the professional ladies
who travelled with us. What crowds assembled on the
landing-place of the stairs, and in the passages of the
Liverpool hotel, to see the troupe pass down to dinner!
What enthusiastic hurrahs at the rise of the curtain, and
as each character in succession made his appearance on
the stage. Of course, in general, the storm of plaudits
was loudest when Charles Dickens was recognized; but
at Birmingham such a rave of delight was heard at an
unaccustomed point of the play, that we in the Green-
room (who watched with interested ears the various
"receptions" given) exclaimed, "Why, who's that gone
on to the stage?" It proved to be George Cruikshanks,
whose series of admirably impressive pictures called
"The Bottle" and "The Drunkard's Children" had
lately appeared in Birmingham, and had been known to
have wrought some wonderful effects in the way of re-
straining men from immoderate use of drink.

Moreover, what enchanting journeys those were! The
coming on to the platform at the station, where Charles
Dickens' alert form and beaming look met one with
pleasurable greeting; the interest and polite attention of
the officials; the being always seated with my sister

Emma in the same railway carriage occupied by Mr. and Mrs. Charles Dickens and Mark Lemon ; the delightful gaiety and sprightliness of our manager's talk ; the endless stories he told us ; the games he mentioned and explained how they were played ; the bright amenity of his manner at various stations, where he showed to persons in authority the free-pass ticket which had been previously given in homage to " Charles Dickens and his party ;" the courteous alacrity with which he jumped out at one refreshment-room to procure food for somebody who had complained of hunger towards the end of the journey, and reappeared bearing a plate of buns which no one seemed inclined to eat, but which he held out, saying, " For Heaven's sake, somebody eat some of these buns ; I was in hopes I saw Miss Novello eye them with a greedy joy :" his indefatigable vivacity, cheeriness, and good humour from morning till night,— all were delightful. One of the stories he recounted to us, while travelling, was that of a man who had been told that slips of paper pasted across the chest formed an infallible cure for sea-sickness ; and that upon going down into the cabin of the steamer, this man was to be seen busily employed cutting up paper into long narrow strips with the gravest of faces, and accompanying the slicing of the scissors by a sympathetic movement of the jaw, which Dickens mimicked as he described the process.

Before the month of June concluded, a second performance was arranged for Birmingham ; and as, in addition to " Merry Wives," and " Love, Law, and Physic," it was proposed to give the screaming afterpiece of " Two o'clock in the morning " (or " A good night's rest," as it was sometimes called), Charles Dickens asked me to dine at his house, that we might cut the farce to proper dimensions. A charming little dinner of four it was,—Mr. and Mrs. Dickens, Mark Lemon, and myself; followed by adjournment to the library to go through our scenes in the farce together. Charles Dickens showed to particular advantage in his own quiet home life ; and infinitely more I enjoyed this simple little meeting than a brilliant dinner-party to which I was invited at his house, a day or two afterwards, when a large company were assembled, and all was in superb style, with a bouquet of flowers beside the plate of each lady present. On one of these more quiet occasions, when Mr. and Mrs. Dickens, their children, and their few guests were sitting out of doors in the small garden in front of their Devonshire Terrace house, enjoying the fine warm evening, I recollect seeing one of his little sons draw Charles Dickens apart, and stand in eager talk with him, the setting sun full upon the child's upturned face and lighting up the father's, which looked smilingly down into it ; and when the important conference was over, the father returned to us, saying, " The little fellow gave me so many excellent reasons why he should not go to bed so soon, that I yielded the point, and let him sit up half an hour later."

On our journey down to Birmingham I enjoyed a very special treat. Charles Dickens—in his usual way of sparing no pains that could ensure success—asked me to hear him repeat his part in " Two o'clock in the morning," which, he and Mark Lemon being the only two persons acting therein, was a long one. He repeated throughout with such wonderful verbal accuracy that I could scarcely believe what I saw and heard as I listened to him, and kept my eyes fixed upon the page. Not only every word of the incessant speaking part, but the stage directions—which in that piece are very numerous and elaborate—he repeated verbatim. He evidently committed to memory all he had to *do* as well as all he had to *say* in this extremely comic trifle of one act an one scene. Who that beheld the convulsive writhes and spasmodic draw-up of his feet on the rung of the chair and the tightly-held coverlet round his shivering body just out of bed, as he watched in ecstasy of impatience the invasion of his peaceful chamber by that horribly intrusive Stranger, can ever forget Charles Dickens' playing Mr. Snobbington? or who that heard Mark Lemon's thundered syllable, " Pours !" in reply to Snobbington's inquiry whether it rains, can lose remembrance of that unparalleled piece of acting?

July brought plans for performances in Scotland, which was to include, besides our previous pieces, the comedietta named in the first of the two following notelets :—

Devonshire Terrace, 1st July, 1848.

My dear Mrs. Clarke,—I enclose the part I spoke of in "Used Up." Will you meet the rest of the Dramatis Personæ here, to read the play and compare the parts on *Monday evening at 7.*

Faithfully yours always,
The Implacable Manager.

[The next (undated) was in very large handwriting.]

The Implacable's reply.

At Miss Kelly's Temple of Mirth, 73, Dean Street, Soho—at 7 o'clock, on Friday evening, July the seventh, eighteen hundred and forty-eight.

On the 15th July we travelled to Edinburgh; and, on our post-midnight arrival there, found a brilliant supper-party awaiting us of several distinguished gentlemen, among whom was the Sheriff of Midlothian, bright super-genial John T. Gordon, and a gentleman who sang Burns' " Mary Morrison " with such exquisite tenderness of expression that Charles Dickens (who had often laughingly observed to me that I did not seem much to admire this kind of pastime) at its conclusion turned to me with eyes that swam as brimmingly as my own, and said, "Why, I thought you didn't care for after-supper singing, Mrs. Cowden Clarke." All I could find words for in reply was, " Ay ; but such singing as this—." To which expressive *break* he nodded an emphatic rejoinder of assent.

The day that followed was spent by some of the Amateur Company in visiting Holyrood, etc. ; while Charles Dickens invited me to go with Mrs. Dickens, himself, and one or two others, to see esteemed John Hunter ("friend of Leigh Hunt's verse ") at Craigcrook. To my infinite regret I was compelled by one of my cruellest habitual head-aches to relinquish this surpassing pleasure, and remain at the hotel, trying to nurse myself into fit condition for acting on the morrow. By that same evening, however, I was well enough to join the merry after-dinner party engaged with Charles Dickens in playing a game of " How, when, and where ;" which he conducted with the greatest spirit and gaiety. I remember one of the words chosen for guessing was " Lemon ;" and of course, many were the allusions to punch and Punch made by the several players. But when one of them ventured in answer to the question, " How do you like it ? " so near as to say, " I like it with a white choker on," Dickens ejaculated, "Madness!" and Mark Lemon, who chanced to be the only gentleman present wearing a white cravat, put his spread hand stealthily up under his chin, and made an irresistibly droll grimace of dismay. On the 17th July we gave in Edinburgh " Merry Wives," " Love, Law, and Physic," and " Two o'clock in the morning ; " and on the 18th, in Glasgow, " Merry Wives," and "Animal Magnetism." As there was to be a second performance given in Glasgow on the 20th, Charles Dickens organized a charming excursion to Ben Lomond on the intervening day, the 19th. No man more embodied the expression "genial" than himself; no man could better make "a party of pleasure" truly pleasant and worthy of its name than he. There was a positive sparkle and atmosphere of holiday sunshine about him : he seemed to radiate brightness and enjoyment from his own centre that cast lustre upon all around him. When the carriages-and-four that he had ordered for the expedition were drawn up in front of the Glasgow hotel, ready for us to take our places in and on them (for some of the gentlemen occupied the box-seats, as there were postillions), we saw from the windows that a large crowd had assembled in the streets and was every moment increasing in numbers. Charles Dickens said hastily, "I don't think I can face this ;" and bidding us go on without them and take them up a little distance, he took Charles Knight's arm, that he might walk out unobserved and pass through the crowd on foot. Charles Knight had joined our party for a few days ; and he afterwards told us that on emerging from the house a lady had come up to him and said, "Could you tell me, sir, which is Charles Dickens?" Upon which Charles Knight —faithful to Dickens' wish to pass on unnoticed—replied, " No, ma'am; unfortunately I couldn't." Though Charles Dickens gave him an expressive pinch of the arm, as he uttered the reply, in token that he recognized his loyalty to friendship, yet, when Charles Knight told us the incident, Charles Dickens laughingly said, "I don't know how you could have the heart to answer her so, Knight, I don't think *I* could have done it!"

The day, that had promised fair, turned out drizzly and misty; so that as we passed the picturesque neighbourhood of Dumbarton, its castle, and banks of the Clyde, they were but hazily seen; and even when we approached the grander scenery of Lake Lomond and the mighty "Ben" of that ilk, it was but greyly and shroudedly visible. I recollect Augustus Egg, who was in our carriage, as he looked towards the hill-sides covered with July fir-trees dripping wet, saying with a true Londoner's travestie of the often-seen placard in a Regent Street furrier's shop-window, *Firs* at this season, half price." We put up at a small inn at mid-day, where we had a lunch-dinner; after which some of the company went down to the shores of the lake (the rain having somewhat ceased) to try and get a glimpse of the magnificent vicinity. Mr. and Mrs. Charles Dickens and I preferred remaining where we were; and, as he owned to being a little tired, we persuaded him to lie down for a short time. In that small inn-room there was of course no sofa; so we put together four or five chairs, on which he stretched himself at full length, resting his head on his wife's knee as a pillow, and was soon in quiet sleep, Mrs. Dickens and I keeping on our talk in a low tone that served rather to lull than disturb him. That modest inn-room among the Scottish mountains, the casement blurred by recent rains, the grand landscape beyond shrouded in mist, the soft breathing of the sleeper, the glorious eyes closed, the active spirit in perfect repose, the murmured voices of the two watching women,—often rise with strangely present effect upon my musing memory.

When the time came for returning to Glasgow, Charles Dickens talked of occupying one of the box-seats; but I ventured to remind him he might take cold. "Oh, I'm well wrapped up," he replied. I said it was not so much a question of warm clothing, as that he could not help inhaling the damp air, and might lose his voice for the morrow's acting. He was not the man to imperil success by any want of precaution, so he laughingly gave way and came inside the carriage again.

That same night, at supper, occurred an instance of one of those humorous exaggerations of speech in which Charles Dickens delighted and often indulged. There was before him a cold sirloin, and he offered me a slice. I accepted, and he exclaimed, "Well, I think I was never more astonished in my life than at your saying you would have some of this cold roast beef!"

During our tours he always sat at the head of the table and carved, I having the enviable privilege of being seated next to him; and he observing [as what was there that ever escaped his notice?] that I ate little—owing to the perpetual state of glad excitement in which I lived—used to cater for me kindly and persuasively, tempting my appetite by selecting morsels he thought I should like. On one occasion I recollect he helped me to a piece of chicken, which 1 took, hailing it in Captain Cuttle's words: "Liver wing it is!" and he instantly looked at me with that bright glance of his. He had a peculiar grace in taking any sudden allusion of this kind to his writings; and I remember Leigh Hunt telling me that once when he and Dickens were coming away from a party on a very rainy night, a cab not being readily

Y

procurable to convey Leigh Hunt home, Charles Dickens
had made him get inside the fly he had in waiting for himself and the ladies who were with him, taking his own
seat outside ; upon which Leigh Hunt put his head out
to protest, saying, " If you don't mind, Dickens, you'll
' *become a demd, damp, moist, unpleasant body !* '" which
was responded to by a blithe, clear laugh that rang out
right pleasantly in the dark wet night.

In the course of the following morning at Glasgow
requests were made that the Amateur Company would
sign their names collectively on some large sheets of paper
produced for this purpose, as interesting memorials of the
occasion; and the persons then chancing to be present
complied.   One of these sheets, filled for my sister Emma,
she subsequently gave to me, and it is still in my
possession.

The performance of " Used up "—thanks to diligent
rehearsals steadily enforced by our " Implacable manager,"
—went with such extraordinary smoothness as to call
forth an expression of astonishment from the professional
manager of the Glasgow Theatre, who said that unless he
had been positively assured the Amateur Company had
never before played the piece, he could not have believed
it to have been a first night's acting.   Charles Dickens's Sir
Charles Coldstream was excellent; but a pre-eminent hit
was made by Mark Lemon, who, as one of his fop-friends,
invented a certain little ridiculous laugh – so original, so
exquisitely inane, so ludicrously disproportioned in its
high falsetto pipe, to the immensely broad chest from
which it issued—that it became *the thing* of all the scenes
where he appeared.   A kind of squeaking hysterical giggle
closing in a suddenly checked gasp,—a high-pitched
chuckle, terminating in an abrupt swallowing of the tone

—first startled our ears and our risibility when Lemon was rehearsing this small part, which he made an important one by this invention; and a dozen times a day, until the night of performance, would Charles Dickens make Mark Lemon repeat this incomparably droll new laugh. I have said how fond Charles Dickens was of a repeated jest: and at this time not only would he never tire of hearing "Lemon's fopling-laugh," but he had a way of suddenly calling out to Augustus Egg during dinner or supper, "Augustus!" and when he looked up would exclaim with a half-serious, half-playful affectionateness, "God bless you, Augustus!" He was very fond of both those friends: and they loved to humour his whimsical fancies and frolics. I recollect on one occasion after dinner at one of the hotels during our tour—on a non-acting night—finding that the evening seemed threatening to become less lively than he liked it to be, and hearing that Mark Lemon had retired early, Charles Dickens went up to Lemon's room, made him promise to get up and come downstairs again; and I shall not readily forget his look of triumphant joy when soon after, the drawing-door opened and Mark Lemon made his appearance, walking forward in his flannel dressing-gown, holding a candle in each hand on either side of his grotesquely-drawn-down visage, as if to show that he had come down stairs in spite of illness to please his "Implacable manager." Well might a grave Scotch gentleman—who called upon us during our stay in Edinburgh, and saw something of the high spirits and good humour in which Charles Dickens and his company were —say, as he did, "I never saw anything like those clever men; they're just for all the world like a parcel of school-boys '

Y

On our last night at Glasgow, after a climax of successful performance at the theatre,—the pieces being " Used up," " Love, Law, and Physic," and " Two o'clock in the morning,"—we had a champagne supper in honour of its being the Amateur Company's last assemblage together. Charles Dickens, observing that I took no wine, said, " Do as I do: have a little champagne put into your glass and fill it up with water ; you'll find it a refreshing draught.   I tell you this as a useful secret for keeping cool on such festive occasions, and speak to you as *man to man.*"   He was in wildest spirits at the brilliant reception and uproarious enthusiasm of the audience that evening, and said in his mad-cap mood, " Blow Domestic Hearth !   I should like to be going on all over the kingdom, with Mark Lemon, Mrs. Cowden Clarke, and John [his manservant], and acting everywhere.   There's nothing in the world equal to seeing the house rise at you, one sea of delighted faces, one hurrah of applause ! "

We travelled up to town next day: he showing us how to play the game of " Twenty Questions," and interesting me much by the extreme ingenuity of those he put to us with a view of eliciting the object of our thought.   He was very expert at these pastimes, and liked to set them going.   I remember one evening at his own house, his playing several games of apparently magical divination,— of course, by means of accomplices and preconcerted signals.   Once, while he was explaining to Augustus Egg and myself the mode of procedure in a certain game of guessing, he said, " Well, 1 begin by thinking of a man, a woman, or an inanimate object; and we'll suppose that I think of Egg."   " Ay, an inanimate object," I replied. He gave his usual quick glance up, at me, and looked at Augustus Egg, and then we all three laughed, though I protested—w h truth — my innocence of any intended quip.

During our journey homeward from Glasgow, Charles Dickens exerted himself to make us all as cheery as might be, insensibly communicating the effect of his own animation to those around him. My sister Emma having produced from her pocket a needle and thread, scissors, and thimble, when somebody's glove needed a few stitches, and subsequently a pen-knife, when somebody else's pencil wanted fresh pointing,—Mark Lemon laughingly said, " It's my opinion that if either of us chanced to require a pair of Wellington boots, Miss Novello would be able to bring them out from among those wonderful flounces of hers."

We were very merry together ; but beneath all I could not help feeling saddened by the sorrowful consciousness that this most unique and delightful comradeship—which I had enjoyed with the keenest sense of its completeness and singularly exceptional combination of happy circumstances—was drawing to a close.

However, I soon had the comfort to receive the following sportively-expressed but truly sympathetic letter, which at least showed me my regret was feelingly shared :—

Devonshire Terrace, Monday Evening,
22nd July, 1848.

MY DEAR MRS. CLARKE,—I have no energy whatever, I am very miserable. I loathe domestic hearths. I yearn to be a vagabond. Why can't I marry [1] Mary ? Why have I seven children—not engaged at sixpence a-night a-piece, and dismissible for ever, if they tumble down, not taken on for an indefinite time at a vast expense, and never,—no never, never,—wearing lighted candles round their heads [2] I am deeply miserable. A real house like this is insupport-

---

[1] A character in " Used Up."
[2] As fairies in " Merry Wives."

able, after that canvas farm wherein I was so happy. What is a humdrum dinner at half-past five, with nobody (but John) to see me eat it, compared with *that* soup, and the hundreds of pairs of eyes that watched its disappearance? Forgive this tear.[3]   It is weak and foolish, I know.

Pray let me divide the little excursional excesses of the journey among the gentlemen, as I have always done before, and pray believe that I have had the sincerest pleasure and gratification in your co-operation and society, valuable and interesting on all public accounts, and personally of no mean worth nor held in slight regard.

You had a sister once, when we were young and happy— I think they called her Emma. If she remember a bright being who once flitted like a vision before her, entreat her to bestow a thought upon the "Gas" of departed joys. I can write no more.

Y. G.[4] the (darkened) G. L. B.[5]

The same kindly sympathy of regret for past dramatic joys is still betokened in the following close to a letter (quoting Sir Charles Coldstream's words) which I received from my dear "Implacable manager," dated "Broadstairs, Kent, 5th Aug., 1848 :"—

" I am completely *blasé*—literally used up.   I am dying for excitement. Is it possible that nobody can suggest anything to make my heart beat violently, my hair stand on end—but no!"

Where did I hear those words (so truly applicable to my forlorn condition) pronounced by some delightful creature? In a previous state of existence, I believe.

Oh, Memory, Memory !

Ever yours faithfully,

Y—no C. G—no D. C. D. I think it is— but I don't know —there's nothing in it.

---

[3] A huge blot of smeared ink.
[4] " Young Gas."   } Names he had playfully given him-
[5] " Gas-Light Boy." }   self.

My sister Emma having helped me with the designs for a blotting-case I embroidered for Charles Dickens, he sent us the accompanying sprightly letter of acknowledgment, signing it with the various names of parts he had played, written in the most respectively characteristic hand-writings. These names in gold letters upon green morocco leather, formed the corners to the green watered silk covering in which I had had the blotting-book bound ; the centres having on one side a wreath of heartsease and forget-me-nots surrounding the initials " Y. G. ;" on the other, a group of roses and rose-buds, worked in floss silks of natural colours.

During the next year my husband and I received the two ensuing playful notes :—

Devonshire Terrace,
13th Jan. 1849.

MY DEAR MRS. CLARKE,—I am afraid that Young Gas is for ever dimmed, and that the breath of calumny will blow henceforth on his stage-management, by reason of his enormous delay in returning you the two pounds non-for-warded by Mrs. G.   The proposed deduction on account of which you sent it, was never made.

> But had you seen him in " Used up,"
> His eye so beaming and so clear,
> When on his stool he sat to sup
> The oxtail—little Romer near,
>   etc. etc.
> You would have forgotten and forgiven all.
> Ever yours,
CHARLES DICKENS.

To C. C. C.

Devonshire Terrace,
5th May, 1849.

MY DEAR SIR,—I am very sorry to say that my Orphan Working-school vote is promised in behalf of an unfortunate young orphan who after being canvassed for, polled for, written for, quarreled for, fought for, called for, and done all kind of things for, by ladies who wouldn't go away and wouldn't be satisfied with anything anybody said or did for them, was floored at the last election and comes up to the scratch next morning, for the next election, fresher than ever. I devoutly hope he may get in, and be lost sight of for evermore.

Pray give my kindest regards to my quondam Quickly, and believe me

Faithfully yours,
CHARLES DICKENS.

Another year came round, and still brought me delightfully sympathetic reminiscences of our happy bygone comradeship in acting, as testified by the following letter. The " new comedy " it alluded to was Bulwer Lytton's " Not so bad as we seem;" and the " book" was the story called " Meg and Alice, the Merry Maids of Windsor" (one of the series in " The Girlhood of Shakespeare's Heroines"), which I dedicated to Charles Dickens.

Great Malvern, 29th March, 1851.

MY DEAR MRS. COWDEN CLARKE,—Ah, those were days indeed, when we were so fatigued at dinner that we couldn't speak, and so revived at supper that we couldn't go to bed : when wild in inns the noble savage ran,—and all the world was a stage gas-lighted in a double sense,—by the Young Gas and the old one ! When Emmeline Montague (now Compton, and the mother of two children) came to rehearse in our new comedy the other night, I nearly fainted. The gush of recollection was so overpowering that I couldn't bear it.

I use the portfolio* for managerial papers still. That's something.

---

* The Blotting-book previously mentioned.

But all this does not thank you for your book. I have not got it yet (being here with Mrs. Dickens, who has been very unwell) but I shall be in town early in the week, and shall bring it down to read quietly on these hills, where the wind blows as freshly as if there were no Popes and no Cardinals whatsoever—nothing the matter anywhere. I thank you a thousand times, beforehand, for the pleasure you are going to give me. I am full of faith. Your sister Emma,—she is doing work of some sort on the P.S. side of the boxes, in some dark theatre, *I know*,—but where I wonder? W.[7] has not proposed to her yet, has he? I understood he was going to offer his hand and heart, and lay his leg [8] at her feet. Ever faithfully yours,

CHARLES DICKENS.

The following note was the invitation I received to the dress rehearsal of " Not so bad as we seem :"—

Devonshire House, 7th May, 1851.

MY DEAR MRS. CLARKE,—Will you come and look at your old friends next Monday? I do not know how far we shall be advanced towards completion, but I do know that we shall all be truly pleased to see you.

Faithfully yours always,
CHARLES DICKENS.

Some account of the rehearsals and performances on this occasion was given by Mr. R. H. Horne in the "Gentleman's Magazine" for February, 1871, therefore I forbear from giving particulars farther than to record my own confirmation of the description there given of the Duke of Devonshire's exquisite courtesy, with as exquisite a simplicity in demeanour towards those who were then assembled beneath his princely roof. He was

[7] Wilmot, the clever veteran prompter, who had been engaged to accompany us on all our acting-tours.
[8] A wooden one.

truly worthy of his title, " Your *Grace*." Nothing more graceful and gracious could be imagined than his mode of standing by Leigh Hunt (who sat beside me), making him keep his seat while he stayed for a few moments in easy talk with him before the curtain drew up ; or his behaviour afterwards in the supper-room, where long tables of refreshments were ranged near to the walls, with the Duke's livery servants in attendance at the back, to dispense what the guests needed. The Duke, perceiving that two ladies were standing a little apart with no gentleman in their company, made a courteous motion of his hand towards Emma and myself, that we should advance towards the table, while he waved his nieces a little aside to make room for us at the board, where tea, coffee, and a thousand delicacies were spread.

The following charming note came to me in recognition of a large basket of choice flowers—sent to me by the same friendly hand that had provided those that greeted our arrival in Manchester—which I had taken to Charles Dickens's house on the morning of the day when the first number of his " Bleak House " was published :—

Tavistock House, 3rd March, 1852.

MY DEAR MRS CLARKE,—It is almost an impertinence to tell you how delightful your flowers were to me ; for you who thought of that beautiful and delicately-timed token of sympathy and remembrance, must know it very well already.

I do assure you that I have hardly ever received anything with so much pleasure in all my life. They are not faded yet—are on my table here—but never can fade out of my remembrance.

I should be less than a Young Gas, and more than an old Manager—that commemorative portfolio is here too—if I could relieve my heart of half that it could say to you. All my house are my witnesses that you have quite filled it, and this note is my witness that I can *not* empty it !

Ever faithfully and gratefully your friend,
CHARLES DICKENS.

I had written to inquire who was the author of the beautiful poem-story that appeared in the Christmas number of "Household Words" for 1852, and he sent me this note in reply. "The two green leaves" was the name he had given to the green paper covers in which the monthly parts of his own serial works appeared ; and "the turning-point" he here alludes to was the one in "Bleak House," where Esther takes the fever from Charley and loses her former beauty.

Tavistock House, Tuesday Evening,
28th Dec., 1852.

MY DEAR MRS. CLARKE,—This comes from your ancient (and venerable) manager, in solemn state, to decide the wager.

The Host's story is by Edmund Ollier—an excellent and true young poet, as I think.

You will see a turning-point in the two green leaves this next month, which I hope will not cause you to think less pleasantly and kindly of them.

And so no more at present from yours
Always very faithfully,
CHARLES DICKENS.

The next note accompanied a presentation copy of "Bleak House," on the title-page of which he wrote, "Mary Cowden Clarke, with the regard of Charles Dickens, December, 1853." The book is still treasured in both places where he wished it might be kept.

Tavistock House, 14th Nov. 1853.

MY DEAR MRS. COWDEN CLARKE,—You remember the flowers you sent me on the day of the publication of the first of these pages ? *I* shall never forget them.

Pray give the book a place on your shelves, and (if you can) in your heart.   Where you may always believe me

Very faithfully yours,
CHARLES DICKENS.

In the summer of 1855 my husband and I received an invitation to witness the performance of Mr. Wilkie Collins's piece called "The Lighthouse," and of Charles Dickens's and Mark Lemon's farce entitled "Mr. Nightingale's Diary."   The play-bill—which, as I write, lies before me—is headed, "The smallest Theatre in the World! Tavistock House" (where Dickens then resided); and is dated "Tuesday Evening, June 19th, 1855." The chief characters were enacted by himself, some members of his own family, and his friends, Mark Lemon, Augustus Egg, Frank Stone, and Wilkie Collins; while the scenery was painted by another of his friends, the eminent Clarkson Stanfield. Choicely picturesque and full of artistic taste was the effect of the lighthouse interior, where Mark Lemon's handsomely chiselled features, surrounded by a head of grizzled hair that looked as though it had been blown into careless dishevelment by many a tempestuous gale, his weather-beaten general appearance, and his rugged mariner garments, formed the fine central figure as the curtain drew up and discovered him seated at a rough table, with his younger lighthouse mate, Wilkie Collins, stretched on the floor as if just awakened from sleep, in talk together.   Later on in the scene a low planked recess in the wall is opened, where Charles Dickens—as the first lighthouse keeper, an old man with half-dazed wits and a bewildered sense of some wrong committed in bygone years – is discovered asleep in his berth.   A wonderful impersonation was this ; very imaginative, very original, very wild, very striking ; his

grandly intelligent eyes were made to assume a wandering look,—a sad, scared, lost gaze, as of one whose
spirit was away from present objects, and wholly occupied
with absent and long-past images.

Among the audience that evening was Douglas Jerrold,
beside whom we sat.

Towards the end of this same year it was announced
that another new serial story—"Little Dorrit"—would
make its appearance on the 1st December : and in anticipation of the event, I designed a white porcelain paper-
weight, with " two green leaves" enamelled in their natural
colours upon it, between which were placed, in gold
letters, the . initials " C. D." The fabrication of this
paper-weight I entrusted to the clever house of Osler at
Birmingham, famous for their beautiful glass and china
manufactory, and known to ourselves for much kindness
and courtesy in old lecturing days. This trifle they
executed with great taste and skill, carrying out my idea
to perfection. It was sent to Charles Dickens on the
day of publication, and brought us the following kind
letter.

Tavistock House, 19th Dec. 1855.

MY DEAR MR. AND MRS. CLARKE.—I cannot tell you
how much I am gratified by the receipt of your kind letters,
and the pleasantest memorial that has ever been given me to
stand upon my writing-desk. Running over from Paris on
Saturday night, I found your genial remembrance awaiting
me, like a couple of kind homely faces (homely please to
observe, in the sense of being associated with Home) ; and I
think you would have been satisfied if you could have seen
how you brightened my face.

Always faithfully your friend,
CHARLES DICKENS.

Among the many regrets for what we left behind us in

our beloved old England, on going to settle at Nice in the Autumn of 1856, was that we just missed being present at the next Tavistock House performance, which consisted of Mr. Wilkie Collins's drama, "The Frozen Deep" and the farce of "Animal Magnetism."

The best consolation we could have had for our disappointment was the receipt of the following letter, giving evidence that we had friendliest sympathy in our keen sense of lost pleasure.

Tavistock House, 10th Oct 1856.

MY DEAR MR. AND MRS. CLARKE,—An hour before I received your letter, I had been writing your names. We were beginning a list of friends to be asked here on Twelfth Night to see a new play by the Author of "The Lighthouse," and a better play than that. I honestly assure you that your letter dashed my spirits and made a blank in the prospect.

May you be very happy at Nice, and find in the climate and the beautiful country near it, more than compensation for what you leave here. Don't forget among the leaves of the vine and olive, that your two green leaves are always on my table here, and that no weather will shake them off.

I should have brought this myself, on the chance of seeing you, if I were not such a coward in the matter of good-bye, that I never say it, and would resort to almost any subterfuge to avoid it.

Mrs. Dickens and Georgina send their kindest regards. Your hearty sympathy will not be lost to me, I hope, at Nice ; and I shall never hear of you or think of you without true interest and pleasure. Always faithfully your friend,

CHARLES DICKENS.

"The Story" alluded to in the next letter was "A Tale of Two Cities ;" and the promised copy, when it could "be read all at once," faithfully came to us. "The bygone Day" to which he refers, was not at "Glasgow,"

but at Birmingham ; where—during the performance of
" Every Man in his Humour "—I (as Tib) was perched up
at an aperture in the flat scene at the back of the stage,
out of reach of prompter's voice, and Ben Jonson's somewhat disjointed and irrelevant words slipped entirely out
of my memory for some moments. The actor on the
stage at whom I was stated to have "stared," was Mr.
Dudley Costello, who played Kno'well. Forster, as Kitely,
came on later in the same scene, dragging Tib forth from
the house ; and I recollect his doing this with such force
of dramatic vehemence,—swinging me round with a
strong rapid fling—that had it not been for my old (or
rather, *young*) skill in dancing, which rendered me both
nimble and sure-footed, I should have been down upon
the stage. The reader will readily understand how
pleasantly these reminders of our acting-days came to me
abroad,—after a decade had elapsed,—from my " Implacable manager."

Gad's Hill Place, Higham by Rochester, Kent,
21st Aug. 1859.

MY DEAR MRS. COWDEN CLARKE,—I cannot tell you how
much pleasure I have derived from the receipt of your
earnest letter. Do not suppose it possible that such praise
can be "less than nothing" to your old Manager. It is more
than all else.

Here in my little country house on the summit of the hill
where Falstaff did the robbery, your words have come to me
in the most appropriate and delightful manner. When the
story can be read all at once, and my meaning can be better
seen, I will send it to you (sending it to Dean Street, if you
tell me of no better way) and it will be a hearty gratification
to think that you and your good husband are reading it together. For you must both take notice, please, that I have
a reminder of you always before me. On my desk here
stand two green leaves, which I every morning station in

their ever-green place at my elbow. The leaves on the oak-trees outside the window are less constant than these, for they are with me through the four seasons.

Lord! to think of the bygone day when you were stricken mute (was it not at Glasgow?) and, being mounted on a tall ladder at a practicable window, stared at Forster, and with a noble constancy refused to utter word! Like the Monk among the pictures with Wilkie, I begin to think *that* the real world, and this the sham that goes out with the lights. God bless you both.

Ever faithfully yours,
CHARLES DICKENS.

The " Sonnets" mentioned in the following letter were the six sonnets on " Godsends ;" and, at my request, they were published all six at once (instead of by " two " at a time) in No. 74 of " All the Year round" for the 22nd September, 1860 :—

London, 23rd April, 1860.

MY DEAR MRS. COWDEN CLARKE,—I lose no time in acknowledging the receipt of your very welcome letter. I do so briefly—not from choice but necessity. If I promised myself the pleasure of writing you a long letter, it is highly probable that I should postpone it until heaven knows what remote time of my life.

I hope to get *two* of the sonnets in shortly; say within a month or so.

The Ghost in the Picture-room, Miss Procter—The Ghost in the Clock-room, a New Lady, who had very rarely (if ever) tried her hand before—The Ghost in the Garden-room, Mrs Gaskell.

Observe, my dear Concordance—because it makes the name of my Gad's Hill house all the better—the name is none of my giving; the house has borne that name these eighty years—ever since it was a house.

With kind regards to Cowden Clarke,
Ever your faithful friend,
CHARLES DICKENS.

A letter to me, dated " Friday 25th January, 1861," has the following playful and friendly conclusion ; the " Property house-broom " refers to the one with which I used busily to sweep, as Dame Quickly, when her master, Dr. Caius, unexpectedly returns home :—

I am glad to find you so faithfully following " Great Expectations," which story is an immense success. As I was at work upon it the other day, a letter from your sister Emma appeared upon my table. . . . . . Instantly, I seemed to see her at needlework in the dark stage-box of the Haymarket in the morning, and you swept yourself into my full view with a ' Property ' house-broom. With the kindest regards to Cowden Clarke, whom I have always quoted since " The Lighthouse " as the best " audience " known to mortality,

Believe me ever affectionately yours,
CHARLES DICKENS.

In the summer of 1862 my husband and I went with my brother Alfred and sister Sabilla for an enchanting visit to England, to hear the Handel Festival and to see the International Exhibition. Many other delights of ear and eye then fell to our share : such as our dear old Philharmonic and other concerts, as well as Exhibition of Old Masters at the British Institution, Royal Academy Exhibition, National Gallery, Kensington Museum, John Leech's collected oil sketches, Rosa Bonheur's pictures, Burford's Panorama of Naples, Messina, and top of the Righi, a very feast of sounds and sights after our long fast from such dainties. For though abroad we had occasionally heard music and seen paintings, it had been at sparse intervals ; not a daily recurring artistic banquet such as we enjoyed that never-to-be-forgotten season. Among the delights we came in for, were two readings by Charles Dickens at St. James's Hall : one on the 19th June, " The Christmas Carol " and " Trial from Pick-

z

wick ;" the other on the 27th June, from "Nicholas Nickleby," "Boots at the Holly-Tree Inn," and "Mrs. Gamp." In reply to our letter telling him what a surpassing treat we had enjoyed on both evenings, he sent us the following note of affectionate reproach :—

Gad's Hill Place, Higham by Rochester, Kent,
7th July, 1862.

MY DEAR MRS. COWDEN CLARKE,—I am very angry with you and your other half for having the audacity to go to my readings without first writing to me ! And if I had not been in France since I read last, and were not going back there immediately, I would summon you both to come to this Falstaff-Ground and receive the reward of your misdeeds.

Here are the two green leaves on my table here, as green as ever. They have not blushed at your conduct at St. James's Hall, but they would have done it if they could.

With indignant regard, believe me ever faithfully yours,
CHARLES DICKENS.

On our first coming to reside in Genoa, my husband and I made a point of going over to Albaro at the earliest opportunity, to find out the Villa Bagnerello (the "Pink Jail," as he calls it in his "Pictures from Italy") where Charles Dickens once lived. We took with us some of the simple bread-cake, called *pan dolce di Genova*, for which the place is famous, and ate it together as a kind of picnic lunch, under some trees by the road-side in the lane where the "Pink Jail" stands, that as festive an air as possible might be given to our expedition in honour of one who was so peculiarly endowed with the power of making a party of pleasure go pleasantly and who was so intimately associated with the most holiday episode of my life. We subsequently went also to see the Palazzo Peschiere and gardens [see the charming description of them at pages 72—75 of "Pictures from Italy"], where Charles Dickens

lived after he left the " Pink Jail:" and of these two
loving pilgrimages we told him in a letter to which the
following is a reply.   The "plan" to which it refers was
one of Genoa, which formed the printed heading of the
paper upon which we wrote to him; and "Minnie's
Musings," is the name of a little verse-story which he
published in "All the Year round" for 29th December,
1866 :—

Office of "All the Year round," London,
3rd Nov. 1866.

MY DEAR MRS. COWDEN CLARKE,—I am happy to accept
"Minnie's Musings" for insertion here.   When it appears
(unless I hear from you to the contrary) Mr. Wills's business
cheque shall be enclosed to Mr. Littleton in Dean Street.

This is written in great haste and distraction, by reason of
my being in the height of the business of the Xmas No.
And as I have this year written half of it myself, the always
difficult work of selecting from an immense heap of contributions is rendered twice as difficult as usual, by the con-
tracted space available.

Ah ! your plan brings before me my beloved Genoa, and
it would gladden my heart indeed to look down upon its bay
once again from the high hills.

No green leaves in present prospect.

Affectionately yours,
CHARLES DICKENS.

The next notelet serves to show the grace and cordiality with which he wrote even when most briefly :—

Office of "All the Year round,"
17th June, 1867.

MY DEAR MRS. COWDEN CLARKE,—I have great pleasure
in retaining "The Yule Log" for the regular No. to be published at Xmas time; not for the Xmas No. so called
because that will be on a new plan this year, which will not
embrace such a contribution.

Z 2

With kind regard and remembrance to your husband,
Believe me always
Your faithful old Manager,
CHARLES DICKENS.

Your two green leaves are always verdant on my table at Gad's Hill.

And the next—the *last*, alas, we ever received from him !—was in answer to a " Godspeed " letter we had written to him upon learning that he was going for a second visit to America :—

Gad's Hill, Higham by Rochester,
2nd Nov. 1867.

Heartfelt thanks, my dear Quickly and Cowden Clarke, for your joint good wishes.   They are more than welcome to me, and so God bless you.

Faithfully yours always,
CHARLES DICKENS.

The hearty kindness, the warmth of farewell blessing, formed a fitting close to a friendship that had brought nothing but kindly feeling and blessed happiness to those who had enjoyed its privilege.   In June, 1870, I read four words on the page of an Italian morning newspaper, which were the past night's telegram from England,—- " *Carlo Dickens è morto*,"—and the sun seemed suddenly blotted out, as I looked upon the fatal line.   Often, since, this sudden blur of the sunshine comes over the fair face of Genoese sea, sky, harbour, fortressed hills, which he described as " one of the most fascinating and delightful prospects in the world,"—when I look upon it and think that his living eyes can never again behold a scene he loved so well : but then returns the broad clear light that illumined his own nature, making him so full of faith in loveliness and goodness, as to shed a perpetually beaming genial effect upon those who knew him,—and one's spirit revives in another and a better hope.

Three of his portraits—the one by Samuel Lawrence, the one by Maclise, and the one published by the "Graphic" in 1870 — together with those of others whom we cherished in lifetime and cherish still in memory— are placed where we see them the last thing before we close our eyes at night and the first thing on awaking in the morning : and in that Eternal Morning, which we all trust will dawn for us hereafter, the "*Author* Couple" hope to behold the dear originals again, and rejoin them for evermore in immortal Friendship and Love.

M.

Macirone, Clara Angela, 115.
Macready, William, 65, 74, 85, 295, 302.
Main, Alexander, 112.
Mars, Mdlle., 75.
Marsh, His Excellency George Perkins, 112.
Marston, Westland, 103.
Martin, Mr., 91.
Martin, Miss, 91.
Massey, Gerald, 112.
Mathews, the elder, 81.
Mayer, Mr. and Mrs. Townshend, 111.
Mazzini, Giuseppe, 290, 293.
Meadows, Kenny, 308.
Mellon, Miss, 48.
Mendelssohn, Felix, 68, 69.
Moore, Thomas, 17.
Moritz, Mdme. Henrietta, 115.
Mulock, Miss, 103.
Munden, Joseph, 19, 185.
Murray, Lord, 98.

N.

Nesbitt, Mrs., 62, 288, 289, 303.
New, Herbert, 115.
Norton, the Hon. Mrs., 42, 289.
Novello, Vincent, 1, 18, 19, 29, 68. 201.
———, Mrs., 21, 23, 24, 25, 205, 220.
———, Francis, 38, 39.
———, Alfred, 70, 337.
———, Cecilia, 79.
———, Emma, 299, 325, 329, 337.
———, Sabilla, 277, 278, 337.
Novellos, the, 37.
Nugent, Lord George, 91, 292.

O.

Ollier, Charles, 17, 137, 192.
Ollier, Edmund, 111, 334.
O'Neil, Miss, 14.
Osler, Mr. and Mrs. Follet, 99, 333.
Oxenford, John, 84.

P.

Paganini, 75.
Paton, Miss, 65.
Payne, Howard, 183.
Payne, Mrs., 222.
Peacock, Dr. Beddoes, 100, 101, 102.
Peacock, Henry Barry, 100, 255.
Peake, Richard, 81, 82.
Perlet, 75, 76.
Phillips, Colonel, 183.
Pickering, Thomas, 108, 109.
Pillans, Professor, 98.
Plessy, Mdlle., 75.
Potier, 64, 65, 75.
Power, 201, 202, 205.
Priestly, Dr., 5.
Pritchard, Mrs., 8.
Procter, Bryan Waller, 28, 36, 116, 201.
Procter, Miss, 339.
Publishers, 107.
Pulszky, Mr. and Mrs., 114.

R.

Rachel, Mdlle., 76.
Reade, Edmund, 63.
Richards, Tom, 17, 201.
Robertson, Henry, 17, 39, 192, 195, 231.
Robinson, Henry Crabbe, 36.
Rolt, John, 103, 104.
Rossini, 66.